THE SEVENTH TOWER™

Volumes 4-6

Garth Nix

THE SEVENTH TOWER™

Volumes 4-6

LUCAS BOOKS

www.theseventhtower.com

SCHOLASTIC INC.
New York Toronto London Auckland Sydney
Mexico City New Delhi Hong Kong Buenos Aires

Above the Veil, ISBN 0-439-17685-9
Copyright © 2001 by Lucasfilm Ltd. & TM

Into Battle, ISBN 0-439-17686-7
Copyright © 2001 by Lucasfilm Ltd. & TM

The Violet Keystone, ISBN 0-439-17687-5
Copyright © 2001 by Lucasfilm Ltd. & TM

12 11 10 9 8 7 6 5 4 3 2 1   3 4 5 6 7 8/0

Printed in the U.S.A.

This edition created exclusively for Barnes & Noble, Inc.
2003 Barnes & Noble Books

ISBN 0-439-62433-9

First compilation printing, September 2003

ABOVE THE VEIL

*To the total Seventh Tower team: All the people at
Scholastic and Lucasfilm who have worked so hard on
publishing the books and getting them to readers.*

·CHAPTER·
ONE

The Chosen rarely entered the Underfolk levels of the Castle. As long as their servants continued to work, they ignored them. Long ago there had been Chosen overseers who regularly inspected all seven Underfolk levels and even the odd chambers and workrooms below the lowest level. But in the past hundred years or more, only the occasional adult Chosen would wander through, though bands of Chosen children would sometimes explore for a few hours.

All that changed in a moment. Without warning, scores of Chosen were spreading out across the seventh and lowest of the Underfolk levels. Most of them wore the gold Sunstone-set bracers of the Empress's Guard and held naked swords in their hands.

As they pushed open doors and ran down corridors, their shouts filled the air and their Spiritshadows flickered across every floor and wall. Sunstones flashed brightly, illuminating dark corners and possible hiding places. If anything moved, the light was followed by bolts of incandescence that incinerated caveroaches, rats, and whatever else fled from their intensive search.

The Underfolk stopped and stood still as stone while the hunting parties of Chosen scoured their workrooms and caverns. They knew that this was the safest thing to do. But not all Underfolk realized the danger, or were quick enough to stop and identify themselves. One old, very deaf woman did not hear the command to stop as she limped along a dimly lit corridor. The guard did not shout twice, but followed the command with a Red Ray of Destruction from his Sunstone.

When the body was revealed to be an old woman — not one of the fugitives the guards sought — there was no apology or explanation. The guards simply moved away, their needle-waisted Spiritshadows sliding after them. The body, like everything else destroyed, ruined, or discarded by the Chosen, would be cleaned up by the Underfolk.

In the chamber where the Castle's fifty-six level laundry chute ended, the Chosen in charge of this unprecedented search of the Underfolk levels sat at ease on a pile of laundry bags, eating dried shrimps from a pocket in his sleeve.

At first sight he seemed like a normal Chosen. His Sunstones and glowing staff declared him to be a Brightblinder, the Deputy Lumenor of the Orange Order, and a Shadowmaster of the Empress. His face was plump and his mouth was small and cruel, but he was otherwise undistinguished.

His Spiritshadow was more imposing. A thing of spikes and sharp edges, it was taller than a man. Its head bore two horns and, in addition to a mouth of many fangs, it had four upper limbs that each ended in a cluster of hooked claws. It stood upright on two lesser-clawed legs and paced behind its master's seat of laundry bags, as if it cared more about the objects of this search than his master. In the light of so many Sunstones, it almost seemed to be made of solid, jet-black flesh, rather than shadow.

The fat, shrimp-eating man was not a normal Chosen. He gave orders to the guards as they came and went, and all of them were Chosen of higher Order and rank. There were Chosen of the Blue, Indigo, and Violet, but all bowed their heads before this Orange Chosen and gave a respectful flash of light from their Sunstones.

Most bowed low enough that they did not have to look at the gaping wound in his chest, a ghastly fist-sized hole that they could see right through, from front to back. The hole did not bleed and this strange Chosen showed no discomfort from it, though the Merwin-horn sword that had punched so easily through bone and flesh had been withdrawn less than an hour before.

That sword lay at his feet now, gently glowing. There was no blood on it.

Shadowmaster Sushin settled farther back on his makeshift seat and ate the last of the shrimps. Then he rubbed his hands on a Yellow robe that was poking out the top of one of the laundry bags and looked at the latest guard who had come back to report — a Shadowlord of the Violet.

"We've lost them," said the guard, her head bowed. "They went into a belish root forest and disappeared. We're clearing the roots, but there is no sign of them."

The guard's Spiritshadow shrank back as its mistress spoke, so that it almost hid behind her, though its broad shoulders were wider than any human's by at least a stretch.

Sushin frowned.

"Keep searching, Ethar," he said. "Make sure the Underfolk understand that they are to report any sign of the fugitives. I am returning upward to attend to . . . other matters. Remember, I want them both dead and the bodies and clothing destroyed. But their Sunstones are to be returned to me. That is most important. We must not risk losing their Sunstones."

Ethar looked up, straight at the hole in Sushin's chest. She seemed about to speak, but Sushin stopped her. He raised his hand, displaying a particularly large and vibrant Sunstone ring that shone with the purest Violet, dimming the light from the other rings on his hand.

"Do you question my orders, Shadowlord — or my authority?"

Ethar stared for a second longer, then looked away.

"No, Sushin," she said finally. "I know with whose voice you speak."

She turned away and gestured to the guards who were keeping a respectful distance. As they left, Sushin chuckled and mumbled something too soft for Ethar to hear.

"Do you, Ethar? Do you really?"

·CHAPTER·
TWO ⊙

"No, you push the lever in and turn it at the same time," said Tal as Adras, his Spiritshadow, once again pawed ineffectually at the handle of the hatch. "Look, I'll do it."

He started to climb back, but Adras finally managed to work the handle out. The hatch shut behind them.

"Now I want you to twist the handle off," said Tal. There wasn't any lock on the hatch, but if Adras pulled the handle off it might jam the mechanism. Nobody would be able to follow them down.

"Need light," Adras puffed as he wrenched at the handle. "Not strong enough."

Tal made sure his foothold was secure before extending his hand. The Sunstone set in the ring he wore flashed orange and then turned to white, steadily growing brighter and brighter.

With the light, Adras became more clearly defined. A Storm Shepherd from the spirit world of Aenir, here on the Dark World he was a free Spiritshadow, bound to be with Tal, but not necessarily to obey him. It was a situation Tal regretted most of the time.

The billowing cloud of shadow was vaguely manlike, but twice the size of Tal. One mighty arm heaved and the lever broke off in his hands. He was about to drop it when Tal shouted.

"No! Pass it to me! Milla and Odris are below us, remember?"

"Sorry," Adras said as he passed the broken lever to Tal. Tal put it in his pocket, sighed, and recommenced his downward climb.

Tal had found the hatch only by accident, stubbing his toe on the lip as they raced through one of the vast caverns where the Underfolk cultivated thousands of ugly strings of the root vegetable they called belish. Tal had never liked eating belish and pushing through a thick forest of muddy belish roots wasn't much fun, either. But the accidental discovery of the hatch had made it all worthwhile. The guards had been closing in.

Now Tal was in a narrow tube leading down at a forty-five-degree angle. There was no proper ladder, but spikes had been driven into the stone close enough together to use as foot- and handholds. There was no permanent light, either, no Sunstones set in the walls, floor, or ceiling. To get light, Tal pointed his Sunstone down and an answering light flashed back up from Milla's Sunstone, twin to his own.

Milla was descending quickly, wasting no time. The Icecarl girl was now totally focused on leaving the Castle and returning to the ice. She believed that she had made wrong decisions and sailed a wrong course. The Spiritshadow at her side was a constant reminder of her pride and failure. Only on the ice could she atone for her misdeeds.

That Spiritshadow followed her now. Like Adras, Odris had been a Storm Shepherd less than a day before, but that had been in the spirit world of Aenir. Here in the Dark World she was Milla's Spiritshadow — and having a Spiritshadow was against every Icecarl rule and custom.

Milla believed the loss of her ordinary shadow meant the end of her dream to be a Shield Maiden . . . and probably the end of her life as well. Only the need to inform the Crones about what was going on in the Castle and Aenir would prevent her from giving herself to the Ice as soon as she got out of the Castle.

But first they all had to get away from Sushin and the guards. Then they had to find Tal's great-uncle Ebbitt and try to make sense of everything they'd learned. Not that Ebbitt was ever much help in making sense of things, Tal thought. But he might be able to explain what the Keystones were, how they controlled the Veil, and how Tal's father, Rerem, could be affected by the Orange Keystone . . . What was it the Codex had said?

He is the Guardian of the Orange Keystone. It has been unsealed and so he does not live. Until or unless the Orange Keystone is sealed again, he does not live. If it is sealed, he will live again.

There was also Gref — Tal's brother — to think about. Tal had almost rescued him, but was foiled at the last moment by Sushin's tricks. Gref had been poisoned or somehow put into a coma. Just like Tal's mother, Graile . . . though she had been sick for a long time.

Tal had tried so hard to help his family, to live up to his father's wish that he look after them. But whatever he did, something always went wrong. In the beginning he thought all he had to do was get a new Sunstone, and that was hard enough.

Life was *a lot* harder now.

Distracted by these thoughts, Tal didn't hear Milla call out to him from down below, until his Spiritshadow tapped him quite hard on the head.

"Ow!"

"Milla says there's a drop into water," Adras reported, his voice too loud, as usual. Even as a Spiritshadow, he retained the characteristics of a Storm Shepherd. He boomed rather than spoke, and shadow-lightning crackled around his eyes and fingers.

Tal looked down, shining his Sunstone. Milla had stopped and was shining her Sunstone farther into the tunnel. Something reflected back, quite a long way from them. What water could it be? Tal frowned, trying to remember long-ago lessons about the layout of the Castle.

They were climbing down from the seventh Underfolk level, which was filled with various workrooms, vegetable and fungus farms, and manufactories. The seventh was the lowest complete Underfolk level, except for some isolated forges and . . . the fish pools.

That was what lay underneath them. One of the huge pools where the Underfolk farmed fish. Yellowscale and finners for the Chosen's tables, and the translucent shrimps that were such a delicacy when dried. Sometimes there were eels in the ponds, too, but they were considered vermin by the Chosen, left to the Underfolk to eat.

"It's shallow!" Tal shouted down to Milla. "Don't jump."

Milla scowled back at him, and jumped anyway.

But she jumped holding on to Odris. Even as Spiritshadows, the Storm Shepherds retained some of their cloud characteristics. Milla floated like a feather, with Odris spread out in a great billow of darkness above her.

Milla splashed down gently, the water only up to her waist. She raised her hand and increased the light from her Sunstone. She hadn't had the stone very long, but Tal noticed she was rapidly gaining better control of it, even though he'd given her only the briefest of lessons. He found this unsettling. Only the Chosen were supposed to be able to use Sunstones.

It was yet another part of his world and his beliefs that had started to come apart at the seams. Tal wasn't sure what was true anymore. Most of what he'd been taught in the Lectorium seemed to be half-truths or only part of the whole picture. It was almost as if the main purpose of his schooling had been to blind him to wider knowledge, rather than teach him.

"Come on!" Milla ordered.

Tal sighed and climbed down to the last spike, then reached up to take Adras's hand. The Spirit-shadow accepted it absently and let go just as Tal was about to drop.

"Hold on to me!" Tal said. "And you need to puff up, so we can float down."

"Sorry," boomed Adras. "I was thinking about home."

"Well, don't," Tal muttered.

This time, the Spiritshadow did as he was told, hanging on to Tal and puffing up so they made a controlled descent.

Even so, Tal cried out as they hit the water. In the dash to escape, he'd momentarily forgotten the pain from the Waspwyrm sting. The jar of landing and the cool water sent a jab of pain right through him, and he stumbled forward, almost sinking under-water.

Adras hauled him up, and Milla and Odris looked around.

"Are you all right?" Odris asked. Characteristically, Milla didn't say anything. Tal knew that she would never have cried out from something as simple as pain. He gritted his teeth and stood upright, wincing as his leg spasmed.

"I'm fine," he said, though it took an effort to speak. "Let's go."

"Where?" asked Milla. She held her Sunstone ring high so that its light spread out all around them, illuminating a wide circle of shimmering water. Beyond that circle was darkness.

Tal turned his head, looking all around. The fish ponds were extremely large, he knew, some of them two or three thousand stretches in diameter. But there would be a dock or platform somewhere, so the fish, once caught, could be boxed and transported up to the storehouses and kitchens.

The only problem was knowing in which direction that dock lay.

·CHAPTER·
THREE

"Douse your light," Milla said suddenly. She stared at her Sunstone ring. When the light did not fade fast enough, she covered it with her other hand. Tal, who was properly trained, made his wink out in a second.

"Why?" Tal whispered as they stood in the darkness. For some reason the whole cavern seemed much quieter without light, and he didn't want to disturb that silence.

Milla's only answer was a slight splashing sound. She was moving around.

"I don't like this," said Adras. "I feel weak."

"I feel sick," said Odris. "Like being thirsty back on Aenir."

"It's only for a moment," Milla told them. Her voice startled Tal, coming from behind him and farther out than he expected. "Ah, I have it now."

Light flared on her hand again. Tal let his Sunstone surge in answer.

"Have what?" he asked.

"There is light over there," said Milla, pointing. "And I heard something, too. But it is distant. This cavern . . . this fish pond . . . is very large."

"It could be the biggest one," said Tal. "There are three, I think."

Vague and unpleasant memories of childhood tales were coming back to him. Something about the big fish pond and enormous eels, each ten stretches long and with an appetite to match.

He remembered laughing as a child at the thought of Underfolk being surprised by a giant eel. It didn't seem so funny now that *he* was wading in the fish pond.

Something brushed his waist and Tal yelped and leapt back. In that same second, he recognized what it was. A weed. A thick black rope of seaweed, with huge bulbous air nodes that kept it floating on the surface.

Milla lifted up a strand. "This is different from the seaweeds we harvest under the Ice. I don't think this can be eaten."

15

"Definitely not," said Tal, grimacing in distaste. He pushed the weed away. It was slimy, it smelled bad — and there was a lot more of it to wade through.

As Tal moved the weed away, he saw a face in the water. He almost flinched as he saw it, thinking someone else was creeping up behind him, before he realized who it was.

It was his own reflection, but so different from the last time he'd looked in a proper mirror that he almost didn't recognize himself. That had been only a few weeks before, but so much had happened.

The young Chosen boy with the slightly scraggly dark brown hair and lopsided smile was gone. In his place there was someone Tal would have once described as a wild man. His hair was crazier and dirtier and there was a broad stripe down the middle that was bright green, the result of an encounter with a monster in Aenir. His face appeared to be permanently set in a tense expression that was half scowl and half frown. He looked quite a lot older than his almost fourteen years.

"Come on," said Milla.

Tal realized he'd been staring at his reflection. He looked across at Milla and noticed that she had changed, too. She had discarded her temporary disguise of a Chosen matron's Yellow robe, and openly wore her Icecarl furs and Selski-hide armor. She still had her white-blond hair tied back. But something had changed.

It took him a moment to realize that the change was in her gray eyes. The fierceness had gone out of them, as if some spark had been lost.

Only then did Tal understand that she really was going to give herself to the Ice. When he'd thought he was saving her life — and his own — by agreeing to take the two Storm Shepherds as Spiritshadows, he had only postponed Milla's fate. She *would* take her own life because she had lost her own shadow and gained a Spiritshadow instead.

"Come on!" Milla repeated. She started wading off through the water, pausing every now and then to push apart particularly difficult strands of the bulbous seaweed.

Tal followed more slowly. He felt incredibly tired all of a sudden. Everything felt like it was too hard. No matter what he did, he made things worse. Now he knew he had to make sure Milla survived. The only way he could think of doing that was to stop her leaving the Castle, which would be totally against her wishes. And going against Milla's wishes was almost never a good idea.

Perhaps Ebbitt would be able to figure something out, Tal thought wearily.

Ebbitt. They had to find Ebbitt — wherever he was — before the guards caught up with them.

Or caught up with Ebbitt, Tal suddenly thought. That hadn't occurred to him before.

He groaned. Milla, Adras, and Odris all stopped and looked at him.

"What is it?" Milla asked. She already had her bone knife in her hand, drawn in an instant.

Tal shook his head.

"Nothing. I just realized how stupid this is. We're looking for Ebbitt but we don't know where he is or what we can do once we find him. There are guards everywhere, not to mention Sushin, whatever in Light's name *he* actually is. We're in a scum-filled fish pond. I haven't done anything right and I don't understand what's going on. . . ."

His voice trailed off as Milla stared at him. It was not the Icecarl way to complain, he knew. It *was* the Chosen way, though. Chosen complained about Underfolk servants, about food quality, about their clothes, about anything.

Anything trivial, Tal thought. Did he really want to be like that?

He looked down at his reflection again and tried to force a smile. It came slowly and for some reason it no longer had that annoying crooked curve on the left side.

"On the other hand," he said slowly, "I have a new Sunstone, which is all I wanted to start with. And a Spiritshadow —"

"That's me," said Adras proudly.

"And we have the Codex hidden up in the Mausoleum," Tal continued. Saying the positive things made him feel a bit better about the whole situation. "So what am I complaining about?"

"I don't know," said Milla. She frowned and added, "You are alive. Be grateful for the gift of life, till you have it no more."

She turned and plowed off through the weed again, faster than before. Tal followed, wincing at the pain in his leg. She was going faster than was comfortable for him, but he didn't complain.

It was hard going, wading through the seaweed. There was a lot more of it than Tal would have thought was healthy for a working fish pond. For that matter, there didn't seem to be any fish. Or eels. Though it was possible they had scared the fish away, or couldn't see them in the dark. Milla had insisted that they keep their Sunstones down to dim sparks so they didn't give themselves away. Adras and Odris had complained at first, but seemed to have gotten used to feeling weak from the lack of light.

Tal waded for at least fifteen minutes without a single thought and without being aware of what he was doing. He just pushed through the seaweed, following Milla. He would have mindlessly kept on doing it, too, except she stopped.

"What is it?" he whispered, edging around her.

"Look," Milla whispered back.

Tal looked. There was some light ahead. But it wasn't the clear, steady illumination of Sunstones. The light was flickering and fairly weak, changing color quite a bit. A couple of oil lamps, Tal thought — the ones the Underfolk used in the parts of the Castle where there were no fixed Sunstones. Underfolk couldn't use Sunstones, of course, so they had to make do with oil lanterns and similar devices.

In the dim light, Tal could see four . . . no . . . five people hard at work. Two were in the water, passing loads of something up, while the others were taking whatever it was and putting it in barrels.

"Underfolk harvesting fish," Tal said, not bothering to keep his voice down. "We can just walk past —"

A cold hand across his mouth cut him off.

"Quiet," Milla whispered fiercely. "They're not normal Underfolk. And they're not harvesting fish."

For a moment Tal was tempted to bite her hand, but the moment passed and Milla took her hand away. Besides, as he squinted at the dock, he realized there *was* something funny about these Underfolk. They weren't wearing regular white robes, for a start. And they weren't harvesting fish. It was the seaweed they were dragging up, cutting it into lengths on the dock before putting it in the barrels.

"They have spears," said Milla quietly. Her eyesight was much better than Tal's, particularly in the dark or near-dark. "And one of them has a long knife. Ah —"

One of them had stopped exactly where the lantern light fell most brightly. He was a boy not much older than Tal, but taller and more muscular. He wore Underfolk whites, but something had been painted or embroidered on the cloth — some sort of pattern or writing that Tal couldn't make out from the distance. He also wore a strange triangular hat, with the sharpest peak at the front. It had several long black or deep blue feathers stuck to it at a jaunty angle.

He looked vaguely familiar. Tal felt sure he'd seen him somewhere before, but he couldn't work it out where.

Milla could, though.

"It is the one called Crow," she said. "The leader of the people who brought us up from the heatways, when the air went bad."

"Them?" asked Tal. He'd been partially unconscious, or delirious, from the fumes in the heatway tunnels. If they hadn't been rescued they would have died down there. He hadn't had time to think about the people who'd carried them out. Now it was all coming back.

"Yes," said Milla. "We had better be careful. Most of them wanted to kill us. And they hate the Chosen."

"What?" asked Tal. "They're Underfolk! They can't hate the Chosen! It's . . . it's not allowed."

"They are not normal Underfolk. It is like I said before. They are Outcasts."

Tal stared at the Underfolk. It was true they were wearing very odd clothes. And no Underfolk had any business to be in the heatway tunnels, where they'd rescued Tal and Milla. He had heard that some Underfolk rebelled against the Chosen and lived below the normal levels. But he'd never really believed it.

"There are only five of them," he said finally. "We both have Sunstones, and Adras and Odris."

"But we're weak," said Odris, a plaintive voice in the darkness. "I couldn't crush a caveroach the way I feel at the moment."

"I could," Adras chimed in. "I could easily crush a caveroach and maybe something about as big as a Dattu, or, say, a Lowock —"

"I was *exaggerating*," interrupted Odris. "Of course I could crush a *caveroach*. But I wouldn't be much use in a proper fight —"

"I would be," Adras said proudly. "But if there was more light —"

"Quiet, both of you," Milla ordered.

"We have to get past them," said Tal. "There's no other way out of this lake. And the guards will probably find that trapdoor soon."

"We owe them life," said Milla, the words coming out slowly as if she were thinking aloud. "That means we must talk to them first. They may know where to find your greatest uncle Ebbitt."

"*Great*-uncle, not *greatest*," Tal corrected. "I

doubt it, though. Underfolk don't normally know anything except their jobs. I wonder what they're planning to do with that weed?"

"Adras, Odris, be prepared to defend us if they attack," said Milla. "We'll give you more light. Let's go."

·CHAPTER·
FOUR

They were only a dozen stretches from the dock when the Underfolk noticed them. It was Crow who glanced across the water, alerted by a splash. Shock flicked across his face but it was gone in an instant as he shouted and grabbed his spear.

"Look out! In the water!"

The other two Underfolk on the dock went for their spears as well, while the two in the water splashed in a panic to the steps. Weed went flying through the air as the Underfolk threw it aside in their haste to get weapons or get out of the water.

"Peace!" shouted Milla. "A truce!"

"Talk!" shouted Tal. "We just want to talk!"

Unfortunately, Adras decided at the same moment that he would help with a thunder shout. It broke across the water with all the strength of real thunder, drowning out everyone's words and momentarily stunning the Underfolk.

As the thunder echoed through the pool, Crow threw his spear straight at Tal. Milla leapt forward and snatched it out of the air.

Tal fell into the water, up to his neck. But he kept his hand and Sunstone ring above the surface. Suddenly angry, all his thoughts focused on bringing forth blinding brilliance.

Light exploded out of the stone, banishing the darkness. Adras and Odris roared with delight, suddenly visible as hard-edged shadows, huge humanlike figures of billowing cloud. They rushed at the other Underfolk, who threw their spears uselessly at the Spiritshadows. Adras and Odris batted them away.

It looked like a full-scale battle was about to develop when Milla shouted, using the voice that she had been trained to use aboard an iceship at the height of a gale.

"Stop! Everybody stop!"

Everybody stopped. They might have started again if Milla hadn't kept on shouting.

"Adras! Odris! Come back here. You Underfolk, stay where you are. We just want to talk! We're not Chosen!"

Tal dragged himself up from the water, pushing the weed off his shoulders. He kept his Sunstone burning bright, but deflected the light off the distant ceiling so it didn't blind anybody.

"It's them," said one of the Underfolk, a tall blond-haired boy . . . no . . . girl who Tal suddenly remembered was called Gill. "The two we dragged up from adit three. I told you we should have killed them."

"Close it," said Crow. He was looking at Tal and Milla, but his eyes kept shooting across at Adras and Odris. He had a knife in his hand, held low at his side.

"We aren't Chosen," repeated Milla. She ignored Tal's furious look at her. She might not be Chosen, but he was and he couldn't see any point in pretending otherwise.

"No?" asked Crow. "You have Sunstones and Spiritshadows."

"I am Milla, an Icecarl, from outside the Castle. Tal . . . used to be a Chosen but he's not anymore. The Chosen have cast him out. The guards are after him."

Tal opened his mouth to protest, then shut it again. Milla was describing what had happened to him in her terms, but it was still true. He *was* effectively an Outcast. He hadn't really thought it through before.

Crow listened without changing his expression. Even the news that Milla came from outside the Castle didn't seem to perturb him. The others shifted nervously and looked behind them to the open door and the tunnel beyond.

"We're looking for my great-uncle Ebbitt," said Tal. "An old Chosen. His Spiritshadow has the shape of a maned cat. Have you seen him down here?"

"Maybe," said Crow. Tal noticed that the other Underfolk seemed to recognize Ebbitt's name, and they wouldn't meet his eyes. It was also clear Crow was their leader and they would stand silently while he did the talking.

"Can you take us to him?" asked Milla.

"That depends, doesn't it?" said Crow.

"On what?" Tal asked. He was getting more and more angry. "Why don't you . . . why don't you just do as you're told?"

Even as the words left his mouth, Tal regretted them. This was exactly how he'd gotten in trouble with the Icecarls. His mind knew better, but it was slower than his tongue.

Crow stared at him, his dark eyes shining with a deep hatred.

"You're still a Chosen, aren't you?" he said, raising his knife. "Do this, do that! We're not your servants down here! We're Freefolk, not Underfolk. And you can wander around down here like little lost light puppets until the guard gets you, as far as I'm concerned!"

Tal raised his Sunstone, his mind concentrating on a Red Ray of Destruction. If Crow sprang at him or tried to throw the knife, he would unleash it.

Crow saw the Red light swirling around the stone, and hesitated. Before either of them decided to break the momentary stalemate, Milla sloshed between them and looked up at the Underfolk on the dock.

"There should be no fighting between us, when the real enemy is close," she said. "Afterward, when the storm is done, we can settle scores."

Crow stared down at her, the fury still obvious in his face. It looked like he was going to attack anyway, until one of the other Underfolk sidled over and whispered something to him.

"Close it, Clovil!" said Crow, pushing the other boy, hard enough that he fell over a barrel and into a pile of seaweed.

"All right, I'll say it so everyone can hear," shouted Clovil. He was angry now, too, as he clambered out of the seaweed. "We've orders to bring anyone who wants to see Ebbitt to —"

"Close it!" Crow repeated. But he seemed to have lost the heat of his anger, for there was no strength in his words.

"So you *do* know Ebbitt," said Milla. "And there is someone who gives you orders. Lead us to your Crone."

"Our what?" asked Gill, as Crow frowned and did not answer.

"Whoever is in charge," Tal explained. He'd managed to calm himself down and was remembering his first introduction to Milla and the Icecarls. Obviously these Freefolk weren't normal Underfolk and couldn't be treated like them. He'd have to be more polite. He'd learned at least that out on the Ice.

"I'm sorry about what I said," Tal added, looking at Crow. Crow stared at him, expressionless. There was no knowing what thoughts lay behind those unblinking eyes. Tal didn't know whether his apology was accepted or not.

"Clovil, Ferek," Crow ordered, "lead out. We'll go via forge country and across holding tank four."

"Four?" asked Ferek. He was a small and seemingly nervous boy. He twitched as he spoke. Tal had seen that sort of twitch before. Ferek must have spent time in the Hall of Nightmares.

"I said forge country and holding tank four," snapped Crow. "Do I have to repeat every order?"

"Only the stupid ones," muttered Gill, too soft for anyone but Milla to hear. The Icecarl glanced at the girl, who was surprised to have been heard. She scowled and looked away.

Milla and Tal climbed out of the water and onto the dock, their Spiritshadows rising up close behind them. The Underfolk stepped back, unconsciously forming a line.

"As I said, I am Milla, of the Far-Raiders clan of the Icecarls. What are your names?"

The Underfolk all looked at Crow, who shrugged. Evidently this was permission. Even so, it took a moment before they mumbled their names.

"I'm Gill," said the blond girl. Like all of them, she wore a mixture of Underfolk white robes and odd bits and pieces. In her case, that included the belt from a Blue Brightstar, though the belt was so dirty it could be black instead of blue. She needed it because she was so skinny.

Up close Tal saw that her white Underfolk robes had crude writing on them, as did all the others. He had to crane his head sideways before he could work out that it was the letter *F* from the standard Chosen alphabet repeated over and over.

"It stands for Freefolk," said Clovil, who had seen what Tal was doing. "Free of the Chosen. It shows who we are, to separate us from the Fatalists."

"The Fatalists?" asked Tal. "Uh, that starts with *F*, too. . . ."

"But they don't have writing on their robes," Clovil explained.

"You mean the . . . the regular Underfolk?"

Crow made a cutting movement with his hand and Clovil didn't answer. Tal didn't press it. There was still a lot of tension in the air.

"You are called Clovil?" asked Milla, when no one else introduced themselves.

Clovil nodded. He still had seaweed on his shoulders. He was almost as tall as Crow, and from the way he'd behaved before it looked like he thought he should be in charge. His long sandy hair was held back by a comb made from a large white bone. Possibly a human one, though the Underfolk kept all sorts of livestock for the Chosen's tables so it could easily have come from an animal.

"And you are Ferek," continued Milla, pointing

at the twitching, small boy. He nodded and smiled eagerly. Crow frowned at him, and the smile disappeared.

Apart from Crow that left a single, stout girl, who had stood silently by the whole time. Unlike the others, she wore a heavy hide apron over her Underfolk robes and had a large number of pouches hanging from her belt.

"That's Inkie," said Gill.

Inkie nodded to them. There was no explanation of why she didn't talk.

"I am Odris," said Odris, after another momentary pause.

As the Spiritshadow spoke, all the Underfolk — even Crow — jumped in surprise and Ferek stepped back, shaking uncontrollably, as if he had a sudden fever.

"What?" asked Odris, looking at Milla and Tal. "All I said was my name!"

"Spiritshadows don't usually talk to anyone but their masters, in private," said Tal. He'd become so used to Adras and Odris talking away that he'd forgotten this was yet another way in which the Storm Shepherds were different from other Spiritshadows.

"Odris and Adras are not normal Chosen Spiritshadows," explained Tal to the Underfolk. "They are . . . um . . . friends, I suppose, rather than . . . er . . . servants."

Milla didn't say anything. She was looking back across the lake, into the darkness. Lights had flared there, a sudden show of distant flashes and stars. There was also the very faint echo of shouts.

"The guards," she said urgently. "They've found us. We have to move quickly."

"Right," said Crow. "Like I said — through forge country and then across holding tank four. Clovil, Ferek, you lead."

The two named Underfolk ran along the dock to a door in the cavern wall and slipped through it.

"After you," said Crow to Tal and Milla, gesturing for them to go first.

Milla shook her head.

"No," she said evenly. "We will follow you."

Crow stared for a moment, then shrugged and left, followed by the other Underfolk. On the way, he picked up a long strand of the weed, one with very large nodules, and hung it over his shoulder. Gill and Inkie did the same.

Milla and Tal waited till the Freefolk were well in front before they followed. Nothing was said, but both Milla and Tal didn't want Crow behind them.

·CHAPTER·
FIVE

The Freefolk led Milla, Tal, and the two Spirit-shadows through winding, narrow pathways that were carved roughly through the pale yellow stone of the mountain. Every now and then a single, fading Sunstone would show that these ways had once been lit and used by the Chosen. But for the most part they were dark, stained with the smoke from Underfolk lanterns, and the only Sunstones were long dead, nothing more than blackened pits in the ceiling or walls.

Clovil and Ferek kept up a fast pace, which pleased Milla, since she knew the guards or their Spiritshadows would soon work out where they'd gone. It would have pleased Tal, too, if his leg didn't hurt so much. He wanted to use his Sunstone to ease the pain, but they never stopped long enough for him to cast any of the healing glows he'd learned in the Lectorium.

After an hour of traveling through the narrowest, most winding ways, Clovil and Ferek slowed down and stopped a few stretches before the next corner. As the others moved up, Tal and Milla heard strange water noises — or something — gurgling and splashing, almost as if a herd of giant animals were drinking and then spitting.

There was also a strange light spilling into the tunnel — a hot, yellow-and-blue-tinged light that Tal had never seen before. At least, never so intensely. It reminded him of something he couldn't quite place.

"We have to time this bit carefully," said Gill. "Wait for the backflow."

"Backflow of what?" asked Tal.

"The crystal," said Gill. "This is forge country."

"Close it, Gill, and see whose shift is on and how long till the backflow," Crow ordered suddenly.

Gill sniffed and edged up to the corner. As soon as she stuck her head around, her skin was bathed in the yellow-blue light, so she seemed to have changed color. She looked for a minute and then ducked back.

"It's the Thrower and his gang," Gill reported.

"I reckon the backflow's not far away. The crystal's already changing color."

Her mention of the Thrower's name was met by groans from the other Freefolk, except for Crow. He simply frowned slightly and kept looking at the spill of light around the corner.

"Who is this 'Thrower'?" Milla asked. "Is he an enemy?"

"Not exactly," explained Clovil. "He's a Fatalist, like most of them —"

"Close it!" snapped Crow.

"Close it yourself!" Clovil snapped back. "Like I said, he's a Fatalist, what you call an Underfolk. They think we're all meant to work for the Chosen, that's the way life is meant to be —"

Crow made a threatening move toward Clovil, who immediately closed his mouth with a grimace. He opened it again once Crow had stepped back.

"We call him the Thrower because he throws liquid crystal at anyone who interferes with the work."

"Liquid crystal?" asked Tal. "What's that?"

"You'll see!" Crow announced. "It's going green. Get ready to run, everyone. Tal and Milla, stay exactly behind us. Don't leave the path."

The light ahead was changing, going from the yellow-orange into a cooler green. When only a few flickers of color remained and the light was nearly all green, Crow shouted, "Backflow!"

Clovil and Ferek suddenly leapt forward and rounded the corner at a run, the others close behind.

They burst out into a huge cavern. Tal had only a moment to take it all in before he had to concentrate on following the Freefolk.

A narrow, meandering path was appearing in the center of a huge sea of molten green crystal that was ebbing back toward the sides of the giant cavern. Heat rolled off the crystal in shimmering waves, but it was bearable. Tal couldn't work out why they hadn't all been incinerated immediately, as surely such a lake of molten crystal would have set their clothes alight at least. Then he saw the enormous, ancient Sunstones in the ceiling and the light that they projected.

The Sunstones were melting the crystal liquid at each side of the cavern, but they were also cooling this central path. Other Sunstones were projecting lines of blue force that stirred the crystal, creating eddies and currents.

There were other safe paths appearing as the liquid ebbed, paths that formed around deep pools of crystal. Underfolk clad in heavy protective robes and boots, hurried out along the paths to scoop molten crystal from the deeper pools with long-handled ladles. Once their ladle was brimming with liquid crystal, they ran back to one of the three raised islands that were permanently safe from the molten mass. On the island, they poured the liquid crystal into a waiting mold and then ran back out for more.

Tal was busy looking at what the Underfolk were doing and didn't realize he'd fallen behind until he heard Gill scream at him, "Hurry up!"

At the same time, he felt one of the Sunstones above switch off. Without its beneficial blue light the temperature shot up until it was searing. Tal jumped forward and sprinted to catch up with the others, who were just climbing onto the third island. As he landed, his leg spasmed and he half fell, half sat down. He pushed his thumbs into the muscle, grimacing in pain.

"Let me do that," said Adras, reaching his huge, puffy shadow-fingers down. Tal hastily pulled his leg away.

"No! No! You'd probably break my leg."

"This is halfway. We have to wait here for the next backflow," said Gill. "Let's hope the Thrower leaves us alone."

Tal kept massaging his leg and looked out across the cavern. Molten crystal was flowing back across the path, and the light was once again growing more intense. It was cool enough on the island, but Tal could tell that this was totally dependent on a single, very old Sunstone. Looking around, he saw charred, corroded lumps of high ground. There had once been more than three islands, but their Sunstones had failed.

"So this is where all the cups and plates are made," Tal said as he watched the Underfolk on the closest island turn the molds over and tap them to remove the highly durable crystal cups, plates, and other utensils he was so familiar with. "I had no idea."

"You wouldn't," said Crow. "The robes and boots those people are wearing are nearly as old as the Sunstones in the ceiling. Do you know how many people burn to death here every year, just so some Chosen can have plates of different colors?"

Behind him, Gill held up her thumb and forefinger to show "zero." Crow must have seen some hint of that in Tal's eyes, because he whirled around angrily. Gill's hand dropped instantly and she looked away. She was clearly afraid of Crow.

"Dark take it," swore Clovil. "It's the Thrower."

He pointed. Through the distorting heat haze above the steadily spreading crystal, now once again mostly a fierce yellow tipped with blue, Tal saw someone wading through the molten mass.

"How's he —" Tal started to say, before he saw more clearly. The man was wearing the same sort of heavy suit that Tal had seen on the other Underfolk workers, but this one had active Sunstones worked into it. They were wreathing the figure in cool blue light.

"The only armor that still works," said Clovil nervously. "I hope we get the backflow before he gets close enough to throw."

It was slow going through the molten crystal. There were currents and deep holes that had to be waded around. But the Thrower knew them all, and he kept on coming. He carried one of the long-handled ladles over his shoulder.

"Maybe he'll only warn us," said Ferek. He was twitching again.

"He warned us last time," said Clovil. "He'll burn us for sure."

"No he won't," said Crow. "Use your head."

He gestured scornfully at Tal and Milla.

"As soon as he sees these two with their Sunstones and Spiritshadows, he'll be licking their hands and wanting to show them around."

Ferek sighed with relief and relaxed. But Clovil kept watching the approaching Underfolk. As the

Thrower drew closer, he took the ladle off his shoulder and started scooping and throwing big globs of molten crystal in their general direction.

"I don't think the Thrower can see too well," Clovil announced as one of the lumps of crystal splashed down twenty or thirty stretches short of the island. "He's pretty old and he's got a hood and goggles on."

Another superhot glob of crystal hurled through the air, landing even closer.

"I don't think he can see the Spiritshadows or the Sunstones at all," said Clovil, his voice growing more anxious as they all edged to the farthest point of the island. "How long to the backflow?"

"A couple of minutes," said Crow calmly, looking at the color of the crystal.

Even as he spoke, a lump of molten crystal crashed down on the other end of the island, exploding into sparks and spraying superhot fragments in all directions. Some came within a few stretches of the group. In response they all pressed up against one another on the far end.

"Adras," Tal commanded, "you and Odris go out and tell this Thrower to stop. Stay above the crystal, and don't get hit if you can help it. Whatever you do, *don't* try to catch the crystal or bat it away. Since it's infused with Sunstone light it might be able to hurt you."

"Really?" asked Odris. "We're better off staying here, then."

Adras had already started to glide out, but she reached out one billowing shadow-hand and pulled him back by the ear.

"Ow!" exclaimed Adras.

The Thrower paused again to scoop up liquid crystal and then expertly hurled it. This time it splashed down to the left of the huddled group, off the island. They were struck with tiny, falling sparks and specks of molten crystal.

Everyone except Milla and Crow jumped and swatted at the burning specks, trying to get them off their clothes before they burned through to the skin.

"Hurry up, Odris," snapped Milla. The Thrower was scooping up crystal again. "You're fast enough to avoid getting hit."

"Oh, all right," grumbled Odris. "I know you just want to get rid of me, anyway."

She launched herself up into the air, arms and legs losing definition to become more cloudlike. The cavern was so bright that her shadowflesh was well defined. She looked almost like she had back in Aenir, as a jet-black storm cloud.

Adras followed her, but had to put one foot down on the island and give himself a boost to get into the air. Tal sighed as he saw the clumsy maneuver. Disobedient, not too clever, and clumsy — that was his Spiritshadow.

The two Spiritshadows floated out toward the Thrower. He had the ladle out of the crystal and was twisting his body to start flinging when he saw the Spiritshadows coming his way.

Surprised, he kept swinging the ladle back, until he lost his balance. He dropped the ladle, his arms flailed at the air, and then he fell backward — into the molten crystal. There was a huge splash, a hand clawed above the surface, and then he was gone.

There was only the flowing crystal, color already changing to blue, and the heat haze shimmering above it.

"He's dead for sure," said Clovil as he stared where only seconds ago there had been a man. "Even with the suit."

The Spiritshadows returned and grew their legs down to walk on the island once more.

"We didn't do anything," said Odris anxiously. "He just fell over."

"He *was* throwing molten crystal at us," said Gill, without much conviction. For a supposedly bloodthirsty rebel, she seemed greatly shocked by this sudden accident.

"Almost backflow," said Crow. He was the only one who seemed unconcerned. "Get ready. We have to get across the rest of the cavern this time."

But everyone was still watching the point where the Thrower had fallen into the crystal. It was cooling now, turning blue-green, and the liquid was ebbing back. No one spoke, but obviously everyone was hoping that the Thrower would have somehow survived, that he would stand up.

The molten crystal continued to flow back to the sides, and the paths started to appear. The Thrower's body became visible, a motionless lump, a tiny island.

"The Sunstones are still working in his suit," said Tal, noting the blue glow. "Maybe we should help him up. He might be all right."

"We haven't got time." Crow pointed to the path that was slowly appearing as the crystal retreated. "It's backflow *now*!"

He started off to the far side of the cavern. The other Freefolk hesitated, then took off after him. Milla grabbed Tal by the arm and pulled him to follow.

"There's no time," she said. "He was an enemy. The guards are still after us, remember. Come on!"

Tal followed her. He couldn't work out why he felt so upset. The Thrower was only an Underfolk, and Underfolk died all the time. But it was all so sudden. One second he was alive, and then he was drowning in molten crystal. . . .

Perhaps he would still get up, after they'd gone. Perhaps his armor was good enough to keep him alive while he recovered his strength . . .

Tal's leg started hurting again then, and he had to focus his mind on running. It was a good two hundred stretches to the far side of the cavern, and the others were well ahead. Except for Adras, who kept pausing to look back.

Once again, Tal felt the protective rays of the ceiling Sunstones begin to fade. The others were already climbing a steep stair that led out of the cavern. Suddenly the molten crystal began flowing back. Tal was fifty stretches short, and he had a moment of panic as a sudden surge of crystal flowed across the path. But it was narrow, and he managed to jump it and land without his leg giving way. Even so, he felt the heat, a sudden flash that would have been dangerous if it lasted for more than a split second.

When he gained the steps, Crow looked down at him with a sneer.

"Too much eating and not enough exercising," he said. "Typical Chosen."

"Tal is wounded," explained Milla in a matter-of-fact tone. "A Waspwyrm sting to the leg."

"A what?" asked Clovil.

"Waspwyrm," said Tal. "In the spirit world, Aenir."

"Aenir?" Clovil looked confused. "But I thought the Chosen's bodies stayed behind when they go to Aenir."

"They do," said Tal. "But whatever happens there affects your body here."

"Does it work the other way, too?" asked Crow, with a sudden intensity. "If a Chosen's body is hurt here when they're in Aenir, do they hurt there?"

Tal looked at the glitter in Crow's eyes. It was clear that he really hated the Chosen.

"Their bodies are guarded by their Spiritshadows here," Tal said shortly, not really answering the question.

"But what if they weren't protected?" Crow continued. "Say I stabbed a Chosen's body, would he or she die in Aenir?"

"They are guarded by Spiritshadows, so who knows?" replied Tal.

"Maybe I'll find out one day," Crow taunted menacingly.

"Enough talk," commanded Milla. "We can talk later. We need to find Ebbitt."

Crow nodded and jerked his head at Clovil and Ferek, indicating that they should lead off again.

The stair continued up almost to the top of the cavern, where it ended in a set of very large metal doors. They were slightly ajar, just enough for people to slip between, though someone as fat as Sushin would have trouble.

Milla paused at the doors, brushing the dust from a small patch. As she'd thought, the doors were made of the same dull golden metal as the Icecarls' Ruin Ship, and Asteyr's Orskir, in the spirit world. Further evidence of the connection between the Icecarls and the Chosen, way back in distant times.

Tal paused, too, but it was to look down at the forge country's molten sea. Even this high up, he could feel the heat coming off the crystal, and the counterbalancing cool of the Sunstones set in the ceiling, which was still higher than the top of the stair.

He scanned the area near the central island, hoping to see some sign of the Thrower. But there was no one there. There were only Underfolk on the other islands, busy at their work.

It was possible that the Thrower had gotten up and made it back to one of those other islands as they climbed the stairs. But it was unlikely.

"Tal."

It was Milla calling. She waved her hand, telling him to hurry.

Tal kept looking. Adras was next to him, looking down as well.

"Pretty colors," said Adras. "Like rainbows."

Tal couldn't see anything pretty in the molten crystal. Just the memory of a human hand clawing for support, desperate for help, the last action of a dying man as he sank beneath the burning surface.

"Tal!"

49

"I've never seen anyone die," whispered Tal. "Not like that. So suddenly."

Milla came back, frowning. But it was not a frown of anger.

"Death is the end of a song," she explained quietly. "But it is not the end of *all* songs. Here, a man has died. Somewhere, in your castle or out upon the ice, a child has been born. One song ends, another begins."

Tal looked at Milla. She had surprised him again.

"Did you just make that up?"

"No," replied Milla. "I learned it, long ago. Hurry up!"

·CHAPTER·
SIX

The Freefolk led them through another maze of narrow passages, all of them dark. Some were partially flooded, requiring wading. Others were packed with long-forgotten boxes and barrels, rotting away in the darkness. Occasionally bright patches of luminous mold shone like pale beacons, and once a Sunstone flickered high on a wall, a stone in its dying days.

They saw no other Underfolk and it was clear that the paths Crow chose were rarely used by anyone. More than once, Clovil and Ferek hesitated before a choice of ways, and there was a quick conference with Crow before they moved off again.

After several hours, they climbed down a switch-backed series of rough-hewn steps, to enter a large cavern with a sandy floor. Crow led them to the center and declared they would take a rest.

"We don't need a rest," said Milla. "We need to meet with Ebbitt. Then I have to go on."

Tal didn't say anything. He needed a rest. His leg was aching and he wanted to take the pain away with some healing light. He gratefully sat down on one of the stones Crow had indicated in the center of the cavern and stretched out his leg.

The others kept standing, a few stretches away. Adras slid over and copied Tal, stretching out his puffy leg.

"My leg hurts, too," he announced.

Odris came over to look at it, while Tal focused on his Sunstone to summon a Blue Glow of Healing. It wasn't as powerful as the full Blue Ray, but at least it would take the pain away.

Concentrating on the light magic, Tal didn't really pay attention to what the others were doing. Milla was arguing with Crow about the delay, and the other Freefolk had drifted over to stand behind him, except for Inkie, who had wandered over to the far side of the cavern and appeared to be looking at the rock wall.

Tal was unprepared when, in midsentence, Crow

leapt forward and pushed Milla as hard as he could. She flew back, turning into a flip as she fell. She landed on her feet, knife suddenly in her hand.

Before she could do anything, Crow shouted, "Now!"

Even before he shouted, Inkie pulled a concealed lever in the wall.

The floor below Tal suddenly opened, sand cascading down. Tal yelled and tried to jump up and across, but it was too late.

The whole center of the cavern was a trapdoor. Tal went down with the cascading sand, Adras following him with an excited shout.

Milla was quicker. As the floor shifted, she threw herself forward and got a handhold on the lip of the huge trapdoor — but she had to drop her knife. Odris flew up behind her, and gripped her around the waist, easily lifting her onto solid ground.

Crow charged her immediately, with Clovil and Gill coming on each side. Ferek ran around the outside, yelling excitedly.

Milla met Crow's charge with a flurry of punches and kicks. Crow surprised her by blocking or dodging most of them, until she got a lock on his arm and used it to swing him around to collect a blow from Clovil.

Milla had to let Crow go then, as Gill tried to grab her around the knees and push her over into the hole. Milla jumped clear and followed up with a kick that knocked Gill out.

"Odris!" she shouted. "Attack!"

"But Adras has gone down there," said Odris, pointing at the hole. She didn't attack.

Milla scowled in anger. Crow and Clovil circled her warily. Ferek had retreated to join Inkie. Gill was groaning on the ground.

"Why?" asked Milla. "We had an agreement."

"Can't trust a Chosen," said Crow. He drew a long, sharp knife. Clovil looked at him, then hesitantly drew his own knife.

"What about Ebbitt?" said Milla. She didn't take her eyes off either knife-wielding opponent. "And your Crone? Your leader?"

"What they don't know won't bother them," Crow replied.

Clovil glanced across at his leader. Milla saw the uncertainty there.

"Someone will tell them," she said. Crow smiled and edged forward, his knife weaving slightly from side to side.

"I could let you go," he said, "if you promise to just get out of here. We'll take you to the heatways.

You aren't a Chosen. I've got the one I wanted. That Tal. Once a Chosen, always a Chosen."

"We have to help Adras," said Odris. "He hasn't come back up."

Milla thought about it for a moment. She could feel Odris's desire to fly down to see what had happened to Adras.

Inkie moved. For a fraction of a second, Milla was distracted.

In that moment, Crow reversed his knife, revealing a Sunstone in its pommel. The stone flashed white. Milla and Odris cried out and shielded their eyes.

At the same moment, even more of the floor opened up. Milla fell back, flailing her arms and legs. Accompanied by a torrent of sand, she slid down into darkness, Odris fleeing after her.

Behind them, Milla heard a panicked shout and saw someone else tumble into the sandslide above her.

It was Gill. She had been caught, too, and she, Milla, and Odris were all plummeting down.

·CHAPTER·
SEVEN

There was no way to break their fall, though Milla did manage to turn herself around so she was sliding feetfirst. And she called up light from her Sunstone.

As she spun and slid along with a large quantity of sand, she saw they were on some sort of steep ramp. A very long, steep ramp. Already she'd lost sight of the trapdoor above them, though it had probably closed again.

Gill was twenty or thirty stretches behind her, upside down and screaming as she tumbled.

Odris was ahead, on her back, her arms and legs spread out wide. She appeared to be enjoying the ride.

"Odris! Slow me down!" Milla shouted.

For once, the Spiritshadow obeyed. She made

herself puffier and flew back against the sliding sand. Milla put her feet on the Spiritshadow's shoulders and felt herself slow. A few seconds later, she caught Gill as the Freefolk girl slid past.

An immediate headlock indicated that Milla hadn't grabbed the other girl out of kindness.

"Where does this go?" Milla demanded. The rushing sand was very noisy, as well as uncomfortable. They would be minus some skin by the time they got to the bottom.

Gill coughed and spluttered, unable to answer. She'd gotten a lot of sand in her face. Milla contented herself by keeping hold of the girl. Questions — and answers — could wait till they got to the bottom.

They didn't have long to wait. The ramp suddenly grew steeper and Odris groaned at the extra effort of slowing them down. Then suddenly they shot out into open air, high up in some vast cavern.

"Odris!" Milla shouted again as she fell off the Spiritshadow's shoulders and lost her grip on Gill. She was falling, and the ground was a hundred stretches below. Milla concentrated on keeping her eyes open. Icecarls always faced death with their eyes open.

Odris grabbed her a second later. She had Gill in her other hand, but the combined weight of both girls was too much for the Spiritshadow to fly. They continued to fall, too fast for comfort.

A few seconds later, they hit.

Not solid stone or sand, but warm water. All three went under with a huge splash, and all three came back up again.

Milla spat out a mouthful of water and swam a few strokes in a circle, looking around. She could see Gill coughing and spluttering, but she was all right. Odris was puffing herself up, climbing out of the water into the air.

There was no sign of Tal at first. Then Milla saw a bright Sunstone light, fifty or sixty stretches away and higher up.

"Over here!" shouted Tal. "Hurry!"

Milla spat out even more water and started to swim. Her furs were heavy and already water-logged, but she had learned to swim that way, in the warm pools around the Smoking Mountain.

"Hurry!" Tal yelled again. He sounded scared. Milla looked around, wondering why. Gill was already swimming as fast as she could toward Tal. Odris was floating above Milla, unconcerned.

What could Tal see that she couldn't? And what did Gill know about this place that was making her swim so fast?

"Spiders!" Tal shouted. "Hurry!"

Milla focused on her Sunstone, making it brighter, and swung her hand behind her, sending the beam of light flashing across the water. It was met by many sparkling reflections, clusters of bright eyes.

Water spiders. Lots and lots of water spiders.

Milla twisted in the water and started swimming as fast as she could. There were too many reflecting eyes behind her. The whole place was thick with water spiders. She remembered Ebbitt talking about them. They were about half her size, their bulbous bodies were thick-skinned and hard to damage, and they could walk on the water as well as swim in it.

They were also very poisonous.

Milla turned to take a breath and saw a ray of Red light shoot over her head and strike somewhere behind her. She heard the hiss of steaming water and a weird clacking noise, like the grinding of bone planks in an iceship as it ran over rough ground. It took her a moment to realize that it had to be the noise of the spiders' multijointed limbs.

They were racing after her, legs skimming the surface. Tal was trying to keep them at bay with his Sunstone. She saw more Red Rays zap overhead, and more steam spouted up behind her. But the clicking was louder, too, and she redoubled her efforts, kicking harder and pushing all the strength of her shoulders and arms into her stroke.

Somewhere along the way she overtook Gill, who was struggling, her arms and legs flailing, all rhythm lost.

Milla slowed momentarily, and looked back. Red Rays of Destruction from Tal's Sunstone crisscrossed the water, sending up gusts of steam. She could feel the heat of them passing overhead. In their light, she could see hundreds of water spiders. A solid line of them, skittering and dancing on the surface. Constantly edging forward, hesitating as Tal's rays struck them, then coming forward again.

"Odris!" called Milla. She couldn't see the Spiritshadow, but she shouted anyway. "Help Gill!"

Something erupted from the water near here, and Milla almost struck at it before she realized it was Odris.

"Too dangerous up there," said the Spiritshadow, indicating the Red Rays flickering off and on above their heads. She reached out and grabbed Gill, who shrieked and went under for a moment, then reemerged, coughing, as Odris lifted her partially out of the water.

Milla grabbed Odris, too. The Spiritshadow had formed her back half into one energetic tail, which was propelling her far faster than Milla could swim.

That was only a fraction faster than the water spiders. They reached the ledge where Tal was kneeling in deep concentration, his Sunstone ring bright Red, rays bursting from it every few seconds. Adras leaned down and pulled Gill out, and Milla leaped up, using Odris's shoulder as a step.

"Too many!" Tal gasped. He waved his hand across the whole front of the ledge, creating a continuous Red Ray that touched the water so that a curtain of steam rose all around the ledge. Water spiders clacked and there was a multitude of splashes as they fell back.

For a moment or two more kept crawling up, even as Tal shot them down.

The ledge was narrow, a crumbling shelf in the cavern's side. It went back only five or six stretches. There was a corridor beyond it, through the cavern side, but the way was barred by a portcullis of golden metal — a heavy grille of cross-hatched bars, set too close together to crawl through.

"Odris! Adras! Help me open this!" Milla shouted. She strained at the portcullis, trying to lift it. But it didn't budge.

The two Spiritshadows flowed across to join her. But when their hands met the golden metal, their shadowflesh went straight through. They couldn't get a grip on it.

"Aarrggghh!"

It was Tal screaming.

Milla spun around to see a huge, bloated spider leap on top of Tal. He fell back and its eight hairy legs wrapped completely around him. A second later it struck at his chest with its two huge fangs, venom dripping as it pulled away.

Milla rushed at the spider and kicked it in its disgustingly swollen abdomen, until its legs uncurled and Tal rolled out. Then she spun on her heel and kicked it again, knocking it back into two other water spiders.

"Adras! Odris! Help!"

Without Tal's Red Rays of Destruction to keep them back, the water spiders swarmed the ledge. Milla stood over Tal's body, kicking and punching, and the Spiritshadows stood at her shoulders, their massive arms whirling to knock the spiders back into the water.

Gill hung on to the portcullis, screaming for help. But no help came. Only more spiders.

·CHAPTER·
EIGHT

With the help of the two Spiritshadows, Milla managed to beat back the spiders' assault and drag Tal to the portcullis, to gain some slight shelter at their backs. But as the water spiders withdrew, it was clear it was only a temporary respite. They were climbing up the wall, spinning sticky threads of web behind them.

"They're getting ready to drop down on us," said Milla, watching the spiders climb. "They'll attack from above as well as in front. Gill! How do you open this portcullis?"

"From outside," sobbed the girl. "Crow will come and get us."

Milla scowled and looked back at the massed ranks of spiders. All those glistening eyes, reflecting in the light of her Sunstone. If only she knew how to create the Red Ray of Destruction, or some of the other light magic Tal had told her about. Even better would be her Merwin-horn sword or an Icecarl battle-ax. Then the water spiders would keep their distance.

But she had only her fists and feet. Even her knife was lost.

A sudden thought came to her. The other Freefolk had knives. Perhaps Gill did, too.

"Gill, give me your knife," she ordered. The Freefolk girl was still screaming through the bars of the portcullis, so Milla had to shout at her twice. Numbly, the girl pulled a long, thin knife from the side of her boot and handed it to Milla.

Milla smiled as she brandished it. The knife was metal and sharp, and it glistened in the light more brightly than the spiders' eyes.

She would make the spiders pay dearly for her life. She hadn't managed to kill any spiders with her blows, but she would now.

"Ten," she whispered. That seemed a reasonable number of spiders to take as a death-due for her own life. "And five for Tal."

The water spiders were almost directly above Milla. A thin wisp of spider-silk fell down across her shoulders. The front rank of spiders began to click and rustle as they moved forward in a single line. Their horrible hairy legs rose and fell in near-perfect synchronization as they edged forward, their fangs twitching and dripping with venom.

Their eyes, thought Milla. She would have to stab them in the eyes.

"Adras, Odris. I want you to hold each one in front of me, so I can stick them. Then throw it back and grab the next one."

"I feel sleepy," said Adras, yawning. "Very sleepy."

"Not now!" exclaimed Milla. But even as she spoke, the huge Spiritshadow slipped down the wall and spread out on the ground, across the still form of Tal.

"Adras!" exclaimed Odris and she slid down, too, to see what was wrong with him.

The spiders chose that moment to attack. Dozens of them rushed forward, running on one another's backs and getting tangled in their eagerness to get at their prey. Others dropped straight down, or swung in on webs.

Milla shouted her war cry, Gill screamed something — and suddenly the water spiders stopped and reeled back. Milla stared at them as they fell over each other trying to get away.

Surely her war cry wasn't that effective?

A moment later a great cloud of foul-smelling mist rolled past her. It was a foul smell she recognized, though she had last experienced it as a yellow ointment.

Ebbitt's water spider repellent.

She turned around. The portcullis was up, and there was Ebbitt and his maned Spiritshadow. The old man had a small barrel under his arm and a pumping device. He was working vigorously to spray repellent everywhere.

Gill was dragging Tal through the gate, and Odris was dragging Adras.

"Hurry up, hurry up, don't be late for the gate," said Ebbitt. Milla hurried through. Ebbitt backed after her, still spraying. When he was through, the portcullis rumbled down.

"A spider bit Tal," said Milla. "I couldn't stop it."

"Well, now, I don't suppose you could." Ebbitt didn't appear to be terribly concerned. "They're awful biters when the mood strikes them. Which is most of the time. You and young Gillimof will have to carry him."

"I told you not to call me that," Gill protested.

Milla was about to ask Ebbitt how he knew where they were. Then she saw Crow and the other Freefolk standing by a large wheel that obviously raised and lowered the portcullis. Instantly she pushed past Ebbitt, knife held low for a savage cut.

"Traitor!"

Before she could reach him, Ebbitt's Spirit-shadow reared up between them and a sparkling loop of Indigo light wrapped around Milla's torso and pulled her back.

"Let me go!" roared Milla. "He promised to bring us to you and then dropped us in with the water spiders!"

"That's what we're supposed to do for suspicious visitors," said Crow easily. "And *all* Chosen. So we can leave them in with the water spiders if we need to."

"That's true," said Ebbitt. "A precaution insisted upon by the leader of the Freefolk. Only the blue-tufted flowershrike here was a little slow letting me know."

"Crow!" corrected Crow, touching the black feathers in his hat. "You know I'm called Crow!"

"What about Tal?" asked Milla. "I told you a spider bit him."

"And something's happened to Adras as well!" added Odris. "I can't wake him up!"

Ebbitt peered at Odris, who had her fellow

Spiritshadow draped over her shoulders. He looked at them through both eyes, then only through his left eye, shutting the right. He tried looking with his left eye shut and right eye open, then with both shut.

Finally he opened both eyes again and said, "Storm Shepherds, I believe? And in free association, not bound?"

"Yes," said Odris.

"Well, won't lots of Chosen be running around gibbering when they hear about you!" Ebbitt exclaimed. "Now, don't worry about Tal and . . . um . . . Pladros. The spider venom is only a soporific in small doses, and the Fleefolk have an antidote."

"That's Freefolk, not Fleefolk!" corrected Crow.

"What is a soporific?" asked Milla. The word was unfamiliar to her, though much of the Chosen and Icecarl language was the same.

"Something that puts you to sleep," explained Ebbitt. "It can be a drug or something else, as in the sentence 'Blueshrike's tales of his bravery were extremely soporific.'"

Gill and Clovil laughed, but choked it back as Crow glared at them.

"Come on, then," said Ebbitt, clapping his hands. "Milla and Gill, you can carry Tal. We must be off to the Leefolk's lair. I mean the Weefolk's weir. That is, the Freefolk's fortress. Where is the Codex, by the way? Under your coat, perhaps? We'll need it for the meeting."

"It's up in the Mausoleum," replied Milla. "We had to hide it there. It was too big to carry."

Ebbitt stopped and a look of genuine consternation spread across his face.

"You mean you left it behind? It's the one thing we really need! You should have left yourselves behind!"

"We brought it back from Aenir, and that wasn't easy," retorted Milla. "But we hid it. It will still be in the Mausoleum."

"No, no, no it won't!" Ebbitt howled. He started jumping up and down on the spot. "It can move of its own accord in the Castle, at least, if not farther afield. It will wander off! It could be anywhere!"

"It was too big to carry," said Milla angrily. "We were lucky to get away ourselves. Besides, it is nothing to me. I am returning to my people."

"It shrinks," said Ebbitt mournfully. "You could have carried it. Or asked it to follow you."

"I don't care," said Milla. "I will help carry Tal to your Freefolk Fortress and then I am leaving. I am going back to the Ice."

·CHAPTER· NINE

The Freefolk Fortress, as Ebbitt called it, lay on the far side of a deep chasm that went all the way down to the lava pools that the Chosen had tapped long ago for their complex heating systems of steam and hot water. As they approached the lip of the chasm, Milla could feel the heat rising up from the depths and could see the red glow.

The only way across was a narrow, makeshift bridge that precariously spanned the fifty-stretch gap. The basic structure of the bridge was two very narrow rails of the same golden metal as the Ruin Ship. But all the planking and the handrailings were made of crystal, metal, and scavenged material of all kinds that could easily be dismantled so that the bridge would be almost impossible to cross.

Fortunately it seemed solid enough as they

crossed it, though Milla was careful to watch where she stepped and not put any undue reliance on the handrails. She and Gill were carrying Tal between them, so it was a slow progress. Odris was carrying Adras and complaining about it every ten or twelve steps.

Ebbitt led the way in his own peculiar fashion, stopping every now and then to spin around, or suddenly crouch down, or just stop and stare into space. His maned Spiritshadow watched him indulgently, itself always regal and controlled.

Across the chasm, they passed through a narrow, winding tunnel. Milla noted holes in the ceiling, useful for throwing stones or pouring hot liquid on intruders. With the chasm and this narrow way, the Freefolk were well defended. Though Milla doubted any of it would be much use against determined Chosen, with their Spiritshadows and Sunstone magic.

Since Tal had never mentioned the Freefolk, she suspected that the Chosen either didn't know about the Underfolk rebels or simply didn't care about them, as long as they didn't cause too much trouble.

The narrow tunnel finally opened out into a vast cavern, easily three or four hundred stretches in diameter and more than a hundred stretches deep. A few old, pinkish Sunstones shone in the distant ceiling, creating an effect like an Aeniran twilight.

There were six or seven fairly dumpy cottages arranged in a circle in the middle of the cavern, centered on a large open well, with clear water lapping over its sides into a gutter. A few buckets were stacked next to the well, and there was a pile of barrels, boxes, and other containers in a walled pen behind the houses.

It didn't look like much. It certainly didn't look like a fortress.

"The Fortress of the Freefolk," announced Ebbitt, with a grand gesture. "Or Temporary Digging Camp Fourteen as it was once known many, many, *many* caveroach lives ago."

"Where do we take Tal?" Milla asked. The Chosen boy was heavy and, though she would never admit it, Milla was tired.

"Oh, I suppose I can give him the antidote here as well as anywhere," said Ebbitt. He took a small vial out of one of the deep pockets of his multilayered robe and added, "Just lay him down and support his head."

"You have the antidote on you?" asked Milla. "You had it all the time? Why didn't you use it before?"

"The poor boy clearly needed his rest," said Ebbitt, looking down on his great-nephew.

Milla shook her head. She knew there was no point in getting angry with Ebbitt. He was like some of the older Crones. His mind was traveling somewhere else where no ordinary Icecarl — or Chosen — could follow.

She and Gill laid Tal down and then held up his head. Ebbitt bent down and opened the sleeping boy's mouth with two fingers, poured in the contents of the vial, pinched Tal's nose, and said, "Shake him up and down a bit."

Milla and Gill followed his instructions. Nothing happened at first, then Tal coughed. The cough was followed by a sneeze, suffocated by Ebbitt's nose-clasping fingers. Then Tal's eyes slowly opened. He was groggy, but after a minute or so he could stand up on his own.

At the same time, Adras came around and sat up, scratching his head.

"Why did you wake me up?" he said aggrievedly to Odris. "I was having such a good dream. I was shooting lightning at moths and every time I hit one they exploded with smoke and sparks —"

Odris slapped him, shadowflesh meeting shadowflesh with a strange rasping sound.

"I thought you were dying!" she said. "And you're worried about a stupid dream!"

"Where are we?" asked Tal. His voice was weak and he felt terrible. He was sick in the stomach and shivery all over.

"The Freefolk Fortress," said Ebbitt.

"The Cavern of the Freefolk," said Crow at the same time. "Call it by its proper name."

He pushed past Ebbitt and stalked off toward the largest of the cottages. Inkie scuttled after him. Clovil and Ferek hesitated, then followed. Gill stayed behind.

As Crow approached the cottage, the door opened and two grown men in the painted Underfolk robes came out. One was quite old, as old as Ebbitt, but he was much shorter and quite shriveled and dried-up-looking. He had gray hair, cut so short it was a stubble. The other man was about the same age as Tal's father, Rerem, though he was much brawnier. He looked like the sort of Underfolk who did the heavy carrying around the Castle. His chest and upper body were easily twice the size of Tal's. His hair was black and long.

As Tal looked at the younger man, he realized he had to be related to Crow, and might even be his father. There was a strong facial resemblance and though Crow was not physically as big yet, there was every indication he would be one day.

Crow raised his hand in a formal-looking salute, but only the older man waved back. Tal was surprised to see Crow lean forward and hug his brawny relative, but the man did not hug him in return.

"We have brought four prisoners," Crow said to the older man, loud enough for Tal and Milla to hear easily. "Two Chosen and two Spiritshadows."

"I'm not a Chosen," Milla declared. "And I'm *not* a prisoner."

Tal didn't say anything. He didn't feel up to it. Besides, after his experience with the Icecarls he had started to think that silence was the best policy when meeting anyone new.

"Neither am I," said Odris. "And Adras isn't one, either."

"One what?" asked Adras. He was rubbing his stomach and hadn't been listening.

"Prisoner. You're not a prisoner of anybody!" said Odris.

"Sure." Adras looked across at Tal and said, "Can you try to feel better? Your shadow is making me feel sick. It made me sleepy before."

"It's the spider bite," Tal explained. "So you were unconscious, too?"

"And asleep," Adras answered. "I fell over right after you did."

Crow and the other Freefolk were talking to the old men, but Tal didn't listen. He was too interested in what Adras had just said.

"I wonder if this spider poison . . ." he said aloud. Then he turned to Ebbitt and said, "Uncle Ebbitt? Could my mother be ill because she's being poisoned with water spider venom?"

Ebbitt scratched his head, and discovered a blue crayon that had somehow gotten tangled there. He looked at it in a puzzled way and said, "Yes. I hadn't thought of that! I don't know how you would get the venom out of the spider. But constant small doses would make her very sleepy, and if continued, would force a coma. Yes, it explains the symptoms. But how to milk the spider? I suppose some sort of harness and then a vacuum apparatus. Good thick gloves, a stick to whack the critter with . . ."

His voice trailed off into a mumble as he continued to think aloud.

"Gref must have been poisoned, too," said Tal. He was thinking furiously as he became more alert. Both his mother and Gref poisoned with water spider venom . . . Sushin must have access to the spiders. Perhaps he even had some tame ones somewhere. . . .

Tal shuddered at the thought of Sushin cuddling up with water spiders. But he was also suddenly hopeful. Now that he suspected what was being done to Graile and Gref, he could possibly get them the antidote.

His thinking was interrupted by Crow shouting something and stalking off to one of the other cottages. He opened the door viciously, went through, and slammed it shut so hard that some rock dust fell from the distant ceiling of the cavern.

The two men watched him go for a moment. Then the older man walked up to Tal, with the black-haired giant following him a pace behind. As they approached, Tal realized the leader looked familiar, though he had never seen him in the robes of an Underfolk . . . that is . . . a Freefolk.

"Greetings, Tal and Milla, Odris and Adras," the man said. As Tal heard his deep, measured, vibrant voice, so out of place coming from the little body, he remembered where he'd seen him before.

"I am called Jarnil, and I am the leader of the Freefolk," said the old man.

Tal blinked. He knew this man by his full name. He was the Brilliance Jarnil Yannow-Kyr of the Indigo Order, once Chief Lector. He had taught Tal when he was a little boy.

He had also been dead for at least five years.

·CHAPTER·
TEΠ

Tal still remembered the announcement at the Lectorium of the Chief Lector's demise. An accidental death, they'd said, without giving any details. Since any sort of fatal accident was unusual for a Chosen, the children had talked about it for some time, trying to imagine exactly what had happened.

"You're supposed to be dead," Tal burst out.

Jarnil smiled, but it was a bitter smile that did not light up his eyes.

"That was the story they spread," he said. "It was almost true."

He raised his arm and Tal saw that his hand twitched and jerked as if it had a life of its own, beyond Jarnil's control.

"I was taken to a place you . . . you know of," said Jarnil. "After Fashnek had finished with me, my supposedly dead body was thrown out to be removed by the Underfolk. That was Fashnek's mistake, for I was dying, not dead.

"For many years I have secretly coordinated the activities of those Underfolk and Chosen who wish to change the way we all live in the Castle. Some of the Underfolk who knew me were on the burial detail. They brought me here and nursed me back to . . . well, I suppose you could call it health."

"What do you mean Underfolk and Chosen who want to change the way we live?" asked Tal. He was shocked by the idea. He didn't want to change anything. He just wanted everything to go back to normal, with his father and mother at home, with Gref and Kusi. Obviously things would have to change with the Underfolk — and the Icecarls — but perhaps it could be a slow change. Though even as Tal thought that he knew it was too late. Everything *was* going to change and he might as well get used to it.

"Exactly that," said Jarnil. "This is Bennem, by the way."

Bennem gave a kind of grunt and nodded a fraction. He seemed about as friendly as Crow. Now that he was closer, Tal thought he wasn't old enough to be Crow's father. Perhaps he was an older brother.

Jarnil kept on talking as he led them to the nearest

cottage. Surprisingly, inside the door there were steps leading down to a comfortable, Sunstone-lit cellar room that was much larger than the cottage above it. A thick red rug in the center of the room was surrounded by low cushions of white and gold. Jarnil sat down and gestured to everyone to sit as well. They all did so, except for Ebbitt, who prowled around the outside, and the Spiritshadows, who floated up to the ceiling to circle the Sunstone set there.

"Where was I?" continued Jarnil. "There is sweetwater in the jugs over there. Help yourselves. Ah, yes. There have always been some Chosen who believe that the Underfolk are no different than we are, save for the accident of their birth. Why should they be kept in ignorance of Sunstone magic, and of Aenir? We called ourselves the Sharers of Light. Similarly, there have always been some Underfolk who have questioned why they should be servants of the Chosen. Though there is some, ah, variation in their aims, they generally call themselves the Freefolk. Together, we hope to change things so that it is possible for capable Underfolk to rise up to Red and become Chosen."

"But you will still have your thralls," said Milla. Her tone of voice showed that she didn't think much of the Sharers of Light.

"Thralls?" asked Jarnil.

"Slaves," replied Milla.

"No, no," said Jarnil. "You don't understand. We cannot change everything. Change must be introduced slowly. We are still loyal to the Empress. All we want to do is test and train Underfolk, and those who show potential to become Chosen will be raised up. Then they may begin their climb to Violet."

Tal shook his head. This all sounded like a Lector's theory, not something practical. Even after only a few moments of thought he knew it wouldn't work

"Why were you taken to the Hall of Nightmares?" he asked.

Jarnil coughed and a faint hint of redness touched his cheeks.

"I made . . . er . . . two serious errors of judgment," he said quickly. "Progress was slow in recruiting Chosen to the Sharers of Light, and I had made contact with only a few isolated bands of Freefolk in the lower depths. So I decided to put my plan for raising up Freefolk to the Empress. My first mistake was to share the exact nature of my plan with the Dark Vizier who recorded my request for an audience with Her Majesty. I *was* granted an audience for the following day. But that night, I was taken . . ."

His hands shook even more and he had difficulty getting out the last words.

"To the Hall of Nightmares."

"The Dark Vizier?" asked Tal. He'd never heard of that office. "Who is that?"

"What are they teaching in the Lectorium these days? The Empress has always been served by both a Light Vizier and a Dark Vizier, one for the day and one for the night. Traditionally the Light Vizier deals with ceremony and celebration, while the Dark Vizier deals with matters less pleasant, those best left unseen in darkness. The identity of the Dark Vizier is always kept secret, and he or she is disguised as a Chosen of lesser rank, while secretly holding the highest rank in the Violet Order. As is traditional, I met the Dark Vizier in a room where I stood in brilliant light and he in darkness. It was there I made my second mistake. . . ."

"What was that?" asked Tal as Jarnil stopped speaking and stared into the distance.

"I looked back at the doorway as I left," said Jarnil. "The Dark Vizier was careless. He had stepped half out of the shadow, so that the light fell upon his face. I recognized him, and I was fool enough to show it."

"Who was it?" asked Tal.

"I think you know," said Jarnil. "Someone who can speak with the authority of the Empress, command her guards, make other Chosen do his will, all without Her Majesty's knowledge?"

"Sushin!" Tal exclaimed. "But why? What does he hope to gain?"

"Good question," interrupted Ebbitt. "Very good question. When you find out the answer, let me know."

"We do not know what drives Sushin," said Jarnil. "Or to what end. But he has clearly been working toward some evil purpose for many years. I thought I knew him once, but even before my 'disappearance' he had become strange and distant. A different man from the one I used to know."

"He is not a man," said Milla, stirred by the image of Sushin laughing with the Merwin-horn sword thrust through his chest. "I think a Spiritshadow lives inside his flesh. An old shadow that has not forgotten the ancient war between our world and Aenir. A shadow that wants to lower the Veil and remove the darkness that protects us. I am sure of this, and I will tell the Crones, so that we Icecarls can do what must be done. I must go back to the Ice."

·CHAPTER·
ELEVEN

Silence greeted Milla's words, but it was the silence of disbelief, rather than shock. Jarnil even smiled a little, the same smile Tal had seen when a Chosen gave a particularly stupid answer in the Lectorium.

Tal opened his mouth to say something, but no words came out. Half of him wanted to protest, to say that Milla was mad, that she had no idea what she was talking about. But the other half wanted to scream out, "Listen to her!"

What she had said *did* make sense. Maybe Zicka the lizard in Aenir *had* been telling the truth about an ancient war between the Aenirans and the peoples of the Dark World — Chosen and Icecarls. Something *was* being done to the Veil, something that Tal's own father had been caught up in, as

Guardian of the Orange Keystone. But what was a Guardian? What did the Keystones do?

Tal was about to ask a question about Keystones when he finally noticed something else.

Jarnil had a natural shadow. His Spiritshadow was gone.

"Your Spiritshadow!" gasped Tal, his question forgotten. "What happened to it?"

Jarnil looked down, his natural shadow mimicking the movement exactly, better than any Spiritshadow ever could. No Spiritshadow was that flexible, unlike the shadowguards of children.

"I don't know," he said, the pain of his loss clear on his face. "I believe it was somehow forced to return my natural shadow, which bound it to me, and was then killed, or returned to Aenir, or —"

"Or signed on to serve the good ship Sushin," interrupted Ebbitt gloomily. "Or Fashnek."

"What?" asked Tal. "You mean they took your Spiritshadow and made it serve Sushin?"

"I fear so," said Jarnil. "Fashnek certainly had more than his own Spiritshadow to do his bidding."

"He has three by my count," said Milla. "As well as the one that carries him. You Chosen have let these shadows in, and they will destroy the veil and let in the sun. I must go swiftly to tell the Crones. Who will guide me to the heatway tunnels?"

"All in good time, all in good time," soothed Jarnil. "Let us share our knowledge first. What is this talk of the veil being destroyed?"

"Drunkards talk while warriors work," spat Milla. She got to her feet and glared at the Freefolk. "I know what must be done."

"Yes, yes," said Jarnil. "Gill will take you in due course. Do we have plenty of airweed?"

The last question was directed at the Freefolk girl. She nodded and showed the strand that was tucked through her belt.

"The others have more, too," she said. "And there are six barrels to pick up later."

"Airweed?" asked Milla. "What for?"

"Like it says. Airweed for air," said Gill. She indicated one of the bloated nodules. "These hold air. You can tap them with a knife and breathe from them when there is poison air or smoke in the tunnels. That's how we rescued you before."

"Good," said Milla. "Then we will go."

"No!" Tal shouted out. "Wait! Maybe you're right about the Aenirans, and the ancient war and everything, but shouldn't we at least see if Ebbitt,

Jarnil, and Bennem know anything the Crones need to know?"

Bennem grunted as his name was mentioned again. Tal looked at him in surprise. The surprise turned to pity as he realized that Bennem's eyes were empty, that they were not focused on anything.

Ebbitt noticed him looking.

"He was carried to the Hall with a cry and a shout," Ebbitt explained. "Twice he went in, and twice came out. But what went in was more than this, and what didn't come out we'll sorely miss."

"He means that my brother was taken to the Hall of Nightmares twice. His body came back but inside he is dreaming. He knows his name and simple things. Sometimes he wakes fully, but only for a minute or two."

It was Crow speaking. He stood halfway down the steps, with the others behind him. Tal had not heard them come in.

"Our parents did not come out of the Hall," he added, looking straight at Tal. "So you see we have much to thank the Chosen for."

Tal couldn't meet his gaze. He couldn't look at Bennem, either. A strange feeling gripped him, a coldness in his stomach. It was guilt, he knew.

"Tal is no longer a Chosen," said Milla. "He is an Outcast. You cannot blame him for the evil of his former clan."

Tal looked at her. Why was she standing up for him?

Crow ignored Milla and turned to Gill, who stepped back a little.

"Come on, Gill. We've got to go back for the barrels."

Gill shook her head. "I'm showing Milla how to get to the heatways."

Crow scowled. "We need you to help with the airweed. She has a Spiritshadow. Let *it* find the way for her. Let her get lost, if it comes to that."

"I'm not an *it*," growled Odris. She billowed down, and Milla slipped into a fighting crouch. Suddenly conflict seemed seconds away.

"No, no!" said Jarnil. "This is all going wrong! Crow, we need to talk to these people, not fight them! Why don't you get Korvim to help with the weed?"

"Korvim and his lot have gone back," Crow replied. "To rejoin the Fatalists. Just like Linel and Drenn and all the others, because we sit around talking all the time instead of killing Chosen!"

"How many Freefolk are there?" asked Tal.

All the Freefolk began to speak at the same time.

"Well, the numbers fluctuate —" began Jarnil.

"Don't tell the spy —" spat Crow.

"Seven right now," said Ferek. "Counting Jarnil."

"Close it!" roared Crow. Ferek flinched, but the older boy did not follow through with any action to enforce his words.

"Close it," repeated Crow, but softer. For a second Tal thought he caught a hint of kindness in Crow's voice, as if he was sorry he'd shouted at Ferek.

"*Seven* Freefolk?" asked Tal. "That's all? Counting Jarnil? What about the other Sharers of the Light? How many of them are there?"

Jarnil looked down and mumbled something.

"None left?" repeated Milla, who was the only one who had heard his words. "None at all?"

"There were only ever twelve of us," said Jarnil. "Thirteen if you count Ebbitt, though he was never formally in the group and sometimes I wondered . . . anyway, Rerem — your father — was one, Tal. After I . . . began my new life down here, I made contact with them. But then over the years, they disappeared, one by one. Rerem was the last to go. I'm sorry, Tal, but I am sure that like the others . . . like the others, he must be dead."

"No, he isn't," said Tal, shaking his head. "I asked the Codex. It said '*He is the Guardian of the Orange Keystone. It has been unsealed and so he does not live. Until or unless the Orange Keystone is sealed again, he does not live. If it is sealed, he will live again.*'"

Tal took a deep breath and got to his feet before continuing, the words coming faster and more forcibly as he spoke.

"That's why I want to know what the Keystones are, and how they get unsealed, or sealed. And I think Milla needs to know, too, because there is something terrible going on, and we all need to sit down and talk because no matter whether we're Chosen, or Un . . . Freefolk, or Icecarls, or something in between, if the Veil is destroyed and the sun breaks through and shadows swarm in from Aenir, they'll kill all of us! We should be working *together*, instead of fighting and arguing and *helping* Sushin and the Aenirans take over!"

Tal's impassioned words had the strongest effect on Ebbitt. The old man stopped pacing as he spoke and stood taller and straighter than anyone had ever seen him stand. His Spiritshadow stood at his side, a regal companion. And Ebbitt spoke with a voice that Tal had not heard from him before, an assured and somehow noble voice, without the wandering and strange humor. For a moment, Ebbitt was once again the Shadowlord of the Indigo he had once been, a great man among the Chosen.

"Seven Keystones stand in Seven Towers, forming the foundation of the veil," he pronounced. "Seven Guardians hold the secrets of the Stones. My nephew Rerem was indeed the Guardian of the Orange Keystone, as was my brother before him. If the Codex has told Tal that the Orange Keystone is unsealed, then the veil is indeed threatened. For if all seven of the Keystones fail, the veil *will* be destroyed."

The room was silent after Ebbitt spoke. Everyone stared at him, even Crow. Ebbitt met their looks, unblinking. Then his eyes seemed to twinkle, and his gaze shifted to the ceiling.

The silence broke as he began to speak again, his voice softer, his stance already shifting. He seemed diminished, more like his everyday, eccentric self.

"Sun and shadows," he said. "Sun and shadows. The veil may block the sun, but it cannot block the pride and greed of the Chosen. We should have obeyed Ramellan's Strictures and never returned to Aenir. Everything that will come we have brought upon ourselves."

"The Orange Keystone unsealed," echoed Jarnil. Beads of sweat had come up on his forehead. "Unsealed. My cousin Lokar was the Guardian of the Red. She disappeared a year before Rerem and . . ."

Jarnil's face went white and his voice almost disappeared. He drank heavily from his cup of sweetwater, as if it might bring relief from some great fear.

"I have just had the most terrible thought," he whispered. "Twenty-two years ago, Shadowlord Verrin of the Indigo disappeared without a trace, just like Lokar and Rerem. He was the first Chosen to disappear without explanation for almost a hundred years. He was probably the Guardian of the Indigo Keystone. The first to go."

Now incredibly agitated, Jarnil leapt up and gripped Ebbitt on the arm.

"Twenty-two years ago, Ebbitt! That same year that the three Chosen overstayed in Aenir!"

Ebbitt gently pulled Jarnil's fingers away, but did not speak. He kept staring up at the Sunstone in the ceiling and Tal could hear him humming some soft and doleful tune.

"What about the Chosen who stayed in Aenir?" Tal asked.

"The only one who came back was Sushin,"

whispered Jarnil. "He never explained what had happened, and disclaimed all knowledge of the other two. He was more than a month late returning, but he was not punished. Verrin disappeared soon after he came back. I would never have thought to connect them before."

"This is Chosen business," interrupted Crow, sneering. "You talk of the veil being destroyed. What does that matter to the Freefolk? We have never seen the sun in your Towers, or in your private world of Aenir. Maybe it is good the veil will be destroyed."

Milla looked at him angrily.

"You speak faster than you think," she said. "The veil is a defense, a ship-wall against shadows. It is not just the sun that would be let in, but also the many creatures of Aenir who hate and fear us. They are the ancient enemies of all our people, and they will slay Freefolk, Underfolk, Chosen, and Icecarls."

Crow shrugged, as if he could shake off Milla's words. But he did not speak, and she could tell that he didn't want to admit that he heard truth in her voice.

"How is a Keystone unsealed?" asked Tal.

Jarnil wiped the sweat from his forehead and folded his hands together before he answered, a habit Tal remembered from the Lectorium. It meant that Jarnil didn't want to admit he didn't know the answer and would talk a lot to disguise that fact.

"While the secrets of the Keystones are kept only by the Guardians," Jarnil began, "I understand that certain lengthy rituals and incantations —"

"Balderdash," interrupted Ebbitt. "Also codswollop and shadowpoop. No one knows, except the six Guardians."

"Seven," corrected Jarnil, angry at being so rudely interrupted.

Ebbitt smiled and held up six fingers, closing each one in turn into his fists as he counted.

"Red, Orange, Yellow, Green, Blue, Indigo."

"And Violet," added Tal. He was used to Ebbitt's eccentricities and weird lapses of ordinary knowledge, but this was so obvious he was embarrassed for his great-uncle.

Ebbitt shook his head and smiled, a secret smile.

"The Violet Guardian is the heir of Ramellan," he said. "Not the toe, not the ear, nor the fingernail, but the heir of Ramellan. The in-hair-itor."

"The Empress," said Jarnil. He seemed relieved. "Then we need not fear for the veil so much. It would be truly terrible if Sushin and his cohorts already had the Violet Keystone."

"Why?" asked Milla.

"The Seventh Tower holds all the ancient secrets of Ramellan, all the devices and machines of the ancient magic," said Jarnil. "Whoever controls the Violet Keystone controls the Tower. Fortunately, while the Empress is obviously unaware of the machinations of her Dark Vizier, she would never entrust control of the Violet Keystone to anyone but herself. We can rest easy on that one Keystone, at least."

Ebbitt held up an imaginary book and turned some imaginary pages. It seemed that he had no trouble seeing the book himself, because he traced the first line with his finger, reciting.

" 'The Empress Kathild, first of her line, came to the throne of Ramellan in unusual circumstances. Controversy surrounded the death of Emperor Mercur, and his funeral was irregular and rushed, with no lying in state, giving rise to talk that he had been hideously assassinated and the body was not fit to view.' "

"That's from Kimerl's *History*," protested Jarnil. "She was totally discredited years ago and the book banned. I fail to see any relevance in it, or may I say it, in you, Ebbitt. Really, anyone would think you were the one who came out of the Hall of Nightmares!"

"Talk, talk, talk," said Crow. "That's all that ever happens here. If the veil is in danger, and all of us because of it, what are we going to do? And what's in it for the Freefolk?"

"I will take word to the Crones," said Milla. "They will know what to do."

"I think we need to take a look at one of the Keystones," said Tal slowly. He was still thinking it through. "Maybe if we can work out how to seal it again, it would bring back the Guardian. Or if we find one that's still sealed, we could take it away, so Sushin couldn't get at it."

"I doubt if the Keystones can be moved," said Jarnil. "Since they are part of the Towers and the Veil. But your plan has merit, my boy. If we can release even one Guardian, they can tell us what we must do. And the Empress would surely believe us if we had one of the Guardians to tell their story. Even against the Dark Vizier. But who will go, and to which tower?"

"I will go," said Tal. "To the Orange Tower, to free my father."

·CHAPTER·
TWELVE

"That is ill thought," Milla protested. "Where is your battle sense? Sushin has already laid a trap for you with your brother as the bait. There will surely be other traps, and better ones now, laid around your father and your mother. You should seek a different Guardian in a different Tower."

"You will need help to reach the Tower," said Jarnil. "Crow —"

"Forget it!" interrupted Crow. "Like I said, what's in it for us? If we help the Chosen fix the Veil, then everything stays the same. You say the Aenirans will kill us all, but maybe they'll only kill the Chosen."

"You have a Sunstone," said Jarnil. "I have taught you how to use it. Under the plan of the Sharers of the Light, you would become a Chosen.

The Empress will be grateful if we save the veil. I am sure you would be raised up."

"I don't want to be raised up!" Crow screamed. "I want *all* of our people to be free!"

Bennem made a sound deep in his throat and stood up, looking wildly from side to side. Crow immediately quieted and went to his brother's side, sitting the big man back down.

"I want us to be free," he continued, his voice quite soft. "No more Underfolk, no more Chosen. I will only help you save the veil if you all promise to help free my people."

"I will take your words to the Crones," said Milla. "They will weigh them with the other news I bring. I can do no more than that."

Tal looked at Jarnil and Ebbitt. Jarnil was frowning, his face now as red as it had been white a few minutes before. He was obviously very angry with Crow. Ebbitt, on the other hand, was looking at Bennem. Tal looked, too, meeting the man's soft, unseeing eyes.

"I don't know what I can do, and I won't help kill Chosen or anything like that," Tal said hesitantly, still looking at Bennem. "But if you help us, I will do what I can to . . . change things and make sure that the Underfolk become Freefolk."

Crow looked at Tal with suspicion.

"I suppose that's better than nothing," he said grudgingly. "But you'd better do what you say."

Milla drew the knife she'd taken from Gill and said, "Do you wish me to make the cuts for the swearing?"

"No," said Tal, looking away. "That's not the way we do things here."

Crow shook his head, too.

"A bond without blood is a bond soon broken," warned Milla. "And Crow has not spoken his part of the bond."

Tal looked back and met Crow's eyes. He could not see the burning hatred he'd seen before, but neither could he work out what the older boy was thinking.

"I'll help you get to the Tower," said Crow, but he hooded his eyes as he spoke. "And seal the Keystone or whatever it is we have to do."

Tal nodded. He noticed that Crow had not mentioned helping him come back from the Tower. But perhaps that was simply an oversight, not a thinly shrouded threat.

"And you, old man?" Crow asked Jarnil. There was little respect in his voice now. "Are you still dreaming about good little Underfolk lining up to be tested and joining the Chosen?"

"No," whispered Jarnil sadly. "You were a good boy, Crow. I fear you will not be a good man. All I ask is that you help Tal now. As you say, I am too old and broken, and I can only hope that we will save the Veil and nothing worse will come to either of our peoples. Come, Bennem. It is time to rest."

"I will leave after a short sleep," said Milla. "If Gill will still guide me."

Tal looked at her. In all the talk about the Veil and the Keystones, he had forgotten about Milla and her desire to return to the Ice. But he couldn't think of any way to stop her. Besides, a small part of his mind was telling him they might need the help of the Icecarls, though he was reluctant to admit that.

"We could use your help in the Tower," Tal said, as he desperately tried to think of something that would convince Milla she should not go. "That might be more important than telling the Crones."

"No," said Milla, very firmly.

"What about if . . ." Tal said, racking his brains. It was his fault Milla had lost her own shadow. If she was punished — or punished herself later — it would almost be as if he'd killed her himself.

"What if the Crones want to know more?" Tal said, an idea suddenly coming to him. "I mean, they can talk to one another in their heads or something, can't they? So if one needs to come back here, you'll have to guide her."

"I can tell others the way," said Milla. "If a Crone comes, she will choose Shield Maidens to guide and protect her. I am not a Shield Maiden."

Only Tal caught the slight shiver in Milla's speech as she said "I am not a Shield Maiden." For a moment he thought he'd imagined it, but it was there, the only sign he had ever seen of Milla almost losing control. It was almost as if he had seen her cry, something she had never done, even when terribly wounded by the Merwin.

"I don't think we should be inviting anyone to the Castle," said Jarnil nervously. "While I'm sure Milla and her people mean well, I think the situation with the Veil is best left to us here to deal with."

Milla looked at him, and then around the room at the pitifully small gathering. There was Jarnil, an old man and, as he had said himself, broken by the Hall of Nightmares. There was Ebbitt, who was a force to be reckoned with, but not to be depended upon. There was Bennem, who looked like a mighty warrior, but was a permanent sleepwalker, trapped inside his own head. There was Tal, whom she half hated for what he had done, but who was as close to her as anyone had ever been, an alien brother who was neither predictable nor easily understood. But he was brave, and had growing powers. There was Crow, whom she knew little about, save that his bitterness and anger boiled so hot that he was a danger to friend as well as enemy. There were the other four Freefolk, hardy and resourceful, but hardly trained warriors.

Taken together, they were little to pit against the Sushin monster, his guards, Fashnek, and who knew how many Spiritshadows.

"I think you do not know the true strength and nature of the enemy," said Milla to Jarnil. "The Crones will decide what the Icecarls must do. After all, it was not just your Ramellan that defeated the Aenirans so long ago. It was our Danir, too. You should not fear our help."

But they would fear, Milla knew, and perhaps they were right to do so. She was fairly certain what the Crones would do when they heard the news of free shadows in the Castle and the unsealed Keystones.

They would summon every Shield Maiden, Sword-Thane, and available hunter to the Ruin

Ship. A great host of Icecarls would be gathered, with a single aim:

To take control of the Castle and return all shadows to Aenir.

She doubted that any Chosen, whether under Sushin's sway or not, would let that happen without a fight.

Soon, there would be war upon the Mountain of Light.

Milla was not sure whether to be glad or sorry that she would have no part in it. By then, she would have long since paid the price of her failings out on the Ice.

·CHAPTER·
THIRTEEN

There were many beds to choose from in the Freefolk Fortress. Obviously there had once been many more people to sleep in them. But Tal was too tired to think about that. His wounded leg and the aftereffects of the water spider venom still troubled him. He was able to stay awake only long enough to complain about the Freefolk's primitive toilet and washing facilities (a stinking privy and cold water) before collapsing gratefully into a bed that was superior to most of the places he'd slept in the last few weeks.

When he woke, ten hours later according to his Sunstone, Milla was gone, with Odris. Adras was also missing. Tal woke feeling strangely stretched, with a splitting headache. It took him a little while to realize that this was due to his Spiritshadow's absence.

Adras returned only a few minutes later, drifting dejectedly into the central courtyard around the well.

"Where have you been?" asked Tal grumpily. He was cross from his headache, and because Milla had gone without saying good-bye. He was also grappling with guilt. Milla's fate was entirely his fault.

"Following Odris," replied the Spiritshadow. "But I had to come back, because of this stupid connection between us. Ow!"

He stabbed at his chest with one great puffy finger, his third jab a little too hard.

"Did you see any guards or other Chosen?" asked Tal, rubbing his own chest. He'd developed a sympathetic pain there as well.

"No," replied Adras. "Only red glows, like a distant sunset."

"That's good, I guess," said Tal. "Hopefully they've given up looking for us."

"Perhaps they have," said Jarnil. He came over to the well and used his good hand to scoop up a handful of water to splash upon his face. "The Day of Ascension dawns just hours away, and all Chosen will be preparing for the journey to Aenir."

"Hours away?" asked Tal. He'd lost track of the days since his initial fall from the Castle. Time also flowed differently in Aenir. He looked at his Sunstone. It was the second hour of the morning, still the middle of the night, at least above the Veil. "That's great! It will be so much easier to get to the Red Tower."

"Don't forget that the Spiritshadows remain behind," warned Jarnil. "Once I would have said they will stay close to their masters' bodies, but now I am not sure."

"Have you . . . have you thought of going to Aenir to get a new Spiritshadow?" asked Tal.

Jarnil shook his head.

"It would not be safe for me. Remember, all the Chosen think I am dead. Anyone who saw me would think I was a creature that had taken on the shape of Jarnil Yannow-Kyr, and they would blast me to cinders. Besides, I am not sure I could bind a Spiritshadow now."

Tal nodded. Adras nodded, too.

"Crow and Ebbitt are preparing clothes and equipment for you," Jarnil continued. "Crow has decided that it is best if only the two of you attempt the Tower."

"What about me?" asked Adras.

"And you, of course, Master Storm Shepherd," said Jarnil. "I should have said three."

"Master Storm Shepherd! I like that," boomed Adras. "You should call me that, Tal."

Tal sighed. He was missing Milla and Odris already, though he didn't want to admit it.

"I'd better go and get ready," said Tal. "Where are they?"

Jarnil pointed. But before Tal could walk away, he gripped the boy by the sleeve and leaned in close to him.

"I know only what Ebbitt has told me of the Icecarls, and that he gained from you," he whispered.

"Are they as strong and warlike as Ebbitt says? You see, I am not sure we have done the right thing in letting Milla take any news to them."

"They are warlike," Tal answered, his voice low. He bit his lip a little before continuing. "But they are also honorable. They helped me return to the Castle. Milla has saved my life several times."

"I know, it is hard to think of someone who has saved your life as an enemy," Jarnil observed. "But what do you think the Icecarls will do when they hear of a way into the Castle? Ebbitt tells me Milla came here for a Sunstone, that they are rare in the world beyond. I understand that there are many different bands or tribes. What if one of them sees us as a storehouse of riches to be plundered? Would they risk attacking us, even knowing of our superior magic?"

"I don't know," Tal replied slowly. "They might."

"We must be careful, Tal," Jarnil muttered. "These Icecarls are outsiders. While I am keen to raise up suitable Underfolk, they are at least Castle-dwellers. I want you to promise that if the right opportunity comes along, you will warn the Empress, or some safe Chosen, about the possible danger from Icecarls raiding the Castle."

"I'll think about it," said Tal. It was hard not to promise. He still reacted to Jarnil as if he were a Lector, and Tal a small boy. He felt like he should be bowing and giving light in respect from his Sunstone.

"Do so," instructed Jarnil. He let Tal go and stalked away, his bad arm fluttering at his side.

"Forget you heard that," Tal instructed Adras as they went over to the cottage Jarnil had indicated.

"Forget what?" asked Adras.

"Forget it." Tal shook his head.

"What?" asked Adras. "What?"

"Nothing!" shouted Tal. "Never mind!"

Adras snorted and shot up to hover over Tal. A moment later, shadow-rain fell harmlessly on Tal's head. He ignored it and opened the door. Adras stayed outside, rumbling.

·CHAPTER·
FOURTEEN

Inside the cottage, or rather the large cellar room underneath, Crow was sorting through a collection of strange garments. Great-uncle Ebbitt was asleep in a hammock strung up across one corner, his Spiritshadow beneath him. As Tal came down the steps, Ebbitt and his Spiritshadow opened one eye each.

"Beware the voices of sensible men, who sing almost in tune and know all the words," said Ebbitt.

Tal scowled. Sometimes Ebbitt was as bad as Adras.

"Come over here and try these on," instructed Crow. He sounded friendlier than he had in the past.

Crow passed him two sets of white robes. The first was light, probably the standard Underfolk wear, but the other set was made of a heavier, shinier material. Crow also gave him a long-snouted mask that had clear crystal eyepieces, and a pair of crystal clogs.

Tal put on both sets of robes. The outer ones were heavy and hot, as if the fabric did not breathe. The mask was like a giant rat's head, the snout easily as long as Tal's forearm. It had holes in the end, but most of the snout was filled with a spongelike material.

"What is this?" asked Tal, before he slipped it on. The mask fit very tightly to his face and under his chin, and was secured behind with adjustable straps.

"Filter mask," Crow replied. "We're going to be disguised as caveroach sprayers. The masks keep the poison out. Put these gloves on, too."

Tal put on the long, almost transparent gloves. They came up to his elbows and were made of something like the gut of an animal. He was flexing his fingers and being thankful that they were so light when Crow threw him huge, heavy gauntlets made of the same material as the robes.

"Do we have to wear all this stuff?" Tal asked, his voice muffled behind the mask.

"Yes," said Crow. "The caveroach sprayers do all the corridors while the Chosen are away in Aenir. We will be able to get right up to the base of the Red

Tower. But we'll have to spray on the way so we don't look suspicious."

"Your great-uncle thought of the disguise," Crow added reluctantly, nodding at Ebbitt. "It might even work, since he says your Spiritshadow can change its shape enough to be a normal shadow."

"Yes," said Tal. He hadn't really thought about it, but being a Storm Shepherd, Adras was much more malleable than any normal adult Spiritshadow, which had to basically conform to its Aeniran size and shape.

"I always wanted to be a caveroach sprayer," said Ebbitt from his hammock. "But I was doomed to a career as a Chosen."

113

Both Crow and Tal frowned at him, though for different reasons. Since Crow had just put his mask on to adjust it, Ebbitt couldn't see either boy's expression and continued.

"I have often wondered where I might have ended up if I'd been a caveroach sprayer."

"Dead, like most of them," said Crow, taking off his mask. "Even with the suits, the poison gets them after twenty or thirty years."

"Why don't they change jobs?" asked Tal innocently.

Crow stared at him.

"Underfolk can't *change* jobs," he said scornfully. "We get written into the records when we're born. If you're a boy, you get your father's job. If you're a girl, you get your mother's. We don't even have names in the records. Just 'born to Sweeper #1346, a son, Sweeper #3019.' We make up the names later."

"Who keeps these records?" Tal was puzzled. He'd never heard of Chosen doing something so much like work, or of Underfolk having numbers instead of names.

"We do it to ourselves now," said Crow, his lip curling into a sneer. "The Fatalists. The Chosen started it long ago, and the Fatalists are so convinced we are here only to serve that they just keep doing everything as it has always been done. Are you ready?"

The sudden question surprised Tal. He stammered out a yes.

"We'll go, then," said Crow. "It'll take a few hours to get up to Underfolk Seven. We'll have to pick up some poison sprayers on the way."

"We're going right now?" asked Tal. "What about the others —"

"They've gone to get the airweed and scrounge

for food. The sooner we get this over with, the better. That Milla had the right idea. No waiting around. I reckon she'd be a good looker, too, once she washed up."

"What?" asked Tal. He'd never had time to spare any thought to what Milla looked like. He was confused about how he felt about her. He'd just got used to the guarded enmity between them, which was better than when she'd wanted to kill him.

"Milla," said Crow, twisting his face into an exaggerated leer. "I wouldn't mind —"

"She'd kill you," said Tal.

"She liked me," said Crow. "I could tell. You'll see, when she comes back."

"She won't be coming back!" Tal burst out. "After she tells the Crones what she knows, she's going to give herself to the Ice! She'll be dead."

"What!" exclaimed Crow. In his surprise he dropped his odd expression. "Why?"

"It's complicated," muttered Tal. He picked up his mask and headed for the steps. "Are we going?"

"After you," said Crow.

But Tal was stopped at the bottom of the steps by Ebbitt's Spiritshadow. It stood in front of him and yawned, exposing a great mouth of shadow-teeth.

"Tal."

Ebbitt sounded unexpectedly serious. Tal went across to the hammock, while the maned cat stood aside so Crow could climb up and out.

"What is it, Great-uncle?" asked Tal.

"A caveroach does not know the difference between right and wrong," instructed Ebbitt. "Because they have only instinct to act upon. You, on the other hand, have at least some small parcel of thought. Do not be a caveroach."

"What does that mean?" asked Tal. "Do not be a caveroach?"

"It's dangerous to be a caveroach," said Ebbitt. "Particularly when traveling in the company of a caveroach sprayer."

Tal nodded and wondered what in Light's name Ebbitt was going on about.

"The Icecarls cometh," said Ebbitt. "Unless I miss my guess. It's a pity you lost the Codex."

"It's here somewhere," Tal protested. "In the Castle. Maybe it will find you."

Ebbitt brightened at this thought.

"You think so?" he said. "It would be nice to chat to the old thing again."

"Good-bye, Uncle," said Tal. He bent down and hugged the old man, as usual surprised by Ebbitt's lightness. He was more fragile than he appeared.

"Good-bye, Tal," said Ebbitt. As Tal started to straighten up, Ebbitt whispered in his ear, "Bring me back a cake. One of the ones made with almond meal and boiled oranges. And change your mask before you go."

Tal nodded.

"I will, Uncle," he said. "In return for that cake — can I have two doses of the water spider antidote? In advance?"

·CHAPTER· FIFTEEN

Aided by the airweed and Gill's guidance, Milla found the entrance to the heatway tunnels without trouble. Gill wanted to continue on with her, but the Icecarl sent her back and waited to make sure she did not follow. Milla knew that she was the only one who knew the way through the heatway tunnels, and that was how she wanted it. Tal would not remember the twists and turns, and she was fairly confident he had lost the miniature map carved on bone — though there was a slim chance Crow had taken it, when he had found them unconscious the first time.

Odris followed the Icecarl silently through the heatway tunnels, practicing being a normal shadow, as Milla had instructed. Even though Odris had more freedom to change shape than a bound Spirit-shadow, it was still difficult for her, particularly staying smooth. She was naturally puffy, and her arms and legs had a habit of billowing out to be much wider than they should be.

Milla kept her Sunstone low, so there was not quite enough light for Odris to feel entirely well. Being a natural shadow was further complicated by the coil of rope Milla had wrapped around her chest, and the extra blankets and gear she was carrying rolled up in a swag across her back. It all changed her silhouette and Odris had to pay constant attention to match it.

At the skeleton where Milla and Tal had found the Sunstone they now each had part of, Milla stopped and collected the skull and bones, wrapping them in a blanket. She felt that she owed the Chosen that much, for her Sunstone. She would take the bones with her and give them a proper Icecarl funeral, leaving them out in the clean snow and ice of the mountainside.

As she collected the bones, something glinted in the light. For a second Milla thought it was another Sunstone, put to sleep as the previous one had been.

It wasn't. It was an artificial fingernail, made of the same Violet crystal the Chosen used so extensively in the Castle. As Milla held the nail close, she saw it was flecked with tiny Sunstone fragments that picked up the light of her stone and sent it sparkling in currents through the nail.

The nail could be slipped on and was held securely by a thin band of crystal behind it. Milla tried it on. At first it was loose, then the band tightened. Milla tried to take it off, but it would not budge.

Milla shrugged. More Chosen magic. At least the nail was sharp, and could be a useful weapon. Besides, she was already doomed by the Spiritshadow that loomed behind her.

"What is that?" whispered Odris.

"A nail," said Milla. "Remember, you must not talk once we are outside. An Icecarl might be hidden nearby. I will be slain out of hand if anyone suspects you are a Spiritshadow — and I must take my warning to the Crones before I die."

"All this talk of dying," said Odris. "I won't let you, you know."

"The Crones will deal with you," said Milla roughly.

"Hmmph," said Odris. "We'll see."

Just before the exit, Milla found her heavy fur coat, the new one she had been given at the Ruin Ship. She rearranged her equipment to put the coat on and looked down at Tal's coat that had lain underneath her own. She felt a vague uneasiness as she thought of the Chosen boy. It was rude to sneak away without a farewell, particularly from a Questbrother — even if he had doomed her, giving away her shadow.

"Was that Tal's?" asked Odris. "You know, I feel like I miss him as well as Adras. Funny, isn't it? The feeling must be coming from you, because I don't care for him."

"It isn't," snapped Milla. "Tal is of no importance. Now be silent."

The cold hit her as they climbed out of the tunnel entrance. Milla had never left the cold for long before, and now it cut into her, taking her breath away. She had to stop and practice a Rovkir breathing exercise to stop shivering. Fortunately, the weather was fine, at least by Icecarl standards. The wind was strong and steady, and her Sunstone shone brightly out into the permanent darkness. No snow, hail, or sleet fell into the circle of light around her.

Outside, Odris found it even harder to remain a natural shadow. The wind called to her, as it did in Aenir, tempting her to launch into the air and go with it. At the same time, she felt Milla's shadow deep inside her, anchoring her to the Icecarl girl. Somehow Milla's Rovkir breathing also helped the Spiritshadow keep control of herself.

It only took a moment to unwrap the skeleton and cast the skull and bones out into the dark void. With good fortune, Milla thought, something would find them useful, to chew upon or to line a lair.

Just below the entrance to the heatway tunnels was the blue crystal pyramid of Imrir, and past that, the gap in the road. Tal and Milla had jumped across it, coming up. Now Milla stood on the edge, staring down into the darkness.

She considered jumping across. Would it be weakness or strength to have Odris fly her over? She should not use her unnatural shadow. But it was her duty to get the Sunstone back to the clan as quickly as possible and warn the Crones of the danger to the veil.

She had made the mistake of putting her own wishes ahead of her duty before, Milla thought.

She would use Odris.

"I want you to carry me across," Milla said, holding up her arms.

"I'll need more light," said Odris. "And a run up."

Milla nodded and backed up. She concentrated on her Sunstone as she walked. She was getting better at controlling it, but was still much slower than Tal. The stone slowly brightened, the ring of light around her expanding. Odris slipped up into the air and spread out into a puffy shadow-cloud, swaying in and out of the light as she adapted to the breeze.

Milla held up her arms again.

As Odris gripped her, a terrible, penetrating scream startled both of them. Odris lurched forward, even as a huge winged creature came down and thrust its claws through the Spiritshadow and almost into Milla.

"Perawl!" shouted Milla, but Odris held her so tight she could not draw her knife, or even turn and bite. She was totally defenseless and under attack by one of the most vicious predators on or above the ice.

·CHAPTER·
SIXTEEN

Tal was surprised by how the Castle was transformed by the Day of Ascension. With all the Chosen retiring to their rooms to lie down and transfer their spirits to Aenir, and their Spiritshadows going with them, the Castle was left largely to the Underfolk.

It was eerie and still in the corridors. Tal couldn't help but think of what he should be doing. He should be with his family in their quarters lying down on his bed with the specially embroidered cover, waiting for his father to stand over him with his Sunstone, to guide him in the crossing.

He had never felt so alone.

It was strange to see so many Underfolk about too. They chose to use this time in a sudden frenzy to get to work on all the major and intrusive jobs of maintenance, repair, and construction that could not be done while the Chosen were up and about.

Even down on Underfolk Seven, where Tal and Crow stopped to get backpack sprayers of cave-roach poison, there was considerable bustle and preparation. Underfolk storepeople were issuing tools and paint, lumber and screws, brushes and mops, replacement pipes and fixtures, and all manner of other things, to a steady stream of men and women.

As Crow had said, these Underfolk — Fatalists as he called them — seemed very keen to get on with their work. Tal would have thought they would use the opportunity of the Chosen's absence in Aenir to have a rest. But there was no sign of this. They were totally focused on their tasks.

Tal and Crow wore their masks, and Tal noticed everyone gave them a wide berth. Obviously Crow had not exaggerated about the poison. It seemed the other Underfolk feared to touch even the clothes of the caveroach sprayers, and perhaps because this embarrassed them, did not look at Tal or Crow, either.

This was just as well, Tal thought, because Adras was having trouble being a natural shadow. He was always a bit behind, so that when Tal turned a corner, his shadow would keep on going for a moment and then hastily correct itself. No one seemed to have noticed so far, but it was making Tal very anxious.

Still, as long as they stayed out of the Chosen's individual chambers, or some of the specialized areas like the Imperial antechambers, where Chosen slept and their Spiritshadows guarded both them and the rooms, Tal and Adras should be safe from recognition.

It took nearly the whole day to climb up from Underfolk Seven to the highest level of Red, where they could begin the climb to the Red Tower, though it was also possible to get to the Tower from some of the higher color levels. Normally Tal would have taken less than an hour to climb the steps and ramps, but they had to stop all the time and climb into drains or pipes or other out-of-the-way places to spray for caveroaches.

After a while, Tal noticed that Crow was watching him as they sprayed, almost as if he expected something to happen. Tal watched him, too, mindful of Ebbitt's advice to change the mask Crow had given him. But he wasn't sure if that was simply Ebbitt's usual weirdness, or because his great-uncle expected Crow to have picked a defective mask for Tal.

Certainly Crow seemed to be making an effort to

be friendly. His verbal attacks of the previous day were gone, and when he spoke, it was simply to instruct Tal on how to spray, or how to act like an Underfolk. Maybe his watching was also only to make sure Tal was staying in character. Maybe Crow wasn't waiting for him to suddenly pass out and die from the poison.

Tal couldn't make up his mind either way, but he decided to be careful.

From the High Red Commons, the huge chamber that in other times would be full of Chosen of the Red Order meeting to gossip and socialize, Tal thought there would be a stairway that led both to the foundation room of the Red Tower, and a narrow walkway that ran outside around the base of the Tower.

When Tal had climbed the Red Tower before, he'd started higher up in the Orange levels on a similar walkway, then climbed down and across to the Red walkway, where he had launched his assault on the Red Tower.

Though he'd never been in the High Red Commons before, Tal was certain that the layout would be the same as the High Orange Commons. When he saw the huge chamber, he knew that he was correct. Though it was furnished differently, with many low lounges upholstered in bright red cloth rather than the individual crystal chairs of the Orange Commons, the stairway was in the same corner. No more than two stretches wide and without railings, it ran up into the ceiling high above. Like the one in the Orange Commons, Tal suspected it was hardly ever used.

"That's it," he said to Crow, pointing.

"Good," said Crow. He looked around, making sure that the whole chamber really was empty. Then he shrugged off his backpack sprayer and put it carefully upright against one of the lounges. Tal did the same, then they both backed away.

"Don't touch your gauntlets after they're off," instructed Crow. He showed Tal how to loosen both of them and then shake them off, rather than taking one off and then wondering what to do with the other.

They left the gauntlets and retreated again, to kick off their clogs and remove their outer robes. The lighter robes underneath were soaked with sweat and very clammy. Both boys had knives scabbarded on their sashes, and Tal wore his Sunstone ring openly.

Any Chosen or Spiritshadow that saw them would know instantly that they were some kind of enemy.

"Can I stop being a stupid regular shadow now?" asked Adras plaintively as Tal headed for the steps. The Spiritshadow lifted his head up as he spoke, though he kept Tal's basic shape. It looked very strange, as if Tal's shadow had somehow gotten curled up.

"When we're outside," Tal promised.

As they climbed the steps, Crow suddenly asked Tal a series of questions about the Keystones.

"Did your father ever tell you about how these Keystones work?" Crow asked when they were halfway up.

"No," Tal replied. His leg was hurting him again. The steps were steep and it would be easy to fall off. He needed all his concentration.

"I mean, this Guardian job seems to get passed on down the family. He might have mentioned it."

Tal shrugged and shook his head.

"What about old Jarnil's notion that they can't be moved? Do you think he's right?"

"I don't know." They were almost at the top. The door was probably locked, but Tal could melt the lock with his Sunstone. He'd stolen the key to the Orange door, but had long since lost it.

"They had to be put there in the first place," muttered Crow. "I bet they can be moved. We should take it away, so we're the ones who can use it."

Tal ignored him, pausing to get his breath back before he tried to open the door.

It was barred on the inside, but the bar came free easily enough. Tal leaned it on the steps and tried the door again. It was locked.

"I'll open it," said Crow, as Tal peered at the lock and the gap between the door and the door frame. "Let me past."

In his eagerness to get at the door, Crow pushed Tal slightly, and the Chosen boy had to grab the iron staple that had held the bar to avoid falling off. It was a long way to the bottom, far enough to be fatal, and Tal knew Adras probably wasn't smart enough to have caught him if he fell.

But the push had seemed accidental.

"Oh, sorry," said Crow. Tal retreated a few steps down as Crow pulled a ring of keys out of his sleeve pocket and selected one to put in the lock. Then he inserted a strip of thin metal as well, and turned both of them.

The lock turned easily, and the door swung open.

The light from the Sunstones in the chamber spilled out, but was swallowed by the darkness beyond. A freezing wind blew in, rattling the door and sweeping back the two boys' hair, stinging their faces and eyes.

Crow seemed paralyzed. He stood there, his keys in his hand, staring out into the eternal night beyond the narrow walkway.

"Welcome to the Dark World," said Tal.

·CHAPTER·
SEVENTEEN

The Perawl shrieked again and took off, its prey in its huge claws. Unfortunately Odris had made herself quite solid in order to hold on to Milla, so the huge, leathery flying creature could easily grip her shadowflesh.

"Ow!" cried Odris. "Ow! Ow! Ow!"

The Perawl couldn't really damage her, but its great talons were ripping her body, and it hurt.

"Drop me!" shouted Milla. "Drop me now!"

They were still above the road, but the Perawl could swing away at any time, out into open space.

Odris obeyed, but a fraction too late. Milla saw the gap in the road below her, the deep crevasse she had jumped across before. She made a frantic grab and just managed to grip on to the little finger of Odris's left hand.

The finger stretched and stretched into a long rope of darkness as Milla swung below her Spiritshadow. The Perawl beat its mighty wings, taking Odris higher.

Milla focused on her Sunstone, brightening it as fast as she could, and at the same time she screamed, high-pitched and loud. Perawls couldn't stand very bright light, or very loud, high noises. They didn't see or hear like any normal creature.

The Perawl gave a surprised squawk and tried to let go. But its talons were actually embedded in Odris, and the Spiritshadow couldn't make herself more insubstantial without making her finger the same.

133

Milla fell. The Spiritshadow's finger got thinner and thinner, until it was burning through Milla's gloves, and she had to take one last swing and let go.

Immediately Odris thinned herself, slipping off the Perawl's talons like water. But she was already high above Milla. All she could see was a falling light, which was all too soon extinguished.

With the absence of light, Odris immediately grew weaker. She fell from the talons, but did not have the strength to fly. Instead, she plummeted straight down, a blot of formless shadow, indistinguishable in the darkness.

Milla missed the gap in the road by a few stretches, but the impact was hard. She tried to get up straightaway, but the wind had been knocked out of her, so she could only rise to a crouch. She could hear the Perawl squawking in the distance, but there was no sign of Odris nearby.

She could feel her Spiritshadow, though. The connection between them was strong. Milla concentrated on getting her breath and tried to focus on the direction of the feeling.

It came in waves, a horrible, wrenching sensation, accompanied by feelings of weakness and nausea. Milla turned in a circle, to pin it down. After a few turns, she realized that Odris was farther along the road, and down quite a long way.

Milla also felt that the Spiritshadow wouldn't last much longer without light. Already she was fading, and as her strength faded, so did Milla's.

The Icecarl girl forced herself fully upright and started down the road. The smell of the ghalt, the molten stone used in the road, was strong. She drew it into her nostrils, regretting the loss of her facemask for a moment. Then she moved at a steady lope, much faster than she had climbed up with Tal.

She risked a fall going at such speed, but with every passing breath, she felt Odris fading. If she didn't get to her to provide light soon, the Spirit-shadow would die — and from the feel of it, would take Milla with her.

That must not happen before she brought her news to the Crones, Milla thought.

She *must* get to the Crones.

Milla felt another wave of nausea and weakness hit her, and shuddered. It was a familiar feeling, as if the blood were flowing out of her body. Unconsciously, she held her hand to the Merwin-horn scar in her middle, as if to staunch the wound there. But it was healed.

Grimly, Milla increased her pace, leaping over snow-covered stones and irregular chunks of ice. At the same time, she began to breathe the Tenth and Final Rovkir Pattern. The Dead-Walking.

That Pattern was the last resort, and few Icecarls had the mastery of it. The Dead-Walking would enable her to keep going, no matter how wounded or weary, till her task was finally done.

Then she would die.

Lost in the Tenth Pattern, she did not even feel the falls, the tumbles, and the many small bruises and cuts, as she continued to run pell-mell down the road. There was only the breathing, and the constant pull of Odris's slow fade to nothing.

Odris felt the light before she saw Milla. It brought her back from somewhere where she had no thoughts, no feelings. In one moment she was falling from the Perawl, in the next, lying spread across the snow. As the Sunstone drew nearer, Odris felt her shape returning. Her shadowflesh flowed back to her like a tide, from where it had been spread across many stretches.

But Milla didn't really stop when she reached Odris. She paused and reached down. Odris grabbed her hand. The Spiritshadow hardly had a moment to shout hello before Milla ran on, dragging Odris with her.

"Slow down," shrieked Odris, as Milla fell down the far side of a large rock and nearly went over the edge. "You'll hurt yourself."

Milla didn't answer. She kept on running.

Odris flowed up her arm and twisted her head around to have a look. Milla's eyes were glazed and there was a strange light in them, reflected from the Sunstone burning brightly on her outstretched hand.

"I don't like this," whimpered Odris. "What are you doing?"

She heard no answer, but in her head came the sudden echo of Milla's thought.

The Ruin Ship and the Crone Mother. The Ruin Ship and the Crone Mother.

They came to a point where the road switch-backed ahead. Instead of running around the hairpin turn, Milla plunged over the side, sliding down thirty or forty stretches through snow, ice, and stone.

"No, no, no!" shouted Odris. She puffed herself up and lifted Milla, so the girl swooped down instead of sliding. But this only encouraged the Ice-carl. She left the road again and launched herself into space, to go straight down the mountain.

"Stop!" shrieked Odris, as she spread herself out to get the best glide and lift, exerting all her strength against the winds that threatened to dash them back into the mountainside. "Whoa! Milla!"

The Ruin Ship and the Crone Mother . . .

·CHAPTER·
EIGHTEEN

Tal and Crow stood on the narrow walkway, high up on the outside of the Castle. Adras flew above Tal, and above him loomed the huge Red Tower. Beams of light in all shades of red sprang from its many windows and openings, weaving a complex pattern in the sky. Behind it were the other six Towers, all of them taller, each also casting light out into the darkness.

Below them, other lights twinkled in the main bulk of the Castle. But even all these lights could not compete with the essential darkness of the world beyond. The veil lay heavy on the world, and the light of the Seven Towers and the Castle spread only a little way.

"I didn't think it would be so cold," Crow whispered as he looked out on the darkness. "Or so . . ."

His voice trailed off. Then, with an obvious effort, he tore his gaze away and looked up at the Red Tower they were about to climb.

As Tal had found before, there were many spikes, gargoyles, and strange ornaments that could be used as hand and footholds. Even so, it was not an easy climb, and would be impossible if they were not protected against the cold.

Tal concentrated on his Sunstone, and soon warmth was flowing from it, along his arm and then all over him.

"You have a Sunstone," Tal said guardedly. He still wasn't sure about the wisdom of an Underfolk having a Sunstone. "Do you know how to warm yourself with it?"

"I know more than that," replied Crow. He took out his knife and flicked open the thin cover on the pommel, to reveal the Sunstone there. He concentrated on it for a moment, and Tal saw it flash in answer.

"Ah," said Crow. "That's better. Do you want to go first, or shall I?"

"You go first," said Tal warily. "It will take us a few hours to reach the veil. Watch out for the windows. Some are open and there may be Spiritshadows there."

Tal was very much aware of the danger. He could remember his first climb too well, and his brother, Gref, being taken through just such a window.

That climb seemed very long ago, but it was only a matter of six weeks or so. His entire life had changed that day, and not positively. Hopefully this climb would mark a change for the better.

At least this time he had a Sunstone, Tal thought. He looked at Adras, hovering above him. And a Spiritshadow of his own.

Once again, he was reminded of his first climb. There was a chance the Spiritshadow that had thrown him off would still be there, though if he was lucky it would be guarding its master's body while he or she was in Aenir.

The Keeper, it had called itself.

Crow started to climb, easily pulling himself up onto the first gargoyle's broad back. Tal let him get a bit ahead, as he thought about the Keeper. Maybe it was a free shadow. . . .

"Are you coming?" asked Crow. He was already a good twenty stretches up.

"Yes!" Tal called out. He started to climb, then stopped and spoke quietly to Adras.

"Adras. Keep a lookout, and make sure you catch me if I slip."

"Sure," Adras replied. "What about thingummy? Do I catch him, too?"

Tal hesitated.

"Yes," he said finally. "But make sure I'm safe first."

The climb went faster than the first time Tal tried it. Crow was quick, and Tal himself felt stronger and more confident. It only took them an hour to reach the veil.

Tal had been ready to call out to Crow to stop, to prevent the older boy climbing up into the thick layer of ultimate darkness. But Crow had stopped of his own accord. He was crouched on a gargoyle's head, slowly raising his hand, watching it disappear into the veil. With his arm apparently ending in a stump, he tried to play light on the veil from his Sunstone, but the light simply stopped when it hit the dark barrier.

"It feels weird," said Crow. He was unable to suppress a shudder as he withdrew his hand. "What's up above?"

"Sunlight," said Tal. "There may be a Spirit-shadow. A big one. It calls itself the Keeper."

"It spoke to you?" asked Crow. "Isn't that un-usual?"

"Yes," replied Tal. He didn't mention that he suspected the Keeper was a free Spiritshadow.

"So how do we get through the veil? Is there some secret . . . some *Chosen* secret to it?"

He couldn't quite keep the sneer out of his voice when he said "Chosen."

"Not as far as I know," Tal replied. "Just go quickly. I'll go first if you like."

"Good idea," replied Crow. "You can deal with this Keeper, too. I don't mind watching."

"With your help, I hope," said Tal quickly. "We're in this together."

He was still never quite sure exactly what Crow meant. Was he joking?

"Adras, you'd better stay close to me," Tal ordered, as he edged up closer to the veil. "Grab hold of my sash and hang on. You'll probably . . . not like the inside of the veil."

"Why?" asked Adras. He drifted closer and hooked two puffy fingers through Tal's blue sash.

"It's made of absolute darkness," said Tal. "So dark you feel like you will never see the light again."

Adras was silent. Tal could feel him struggling with the concept of absolute darkness. Clearly it was beyond his imagination.

"Wait a minute or two, and then come after me,"

Tal told Crow. "Climb through as quickly as you can. It probably helps to take a very deep breath before you start."

"Why?" Crow asked.

"I couldn't breathe last time," Tal explained. "I'm not sure you can breathe inside the veil."

Crow raised an eyebrow, as if he didn't quite believe Tal. But he didn't speak.

Tal reached up into the veil, watching his hands vanish. For a second he had the sensation that they had truly disappeared. He flexed his fingers in response, and felt something he could grab hold of.

"Hang on!" he said. Then he took a deep breath and pulled himself up.

Into the veil. Into the darkness.

·CHAPTER·
NINETEEN

It was a long way down the Mountain of Light. Odris kept shouting and screaming all the way down, even as she frantically steered them away from fatal gusts and sudden outcrops of stone.

Finally they hit the foothills, plowing a trail through deep snow for at least twenty stretches.

Milla immediately got up to run again, but Odris held her fast.

"Milla! What's the hurry?"

Milla didn't answer. She began to drag Odris through the snow.

"Milla!" Odris tried again, this time stretching a hand around to slap the Icecarl in the face.

"Let me go," said Milla, her voice strangely flat. She hadn't stopped dragging the Spiritshadow. "I must go to the Ruin Ship."

"Something is really wrong with you," replied Odris. She kept hold of the girl and craned her head around again. Milla was breathing very strangely, her nostrils clamping in a curiously hypnotic pattern.

Odris was about to pinch Milla's nose shut when someone else shouted Milla's name.

"Milla!"

Odris whipped back to pretend she was a natural shadow, but it was too late. An Icecarl stood in the snow only a dozen stretches away, already kicking off her skis, her knife in her hand.

"Abomination!"

The Icecarl leapt at Milla, knife flashing at her throat. But Milla dodged, and the knife raked across her shoulder, cutting fur and the skin beneath.

"To me!" shouted the Icecarl. It was a woman, Odris realized. Through her mental connection with Milla she felt a name swim into her consciousness.

Arla. Shield Mother.

Answering shouts came out of the darkness, from not far away.

Arla struck at Milla again, but the younger girl blocked the blow and threw Arla over her shoulder. The Shield Mother somersaulted in the air and landed on her feet, twisting to block Milla's strike in turn.

"I must reach the Ship, the Crones," said Milla in her strange, flat voice. "The Ruin Ship, the Crone Mother."

"Never!" spat Arla. "Shadow-slave!"

There was another quick exchange of blows as the two rushed together. Milla was cut again, across the thigh, but did not react to it. As Arla turned to attack again, Odris saw the Shield Mother was cut on the side of her face, where a blow had knocked off her face mask.

"Stop!" boomed Odris. She rushed in and gripped Arla with one hand and Milla with the other, both around the neck. "There's something wrong with Milla. She needs help, not killing."

"To me!" shouted Arla again. "Abominations!"

Milla said nothing, but lunged forward with her left, supposedly empty hand. But the strange fingernail she wore suddenly extended, slashing through Arla's armor and furs.

Arla choked in midcall. Odris let go of her and dragged Milla back.

The Shield Mother tried to stagger forward, her knife raised. She only managed three or four steps before she collapsed. Dark blood flowed from her, stark against the pure white of the snow.

"To me!" roared Odris, in a fair imitation of Arla's voice. Then she let go of Milla and the girl was off and running immediately.

Odris followed her, wringing her shadow-hands with worry. Milla's mind seemed to have been affected by the cold or the darkness. It was still there, as far as Odris could tell, but was blocked off by this thick layer of thought that endlessly repeated the same thing over and over again.

The Ruin Ship and the Crone Mother.

Another Shield Maiden emerged out of the darkness, running at Milla. Odris swept forward and buffeted her out of the way, before Milla did something worse.

The Shield Maiden shouted some words that Odris didn't know, and the shout was taken up all around them, out in the dark. Odris could see and feel faint glows from weak lights all around, then she saw a sudden explosion of tiny green lights that shot up into the air. It would have been beautiful if it wasn't so obviously a signal.

It was followed a few moments later by the sudden blast of a deep horn, a horn being blown urgently, as if someone's life depended on it. A warning sound.

Still Milla ran on, always finding the hardest-packed snow or the roughest ice. She seemed to skim across the surface, bright golden light from her Sunstone flickering with her, her Spiritshadow flying at her side, in her full Storm Shepherd size and shape.

The Shield Maidens and Shield Mother who had come bursting out of the Ruin Ship in answer to the alarm saw her running down the hill, but it was not Milla they saw. It was a monster, blood-soaked and phantom-lit, with a dark beast of shadow as its companion.

"Ready spears!" shouted the Shield Mother in charge. "Wait! Wait!"

Milla came on, Odris screaming at her to stop, her screams only making them both seem more terrible and dangerous.

"Wait!" roared the Shield Mother. Then, as the light from Milla's Sunstone spilled across the first rank of Shield Maidens, the leader dropped her arm and shouted.

"Throw!"

·CHAPTER·
TWENTY

The crushing, breath-stealing darkness pressed down on Tal. He fought it as he struggled to climb, to find another handhold, to break free and into the light.

Just in time, he remembered to close his eyes, so that when he burst out, he was not blinded. There was just the welcome flash of color under his eyelids, and the sudden warmth on his face.

Slowly, Tal opened his eyes a fraction and climbed completely out of the veil, to sit astride a long bronze pole that thrust out of the wall.

Adras was still holding on to his sash. As the Spiritshadow came into the sun, he let out a surprised gasp, and then stretched and luxuriated in the sudden energy.

"I have missed the sun and the sky," he rumbled,

far too loudly for Tal's comfort. "Look, there are clouds!"

There were many clouds, in fact. It was close to sunset, and the sun was shining red and low through a deep band of cloud on the horizon.

Tal didn't look at the clouds for long. He was too intent on scanning the Tower above. There were no more gargoyles or stone ornaments, only long bronze rods and the golden nets that were suspended beneath the rods, nets that held neophyte Sunstones, Aeniran jewels that slowly absorbed power and light above the veil.

Tal wasn't interested in them today. He was looking for the Keeper.

There was a balcony not far above. That was where he'd seen the Keeper last time. But it was empty now. Nor was there any sign of movement on the walkway even higher up.

Tal looked back down at the veil. It was strange to see it spread right across the sky. It looked solid, like black soil, with the Red Tower growing out of it. If you didn't know what it was, you would never suspect that there was a whole world underneath.

Right at that moment, a hand thrust out of the Veil, fingers scrabbling frantically for a hold on the pole. Tal jumped with shock. Another, apparently disembodied arm followed, then Crow's head burst through.

His eyes were wide open. Tal had forgotten to warn him about the sun.

Crow screamed and flung one arm across his face. His other hand lost its hold. Desperately his fingers flailed to regain it, as his body teetered backward.

Tal reached out and grabbed him around the wrist, and Crow gripped him with amazing, panicked strength.

It was too late. Crow was already overbalancing. He fell backward. Tal let go, panicked himself, but Crow still kept hold.

Tal's own handhold slipped, his grip broken.

Together they fell into the veil, even as Tal threw out his other arm, screaming for Adras.

They were in the darkness for only a fraction of a second. Tal felt Adras grab his arm with a familiar shoulder-wrenching suddenness. Then he was hauled back into the light. Crow came with him, almost wrenching his other arm out of its socket, until Adras reached down and pulled him up as well.

Both of them clutched at the bronze pole as if it were a long-lost friend. It took a few seconds before either of them spoke.

"You should have warned me!" hissed Crow. His eyes were still crinkled up against the sun. "It is so bright!"

"It's sunset," muttered Tal, in his defense. "Hardly that bright. Besides, I told you there was sun up here."

Crow muttered something angrily, but Tal couldn't catch what it was. He kept a wary eye on the Freefolk boy. At least Milla was predictable in this sort of circumstance, he thought. He didn't know what Crow was thinking at all.

"Well," Crow said finally. "Let's call it even, shall we?"

"Call what even?" asked Tal, puzzled.

Crow looked at him scornfully. "Don't give me that pretend stupid act. Who did you learn it from? Ebbitt?"

"I don't know what you're talking about," Tal said.

"Sure," snarled Crow. "Whatever you say. From now on, let's just help each other, all right?"

"I thought that's what we were doing. That's what I want to do."

Crow grunted. Carefully keeping one hand tight on the pole, he shaded his eyes and looked up.

"Darkness!" he swore. "What's that?"

Tal looked up swiftly and groaned. Sure enough, oozing over the balcony was the Keeper.

Tal still didn't know what creature it was in Aenir. The Keeper had a huge, grotesque head, with many eyes and a very wide mouth, full of hundreds of tiny, needlelike teeth. It's body was snakelike, long and sinuous, coiling along behind that horrible head.

It was bigger than Adras.

"Seek not the treasures of the sun," chanted the Spiritshadow as it slid over the balcony. Its voice was high-pitched and screeching, awful to hear. "I am the Keeper, and none may pass here, save those who know the Words."

Tal stared up at it, expecting at any moment to be totally consumed by the panic he had felt in his last encounter with the Keeper. But to his surprise he found himself quite calm. His hand was already coming up, his Sunstone glowing red as he instinctively prepared a Red Ray of Destruction.

"Adras, stand clear!" Tal ordered, his steady voice another surprise. "Crow, if you can do anything to this thing, do it!"

"I can if it gets close enough," said Crow. He was getting something out of the pouch on his belt, but Tal was too intent on the Keeper to see what it was.

The Keeper dropped onto the rod above them, twining itself around as it lowered its head for the next leap — straight onto Tal.

Tal kept concentrating on his Sunstone. He fed it anger and rage, and the Red grew deeper and stronger, swirling in the depths of the stone.

As the Keeper opened its too-wide mouth and tensed to spring, Tal thrust his hand forward and released the pent-up power of the Sunstone.

A Red Ray too bright to look upon shot out, a thin spear of light that punched through the Keeper's head. Drops of shadow spurted out of the back of its head. It screamed and recoiled, in pain and surprise.

Tal's relief died as he saw the droplets of shadow leap from the bronze rod and the Tower wall and fly back into the Keeper. In a few seconds the hole drilled by the Red Ray had closed, and the Keeper was once again preparing to spring.

"None may pass here!" hissed the Keeper.

"Can you hold it still?" shouted Crow. There was no need for shouting, but Tal understood why he was.

"No . . . yes . . . I don't know," he shouted back. "Adras, grab hold of that thing."

Adras had only been waiting for the word. He

roared a battle cry and unleashed two bolts of shadow-lightning at the Keeper. More shadow-drops flew, then Adras was upon it, gripping it in a bear hug with his mighty arms. But its snake body was as quick to wrap around him, and Adras grunted as the thing began to squeeze.

Its head lowered, too, and it bit at Adras's shoulder. Adras howled, squeezed even harder, and bit back.

"It's still moving too much!" shouted Crow. He was getting up on the bronze rod now, intending to climb up to the next one where the two Spiritshadows were wrestling and biting. He had a strange silvery bag in his left hand.

Tal stared down at his Sunstone. There had to be something he could do to immobilize the Keeper. A variation of the Hand of Light. A rope. Something! Anything!

·CHAPTER· TWENTY-ONE

As the spears flew, Odris leapt upon Milla, grabbed her, and glided with her only a half-stretch above the snow. The spears went overhead. Odris, with Milla tucked underneath, plowed through the line of Shield Maidens. Knives cut at the Spirit-shadow's back as she passed, but only sank into the shadowflesh and rebounded.

Odris kept going. Ahead of her, a huge wall of golden metal loomed, part of some giant structure that disappeared up into the darkness. There was a doorway in the side, with fuzzy green lights all around it.

"Ruin Ship, Ruin Ship," Milla repeated. Odris understood that this metal house was Milla's target. Perhaps when she reached it she would come to her senses.

If she reached it. Odris felt several spears strike her in the back, some of them going far enough through her to at least scratch Milla. Even so, the Icecarl did not cry out.

Odris kept on gliding, as close to the ground as she dared, sometimes grazing it a little with Milla. Near the door, she swooped up, dropped Milla, and turned to face their pursuers.

No more spears flew. Thirty or more Shield Maidens drew their long knives and rushed forward in total silence.

Odris drew herself up to her full height and shadow bolts of lightning formed in her hands. She was about to throw them when she heard a voice behind her call out a rapid sequence of strangely familiar words, followed by the shouted command, "Stop!"

The Shield Maidens stopped. Odris would have thrown the shadow-lightning, but she found herself unable to move. Whatever the words were, they had done something to the shadow in her heart, Milla's shadow. It had reached out and stilled her muscles.

Odris couldn't even turn to see who had spoken. Now all she could hear was Milla's voice. Milla was suddenly babbling on about the Aenirans and the veil and Sushin and Odris and Adras, but it was all mixed up and it didn't make much sense.

The voice spoke again.

"Libbe! Go to Crone Dalim, ask her to come quickly with her medicines. Breg, go to the Mother and ask her for a shadow-bottle. Run!"

Odris kept trying to turn around. She could feel the shadow inside her going back to sleep or whatever it normally did, and she was regaining control of herself. Slowly, she began to turn.

A silver-eyed woman in black furs was cradling Milla, her hand placed firmly on the Icecarl girl's heart. As Odris turned, the woman looked at her and rapidly spoke the same words again.

This time, they had less effect. Odris felt the shadow stir inside her, but it could not hold her. She turned completely around and took a step forward.

A glowing knife appeared in the woman's other hand. A shorter version of the Merwin-horn sword Milla had lost when she had impaled Sushin.

"Come no closer, shadow," ordered the woman. "You shall not have this girl."

Odris sighed and sat down.

"I don't want to *have* her," she said.

The woman started, and there was a gasp from the Shield Maidens. Apart from the ones who had run off, they were standing still, as the woman had commanded, in a ring around Odris, none closer than thirty stretches.

"You speak," said the woman. "It is long since we have seen a shadow that speaks."

"Is Milla all right?" asked Odris. "She feels sort of sick to me and she's been acting very strange."

"Milla?" asked the woman, looking down. "If that is her name, she has gone far into the Tenth Pattern. I do not know if we can guide her out. If we cannot, she will die."

"I don't want her to die!" wailed Odris. "What will happen to me?"

The Spiritshadow started to weep, huge shadow-tears rolling on to lie black upon the snow.

"Beware the strategems of shadows," muttered the woman. "Lemel, you had best call the Mother Crone herself, and not just a shadow-bottle."

"No need," said a calm, quiet voice. "I am here."

A very old, tall woman spoke. Odris saw that this one had strangely milky eyes. She walked forward with confidence, pausing to look down at Milla. Another Crone, younger and less bright-eyed than the one with the knife, followed her. She went straight to Milla, took something from the bag she carried, and broke it under the girl's nose.

"Ah, I thought it would be Milla," said the Mother Crone. "She got her Sunstone, I see."

"She spoke of strange things," said the first Crone. "Words she had laid upon herself to deliver, dead or alive. I have them."

"Then I will hear them, in due course," said the Mother Crone. "Can she be saved?"

"If you wish it," said the younger Crone. "She is at the choosing of the ways."

"Bring her back," the Mother Crone instructed. "I think I will want more than a few words. Now, Speaking Shadow, what is your name and kind?"

"I am Odris, Storm Shepherd, once of Hrigga's Hill," said Odris. "Who are you?"

"I am the Mother Crone of the Ruin Ship," said the Mother Crone. "I am the Wisdom of Danir, the Living Sword of Asteyr."

"Oh," said Odris. She got up and bowed.

"No Aeniran is permitted upon the Dark World, by the ancient law of Danir," continued the Crone. "By what right do you come here?"

"I came with Milla," Odris explained. "She wanted to tell you about the Veil being in danger, and the Keystones being unsealed, and —"

"Stop!" ordered the Mother Crone. "We will

speak of this with Milla herself. I say again, by what right do you come to the Dark World?"

"I don't know," said Odris miserably. "I just wanted to get away from the Hill and then I had to follow Milla."

"You must be taken for judgment," said the Mother Crone. "Will you go willingly to your prison, or must I force you?"

Odris looked around. The Shield Maidens probably couldn't hurt her, though there was that Crone with the glowing knife. The Mother Crone also seemed very confident Odris could be made to obey her.

"I'll do what you want, on one condition," Odris answered.

"We do not make conditional agreements," said the Mother Crone. "Yet you can tell me what you want. Perhaps it is not a condition after all."

"I want you to stop Milla from giving herself to the Ice."

The Mother Crone looked down at Milla. She seemed to be merely asleep now, breathing normally, as the younger Crone cleansed and bandaged her wounds.

"We cannot promise that," she said. "It is every

Icecarl's right to go to the Ice. Besides, Milla herself must be judged. Perhaps our judgment will be that she must go to the Ice."

Odris frowned and shot up into the sky. But she knew she couldn't go very far from Milla. Even if she could escape that binding, there was no light out in the world. She would fade to nothing.

There didn't seem to be much choice.

"What is this prison?" she asked. "And the judgment? Will I get to speak my side?"

"Yes, you will be able to speak," said the Mother Crone. "And here is the prison."

She drew a tall bottle of golden metal out of her robes and unscrewed the stopper.

"I can't get in that," said Odris. "It's too small."

"I think you will be surprised," replied the Mother Crone. "Will you try?"

Odris felt a strange power in the old woman's voice. Power that was building, as if the next time she spoke, her words would fly out like a Storm Shepherd's bolts of lightning.

"Oh, all right!" she said.

The Mother Crone held out the bottle. Odris billowed down two legs and trudged over, her head downcast in defeat.

"Are you sure this is big enough?"

The Mother Crone nodded. Odris pushed a finger in the top, then another. Somehow she got her whole hand in, and arm, and then the rest of her was sucked in, like being caught up in a whirling storm.

Strangely, Odris did not feel cramped. There was even some light coming in from outside, so she did not feel sick. But when the stopper was screwed back in, Odris did get a strange feeling. There was the hint of other shadows here, from long ago. Shadows who had never been released, who had long since faded into nothing. . . .

·CHAPTER·
TWENTY–TWO ☉

Tal concentrated on his Sunstone, willing orange light to form. Dimly he was aware of Adras shouting and swearing, and the Keeper hissing, but he blocked them out. The Light was the only thing that mattered.

Slowly, he wove the orange light out of the ring. It came out as a bright, narrow strand that thickened as it rose up. It became a rope, as broad as Tal's arm. He kept drawing more of it out, until it rose straight up above him for twenty or thirty stretches.

Sweat beaded on Tal's forehead as he concentrated on the end of the rope. He directed it into a loop, tying a slip knot. Then he gently lowered the noose of light down toward the struggling Spirit-shadows.

The noose hung there, Tal holding it with his

mind and his Sunstone, as he waited for an opportunity. It bobbed down a few times, but he never completed the cast. Adras always got in the way.

"I can't hold it," whispered Tal, after the fourth attempt stopped suddenly in midair, as Adras swayed back under the noose.

"Adras!" roared Crow. "Push it away!"

Adras grunted. For a second he made no move. Then he suddenly let go and instead of hugging the Keeper, pushed it away. At the same time, Tal dropped the noose. It went perfectly over the Keeper's head. Instantly, Tal tightened it, the rope of light cutting deep into the shadowflesh. Then he quickly wrapped the rope around the rest of its body as Adras leapt free, pinning the Spiritshadow in place against the bronze pole.

"Quick! I can't keep it going!"

This was the moment Crow had waited for. He jumped to the higher pole and swung himself up in front of the struggling Spiritshadow. The bag in his hand was made of gold mesh, and he slipped it over the Keeper's head, though it struggled to evade him.

"Let it go!" shouted Crow.

"What?" screamed Tal. "Are you crazy?"

The Keeper's head was in the strange gold-mesh bag but Tal didn't see how that would help. It would just pull out and knock Crow off, before killing Tal and Adras.

"Let the rope go!"

Tal shook his head. But that had much the same effect. He lost concentration, and the rope began to fade. Tal looked to Adras, ready for a quick get-away.

Strangely, the Keeper did not pull its head out of the bag. Instead it actually slithered farther in. Crow held the bag open until all the Spiritshadow was inside, then closed the drawstrings tight and hung it over the end of the pole.

"Pity it's the last one," he said, sitting astride the pole and dusting his hands in the attitude of a man finishing a job well done.

"Last what?" asked Tal, staring at the bag.

"Shadow-sack," replied Crow. "We only had three. Jarnil found them for us a few years ago, I don't know where. He wouldn't say."

"Can it get out?"

"Only if someone lets it out. Someone real. Shadows can't touch that golden metal. Didn't you know? I thought you'd get all this in your Lectorium."

"No," said Tal. "I'm only beginning to realize all the things I wasn't taught in the Lectorium."

"We'd best move on," said Crow. "That was a noisy fight."

He started to climb up to the next rod. Tal looked at Adras.

"Are you all right?"

"Hah!" boomed Adras. "I would have won. It was weak."

"I guess that means you are," Tal said. There were some holes in the Spiritshadow's shoulder, but he didn't seem bothered by them. Besides, Tal knew Spiritshadows healed very quickly under the sun. "Come on."

On the rod above, Crow had stopped to reach into the nets to fill his pockets with Sunstones. But he had picked up only a handful when he threw them down again.

"These aren't Sunstones!" he exclaimed angrily.

Tal joined him and picked up a handful himself. The stones were shiny black ovals, with only the slightest hint of inner fire.

"Sunseeds," he said, not admitting to Crow that he had never actually seen them before. "Jewels from Aenir. They must have harvested the ready Sunstones just recently, and put these out to grow in power."

"Just my luck," grumbled Crow. "Let's hope the Keystone's still there."

He started climbing again, even faster than he had earlier.

"Anyone would think it's a race," Tal complained. Then he thought, maybe it is. He didn't know what Crow really wanted up here, or what he had really agreed to.

"A bond without blood is no bond," Tal muttered. He reached up to the next pole and swung up. "Adras! Give me a hand!"

It was a surprisingly long way to the top of the Tower, almost as far above the Veil as it was below. With Adras's help, Tal caught Crow before too long, but night had fallen before the very pinnacle of the Tower was in easy reach.

They had been tempted to go onto one of the balconies or walkways and continue up the stairs, but caution had prevailed. So they had kept to the outside, the bronze rods and the nets of spun gold with their carefully arranged Sunseeds. Every now and then Crow had taken up a handful, just in case, but he had yet to find a proper Sunstone.

At last they came to the final bronze rod, half Tal's height below the topmost walkway. They could see the spire of the Tower, not far above, surrounded by a crown of distant stars. Light still spilled out above them, but not the bright red rays of the lower windows, just a dim, pinkish glow.

The Tower had grown slender at its peak, little more than forty stretches in diameter. Tal and Crow sat on the pole, listening, hoping to hear if anything was inside the room above. But all they heard was the wind and the soft rattle of the Sunseeds and the nets.

"There may be traps," said Crow. "I'd better take a look first."

"There may be," said Tal. "Light magic traps. We'd best go together."

Crow nodded. He crouched on the pole, hanging on with one hand as he reached up to the railing above, careful to put his hand between the sharp serrations. Tal moved up next to him and had to reach out farther across. Adras hovered next to him and reached out a steadying hand.

Crow jumped. An instant later, Tal followed.

·CHAPTER·
TWENTY-THREE

Tal and Crow landed on the walkway together. Both were scratched by the sharp railings, but not seriously. They stood carefully at the very edge of the narrow path and looked into the room in front of them.

The top of the Red Tower was a domed room, open to the air, with four arched doorways, one at each cardinal point of the compass, leading to the circular walkway. Inside the room, the ceiling was covered in a mosaic of tiny Red Sunstones, glittering like a seam of jewel-filled rock. The floor was tiled in red and white, but not in any regular or obvious pattern.

Hanging upside down — or perhaps growing — from the very center of the domed ceiling was a tree of red crystal. Its trunk was straight and bare for several stretches, before it branched out into a canopy that covered most of the room. Each branch had a silver bell on the end.

Tal stared at it, trying to figure out what it was for. There was a strange cluster of small silver hands around the base of the trunk, at the apex of the dome. They seemed to have some purpose . . . every hand held a thin wire that went back into the trunk of the tree.

"What is that?" asked Crow. He spoke quietly and pointed at the tree.

"I don't know," Tal whispered. His attention had been caught by what was under the upside-down tree.

On the floor of the room, there was a pyramid-shaped plinth of a darker red, about as high as Tal's chest. Two silver hands were mounted upon it, and between them was clasped a large, slowly pulsing Sunstone. It had to be the Red Keystone.

"I don't like the look of all those bells," said Crow, studying them with a burglar's practiced eye. "Or the silver hands."

Then Crow saw the Keystone. He started forward, and stopped only a step from the doorway.

"Maybe you should send Adras in to get it," he suggested.

"Sure," said Adras, before Tal could speak. The Spiritshadow surged forward, but as he tried to enter the arched doorway, the Keystone flashed and a solid sheet of Red light slammed shut like a door. Adras bounced off it with a startled "oof!"

The Red light faded as he bounced back, and the Keystone was quiet once more.

"No Spiritshadows allowed," said Tal. "There must be other defenses, too."

He looked up at the tree and the bell-branches again, and then at the floor. The red tiles seemed to be placed in line with bells above them.

"I think the bells sound if you step on the wrong tiles," Tal said slowly, as he thought it out.

"Maybe," said Crow. "Let's see. . . ."

He leaned forward and lightly pressed a white tile with his finger. Nothing happened. Crow pressed a little harder. Still nothing.

"Now the red," he said, transferring his finger to the closest red tile.

As his finger touched, a silver hand above twitched slightly, and the bell above rang — a tiny, hesitant ring.

"So the red tiles sound the bells," agreed Crow.

They both looked across at the floor. The arrangement of the tiles seemed haphazard, but now they realized that it would be almost impossible to reach the plinth. The individual tiles weren't big enough to get more than most of one foot on, and the red tiles were cleverly distributed so that there were more of them the closer you got to the plinth, and the white tiles too far apart to stretch.

"There must be a way to silence the tree," said Crow.

Tal shrugged. "The proper words, or proper light. But the wrong thing would set them all going."

Crow looked up at the tree, then down at the floor, and finally at Tal.

"You're lighter than me," he said. "I reckon I can stand just inside on those two white tiles, and boost you up to that branch. Then all you have to do is grab any bell that I might set off."

"That's all!" protested Tal. He looked at the crystal tree dubiously. If it was like the ones in the Crystal Wood it would be quite strong enough to climb. But it would also be very easy to fall off it, or cut himself on the narrower branches.

"Do you have a better idea?"

"I could have another try," said Adras, who was still rubbing his head.

"No," said Tal. "I don't have a better idea."

Even without a better idea, they still walked around and checked the other three entrances, to see if either the tree or the floor looked different or easier to move across.

They didn't, so Tal, Crow, and Adras returned to the western arch. The sun had set completely, but the walkway was lit by the Red light that spilled out from under the dome and through the arches.

The brightest light came from the Red Keystone. It shone between the silver hands on the plinth, pulsating with the uncanny and disturbing rhythm of a human heart.

One that was beating a lot slower than Tal's.

"Ready?" asked Crow.

Tal nodded.

Crow backed up to the arch, and then stepped back, craning his head. Keeping his toe pointed, his foot just fit within the confines of one white tile.

Both boys held their breath. But no bell sounded, no light flashed.

Crow stepped back with his other foot. For a moment it looked like he would lose his balance. He swayed and then recovered, cupping his hands so Tal could use them as a foothold.

Adras helped him, being careful not to step too close.

Held high outside by Adras, Tal put his foot in Crow's hands and ducked under the arch. Adras was still holding the back of his shirt.

"Now!" cried Tal.

Adras let go, Crow jerked his hands up, and Tal pushed.

He went flying toward the ceiling and the closest branch.

It seemed farther away than it had from outside.

·CHAPTER·
TWENTY-FOUR

Milla woke in a dream. She knew it was a dream because she was standing with one foot on the bowsprit of a speeding ice-ship, the wind whistling through her hair. Sunstone light spilled on the ground ahead, and the ship bucked and rolled as its runners met uneven ice.

Just ahead Milla could see a great roiling mass of Slepenish, breaking through the ice. Small icebergs bobbed and splintered as the millions and millions of Slepenish turned the ice into open sea.

The ice-ship was heading straight for the hole in the ice and certain destruction. Yet it was not too late for the ship to turn, if only a warning was given.

Milla tried to shout, but no sound came out of her

mouth. She tried to wave her arms in warning, but they would not move.

She didn't mind meeting her end in the freezing water, but she didn't want to take a whole ice-ship full of her people with her. Even in a dream.

A hand touched her shoulder. With it came freedom. Milla turned, meeting a Crone's silver gaze.

The Crone nodded.

"Ware water!" Milla shouted. "Turn aside! Turn aside!"

She was still shouting the warning when she woke up.

The same Crone she had seen in her dream was leaning over her. Behind her Milla could see the golden sheen of the metal walls of the Ruin Ship.

She had made it, and she wasn't dead. The Crone had brought her back.

"Do not try to get up," the Crone warned. "You were far gone in the Tenth Pattern. You will be weak for some days."

"I must tell the Crone Mother," whispered Milla. "Shadows. Aenir. The veil."

"We know," soothed the Crone. "You told me while you were still in the Pattern. And we have walked in your mind while you slept."

Milla nodded. Now she was done. The Crones knew what they must know.

"I will go to the Ice," she said. "I have the strength for that."

The Crone shook her head.

"You may not go to the Ice. At least not yet. Both you and your shadow companion must first be judged, when you are strong enough to bear the weight of whatever judgment is passed."

"There is no need for judgment," said Milla weakly. "I lost my shadow. I brought a free shadow from the Castle and . . ."

She frowned as dim memories came swirling in.

"Did I fight the Shield Maidens?"

"Yes," said the Crone calmly.

"Arla . . ." whispered Milla. "I seem to remember . . ."

"The Shield Mother is dead," said the Crone bluntly. "She died with a knife in hand, as she would have wished. Yet perhaps she was always too ready with her knife, instead of words."

"I . . . I killed Arla?"

Milla's head fell back. She had only flashes of memory since emerging from the heatways. Now one fragment was clear in her head. The strange nail on her hand, sweeping across Arla's stomach.

"It was not a fair fight," she said, the words choking her. She raised her hand to show the strange, Sunstone-flecked fingernail of Violet crystal. "I had Chosen magic."

The Crone shook her head.

"It was not a trial combat, so why should it be fair? Besides, Arla was a Shield Mother, stronger and more experienced than you. And that strange nail is not Chosen magic."

"What is it?" asked Milla, her voice husky, already fading as she struggled to stay conscious.

"It is ours," said the Crone. "One of two made for Danir long ago. One she kept, and one she gave away. Both have been lost for more than a thousand circlings."

Milla heard the Crone's voice getting farther and farther away. She tried to answer, but could not.

Unconsciousness claimed her.

When she came to, there were three different Crones in her room, and several Shield Maidens.

"The Crone Mother of the Ruin Ship has decreed you will be judged," said the eldest, milky-eyed Crone. "Are you strong enough to bear whatever your fate may be?"

Milla nodded. She was unable to speak and she

couldn't look at the Shield Maidens. They clustered close as she shakily stood up, their hands on their knife hilts.

"Follow me," said the older Crone. She pulled back the curtain of furs and led Milla out. The other Crones fell in behind, but a Shield Maiden remained on either side of Milla.

It was a slow progress. Milla had never felt so exhausted. She could hardly put one foot in front of the other, but somehow she managed to keep going. The Shield Maidens stopped when she stopped, but at no time did they or the Crones offer to help her.

Finally, they came to a wide door, the furs already pulled aside. The Crones went in with Milla. The Shield Maidens did not. They pulled the fur curtain across as soon as the last Crone passed.

Milla's eyes had been firmly on her own feet all the way. Now she slowly raised her head.

They had come to a huge room, as large as the Hall of Reckoning. But this room was almost empty, a great chamber of gleaming golden metal walls, ceiling, and floor. There were no Sunstones present, but hundreds of lanterns burning Selski oil were set in concentric rings around the single item of furniture in the whole hall — a tall chair of white bone, that stood in the center of the room.

Milla was led to it and sat down. The two younger Crones tied her wrists and ankles to the chair with strips of Wreska-hide. The bonds were tight and the knots strong.

Milla did not resist.

Then the Crones turned the ring on her finger so she could not see the Sunstone, and retreated to stand against the walls.

Milla sat silently waiting. It was just her and the three Crones in the huge silent room.

She was too tired to wonder what would happen next. What *could* happen? She had brought a shadow to the Ruin Ship and she had slain a Shield Mother. They would probably use the Prayer of Asteyr on her and send her out to stand before the Selski Living Sea. Her name would become a curse, a word to be spat, a ballast-stone of loathing the Far-Raiders would have to bear for many circlings.

She had disgraced herself, her clan, and her people. Now even a clean end of her own choice upon the Ice was out of her reach.

Milla closed her eyes and let her chin slip forward a little, a small sign of the despair within her.

Then she heard the curtain open and she looked back up.

Crones were entering the room. Many Crones,

more than Milla had ever seen. Scores of Crones, from the bright blue-eyed of the newest to the milky-eyed oldest, all of them clad in black. They spread out along the walls, the only sound the shuffle of their feet and robes.

There were hundreds of them, Milla saw. Crones from every clan and ship. Perhaps even her own Far-Raiders' Crone was there.

Milla hung her head again, ashamed. She did not want to see the Crone who had always had such high hopes for her.

Finally, the Crone Mother of the Ruin Ship entered. While all the other Crones lined the walls, she strode out across the open space, a tall figure, her shadow flickering by her side in the lantern light.

She stopped by the chair, unscrewed a bottle she had under her arm, and laid it down next to Milla. Then she stood behind the chair and raised her arms high.

There was total silence in the hall, and all the Crones were still.

The silence lengthened. No one moved. Milla held her breath.

Finally the Crone Mother spoke, her voice soft, but echoing throughout the vast room.

"Today we decide the Doom of Milla of the Far-Raiders, daughter of Ylse, daughter of Emor, daughter of Rohen, daughter of Clyo, in the line of Danir since the Ruin of the Ship.

"Before that Doom is decided," the Crone Mother continued, "we must hear the words of Milla of the Far-Raiders. For she has brought evil tidings, and the news she bears must be weighed with her fate."

"What . . . what must I say?" asked Milla.

"Everything," said the Crone Mother. "Begin when you left the Ruin Ship, with the Chosen Tal, in your quest for a Sunstone. Tell us everything."

Milla cleared her throat and slowly began to speak. She told the assembled Crones about the journey into the Castle, the skeleton with the Sunstone, Great-uncle Ebbitt and the attack by the guards, the Hall of Nightmares, the Mausoleum, the transfer to Aenir, the Storm Shepherds, Tal's use of the Prayer to Asteyr, how Odris was bound to her while she was unconscious, the riddling pool in the desert, the Dawn House, Zicka the Lizard, Asteyr's ship, the Codex, Sushin and the Merwin-horn sword, the Keystones and the threat to the veil . . . it all came tumbling out of her.

The Crones listened in silence, though occasionally a ripple passed through their ranks, as it did when she spoke of Asteyr's ship.

They listened, their strange blue or silver or cloudy white eyes intent on Milla. And as they listened, they judged.

·CHAPTER·
TWENTY–FIVE

Tal was afraid the bell would ring anyway as he gripped the branch. But it didn't. He swung a leg over and hauled himself up, grateful that the branch was round, without sharp crystal edges.

"That bell," said Crow, pointing to a branch a stretch or so away.

Tal balanced on the branch he was on and leaned across. He ran his hand along the branch to the bell and grabbed the wire that would make it sound.

"Ready," he said.

Crow nodded and jumped across. His foot fell on a white tile and partially on a red. As he landed, the wire twitched under Tal's hand, but he had it fast, and the bell did not sound.

"That one," Crow said again, pointing.

"This one will sound as soon as I let go," protested

Tal. He could feel the tension in the wire. Looking up, the silver hand at the base of the tree was still plucking mindlessly away.

"You can hold both," Crow assured him, without bothering to look.

Tal sighed and examined the situation. If he did the splits across two branches he might just be able to hold both bells, but there was a good chance he would fall off.

"Can't you go another way?" he asked.

"No," said Crow, who was on tiptoes. "Hurry up!"

Tal grimaced and stretched his leg across. He tested his foothold, then shifted his weight, while keeping hold of the first bell.

He made it, though he was now hanging on to the first bell's wire as much for his own balance as to stop it sounding. It was an awkward position, but he could reach the second bell, though not its wire. Instead he reached inside and grabbed its clapper.

"Go!" he panted.

Crow jumped again. Tal felt the first wire and the second clapper shiver under his hands.

"Now that one!" called out Crow. But Tal couldn't see him. He was facing the wrong way, and precariously balanced.

"I can't see," called out Tal.

"Dark take it!" swore Crow. "Let go the first one and swing around."

"I can't!" said Tal. "I'll fall."

"Trust a Chosen to give up!" Crow spat. "I'm only two tiles away! Swing on the clapper of that bell."

"That's easy for you to say!" shouted Tal angrily. He was holding on to the bell's clapper with only three fingers.

Crow didn't answer.

Tal tried to crane his head to see the Freefolk boy, but he couldn't.

Instead he took a deep breath, let go of the wire, and pushed off from both branches, so that all his weight was on his three fingers and their precarious grip on a single bell clapper.

He swung around, got both legs over a higher branch and stopped, hanging upside down with his hand still on the clapper, the bell turned up as far as it would go.

"How is this better?" he asked sarcastically.

Crow looked up and laughed a genuine, unexpected laugh. He tried to say something but the laughter kept getting in the way of the words. He shook so much that he had trouble staying on his tiptoes.

"It's not funny!" shouted Tal.

Crow stopped laughing and wiped his eyes.

"I know," he said, frowning. "I don't know why I laughed. Can you let go of that bell on the count of three, and grab the one across to your left?"

Tal looked at the bell Crow was pointing at. He would have to stay upside down, swing across, and grab the branch with one hand and the bell with the other, all in the time it took Crow to jump.

"I can try," he said. "How will that help?"

If Crow jumped there he would have to balance on a single red square, on tiptoe, keeping his other foot in the air.

"I can do it," said Crow. "On three, right?"

"Ready," confirmed Tal.

"One. Two . . . Three!"

He jumped. Tal swung across. Crow's foot came down a fraction of a second before Tal's hand grabbed the wire.

The bell rang once.

Both boys froze, waiting for the other bells to start, or something else to occur. Besides the wire thrumming under Tal's hand, the tree was silent.

"One more and I'll be there," said Crow, his arms stretched out as he balanced precariously, one foot held out behind him. "If I can make it that far."

Tal looked at the tiles Crow would have to jump. There were no white tiles next to the plinth at all. He would have to balance once again on a single red tile. Worse still, Tal wasn't sure which bell went with which tile — the bells were so close together above that point.

He would also have to swing up and there was a branch in between.

"I don't think I can get to the right bell," said Tal worriedly.

Crow tried to look up, but had to stop as he almost overbalanced.

"You'll have to," he said. "I can't stay here like this. On three?"

"No!" Tal called out suddenly. "What if you jump on to the pyramid itself and grab the hands? Would you touch the floor?"

Crow looked across at the plinth. The hands were about level with his neck. It was a long jump, particularly off one foot. But if he could grab the hands, he could hang from them with his feet drawn up, at least till Tal got to the right bell and stilled it.

"I can do that," he said confidently. "Stay where you are."

He crouched on his one foot, toes aching as he kept them pointed. Slowly he leaned forward, arms quivering to maintain his balance. All his attention was focused on the plinth and the silver hands. He would jump that far and grab them. He would. He must.

It was only when he was already totally committed to the jump that a terrible thought flashed through his mind.

What if the hands weren't securely fixed to the plinth?

·CHAPTER·
TWENTY-SIX

Finally Milla's voice, hoarse and weary, faltered to a stop. She wet her lips and waited for whatever was going to come next.

"Now we will hear from the Speaking Shadow," announced the Mother Crone. She stamped her foot near the bottle, and it rang, metal on metal. The stopper had already been unscrewed.

Odris flowed out in one easy motion, drawing up to her full height next to Milla, overshadowing the Mother Crone. But the old Icecarl woman did not flinch or step away.

"So, Odris, Shadow of the Storm," she said, "you have heard Milla of the Far-Raiders speak. Do you wish to challenge any part of her story?"

"No," said Odris. "Only I want to say that I would be quite happy to give Milla her shadow back, if anyone knows how to do it. Though not if it would kill me or hurt a lot or anything like that," she added hastily. "I mean, I just want to go back to Aenir with Adras."

"You were born after the Forgetting, were you not?" asked the Mother Crone.

Odris nodded.

"Then you cannot be held guilty of making war upon our people," pronounced the Mother Crone.

"Good," said Odris. "Can we go, then?"

"No." The Mother Crone walked back behind Milla's chair and spoke to the assembled Crones over the girl's head.

"Milla of the Far-Raiders, by her own voice, is accused of bringing a free shadow to the Ice and of the slaying of the Shield Mother Arla, daughter of Halla, daughter of Luen, daughter of Rucia, daughter of Nuthe, in the line of Grettir since the Ruin of the Ship. You have heard Milla, walked in her dreams, seen from her eyes. What punishment shall be laid upon her, and what shall be done with the shadow that walks at her side?"

No one moved. Then one silver-eyed Crone came forward, taking a dozen slow and somehow threatening steps.

She stood facing Milla. She did not speak.

"In fairness," the Mother Crone announced after a minute or two, "we shall speak with the voice, not the mind."

The Crone looked cross. But she spoke.

"I am Jerrel, sister to Halla, mother of the Shield Mother Arla. Why speak at all, I say? The crimes are clear. She is not fit to go to the Ice. Let her be broken and fed to the Wreska of her clan, and the name . . . *Milla* . . . be never borne again by any Icecarl."

Milla closed her eyes. This was almost the worst punishment possible, one of the possibilities she had tried not to think about. If only they would let her go cleanly to the Ice!

Another Crone stepped forward twelve paces, advancing to stand level with, but distant from Jerrel. She was older, her eyes still faintly silver, but the milkiness already swimming in.

"I am Kallim, Clir's daughter, sister of Rucia," she said. "I have heard Milla, and walked in her dreams, as I walked in the dying dream of my sister's daughter's daughter Arla. I say that on the slaying, it was an equal combat, not murder, and no punishment is needed. On the bringing of the shadow, it came with Milla, but she did not choose its coming. We must also consider that Milla has done a great service in bringing news of the Chosen's evil and the danger to the veil. The news could not be brought without the shadow, so on that score I say she is also blameless."

Milla listened in bewilderment. This Crone seemed to be saying that there should be no punishment at all!

No more Crones came out to speak. But after a few minutes, they started to gather behind Jerrel or Kallim, lending support to one or the other.

"They're talking," whispered Odris, who had sidled up next to Milla. "In their heads. I can almost hear it. Like the whispers on the wind."

Milla watched. She had given up all hope, but now a faint spark had been lit inside her. Maybe there was a chance she would be forgiven, that she could be a Shield Maiden after all. . . .

Only an awful lot of Crones were lining up behind Jerrel, the one who had called for her to be fed to the Wreska. More than were lining up behind Kallim.

After a few minutes there was no further movement of Crones. Milla couldn't be sure, but it looked as if more than half of them were lined up behind Jerrel. If this worked like a normal ship council, then that meant Jerrel would win.

Milla would die ignobly, and her name would be permanently blighted.

She shut her eyes, then opened them again as she heard the Crones shuffling.

A third Crone, a full milky-eyed Mother Crone, was striding off to the far end of the room. When she got there she spoke.

"I am the Mother Crone of the Eastern Clans," she said, her voice heavy with power. It made the hair on the back of Milla's neck stand up. "I say that there is a third way to settle the Doom of Milla of the Far-Raiders and the Shadow Odris."

A ripple passed through the assembled ranks of the Crones, slight but enough for Milla to notice.

A third way?

"For her misdeeds, I say she should be cast out of her clan," announced the Mother Crone. "And her name shall be taken from her."

Milla suppressed a sob. *This* was the very worst punishment. Even if she had been fed to the Far-Raiders' Wreska, she would still be one of the clan, and her name, though not to be used again, would be remembered.

To be cast out was to be erased, to have never been an Icecarl at all.

"For her deeds, and for the blood she bears," the

Mother Crone continued, "let the Outcast then be taken into the Clan of the Ruin Ship and given the name Milla, and confirmed in her ancestry."

Milla choked. How could she be cast out of the Far-Raiders one minute and then adopted by the senior clan of all the Icecarls in the next?

"Further, let this new Milla, Milla of the Ruin Ship, Wielder of the Talon of Danir, be given command of the Expedition we plan," said the Mother Crone of the Eastern Clans. "But as she has trafficked with shadows, let us bind both her and her shadow-companion to the task ahead."

"What Expedition?" asked Milla. "How can I be cast out and then taken in? What . . . what does it all mean?"

No one answered her. All the Crones were moving across to stand with the Mother Crone of the Eastern Clans.

·CHAPTER·
TWENTY-SEVEN

Crow grabbed the silver hands and his knees crashed into the plinth. It hurt, but his feet didn't touch the tiles, and the hands did not give way. He hung from them for a moment, then pulled himself up and rested his forearms across the top of the pyramid, on either side of the hands.

Above him, Tal managed to get in a more comfortable and secure position astride a branch that was positioned so he could look straight down at the Keystone.

They both stared at it, Crow from a handsbreadth away, Tal from four or five stretches above.

The Keystone was a large Sunstone, about the size of a circled thumb and forefinger. It was deeply red, and continued to pulse with the slow regularity of a heartbeat.

Crow suddenly craned forward and studied the stone more closely.

"There's . . . there's someone inside it!" he said. "I can see a woman!"

Tal leaned down lower. He was too far away to see any detail. The stone just looked red to him.

"And there's a shadow with the woman," said Crow. "Smaller than her, some sort of hopping animal . . . with a long tail."

"It must be the Guardian," said Tal. "Jarnil's cousin Lokar and her Spiritshadow. What's she doing?"

"Just floating, as if the stone is filled with water." Crow shook his head in bewilderment. "And her Spiritshadow just keeps hopping in a circle around her."

"Can you touch the stone?" asked Tal. There had to be some way of getting the Guardian out, or of communicating with her.

Crow nodded and transferred his weight to one hand. Then he quickly reached across and tapped the stone.

It shifted sideways in the grip of the silver hands and almost fell onto the floor.

A moment later, the Red light grew in intensity, and a voice came from the Keystone.

"Who wakes me? Who is there? Speak to me!"

"I am Tal Graile-Rerem," Tal called out. "With me is Crow of the Freefolk."

"Who?" came the voice from the stone. "Rerem's son? And Crow, Bennem's brother?"

"Yes," answered Crow, surprised she knew of his brother.

"Are you Lokar, the Guardian of the Red Keystone?" asked Tal.

"I am," said the woman in the Keystone. "Be quick, and focus my Sunstone on the Keystone. Red light in the second intensity will release me."

"Uh, we don't have your Sunstone," Tal replied. "Can I use mine?"

Silence answered him, and a suppressed sob.

"No," Lokar said eventually. "I had hoped you had been sent to release me."

"We would if we could," said Tal. "Where is your Sunstone?"

"I don't know," replied Lokar. "But I used it to unseal the Keystone and it was taken as I did it, so whoever imprisoned me here probably holds it still. Has the veil . . . does the veil . . . ?"

"It's still working," Tal told her.

A sigh of relief came from the Keystone.

"Then the Empress still guards the secrets of the

Violet Keystone," said Lokar. "At the least — perhaps there are other Keystones still sealed. Rerem may know. Was it he who sent you?"

"No," said Tal, his throat suddenly dry. "We think he is trapped like you, inside the Orange Keystone. How . . . that is . . . how did you get in there?"

"The Keystones are sealed to the veil and the Guardians to the Keystones," explained Lokar. "I came here to tune the Keystone, as must be done every year. I unsealed it, but somehow my Sunstone was taken from me as I went within. There was no way back without my own stone, and I could not reseal the Keystone from inside."

"Who took your Sunstone?" asked Crow.

"I do not know," replied Lokar. "Someone who could pass the barriers and the bells of the Tower. Someone with ancient knowledge, a true adept of Light magic."

"The Dark Vizier?" asked Tal. "Sushin?"

"Sushin is the Dark Vizier?" asked Lokar, obviously startled. "I did not think . . . surely the Empress would not appoint someone like him . . . What is happening in the Castle?"

"There's no time to talk about that," Crow interrupted. "Can I take the Keystone out of here?"

"Yes," said Lokar. "But it needs to be here to power the veil. It might be lost or destroyed outside the Tower. Leave it here and find my Sunstone."

"I don't take orders from the Chosen," said Crow. He shifted his weight again, and reached between the silver hands to take the Keystone.

"No!" shouted Tal. "Leave it!"

Crow ignored him. As he lifted the Keystone free, the silver hands opened, palms up.

Crow lost his balance. Desperately, he clutched at the plinth with his knees and tried to keep hold of the Keystone as well.

He failed. One foot slid down the plinth and pressed hard on a red tile.

Tal saw it about to happen and jumped at the branch that held the appropriate bell. Or what he thought was the right bell. But it was the wrong branch and even as Tal grabbed the wire, another bell sounded only half a stretch away.

The bell jangled discordantly, the sound echoing throughout the room. Then the bell next to it started to sound, and the next. Within a few seconds every bell in the tree was ringing furiously, save the one Tal had in his grip.

He let it go, hung from his hands, and jumped down. Crow was already running to the walkway, the Keystone in his hand. Tal followed him. They would have to climb down as quickly as they could, before whatever was alerted by the bell came up the stairs.

Adras had clearly been asleep as they burst out of the archway. The Spiritshadow was lying on the floor of the walkway like a thick blanket of shadow fog, and it took him a few seconds to pull himself together.

"What's happening?" he boomed.

Tal ignored him and rushed to the rail, ready to climb over. Crow was already there, but he had stopped and was staring down.

Tal looked.

His heart seemed to stop.

Light was pouring out of every window, stark shafts of light spreading in all directions. It grew brighter as he watched, as Sunstones inside the Tower activated.

It was not the light that scared Tal.

It was the shadows.

Hundreds of Spiritshadows were issuing out of the windows. All kinds of Spiritshadows, all manner of Aeniran beasts. Most of them were creatures Tal had never seen before outside of a game of

Beastmaker, and they were certainly not companions of Chosen.

Tal couldn't believe his eyes. The Red Tower was housing Free Shadows, Aeniran creatures that should not have been there, but were.

Now they were all swarming up in answer to the tree of bells.

Tal shouted, "Adras!" ready to order the Spiritshadow to fly them across and away. But the command died on his lips as he saw two Waspwyrm shadows launch themselves out of a window and up.

There would be no escape by flying.

They were trapped.

·CHAPTER·
TWENTY-EIGHT

Everything happened very quickly for Milla once the Crones came to their decision. She was cut free from the chair, but told to say sitting there. Odris was ordered to stand behind her.

Then the Crones quickly moved to form a circle around them both. Milla tried looking out at them, but all the strange eyes focused on her were too much and she had to look down.

When the circle was complete, the Crone Mother of the Ruin Ship slowly raised one scarred, pallid hand.

A wind rose with her hand, though this was unnatural inside the Ship. It grew stronger as the hand rose.

A whistling, howling wind circled all around Milla, coming from no single direction. It was strangely cold and hot by turns, unlike any breeze Milla had ever felt upon the Ice.

Milla looked up and saw that the Crones were whistling, their lips pursed, their glowing eyes all centered on her.

Somehow they had called up the wind.

The wind grew stronger, and the lanterns blew out.

The Crones' eyes kept glowing in the darkness.

Then they all spoke together, in a giant voice that was even louder than the wind.

"Milla of the Far-Raiders," roared the collective voice. "For the first time, you are cast out!"

Milla felt the wind pick her up, out of the chair. She was hurled high into the air, above the Crones, almost to the ceiling. Her clothes were stripped from her body, and she flew naked through the air.

The wind took her toward the far wall, and for a moment Milla thought she would smash into it. At the last moment, the wind dropped and she was hurled through a fur-curtained doorway instead, into a corridor.

Still the wind carried her, and the Crones came in a great mass behind, filling the corridor.

"Milla of the Far-Raiders!" shouted the vast voice again. "For the second time, you are cast out!"

Milla was hurled through another doorway. She felt the wind that carried her meet another, more natural breeze, and for a moment she hovered as the two forces of air did battle. But the Crones' gale was stronger, and Milla was pushed on again.

She came to another doorway closed by hung furs. The Ice lay outside, Milla could feel.

"Milla of the Far-Raiders! For the third time, you are cast out!"

The wind cast Milla out through the door, and left her. She catapulted through the air and came crashing down into a deep snowdrift.

The shock of the sudden cold knocked the breath out of her. She lay in the snow, the natural wind spraying ice crystals through her hair. Her skin burned with the cold, and a deep pain stabbed her through the deep Merwin-horn scar on her stomach.

Her heart seemed to slow down and she felt the blood pumping deep in her ears. It grew slower and slower, but she wasn't frightened or worried. Whatever was happening now, this is what was meant to be. Here, out on the Ice.

Milla's heart stopped.

All was silent. She could no longer hear even the wind.

The silence continued for one second. Two seconds. Three seconds.

Then the Crones spoke again.

"Milla of the Ruin Ship, come to your clan!"

Milla's heart restarted with a shiver she felt from the top of her head to her toes.

Hands delved into the snow and gripped Milla, pulling her from the snow. Her arms were put through a coat of silver Ursek fur — one fit for a Sword-Thane of legend — and it was pulled over her head.

Ice crystals were brushed from her hair and a circlet of Selski bone set there, even as she was momentarily lifted up so her feet could be put into thick boots of fur-lined hide. A belt was tied around her waist, silver and black, with a golden buckle in the shape of a leaping Merwin.

Still dazed, Milla was rushed back inside in the middle of a great crowd of Crones. She felt curiously light, almost as if the wind that had carried her was still doing so. The weight of her past worries had disappeared. She no longer felt that she should go to the Ice and die for her misdeeds.

Back in the judging chamber, Odris rushed to meet her, the Spiritshadow babbling with relief.

"What happened, Milla? I felt you . . . disappear . . . and then you were back. I don't like it here. When can we go back to Aenir? It's better there, for both of us. . . ."

"Hush, Odris," said Milla calmly. "We are not finished here. Come stand by me."

She walked to the chair and sat upon it. But in her silver fur and bone circlet, with the Talon of Danir shining on her finger, she did not look like someone come for judgment.

"Welcome, Milla of the Ruin Ship," said the Mother Crone. "We have a heavy responsibility to lay upon you. Do you accept it, for you and your shadow?"

"I do," answered Milla regally. She raised her hand to quiet Odris, who was about to speak.

"Then we shall speak the Prayer of Asteyr to bind you to it," announced the Mother Crone.

Again, the Crones spoke together as a single, giant voice.

A woman's voice.

The power of the voice overwhelmed Milla and Odris, so that after the first few words they did not hear them, but rather felt themselves being caught up in a poem or song, one that reached into their very bones, real and shadow.

With the prayer came a deep instruction, one that

they could never break. It spoke of absolute loyalty to the Icecarl people, a loyalty that would be defined by the voice of the Icecarls.

The Crones. They would speak together in their silent way, and make their decisions in the great mind they shared. Whatever decisions they made would be laid upon Milla, and she must obey, as must the shadow that was bound to her.

The Prayer changed, and the voice grew quieter. Finally only the Mother Crone of the Ruin Ship spoke. Even alone, her voice was binding.

"Three things we lay upon you," said the Mother Crone. "The first is your life-name, so I call you Milla Talon-Hand. The second is the office I have held before you, that of the Living Sword of Asteyr. The third is a title and a responsibility that no Icecarl has borne for two thousand circlings."

She paused and took a deep breath before continuing.

"Milla Talon-Hand, we name you War-Chief of the Icecarls, and charge you to finish what was begun long ago. We charge you to secure our world forever from the Shadows of Aenir."

·CHAPTER·
TWENTY-NINE

Tal looked at the great tide of Spiritshadows rising toward them. They only had a few minutes before they would swarm over him.

He looked at Crow, but the older boy was paralyzed, staring down at their enemies, the Red Keystone loose in his hand.

Tal saw it and had a sudden thought.

He acted quickly, snatching the Keystone from Crow's slack grip.

Instantly, Crow turned, his knife in his hand.

"Give it back!" he snarled.

"What's happening?" came a plaintive voice from the Keystone, as Tal backed away.

"I need it to get us out of here," Tal explained, speaking as fast as he could. "Unless you want to meet those Spiritshadows?"

Crow hesitated, then lowered his knife.

Tal stared at the Keystone. He could see Lokar, suspended in Red light. She looked like she was treading water. Obviously it took some effort to make contact with the outside world.

"Lokar," he said urgently, "there are heaps of Spiritshadows coming up the outside of the tower. Is there anywhere here we can hide, that will be safe from them? Can they come through the arches?"

"Yes, if they have been given the Words," said Lokar, frowning in thought. "You will not be safe here. What is your Spiritshadow? Can it fly?"

"A Storm Shepherd, so yes, but there are flying shadows, so we will be pursued." Tal looked up at Crow, who was still standing there, watching him suspiciously. "Crow! Keep watch. Tell me when they're about fifty stretches away!"

Crow reluctantly went to look over the side.

"You look young," said Lokar. "Have you mastery of the seven colors?"

"Not exactly mastery," replied Tal. "But I can do things . . . I've done things . . ."

"Ninety stretches," shouted Crow. "There are hundreds of them!"

"Can you combine all seven?" asked Lokar.

"Yes," said Tal, almost before Lokar'd stopped speaking.

"Then you can make a miniature dark veil to hide beneath," said Lokar. "Find a corner, crouch in it, and I will tell you how to weave a veil. Quickly!"

Tal looked around widely.

"Fifty stretches!" shouted Crow. He looked at Tal, wide-eyed and clearly frightened. "Whatever you're going to do, do it quickly."

"Let's fight!" boomed Adras. He leaned over the railing and fired off a bolt of shadow-lightning. A sudden, ghastly squeal announced that it had found its mark.

"No, Adras!" shouted Tal. He went to the wall and tugged at a downpipe that carried rainwater from the dome high above. "Help me pull this off!"

The downpipe was set into a recess in the wall. If they could crouch down there and weave a veil, there was a chance the Spiritshadows wouldn't be able to find them.

Crow didn't know what he planned, but he rushed to Tal's side and pulled at the pipe, too. It gave a little, but it wasn't until Adras reached above them both and tugged that it tore away with the screech of metal on stone.

"Quick!" instructed Tal. "Crouch down here, as close as we can get!"

He pushed into the recess with Crow. Adras made himself as thin as possible and slid in behind Tal and up the wall.

"What now?" said Crow.

Tal didn't answer. He was looking at the Keystone, watching Lokar, and focusing on his own Sunstone at the same time.

Crow and Adras watched the railing, expecting to see a Spiritshadow leap over and attack at any moment.

"Hurry up!" Crow murmured. Tendrils of differently colored light were starting to rise out of Tal's Sunstone, but very slowly.

The tendrils issued out and wove together in front of the pressed-in trio. As they wove together, a patch of darkness formed in the air. It spread rapidly, curving up, down, and around.

"Faster," whispered Crow. He saw a taloned shadow-hand grip the railing, behind the forming veil. "Faster!"

A Spiritshadow leapt over the railing — a huge Waspwyrm, shadow-wings still beating, sting looking all too solid in the Red light.

Crow saw it, and he stopped breathing as its head slowly swiveled in his direction. The veil was almost blocking his view. It would be so close. Would the Spiritshadow look first or would the veil be formed in time?

The miniature veil spread across and seamlessly joined to form a perfect sphere around them, a fraction of a second before the Spiritshadow turned its head.

Crow shivered and was startled to find he needed to take a very deep breath.

"Don't do that," said Tal sharply.

"What?" Crow asked softly. He wasn't sure if sound traveled through the veil.

"It's fine to talk," said Tal. He touched the veil, and his finger rebounded as if the veil were tightly stretched cloth. "Just don't breathe too much."

"Why?" asked Crow.

"I was in a hurry —" Tal started to explain.

"What?" asked Crow.

"I made it too solid," said Tal. "I don't think there's any air getting through."

"What?" Crow gasped. He reached out and his fingernails scraped down the veil.

It was solid.

"We have to get out," Crow whispered. "We'll die in here."

"There's enough air for a while," said Tal. He was fighting to stay calm. Just knowing that their air was running out was making him feel terrible. Weak and pathetic. "We have to be still."

Crow looked at him, panic in his eyes. He raised his hand and Tal cringed thinking he was going to punch him. Then Crow pulled back.

"Sorry," he said. "I'll . . . I'll be still."

They sat in silence for a while, then Crow suddenly looked at Tal.

"Where's Adras?" he asked, craning his head around.

There was no sign of the Spiritshadow.

All the color drained from Tal's face. No wonder he felt so terrible.

"He must be outside! They're killing him!"

"No, he isn't!" said a small voice from the Keystone. Tal hurriedly peered down at it.

"He's in your veil!" exclaimed Lokar. "You wove him into it and he has no light!"

·CHAPTER·
THIRTY

"No air for us, no light for Adras," muttered Crow.

"It's better than getting killed by Spiritshadows!" Tal retorted. "Besides, we only have to wait till they're gone."

"We might be dead by then," said Crow. "How will we know when they do go, anyway?"

Lokar said something both boys missed. They leaned down at the same time to hear better, and cracked their heads.

"Dark!" swore Crow. He snatched the Keystone back and said, "Be more careful!"

Tal raised his Sunstone for a second, then thought better of it. He didn't want Crow to have the Keystone but there wasn't much he could do about it now.

"What was that?" Crow asked Lokar.

Tal leaned forward again, more carefully.

"You both need to save your breath," said Lokar. "As far as I can tell from in here, Tal has made this veil too well."

"What do you mean?" asked Tal.

"Not only is it too solid," said Lokar. "I doubt that you can unthread it. You'll have to wait till it frays of its own accord."

Tal and Crow looked at each other. Words seemed at the tips of their tongues, but neither spoke. Instead they settled back and exhaled slowly at the same time.

I wish I'd learned Milla's Rovkir breathing, thought Tal, as the minutes slowly passed, marked by the spark of his Sunstone. It was getting warmer and stuffier, and it seemed to him that Crow was using up too much of their air.

He glanced across and saw Crow's eyes glittering. His hand was on his knife. Clearly he had the same thought. There might only be enough air for one of them to survive.

One must die for the other to live.

Crow pulled his knife out an inch.

Tal raised his Sunstone though it felt like a great weight and shook his head.

Crow eased the knife back in. Tal lowered his hand.

Both kept watching each other, alert for the slightest movement.

At least Tal thought he was alert. But he suddenly realized his head was on his chest. He snapped it up, only to see Crow's head lolling sideways.

The Freefolk boy seemed to be unconscious.

For a moment Tal was tempted to finish him off, so he would have more air. But only for a moment. What was it his great-uncle had said to him?

"Do not be a caveroach."

It would be a caveroach thing to do, to kill Crow for a few breaths that might not be enough anyway.

Instead, Tal feebly pressed at the dark veil. As before, his fingers bounced off it. It seemed as strong as ever, and he could *feel* Adras trapped inside. Fading with every moment.

Tal took a shallow breath and closed his eyes.

It was much easier just to go to sleep.

As Tal's eyes closed, Crow's opened. He touched his knife once . . . twice . . . then slowly closed his eyes again.

Tal awoke in sudden panic, Red light on his face, fresh air in his nostrils, and a terrible headache throbbing above his eyes. Crow was stirring at his side, but there was no sign of Adras.

Or of the enemy Spiritshadows.

Tal looked at his Sunstone. Over an hour had passed. They were very lucky the veil had unraveled when it did. Judging by how terrible he felt, another few minutes would probably have asphyxiated them.

A low groan came from the other side of Crow. Tal crawled over and stared aghast at the tiny, shriveled shadow that was all that remained of Adras.

"Light!" whimpered the mere dab of darkness that was about the size of Tal's foot. "Light!"

There was plenty of Red light around, but Tal lowered his Sunstone, shielded it with his hand, and directed a bright beam of light matched to the color of Aenir's sun upon his stricken Spiritshadow.

Slowly, the shadow thickened and began to spread out across the stones. As it grew, Tal's headache lessened.

He was so intent upon revitalizing Adras that he didn't notice Crow had recovered, too, until the Freefolk boy was standing next to him. He had the Keystone raised almost to his chin and was whispering to it.

"Lokar says there is a secret stair that starts two

levels below," he said to Tal. Obviously he had decided to ignore what had gone on inside the miniature Veil. "If we can climb down to it, she can guide us through the traps. It comes out . . ."

He listened to the Keystone again and continued, "It comes out in a White Corridor, between Red One and Orange Seven. It shouldn't be too hard to get from there to an Underfolk store and then back to my domain."

Tal nodded, though he secretly flinched at Crow calling any part of the Castle "his domain." If there was anything he had learned since his fall to the world outside, it was the importance of keeping his mouth shut — until the time was right.

"Weak," said Adras. He had regained his usual form, but his shadowflesh was almost transparent, barely visible.

"He will be slow to recover," said Crow, repeating Lokar's words. "You must give him light for as long as you can, and lots of it before we go through the Veil proper."

Tal nodded.

"Where are the Spiritshadows?" he asked. "Can you see any?"

"I guess they've gone back into their hidey-holes," said Crow. "At least I couldn't see any when I looked over the side."

"They're there somewhere," said Tal. "Hiding. Waiting. I would like to know what for."

Crow shrugged. That was a problem for another time. He had what he'd come for. He tucked the Keystone carefully into a slim leather pouch he wore on a chain around his neck.

"Come on," he said, as he carefully climbed over the railing. "Stay close. You might need to make another veil. But we'd better be able to breathe in the next one."

Tal watched Crow go over. He was more suspicious than ever about Crow. It was clear the Freefolk boy only wanted him around for what he could do. Crow hated the Chosen so much that he wouldn't hesitate to get rid of Tal if he thought he was of no more use.

The worst thing about it, Tal thought sadly, was that he couldn't really blame Crow. He had a lot to hate the Chosen for.

"Adras," he said, raising his hand, "wrap around my Sunstone and arm, and get as much light as you can."

Adras nodded, too weak to boom a reply. Tal felt

him move onto his arm, a cool touch that made the hair on his skin prickle with small lightning bolts. His Sunstone dimmed as Adras covered it, though the light still blazed under the shadow.

Tal climbed over the railing and gingerly felt for a foothold.

·CHAPTER·
THIRTY-O*NE

Milla stood in the Hall of the Reckoner, the Mother Crone at her side. Both looked down at the complex puzzle of hundreds of tiles and models that depicted the entire world of the Ice and the Icecarl clan-ships that moved upon it. Shield Maiden cadets moved across the huge map, moving the ship models, and, less frequently, exchanging the tiles that told of the quality and condition of the Ice. Seven Crones, seated on tall chairs of woven bone, directed the cadets.

When Milla had last seen the Reckoner, the clan-ships of the Icecarls had been spread all over the world, in no apparent pattern. Now there were clumps of ships forming at various parts of the maps. As Milla watched, a Crone summoned a Shield Maiden cadet and spoke to her. The young girl listened, then stepped lightly across the tiles to one of the gatherings of ships and selected one of the smallest, that had a Sunstone chip set in its prow. This ship she picked up and moved to an adjacent tile.

Milla noticed it was moving toward the tile at the center of the Reckoner, a tile that had the model of a mountain upon it, and a miniature Ruin Ship at its side.

"Yes," said the Mother Crone. "The clans are gathering where they may, and one ship in every seven is bringing all the Shield Maidens and hunters the clans can spare from following the Selski. We have summoned the Sword-Thanes, too, though they do not appear upon the Reckoner, and we cannot know how many will be able to answer the call — or will choose to."

Milla nodded. It was all a bit much for her. She had been cast out, reborn as Milla Talon-Hand, and named War-Chief only that morning. Now everyone expected her to take charge and do whatever had to be done to take over the Castle, force the Chosen to give up their Spiritshadows, and then to . . . she didn't know what . . . cross over to Aenir and do the Forgetting all over again?

"The ships will come as quickly as they can," the Mother Crone was saying. "Yet it will be many sleeps before the full host is gathered. Is it your wish, War-Chief, that the Shield Maidens and hunters we have here be gathered for an initial attack upon the Castle, to secure the passage into it?"

"Um, yes," Milla replied.

The Mother Crone smiled, a smile so brief Milla nearly missed it. The Crone wasn't really asking her, Milla realized. She was helping her work out what to do, but making it look like she was in charge of the military detail. Though everyone knew both she and Odris had to do what the Crones told them.

"Yes," Milla said more firmly. "Let them prepare. I will lead them out after the main sleep. I need . . . I need to rest a little."

"They will be ready," answered the Mother Crone. "Before you go to rest, War-Chief, I would have you meet Malen. She is the youngest of the Crones, and so best suited for the arduous task of accompanying you on this first attack."

Before the Mother Crone finished speaking, a young Crone stepped through the curtains of the door and approached. She *was* young, Milla saw. Blue-eyed, as all beginning Crones were, with a luminosity in the blue. But she didn't look much older than sixteen circlings, hardly older than Milla. She felt a stab of jealousy in her heart. This Icecarl girl had found her place without trouble, Milla thought. She was not constrained by the Prayer of Asteyr, an untrustworthy but necessary evil the Icecarls were prepared to put up with due only to the greater danger that threatened them.

"I greet you, War-Chief Milla Talon-Hand," said Malen. She clubbed her fists together, as did Milla.

Even her voice was perfect, thought Milla. She had a clear, bell-like voice, perfect for singing or chanting the old epics. Everyone must have loved her in her clan, and now they would be so proud of her, a Crone at so young an age.

"I will come with you as the Voice of the Crones," said Malen.

Milla nodded. That was even worse. When Malen wanted to, she could speak with the authority of all the Crones and Milla, bound by the Prayer, would have to do what she said.

Unless she told Milla, Milla wouldn't know if Lornir wasn't connecting with the other Crones, or speaking only for herself.

For a moment Milla considered asking the Mother Crone if someone else, someone older and more experienced, could come with her as the Voice of the Crones. But she didn't.

"We leave immediately after main sleep," said Milla briskly. "I must rest now. Come, Odris."

All the Shield Maiden cadets in the room clubbed their fists as Milla left, but she noticed many seemed reluctant to do so. The Crones had made her War-Chief, but it was not as easy as that. She would have to earn the respect of the cadets and the Shield Maidens and the hunters and Sword-Thanes who would come.

She would also have to work out how to get through the bad air of the heatways, counter Chosen Sunstone magic, and secure the way from Mountain to Castle in order to bring in reinforcements once she had established a foothold in the Underfolk levels. Then there were the Underfolk themselves to consider, and the likelihood of Ebbitt, Jarnil, and the Freefolk aiding the Icecarls or turning against them.

And there was Tal. Milla wondered what he was doing, and whether he had been successful in gaining the Keystone. She wasn't sure if she wanted him to succeed or fail. If Tal did get the Keystone and somehow managed to turn the Chosen against Sushin and the free shadows, he might be able to secure the veil. But knowing him as she did, she was sure he would not want to send all the Chosen's Spiritshadows back to Aenir.

So he would be an enemy and there was only one absolutely sure way to deal with an enemy.

Kill them before they killed you.

·CHAPTER·
THIRTY-TWO ☉

The climb down was nerve-racking. Both Tal and Crow expected to meet hostile Spiritshadows at any moment. Every flicker of light startled them — and sometimes that was enough to make them almost slip or lose their grip. Then they would have another pang of fear as they nearly fell off.

But no Spiritshadows came out of the Tower, and they made it safely down to the window that Lokar had described to Crow. Climbing through that, they found the secret stair. It was a very narrow stairway, hidden within the thick wall of the Tower. Anyone much larger than Crow could easily get stuck.

There were also frequent traps. Crow had to take the Keystone out of his pouch and hold it close to his ear, listening to Lokar's instructions as he kept up a running commentary to describe to her where they were.

The worst trap was where a rack of razor-edged cleavers swung out across the stairway. The cleavers were positioned at knee, stomach, and neck height, Lokar said. The trap was triggered by treading anywhere but the very center of each of six steps. With every one Tal expected to trip, to hear the "snick" of the mechanism, and then feel the sudden bite of the cleavers.

Somehow he made it through.

Tal followed Crow closely, not trusting the Freefolk boy to tell him about the traps. He figured if he stayed close he would be safe.

Adras was still wrapped around his arm and Sunstone, absorbing light. His shadowflesh was slowly darkening, but he had been very close to death. Tal didn't want to think what would happen to him if his Spiritshadow died.

The veil looked strange when they came to it. It cut through the walls of the Tower as if they weren't there. It looked like the stair descended into a pool of the inkiest, darkest water.

Crow hesitated at the veil and listened to Lokar, the Keystone held to his ear. Then he plunged straight down, his hand tracing the wall.

Tal paused, too, and concentrated on his Sunstone, releasing a burst of incredibly bright and powerful light. Adras absorbed it and only a dull glow spread out from Tal's hand.

"Are you ready for the veil?" Tal asked.

"Yes," whispered Adras. "Go quickly!"

Tal took a deep breath, reached out to touch the wall himself, and stepped down.

One step, two steps, three steps . . . and the veil closed over his face.

Tal was in total darkness. He kept on stepping down, grazing his fingers as he pushed hard against the wall, reassuring himself that it was there.

Ten steps . . . eleven steps . . . twelve steps . . . panic started to rise in Tal. The veil seemed thicker here. Surely it was taking longer than before. This should be easier than climbing through it.

He took the stairs more quickly, almost falling in his eagerness to get through. He lost count of the steps and began to take them two at a time.

He had to get out of the veil!

Suddenly, he was out. Crow looked up at him from farther down the narrow, winding stair, the Red Keystone glowing in his hand.

Tal swallowed and slowly stood upright. He'd

hunched down to an almost animal posture in his desperation to get lower, to get through the Veil.

"Are you all right?" he asked Adras. The Spiritshadow was still wound around his arm, and wasn't moving.

"Yes," came the weak reply. "Sick. Light is good."

"Let's go," called Crow. He was clearly in a hurry.

At the base of the stair, where a secret panel opened out into a colorless corridor, they had to wait for a pair of Spiritshadows to pass. With the panel open a crack, Tal and Crow watched them disappear around the corner.

One was a Klenten Warbeast. It had a massive head armored with flanges of thick bone, set upon immense shoulders. It ran as often on four legs as two. The other was a Dretch, the stick insect-and-spider combination, like his cousins'. But this Spiritshadow was larger and its shadowflesh was stronger and more defined.

Tal bit his lip with worry. All the Spiritshadows in the Castle should be with their Chosen. These two were free shadows, like the ones in the Red Tower. How many Aenirans were already roaming around the Castle while the Chosen were in Aenir? They were confident to simply walk the corridors. They didn't expect to meet any opposition.

"I think Sushin must be very close to destroying the veil," Tal whispered to Crow. "There are so many Spiritshadows already here. We need to talk to Lokar about this as soon as we get somewhere safe."

"Maybe," replied Crow. He seemed distracted. "Look, there's another one!"

Tal bent to look through the gap. The next thing he felt was a terrible shock to the back of his head and an intense pain.

Dimly he realized that Crow had hit him with the hilt of his knife. He tried to get up, but there was no strength in his muscles. He couldn't see properly, either. Everything was blurry and the walls and floor were swaying.

"Nothing personal, Tal," said Crow, his voice coming from high up and far away. "If you weren't a Chosen you'd be all right. But you *are* a Chosen, and I've got things to do with this Keystone that you wouldn't agree with."

Tal groaned. He could feel Adras struggling to form himself and attack Crow, but the Spiritshadow was still too weak.

A glint of steel caught Tal's eye and a terrible jolt of fear shot through him.

233

"No," he tried to say as Crow bent down next to him, his knife in his hand.

"Your people killed my parents and drove my brother crazy," whispered Crow. "My grandparents went into the Hall of Nightmares, too, and were never the same. It is . . . justice . . . to kill any Chosen."

Despite his words, Crow did not make any move with the knife. He just sat there, looking at Tal.

Their gaze met. Tal couldn't see or think properly, but it wasn't hate he saw in Crow's eyes. It was fear, though there was nothing for Crow to fear here.

Except himself. The Freefolk boy looked away from Tal, toward the knife in his hand. The steel glittered, red in the light from the Keystone.

"Sorry," Crow said abrubtly. "Don't come after me."

He stood up, looked through the gap again, then slipped out into the corridor.

Tal groaned and felt his head. There was no blood, but it hurt a lot. Pushing against the floor with his hands, he managed to stagger upright.

Adras tried to help him, but there was no strength in his body. Chosen and Spiritshadow leaned together and fell against the wall.

"What do we do now?" Adras asked plaintively.

"We get the Keystone back," said Tal grimly. Using the wall as a prop, he edged to the panel and looked out. Crow was just disappearing around a corner opposite the one the Spiritshadows had taken.

"Come on," he said, pushing himself off with an effort. He was still dizzy, but he could walk. Crow was not going to get away with the Keystone that easily.

235

·CHAPTER·
THIRTY-THREE

Crow was gone by the time Tal managed to get to the corner. The corridor stretched into the distance, the bright white light of the Sunstones set in its ceiling painful to Tal's damaged head. There were lots of corridors joining it, leading off into Red One or Orange Seven.

But Crow wouldn't have taken those, Tal knew. He would head straight for the closest Underfolk store or service-way.

Still stumbling, Adras hooked onto his belt like a blind follower, Tal weaved his way down the corridor. He was kept going by the fury that burned inside him. How dare Crow hit him! It was a coward's hit, too. At least Milla had always hit him face-to-face.

He flung open the first Underfolk door he came to, Sunstone ring raised, already burning with Red light. But this was only a long closet full of spare robes, cleaning equipment, and the like.

Tal was about to back out when his eyes caught the flash of something behind the robes hanging at the back. A faint glimpse of some Red light, only for an instant. The Red light of the Keystone.

He rushed over and pulled the robes away in a frenzy. There was a door behind them, now closed. It had no handle or obvious means of opening.

Tal didn't look for one. He raised his hand and focused his rage upon his Sunstone. Red light answered, a thick, burning ray that flashed out at the door.

Tal retreated as liquid metal flew. He clenched his fist, ring outward, and directed the beam in a wide circle.

In a moment, he had cut the metal door in half. Whatever lock it had once had was now melted into a blob. Tal picked up a mop handle and used it to smash the remnants of the smoking door aside before going through.

A small room lay beyond, and a familiar, larger metal door, locked by a wheel. It was an entryway to the steam pipes of the castle. A few stretches away on the same wall was another narrow stairway, an inspection-way for the steam system.

Crow was at the top of the stairs. He turned as he saw Tal.

"I told you not to follow me!"

"Give me the Keystone!" ordered Tal. He kept his Sunstone raised. The red glare of it was a clear warning.

"No," said Crow. "The Freefolk need it."

"Why?" asked Tal. "Why bash me in the head? I might have agreed with you."

Crow let out a short, bitter laugh. "A Chosen agree with what I plan! Listen, Tal. I've had a Sunstone for five years. I got it off . . . well, I got it. But no one will teach me how to use it properly. Sure, Jarnil's showed me a few tricks, and your great-uncle Ebbitt. But they're afraid. Afraid to let a Freefolk into their secrets. But now I've got Lokar and she'll teach me anything, just so long as I talk to her. It's lonely inside that stone. Nothing ever happens. You can go crazy in there."

"That's it?" asked Tal. He couldn't believe it was so simple. "I'd teach you, if you want."

"No, that's not it!" Crow screamed. "We've got quite a few Sunstones hidden away. Once we know how to use them, the Fatalists will join us. We'll use the Sunstones to overcome the Spiritshadows who guard the most important Chosen while they're in

Aenir. Once we have the bodies as hostages we can *tell* the Chosen what to do."

"But what about Sushin and the veil?" said Tal. "Crow, our whole *world* is in danger! This isn't the time to fight amongst ourselves."

"It's never the time if you listen to the Chosen," Crow whispered, almost to himself. His knife flashed in his hand and then it was in the air, flying straight at Tal.

It struck the wall behind him in a shower of sparks.

Instinctively, Tal fired back a Red Ray of Destruction.

Crow ducked as the ray cut across the stone above his head, sending chips flying. One cut the Freefolk boy across the face, leaving a trail of blood across his cheek.

Crow cried out and charged at Tal. At the same time, Adras leapt forward. He wasn't strong enough to do much, but he put out one puffy foot and Crow catapulted over it.

Unfortunately, he went straight into Tal.

The two boys rolled around on the ground, punching and kicking. Adras managed to get one shadow-arm around Crow's neck long enough to pull him off. As they split apart, Tal snatched the pouch that held the Red Keystone.

Adras couldn't hold Crow. He flung the Spirit-shadow off and snatched up his knife.

The two boys faced each other across the room. Adras retreated to stand next to Tal.

"Don't make me hurt you anymore," said Crow. "Give me the Keystone."

"No," said Tal. He raised his Sunstone. It swirled with Orange light now, for Tal had a different plan. His anger had cooled. He didn't want to kill Crow. He would use Orange light to push the boy away.

Crow started to raise his knife.

Tal prepared a massive blast.

For a long moment, there was the faint possibility that both of them would back down.

Then Tal heard voices coming up the stairs behind Crow. Freefolk voices. Crow must have arranged this place as a rendezvous, must have planned to backstab Tal.

Tal let the blast of Orange light go, aiming just above Crow's head.

Crow heard the voices, too, but the one his ears picked out was Tal's great-uncle Ebbitt. Ebbitt was a Chosen Adept, and his Spiritshadow was fierce and strong. He would take Tal's side, if he knew what was really going on.

Crow threw his knife.

·CHAPTER·
THIRTY–FOUR

Clovil was at the top of the stairs, with Ferek, Inkie, and Ebbitt close behind. Ebbitt saw Crow's back and he called out to him, just as the blast of orange light struck directly above them all.

The blast knocked the Freefolk boy back, but that wasn't all. At the same time it cracked the great beams of the roof and the lintel above the door. Rock shattered and began to pour down, at first in tiny pebbles, then quickly becoming a great cascade of crushing stones.

Tal saw it all happen. He saw Crow catapulted back into Clovil. He saw the other Freefolk look up in sudden fear as the roof caved in, and he heard his great-uncle's surprised shout.

"Back! Back for your lives!"

Then the stairway was completely buried in a

flood of falling stones. A huge piece of the ceiling fell in front of Tal, shattering into tiny pieces that flew up and cut his face and hands. More rock fell, and dust billowed out in huge clouds.

Despite the danger, Tal rushed forward. He concentrated on his Sunstone to make a Hand of Light to try and shift the great weight of stone.

But even as the Hand formed, a sudden, terrible whistle sounded above and in front of him. Instinctively, Tal ducked, a moment before a great gout of steam exploded out above his head.

The steam pipe had cracked! It was the huge riser that carried vast quantities of steam up from the lava-heated pools deep below.

Desperately Tal focused, to create the Hand before the super-hot steam found its way through the cracks.

The whistle grew even fiercer and more shrill as steam howled out under great pressure. The heat was unbearable, and Tal was forced to crawl back. He lost concentration, and the beginning of the Hand of Light winked out.

Pushed back by the steam, Tal had to retreat into the Underfolk's store. He couldn't see anything now. The room beyond was completely full of steam and dust. Deep inside the killing cloud Tal could hear rocks still falling, with a boom that vibrated through the floor.

"Help!" Tal screamed. He didn't care who came. There had to be somebody who could so something. "Help!"

He tried to enter the room again, but was beaten back. Even at the edges the steam was too hot to bear. Further in, it would strip the flesh from bones.

Coughing, Tal retreated again and screamed once more for help.

But no help came. The Chosen were all in Aenir, and the Underfolk would not look in here until they were sure they were supposed to do so.

Tal couldn't do anything. Adras couldn't do anything.

Tal couldn't believe what had happened.

He had probably *killed* Crow, Clovil, Ferek, Inkie . . . and Great-Uncle Ebbitt.

All in one fatal second.

He hadn't meant to, but it had happened. Even if by some chance they had ducked the falling rock, they couldn't have lived through the explosion of steam.

Adras plucked at his sleeve.

Tal looked down and dumbly saw that Crow's knife was caught in a fold of cloth under his arm. It hadn't pierced the skin, but it had missed his heart by less than a handspan.

"What do we do now?" asked Adras, his voice small, not at all like a Storm Shepherd's. "I wish Odris was here."

Tal stared from side to side. He couldn't think. He didn't know what to do.

A tiny voice coming from the bag he held in his fist finally caught his attention.

"What's going on?"

Tal pulled out the Red Keystone and looked into it. A tear splashed on the stone. Tal wiped it away. He hadn't known he was crying.

"What is it?" asked Lokar. "What's happening?"

"Crow's dead," said Tal woodenly. He didn't mention the others.

"Never mind that," said Lokar. "He was only an Underfolk, and crazy. You must take me to the Empress. It is absolutely the most important thing. Life or death!"

"Life or death," repeated Tal. He felt like someone else was using his voice.

"The only question is how to get to her without going through the Dark Vizier . . . or the light for that matter," mused Lokar. "Tal — are you listening?"

"Yes," Tal mumbled. He couldn't think for himself. He was too deep in shock.

"What is that date? Are we close to any of the Festivals, or anything the Empress would appear at?"

"It's the Day of Ascension," said Tal. "Or the day after. I don't know . . ."

"Aenir!" cried Lokar. "The Empress will be in Aenir. You must take me there, Tal!"

"I've killed —" Tal started to cry out, but Lokar interrupted him.

"Aenir! The Empress. She will sort everything out. She can release Rerem using the Violet Keystone!"

That got Tal's attention. Releasing his father. He had to talk to his father about what had happened.

"Aenir," he mumbled. He would have to find somewhere safe to hide his body, because he couldn't leave Adras behind to guard it. Adras couldn't be trusted to stay on the job.

"The Mausoleum," he whispered. He looked back into the swirling mass of steam and stone dust one last time. Sweat poured off his face, mingling with tears.

"We'll cross to Aenir from the Mauseoleum," he decided aloud.

"Aenir?" asked Adras, as Tal began to run, run away from the terrible place behind him. "What about Odris and Milla?"

Tal didn't answer. He kept running.

"We should wait," the Spiritshadow pleaded. "Odris is coming, with Milla. I can feel it!"

Tal didn't hear him. There was only one thing on his mind.

He had to cross over to Aenir. He must do what he had wanted to do all along.

Tell the Empress everything.

Then *everything* would be her problem.

·EPILOGUE·

Three days after the rock fall in the Castle, but far below on the Mountain of Light, Milla Talon-Hand watched the rope bridge being thrown over the gap in the road. All around her, more than forty Shield Maidens labored, hammering in supports and tying ropes. There were more on the other side, near the pyramid of Imrir, doing the same job. Others stood by with moth-lanterns to light the work, or with spears, to guard against Perawls.

Two Sword-Thanes stood below the heatway entrance, guarding against whatever might come from above or below. They both had great bows of bent bone in their hands, and quivers full of bone arrows fletched with the feathers of the blind Arug bird.

Malen the Crone stood with the Sword-Thanes, her luminous blue eyes intent upon the darkness beyond the Icecarls' lights. What she looked for, Milla did not know.

Soon, provided the Crones could supply them with clean air, her first raiding force would begin the journey through the heatways.

And Milla would lead them.

*To all the readers who have travelled
with Tal and Milla through four books.
I hope you stay for the complete journey!*

·CHAPTER·
☉ПE

High on the road up the Mountain of Light, in a tent made from tightly sewn Wreska hides, Milla sat in a chair carved from the single lower jawbone of an infant Selski. Outside the wind howled, and blown ice and snow struck the tent's walls with a constant rattle.

The bone chair was enormous and made Milla seem smaller than she was, like a child pretending to join her elders. The chair had been carried up the mountain path by eight Shield Maidens, with considerable effort and danger. It was ancient, and the arms, seat, and back were engraved with hundreds of small images from Icecarl history and legend. Next to Milla's hand, for example, there was a thumbnail-sized picture of the fabled Ulla Strong-

Arm wrestling a Merwin, its horn about to be snapped off by the ferocious Icecarl.

Milla felt a twinge in her side as she looked at the tiny picture, the scar aching once again where a Merwin's horn had almost fatally injured her. She knew without a doubt that no one could wrestle a Merwin, but at the same time, she didn't doubt that Ulla Strong-Arm had done it.

Milla looked at some of the other pictures and wondered if the heroes of Icecarl history felt like she did — an imposter who wasn't fit to be the stuff of legend.

She was no longer Milla of the Far-Raiders. She was now Milla Talon-Hand, the Living Sword of Asteyr and War-Chief of the Icecarls. The glowing violet fingernail of magical crystal she wore on her right hand was the legendary weapon of her far ancestor Danir. She was sitting on the ancient Thinking Chair of Grettir. She wore the finest silver Ursek furs. A bone circlet, itself carved with tiny pictures of Icecarl triumph, secured her blond hair in place.

A shield of mirror-bright shell leaned against the throne. It was ancient, too, a relic from distant times when the Icecarls had needed to defend themselves from light magic. Next to it was a Merwin-horn sword. It wasn't the one Milla had left stuck in the shoulder of the Dark Vizier Sushin, back in the Castle, but an older weapon. It still had a faint glow, which would make it effective against Spiritshadows.

Milla sat on the Thinking Chair, wondering what she was doing. She might be called War-Chief, but in practice she spent a lot of time waiting for the Crones to tell her what to do. Since they had bound her with the Prayer of Asteyr she had no choice but to obey, as did her Spiritshadow, Odris.

"It's better than being dead," said that Spiritshadow now, rising up from under the chair to hang in the air in front of Milla's gloomy face.

"Stop knowing what I'm thinking!" snapped Milla, even though she knew it was no use. Odris was linked to her too strongly now, both by the original binding that had been made in the Spirit World of Aenir and by the Prayer of Asteyr. They would be together until one of them died.

"Stop thinking about dying!" Odris snapped back. "I don't know why there's such a fog inside you. You're the War-Chief, the leader of the Expedition against the Castle. Probably the most famous Icecarl alive. They're making up songs about you already. I heard one that goes:

Mighty the one-eyed Merwin   Small the slender
*   Shield Maiden*
Bright the Sunstone's brilliance Darting the
*   dagger drives*
Home it sinks in hoary hide   Milla more than
*   Merwin's match . . .*

"That's all wrong!" interrupted Milla, shaking her head. "I'm not a Shield Maiden and I never will be. Plus, Tal was the one who blinded the Merwin with his Sunstone, not me. And even if I did kill the Merwin, what else have I done right? I broke all the laws, I lost my shadow. I should have been left to die on the Ice."

"You're just sulking because we've had to sit here for too long," said Odris. "Don't worry, the Crones will come up with some sort of airweed soon and then we'll conquer the Castle and send all the Spiritshadows back to Aenir. Then we can go back as well and you can . . . I don't know . . . start a small farm, or get a fishing boat or something. . . ."

"Odris, I'm an Icecarl!" Milla protested. "This is my world. I don't want to live in Aenir. And I am not a farmer or a fisher. I am a warrior!"

"So you should be happy," grumbled Odris. "You make me feel ill with your sadness."

Silence returned, save for the howling of the wind outside. Odris slid back to the floor. Milla brooded on her chair, but only for a few more minutes.

"We have sat here too long," Milla announced.

She leaped up, pulled her heavy outer coat from the back of the chair, and put it on, slipping the white bone mask over her face before raising the hood and pulling it tight. Then she buckled on her sword and slung the mirror-shell shield on her back.

"I take it we're going somewhere?" Odris asked with a sigh. "Can I have some more light?"

Milla raised her hand, and the Sunstone ring on her third finger suddenly shone brightly, eclipsing the greenish light from the moth-lanterns that hung from the massive poles in each corner of the tent.

"Where are we going, by the way?" Odris asked as Milla pulled back the heavy furs that closed the doorway. Together they stepped out into the horizontal waves of wind-driven snow.

"The Crones have had long enough to find air-weed," Milla shouted. "I left some at the heatway tunnel entrance. Enough for me to go back through and organize the Underfolk to bring out a whole lot more."

Odris shrugged as she slipped into place at Milla's heels, a shrug that suggested that going back into the Castle through the heatways wouldn't be as easy as Milla made it sound.

At least they were heading in the right direction as far as Odris was concerned. Back to plenty of Sunstone light and Adras, her fellow Storm Shepherd — now also a Spiritshadow.

Odris hadn't wanted to leave the Castle in the first place. But Milla had been determined to warn the Icecarls of the danger to the Veil, not to mention wanting to give herself to the Ice. Fortunately it had all turned out better than Odris had feared.

It took Odris a few seconds to coordinate herself to Milla's quick movements once they were outside. Although the Crones had allowed Odris a limited freedom, ordinary Icecarls were much more comfortable when she tried to behave like a normal shadow. In her natural form in Aenir she was a cloud and could easily shift shape. She had retained this ability to a certain extent as a Spiritshadow, but she was never fast enough to match her movements to Milla's. No one who saw her sliding along behind or to the side, copying Milla's actions a few seconds late, would ever doubt that she was actually a Spiritshadow.

Even with the bright light from Milla's Sunstone it was hard to see the full Icecarl host camped along the road, as the snow was still falling heavily and swirling sideways into the mountain. Every few stretches there would be a moth-lantern or two tied to a bone stake driven into the side of the mountain, and the corner of a tent would become visible, or a stack of supplies.

There were also many Shield Maidens and Icecarl hunters who would suddenly appear out of the whirling snow. Whatever they were doing, they would stop and clap their fists together in greeting as Milla approached. She had to pause and clap her fists in turn, so it took a long time just to walk a hundred stretches from Milla's tent down the road. Eventually she arrived at the point where the entry to the heatway tunnels was marked by two huge flaming tubs of Selski oil.

The entrance was guarded by a full Hand of Shield Maidens in shell-mirror armor. They carried shadowsacks, shadow-bottles, and spears with tips that were heavily coated with luminous algae. The equipment and the luminous algae had all come from secret stores in the Ruin Ship. The Crones had thrown open the Icecarls' ancient arsenal, releasing many weapons that were specifically designed to fight Aeniran shadows.

The Chosen of the Castle had forgotten the ancient war between the Dark World and the creatures of Aenir, but the Icecarl Crones had not. Through the centuries they had maintained both weapons and knowledge, ready for the war they knew must one day resume.

The Shield Maidens clapped their fists together as Milla approached, but Milla was not fooled. There was a reluctance in their greeting — they were wary of her and Odris. She couldn't see their eyes through the amber lenses of their face masks, but she could tell from the set of their heads that they were ready to defend themselves if she went mad and attacked them.

Milla might command the Shield Maidens, but that was never what she wanted. She wanted to be one of them, and still did. But she knew it was impossible. She had lost her shadow, brought a Spirit-shadow to the Ice . . . and she had slain the Shield Mother Arla. There was no going back for her. She could only go forward.

"We greet you, War-Chief," said the Shield Mother of this Hand. Milla didn't know her name. So many Shield Maidens and hunters had come, and even three or four Sword-Thanes. Many more were still on the way across the Ice, though there were already almost two thousand Icecarls camped all along the road from the Ruin Ship up the Mountain of Light. Another thousand or more were kept busy hunting the Ice below for food to feed the host, and there was a continuous line of carriers and carters taking food and supplies between the Ruin Ship below and the various encampments on the road.

"I am going in to the heatways," announced Milla, raising her voice so it would carry over the wind. "Please tell the Crone Malen that I will be some time."

"No need," said a voice beyond the Shield Maidens. A moment later a figure materialized out of the whirling snow. A slim young woman — perhaps a circling older than Milla, who wore the light black furs of a Crone. She carried no weapons and did not wear a face mask, despite the wind and stinging snow. Her eyes were bright blue and glowed with an unnatural light, marking her as a Crone, the blue signifying she was of the youngest of the three orders. In time her eyes would turn silver, and then cloudy and white.

"What do you intend?" asked Malen.

She spoke easily enough, but Milla grimaced as she heard it. Because of the Prayer of Asteyr, she had to obey the commands of the Crones, who spoke with one voice. In this case, it meant obeying the commands of Malen.

The young Crone was bound to stop her, Milla thought. She tensed, trying to resist the command before it came.

"We are taking too long to find a substitute for the Underfolk's airweed," Milla said as calmly as she could. "I left some near the heatway entrance. Using it, I will go back through the tunnels and find the Freefolk rebels. I am sure they will help me bring plenty of airweed back, if we agree to free them from the Chosen when we take the Castle."

Malen listened in silence. Her eyes clouded a little, the luminosity dimming. Milla knew this meant she was communicating with other Crones. They were seeing through her eyes, listening through the young Crone's ears. Any decision that came would be from all the Crones, or at least all of those who chose to participate. It wouldn't be just from Malen.

Even so, Milla almost hated the other girl. She had everything Milla had always wanted. Not to be a Crone, but to have a proper place. To have the respect of the Shield Maidens. To be adored by her clan.

"Yes," Malen said finally. "We have taken too

long, and there is no sign we will succeed in our search for airweed under the Ice. It is best that you find the Freefolk and get them to bring airweed. I will come with you."

"There's not . . ."

Milla started to say "not enough airweed" but the words never came out, because she knew that there was enough airweed for two, if they were careful, and Malen's eyes were fixed on her own. Milla knew the Crone would feel the lie.

"Come on, then," Milla said gruffly.

Milla climbed up to the heatway entrance as the Shield Maidens clapped their fists together again. This time it was more for the Crone, Milla knew. She ignored that, and crawled inside.

·CHAPTER·
TWO☉

Tal settled back into the sarcophagus, the stone cold against his back. Waves of shivering rocked his whole body every few seconds. He kept seeing the beam of light from his Sunstone strike the ceiling. He saw the stone lintel above the door crack and come tumbling down. He saw the steam howling out from the cracked wall.

Most of all, Tal remembered Crow's sudden look of terror as the avalanche of stone, steam, and dust came down upon him.

Crow's face haunted him, but he had not been alone. Tal had almost certainly killed Clovil, and maybe others of Crow's Underfolk gang, and most horribly of all, his own great-uncle Ebbitt. They had all been directly in the path of the falling rocks and the scalding jets of steam. There was no way they could have escaped the collapse of the ceiling and the rupturing of one of the Castle's major steam risers.

It had only happened an hour before, but it was one of the longest hours Tal had ever experienced. He'd tried to stop the falling rocks and the steam but had been driven back. He'd called for help, but no one came. All the Chosen were away. Their bodies might be sleeping in their chambers, but their spirits, their essential selves, were in the Spirit World of Aenir. So there was no one powerful enough to do anything. The Underfolk would arrive eventually, but they could do no more than clean up . . . shut off the steam somewhere down below . . . and dig the bodies out of the rubble.

A thin, squeaky voice interrupted Tal's awful memories. He craned his neck forward to look at the Red Keystone he held in his hand, flat on his chest. It glowed in the darkness of the sarcophagus. Tal concentrated on it, and the image of Lokar, the Guardian of the Red Keystone who was trapped inside the Sunstone, slowly came into focus. She was talking to him, he realized. He should concentrate on what she was saying.

"Tal! Listen . . . you must listen! We must get as

close to the Chosen Enclave as we can," repeated Lokar. "Do you know how to focus on your arrival point in Aenir, Tal?"

"No," mumbled Tal. He knew he should be concentrating on what she was saying, but he couldn't. His head was full of the disaster he had caused. Lokar kept talking at him, telling him how to focus on his Sunstone so that his spirit would cross to the right place in Aenir.

Aenir was the source of Sunstones and Spirit-shadows. It was also, Tal thought bitterly, the source of all his troubles. He had unwittingly gotten caught up in an age-old struggle between the people of the Dark World — the Chosen and the Icecarls — and the strange creatures of the Spirit World of Aenir. His enemy Sushin was undeniably an agent of the shadows of Aenir, and had trapped Tal's father inside the Orange Keystone, poisoned his mother into a coma, imprisoned his younger brother, Gref, and put his very small sister, Kusi, into the "care" of his awful cousins Lallek and Korrek.

"So close, so close, yet far, very far," muttered Lokar, her voice so strange Tal wasn't sure who she was talking to. Then her voice snapped back to its normal, strident tone. Tal!" Lokar ordered. "There's no time to waste! We must get to the Empress and report on the unlocked Keystones!"

Tal nodded weakly, but he didn't do anything. Something squirmed at the edge of his vision and he flinched, until he realized it was his Spiritshadow, Adras. Adras had been a Storm Shepherd in Aenir, a mighty creature of cloud and air. Normally he would be a very strong Spiritshadow in the Dark World. But he had been starved of light and almost destroyed when Tal had incorrectly created a miniature veil to hide them from hostile Spiritshadows. It had worked, but Tal had never cast one before and had accidentally worked Adras into the Veil. Without any light at all, Adras had shrunk and withered away to almost nothing. Even now, he was very weak.

"Odris!" whispered Adras, close to Tal's ear. Odris was his fellow Storm Shepherd, a companion to the Icecarl Milla, who had left the Castle and gone out onto the Ice. "We should go to Odris. She will help us."

"The Empress," repeated Lokar. "The Empress! The Empress! We must cross to Aenir and inform the Empress! We must! We must —"

"Shut up!" Tal burst out. Why couldn't they be

quiet, just for a minute? He needed to lie there in silence, with just the comforting orange glow of his Sunstone ring mixed with the steady crimson pulse of light from the Red Keystone.

Surprisingly, Adras and Lokar both shut up. Tal lay there, breathing quietly, every now and then pressing his hands against the stone lid of the sarcophagus above his head. Pressing hard against the lid released some of the tension inside him.

He still couldn't get that awful frozen second of Crow's face and the falling rock out of his mind. But he finally felt strong enough to make a firm decision. They would cross to Aenir, find the Empress, and tell her everything. He would make sure that she used the Violet Keystone, the strongest and most important stone, to release his father from the Orange Keystone. Then Tal could tell him everything and he would take over and sort everything out.

Tal felt a little better as he made the decision, until a small voice inside his head reminded him that no one could make Ebbitt and Crow and the others alive again.

"It was Crow's own fault!" Tal said suddenly. Somehow getting angry made him feel better. His head still hurt where Crow had hit him. The Underfolk boy had stolen the Red Keystone, too. If Crow hadn't hit him and taken the Keystone, nothing would have happened. He would still be alive, and so would Ebbitt, Clovil, Ferenc, and Inkie.

"It was his fault," Tal repeated. Crow had started it. The rock fall was an accident that never would have happened otherwise.

·CHAPTER·
THREE

"I will go to the Empress," Tal declared as he stared into the Red Keystone. He could see Lokar in the center of the jewel, the small woman looked like she was treading water, her hands and feet in constant movement. Her Spiritshadow, a hopping Leaper-beast, circled her, never stopping. They were both prisoners in the Keystone, trapped there when the stone was unlocked. They could not be released except with Lokar's own Sunstone or the Violet Keystone of the Seventh Tower.

"Good! Oh, good! Excellent!" babbled Lokar. "To make sure we come out close to the Chosen Enclave, you must first fix an image of the place in your head. Then you need to hold that picture there as you recite the Way to Aenir and concentrate on the correct colors. You do . . . you do know the Way to Aenir? Please, you must . . ."

"Of course I know," said Tal, though he didn't know how to transfer to a particular spot. He thought about it for a second. Of course he could do it. He was better at Light Magic now than most adult Chosen. If he hadn't been he would be dead by now.

He had to pick the right part of the Enclave for his arrival. They would have to be careful to avoid being seen. Since the Day of Ascension had just happened, all the Chosen would be in Aenir. Presumably that would include Sushin. As the Dark Vizier, he was able to command any other Chosen in the name of the Empress. There were also a lot of Chosen who willingly followed Sushin, or were duped into obeying him. Probably none of them knew that Sushin was secretly a servant of the free shadows of Aenir, and that his real aim was to destroy the Veil that protected the Dark World from the Sun and from the shadows of Aenir.

Milla thought Sushin *was* some sort of shadow, one who had taken on flesh, but Tal wasn't sure about that.

"Where do you think we should arrive?" Tal asked.

"Soon!" snapped Lokar. "Oh, where? Where? The rim. The rim of the crater, at night."

"At night?" asked Tal. "You mean I can visualize a time as well?"

"Yes," replied Lokar. "Yes. Two deep breaths. One. Two. Where was I? Besides *here*. Yes. Within a day or so. I do not know what would happen if you tried to cross too far into Aenir's future."

"Where do we go if it is not yet night in Aenir?"

"Who knows? Our bodies sleep here, and our spirits arrive there. We will not notice if our spirits spend time somewhere in between. It doesn't matter!"

Tal didn't like the thought of that. But he had decided.

"Visualize," said Lokar. "Hurry. Oh, darkness take you! Think! Think of the Enclave. Pick a spot where you have spent time, that you know well. Remember it in detail. Paint a picture in your head. . . ."

Tal let his head fall back. Lokar's increasingly shrill voice dropped away to the distant buzz of a tunnel-gnat.

He thought of the Chosen Enclave. He saw it in his mind, imagined it as a Storm Shepherd might see it from high overhead. The vast volcanic crater, the rim rising up a thousand stretches above the Plain of Thorns. On the inside of the rim, a lesser fall, only five or six hundred stretches down to the lake that filled the crater. But this was no ordinary lake. It was not water but a mixture of fine gray ash and millions upon millions of tiny clear crystals.

Strange creatures lived in the ash lake. Most were unknown, though some of the shallower regions had been netted over the years, with the catch made to serve as Spiritshadows back in the Castle.

Sushin had originally had a lake-dweller Spiritshadow, a tall, thin creature with an armored shell and a snapping beak. But Sushin had a different Spiritshadow now, another sign of his treachery and alliance with the creatures of Aenir. Chosen did not change their Spiritshadows.

Tal quickly concentrated, remembering details of the Enclave. The Chosen in Aenir stayed in houses built on stilts across the Lake of Ash, houses joined by raised walkways that kept them safely out of reach of the lake-dwellers.

In the very center of the lake there was a real island, rather than a platform made by the Chosen. Protected by stone walls and Sunstone wards, the island was the Empress's Aeniran residence. It had gardens and a palace. It was not open to other Chosen and was not joined to the network of raised pathways and bridges.

Tal thought about arriving on the Empress's island. But he had only seen it from a distance, from high on the crater wall. He couldn't visualize any details because he didn't know any.

He also had better not arrive on a walkway or house. It would be too easy to be seen. Lokar was right, the crater rim would be the best. But where on the crater rim?

Tal remembered climbing up with his parents as a very young boy, before Gref was born. He remembered grizzling and complaining at the steepness of the path, until his father picked him up and piggybacked him most of the way.

But his clearest memory was from the year before. With a bunch of other boys he had climbed to the Hanging Rock to watch some older Chosen light-diving.

The Hanging Rock was a tongue of stone that projected from the crater rim, in toward the lake. It was at least fifty stretches long, a strange, seemingly unsupported platform that was perfect for light-diving. If anywhere could be considered perfect for light-diving, that is. It was a dangerous sport, frowned upon by senior Chosen. Any child who attempted it, rather than a Full Chosen, would automatically gain four Deluminents . . . if they survived. Four Deluminents was more than halfway to the disgrace of demotion, the beginning of a slide that might end in Red or even the white robes of Underfolk.

Light-diving was simple enough. The Chosen divers would weave themselves a rope of light, tie one end around their ankles and the other end to the "anchor hole" in the Hanging Rock. Then they would simply dive off, down toward the lake. If the lightrope was made properly, they would plummet down about two-thirds of the way, then suddenly rebound and bounce up and down for a while. Once they'd come to a stop, it was usually a simple matter to shrink the rope and be drawn back up.

If the rope wasn't properly made, the Chosen diver might fall into the ash, and drown or get eaten by something. Sometimes, less fatally but more embarrassingly, the lightrope wouldn't shrink, and the diver would be left dangling upside down below the Hanging Rock until friends came to the rescue.

The Hanging Rock would be ideal, Tal thought. He would time it so he arrived at dusk. Then he could sneak down the path at night, and onto the network of bridges and walkways. There were some boats on the lake, and he would steal one of those to get to the Empress's island.

Tal fixed the image of the Hanging Rock in his mind, with the red light of the setting sun just upon it. He could see the Rock and the lake below, the crater wall stretching away to either side to circle around in the distance. It was all very clear in his head.

Tal raised his Sunstone and called forth the first of the colors that would begin his transfer. At the same time, he began to recite the Way to Aenir, his words and the colors from the stone mixing together. He felt the color spread across his skin, felt the difference as Red gave way to Orange and then Yellow.

The inside of the stone sarcophagus faded away, to be replaced by swirling colors. Bright rainbows washed across Tal, blurring into each other as each new one passed.

All the way through, he kept the image of the Hanging Rock in his head, with the sunlight just beginning to fall upon it.

Tal was on his way to Aenir. Whether he'd made a good decision or not, he had chosen his cards. Now he would have to play the beast he had created.

·CHAPTER·
FOUR

A heavy outer coat lay a few paces inside the heatway. It was Tal's coat, where they had left it the first time Milla had entered the Castle. That felt like a lifetime ago, or a dream. Milla had been a different person, honored to be going on an adventure, to get a new Sunstone for her clan. Now she no longer belonged to the clan of the Far-Raiders and everything had changed.

"Hurry up!" whispered Odris. "The Crone is stuck outside."

Milla jumped forward and hurried along the heatway. She hadn't realized she'd actually stopped and was touching Tal's coat. This wasn't how a Shield Maiden behaved. She might have been surprised by an enemy! Even though she wasn't a Shield Maiden she should still try to behave like one.

The airweed was farther along the passage. A long stalk of it lay on the floor. Milla picked it up and examined the four bulbous nodules of air that were left. She had used only one nodule on the way out. Even though it had been the biggest, there should still be plenty left for the two of them to make it through.

Taking out her new knife of golden metal — yet another treasure from the Ruin Ship — Milla carefully cut the strand of airweed in half. Handing two of the four nodules to Malen, she explained how to use them.

"When the time comes, Odris will warn us to use the airweed. You must make a tiny hole at the end, where it is softest, and then press your finger on it. Keeping your finger over the hole, put your mouth onto the airweed as if you were a baby suckling milk, and breathe in. Breathe out through your nose. Keep your finger pressed tight over the hole whenever you are not taking a breath."

Milla demonstrated, without actually cutting the nodule. Malen copied her.

"You do have a knife, don't you?" asked Milla. She couldn't see one, nor see the telltale signs of one hidden in a sleeve or boot.

"Yes," said Malen. She looked at Tal's coat. "Do we leave our outer coats here?"

Milla nodded and started to shrug her coat off. The heatways were aptly named. This tunnel and the network of others like it were actually inspection tunnels for the Castle's heating system. It used lava to heat great lakes of water, and the steam was piped throughout the more than a hundred levels and seven towers of the vast building. Unfortunately, over the centuries the lava had broken out of its assigned channels and had invaded some of the inspection tunnels. That was where the bad air came from.

"Odris, go first," Milla ordered.

"Do this, do that," grumbled Odris. "You might be War-Chief of the Icecarls but you're not War-Chief of the Storm Shepherds."

"You need to go first so you can warn me about the bad air," said Milla patiently.

"How can it tell?" asked Malen.

"It!" exclaimed Odris. "How would you like to be called 'it'?"

"She can taste it," Milla answered. "Odris was a Storm Shepherd in Aenir. They have a particular affinity for air, even as Spiritshadows."

Malen nodded, but she didn't answer Odris, or otherwise acknowledge her. Odris stood waiting, puffing herself up to her full size, a huge shadow that completely filled the tunnel.

"Odris, it would please me if you go ahead," said Milla wearily. It was clear that Malen was not going to lower herself to talk to a free shadow.

"Tell *it* to keep *its* distance," hissed Odris, pointing a puffy finger at Malen. Then she turned and started off down the heatway. She shrunk herself at the same time, her shadowflesh becoming darker and denser.

Milla followed her, ignoring the Crone. She would follow or not. Milla was already remembering all the twists and turns of the heatway passages. Tal had found a map the first time through, and she had committed every turn to memory. Coming out she had reversed it and now must reverse it again. There were more than a hundred turns and several climbs to recall, and she had to get it right. A wrong turning or other mistake could plunge them down into the lava flows or the boiling reservoirs.

Despite the increasing heat, Milla kept up a punishing pace, first in a hunched-over walk and then at a crawl as the ceiling lowered. Odris was often only a few steps ahead of her, and Malen was often ten or even twenty stretches behind. Milla knew the Crone would have had no experience of such heat, and was obviously finding it a struggle. But Malen did not complain. All she did was undo the lacings at her throat and sleeves.

Soon they had to resort to breathing through dampened rags, as the heat continued to build. Still Milla kept on, occasionally pausing to think about the next turning before continuing forward. Her Sunstone lit up the tunnel ahead and also provided Odris with a source of strength.

After a few hours they came to the broken skeleton where Milla and Tal had found a Sunstone that Tal's great-uncle Ebbitt had later split in two. Later, on the way back, Milla had found the strange fingernail that she now knew as the Talon of Danir among the bones.

Milla paused before the skeleton and held her Sunstone high. Malen came up close, and they both gazed down upon the bones.

"This is where you found the Sunstone and the Talon," said Malen. "I wonder who bore them? I do not think the bones are particularly old."

Milla scowled. She hadn't noticed before, but the bones were not as ancient as she had always thought. Trust a Crone — this Crone — to instantly recognize something that might be important.

"Tal said he must have been a Chosen," Milla said. "He wore the Sunstone on a ring."

There was no room for Malen to get past Milla to the main skeleton, but the Crone reached out and picked up a bone that had been scattered farther along. She tapped it against the wall, then pulled out a small sharp stone from her sleeve and pared off a sliver.

"Not more than a hundred circlings," Malen pronounced after examining the sliver. "And not less than fifty. I wonder who could have been wearing the Talon of Danir as recently as that?"

Milla shrugged. The question was of no importance to the immediate task. The skeleton was a pile of bones, and bones could not speak.

"The bad air will probably begin soon," Milla said. "Be ready with your airweed."

Malen nodded. Milla gestured Odris to go on. But the Spiritshadow did not move. Instead she held up one puffy hand and cocked her head to one side.

"Wait," she whispered. "Someone comes. There is movement in the air."

Milla reacted instantly, focusing on her Sunstone to dim it to a weak glow. Then she eased her sword in its scabbard, for a quick draw. Behind her, she heard Malen draw in a nervous breath.

They waited in the near darkness for what felt like a long time but wasn't, before a faint light appeared in the distance. It was not even and bright like a Sunstone, or the red glow of the lava, but a flickering yellow.

Milla and Malen lay completely still, close to the floor. Odris slid up against the ceiling and pressed herself there. All of them looked forward.

The yellow light grew brighter. Milla saw two men in white Underfolk robes crawling down the tunnel. They each carried an Underfolk lamp of the type Milla had seen before, simple globes of unbreakable crystal filled with mineral fuel and topped with a wick.

The lamps shed only a narrow circle of light around the men. It also blinded them to what lay ahead.

The yellow light flickered as the Underfolk crawled, but there were more shadows around the men than could be explained by that. Milla tensed as she realized that the men were being followed by two . . . no, three . . . Spiritshadows. Thin, thorny Spiritshadows, not of any kind Milla had ever seen. They were about the same size as the Underfolk, but had six legs, razored and bulbous bodies, and long thin heads that ended in what would probably be a sharp spike or bloodsucking proboscis in their native Aeniran form.

The Underfolk paused to take breaths from air-weed nodules they had slung around their necks. But the Spiritshadows didn't let them take more than one. Their forelegs whipped the men about the shoulders. Milla saw their shadowflesh get darker and denser and the Underfolk flinch under the blows.

These were free shadows, Milla realized. They were using the Underfolk to provide the light they needed. If only the men realized, they could blow out their lanterns and the Spiritshadows would be helpless. But then, down here, so would the Underfolk. And the Spiritshadows might not fade fast enough. . . .

The Underfolk started crawling again. Thoughts flashed through Milla's mind. She had her Sunstone, but didn't really know how to use it properly against Spiritshadows. Her Merwin-horn sword would cut them. Odris could probably outfight one or two of them. The Crone might also be of some use. The Crones did seem to have some tricks they could use against shadows.

The Underfolk kept crawling on. The Spirit-shadows followed them, but not closely. They kept flitting from side to side, thrusting their shadow proboscises into cracks in the walls and ceiling, reaching out with their forelegs.

"They are looking for something," whispered Malen, just as Milla had the same thought.

Milla looked down at the Talon of Danir on her finger. It was glowing violet and gold. When she had fought the Shield Mother Arla, it had suddenly extended and mortally wounded Milla's opponent.

Milla closed her fist to hide the glow of the Talon.

"When they get close, we will attack," she whispered. "The shadows, not the Underfolk."

·CHAPTER·
FIVE

Tal blinked and opened his eyes. As he always did when he arrived in Aenir he felt lighter, less substantial. The first thing he did was look down at himself. Sure enough, his skin had gained the peculiar glow that all Dark Worlders had on Aenir. He knew that he was also shorter and slighter, another effect of the transfer.

Tal looked around, his eyes adjusting to the twilight. It was exactly as he'd pictured it. He stood on the end of the Hanging Rock, high above the Lake of Ash. Out on the lake there was the Empress's island and then, in a semicircle around it, hundreds of Chosen houses, all built high on stilts and joined by narrow bridges and raised walkways.

The anchor hole was near his feet. He could see through it, see the lake far below.

"I've done it!" he exclaimed. There was a red glow in the distance, behind the far crater wall, the sun setting. He had timed it exactly. Soon the last light would fade and he could sneak down the path behind him.

"Adras, I've done it!" he said again.

There was no reply. Puzzled, Tal looked around. There was no sign of the Storm Shepherd. But Tal knew he had to be there. They were inextricably bound together. Adras *couldn't* have been left behind. He'd die in the dark sarcophagus without Tal's Sunstone light!

A faint cry sounded above him. Tal looked up and sighed in relief. Adras was high above him, a faint white speck in the darkening sky. He was still only a third his normal size, but he was no longer a shadow. Like Tal, he had been transformed, in this case back to his natural form, the puffy cloud-flesh of a Storm Shepherd.

"Water," called Adras, his voice thin and high, like the wind blowing between the cracks of a house. "I must find water. I will return!"

He rose up higher then, and Tal felt a pang in his stomach. It wasn't exactly painful, but it wasn't pleasant, either. He knew it would last until Adras came back, and that the Storm Shepherd would also feel it. They could not stay very far apart for too long.

He looked down again, and realized he was still clenching his fist. He opened it and looked at the Red Keystone. As before, Lokar swam into view as he concentrated upon the stone's sparkling depths.

"We're here," announced Tal. "On the Hanging Rock, at dusk."

"Good," replied Lokar. Her voice was almost a sob. "Oh, I will soon be free of this accursed prison! The Empress will use the Violet Keystone to release me!"

"Is it . . . is it that bad in there? Does it hurt?" asked Tal. He wasn't really thinking of Lokar. His thoughts were with his father, Rerem, trapped inside the Orange Keystone.

Lokar laughed, a laugh tinged with hysteria.

"Hurt? It doesn't hurt. Yet I cannot rest, I cannot sleep, I cannot stop this endless circling inside the stone. Unless someone speaks from outside, there is only my Spiritshadow and me, surrounded by silence. Years and years and years of silence. Is it any surprise that I have been mad?"

Tal stared down at her. Suddenly taking her advice didn't seem so sensible. Lokar said she had been mad. What if she still was?

"Speak!" ordered Lokar. "Speak! Tell me what is happening outside!"

"Uh, nothing really."

Tal stumbled over the words. He didn't know what to say. "Um, Adras has flown off to find some water. I'm going to wait until it's a bit darker and start down the path."

He looked up as he spoke, to see how much light was left. To his surprise, the light on the horizon was brighter than before. It was also less red. Tal stared at it, not listening to the buzzing voice of Lokar.

It took him a full two seconds to realize he'd made a dreadful mistake.

It wasn't dusk.

It was dawn.

In a few minutes, the sun would rise above the crater wall. He would be easily seen on the Hanging Rock, or heading down the path. Sushin's followers, or even just some concerned Chosen, would spot him for sure.

"I made a mistake! It's dawn!" he gabbled to the Keystone. Without waiting for an answer, he tied the stone into the corner of his sleeve and pulled it tight, so there was no chance it could be lost. He already had his two vials of water-spider antidote tied in the other sleeve.

There was only one thing Tal could do to avoid detection and capture. He must weave a lightrope within the next few minutes and dive down to the Lake of Ash. But unlike the regular light-divers who returned to the Hanging Rock by shrinking their ropes, he would have to try and get as close to the ash as possible, cut himself free, and swim ashore.

Tal knew the principles of lightropes. A red strand for strength, a yellow strand for flexibility, and an indigo strand to keep it all together. A few months ago he had never even handled light above the yellow spectrum, but now he didn't hesitate. He would even use violet if he had to.

Tal lifted his Sunstone ring and concentrated on it. A thick line of red light spilled out of the Stone and fell down, coiling as it fell. Tal kept it going and added a yellow strand, thicker than the red. Then came the indigo, winding about the two other strands. The complete rope kept falling and coiling, and Tal realized he had another problem.

He didn't know how long to make the lightrope. If it was too short he'd just bounce up and down and end up hanging too far above the ash to safely drop. If it was too long he'd dive deep into the ash and even though he'd probably bounce out several times, the initial impact would probably kill him.

Desperately he tried to remember watching other light-divers. He tried to recall conversations he'd overheard. Was it three hundred and fifty stretches? It was three hundred and something . . . three hundred and sixty?

Tal decided shorter was safer than longer. Better to be captured alive dangling above the Lake of Ash than killed. He decided on three hundred and fifty. Allowing five stretches for the loose ends before the lightrope wove together, he was almost there.

A thin sliver of sun was already poking over the far crater wall. Behind him, there was sunlight on the closer wall, about fifty stretches above him. He could see the line of sunlight falling every minute, creeping closer down to him.

Tal twisted his hand and directed the end of the rope through the anchor hole, directing the light so it shot under the Hanging Rock and back over to rejoin itself below his hand. Tal pulled back as if he were lifting a weight, tightening the loop until the rope was fast against the rock. Then he cut it off with a thought and went forward to pick up the other end. After cutting off the loose strands with a fine ray of Red light, he used two fingers of Indigo light to tie the lightrope securely around his ankles.

The sunlight hit the top of his head. Tal took a deep breath and shuffled to the very edge of the Hanging Rock.

He looked down. The lake was a long, long way down. The Chosen houses and the walkways between them were tiny.

Sunlight touched his eyes.

Tal shut them firmly and leaned forward. For a moment he hung on the very edge of the Hanging Rock.

Then he toppled forward and fell straight down, the lightrope rippling out behind him.

·CHAPTER·
SIX

The Underfolk crawled closer. The free Spirit-shadows followed right behind them. As the light from the lanterns illuminated a stray bone from the skeleton, the Underfolk stopped and pointed. Instantly, the three Spiritshadows swarmed forward, obviously excited. The Underfolk shuddered as the Spiritshadows slid over and past them, cold shadowflesh chilling them through their robes.

The lead Spiritshadow touched the bone with its proboscis, then with its two front claws. Then it looked at the others, and all three briefly touched their forelegs.

At that moment, while they were distracted, Milla attacked.

She lunged forward in a crouch, her hand extended, trusting that the Talon of Danir would do whatever it did automatically.

She intended to use the glowing fingernail to cut the closest Spiritshadow. But as she leaped forward, the Talon extended itself, until it was as long as her forearm. Bright violet sparks showered from the end, and a long plume of violet light shot out like a whip — a whip of light at least three stretches long.

Milla brought her hand down toward the Spiritshadow, and the whip of light shot around and became a lasso. Without conscious direction from Milla, it settled over the head of the Spiritshadow and pulled tight. It went through the shadowflesh like a wire through cheese, cutting the Spiritshadow's head off in a single sharp action.

Milla flicked the lasso at the next one, and the same thing happened. As she flicked it at the third and last Spiritshadow, the other two were picking up their separated heads and then trying to reconnect them, as they scuttled as fast as they could back down the tunnel.

The third Spiritshadow was quicker and the lasso missed. But before it could attack Milla, the violet streamer undid itself and the free end whipped out to slice through the Spiritshadow's forelegs. The creature crashed to the floor, and wriggled backward, sliding over the Underfolk, who had pressed themselves facedown on the floor. It halted for a moment, then scuttled away.

Odris had rushed forward to grab the shadow, but as she reached out, the light from the Talon whipped back toward her. Instantly, Milla threw her hand the other way, slapping her palm against the wall.

The whip missed Odris by a finger-width.

"Careful!" boomed Odris. She sounded scared.

Milla was shaken, too. She held her hand against the wall, until the violet stream of light slowly ebbed back into the Talon, and it shrank back to its regular size.

"I didn't know it did that," said Milla. No wonder Danir had been such a fearsome warrior, her legend lasting thousands of years. She had worn one of these magical fingernails on each hand.

"Interesting," said Malen. "The Talon seems to act of its own accord against shadows."

"I'm staying back here, then," said Odris, "until you learn to control it."

Milla nodded and cautiously drew her hand back from the wall. The Talon didn't do anything. Perhaps it only worked when she wanted to fight. She would have to be careful to make sure Odris wasn't nearby when she did. In a way it was like being a Wilder, one of the berserk warriors that occasionally emerged in the clans. You had to stay clear of them when they fought, until the blood-craze left them and they knew friend from foe.

"You can get up now," said Milla to the two Underfolk. "Well, you can crouch, anyway."

She crawled up to them, but they didn't move. Milla raised her Sunstone and light flared, the brightness washing out the yellow glow of the lanterns.

"You can . . ." Milla started to say again. Then she scowled and reached forward to touch the closest man. He didn't move.

Milla felt for a pulse in his neck and then repeated the action with the other one.

Neither one had a pulse.

"They're dead," she said slowly. "But I don't see how."

She shuffled up between the two bodies. Only then did she see that they each had a tiny wound in their back of the head. A wound about the same size as one of the Spiritshadow's proboscis.

"The last one must have stabbed them as it passed," Milla said.

She felt strangely affected by their deaths. Death was no stranger to her, even sudden, unexpected, and violent death. But somehow this felt worse than the accidents she had seen, or the fatal encounters with the wild beasts of the Ice.

It took her a moment to realize what it was.

"Shadows have killed," she said slowly. "I do not think I believed it was possible before."

"It is not only possible, it has happened many times before, long ago," said Malen. "The ancient war has begun again. We know it, as do the shadows of Aenir, even if the Chosen do not. You realize what those shadows were looking for?"

Milla nodded.

"The Talon," she said, looking back at the skeleton. "And perhaps the Sunstone. The Spiritshadows expected to find the man's remains — or what he carried — to be here somewhere. That is why they were searching so carefully."

"They have reason to be afraid of the Talon," said Malen. "I wonder how much a shadow can be cut before it cannot repair itself?"

"This is a very morbid conversation," said Odris. "Personally, I don't want to find out."

No one spoke for a moment. Milla carefully rolled the two Underfolk over to look at their faces and fix them in her mind, so she could describe them later and find out their names. She wondered if the

Freefolk would know them. Perhaps they were close family. Certainly they would be someone's brothers, or uncles, or fathers.

"I do not know what the Underfolk do with their dead," Milla said finally, as she folded their arms across their chests and carefully opened their eyes wide so they might see their way ahead. "The Chosen trap them in stone boxes."

"I have spoken to Crone Mother Panul," said Malen. "I have told her the turnings. She will send Shield Maidens to take these Underfolk out and give them to the Ice. There is no likelihood of bad air between here and the outside, is there?"

"I don't think so," replied Milla. She gestured down the tunnel. "It lies ahead. Tell Panul they should take the airweed these men carried. Tell her how to use it."

Malen nodded. Her eyes clouded as she joined the mass mind of the Crones.

Milla looked away, at the tunnel stretching out ahead. The Spiritshadows would have spread the alarm. They would not know who they encountered, but they would tell of the deadly whip of violet light.

Many shadows might be gathering now in the lower Underfolk levels, waiting for Milla, Malen, and Odris. The Chosen should all be in Aenir, but even if they weren't, Milla wasn't afraid of them. They had lived too easy lives. They were not warriors.

Free shadows from Aenir were a different matter.

"Come," she said. "We must hurry. The enemy now knows that the evening breeze brings raiders down upon the ship."

"What?" asked Odris. "Which raiders? What ship?"

"It's only a saying," said Milla. "Anyone would think you were Adras."

"Adras is gone," sighed Odris. "Gone to Aenir, back to being a Storm Shepherd."

"Gone?" asked Milla. "But Tal was to get the Red Keystone. He shouldn't be in Aenir."

"Maybe he isn't," said Odris mournfully. "Maybe . . . maybe he's dead, and Adras was released. I don't know."

"When did this happen? Why didn't you teli me?"

Odris shrugged. "Three sleeps ago. I heard his farewell upon the wind. You were sulking on your stupid chair."

"You must tell me matters of importance," Milla said angrily. "I bet he's got himself into trouble again."

"Adras?"

"No, Tal! Come on!"

·CHAPTER·
SEVEN

Tal plummeted down, the lightrope spilling out behind him. Down and down he fell, his arms spread wide, his head back. He saw the Lake of Ash below, coming closer and closer and closer, and still he fell, the lightrope running free.

Any moment, the rope would run out and he would bounce back, but the moment didn't come and the lake was so close, only ten or twenty stretches below — and this time Adras wasn't nearby to catch him!

The rope was too long. He was going to hit the lake!

Tal wrapped his arms around his head and screwed his eyes shut. He felt his stomach stay behind as his fall was suddenly arrested. He opened his eyes and saw the surface of the lake just beyond his reach — and then he was hurtling up again as the rope jerked him back.

His stomach felt like it was determined to stay on the surface of the lake as Tal bounced up and down. When he finally came to rest, he was hanging about four stretches above the surface of the ash and sixty stretches from the shore.

The surface of the lake was quite smooth. Even though it looked completely gray higher up, from this distance all the clear crystals allowed Tal to see a little way under the surface. It was like looking into very cloudy water. Not that there was anything to see, which was a good sign. He didn't want to see anything there.

Flipping himself up, Tal grabbed the rope. He used his Sunstone to unravel the indigo binding thread. He hung from his hands for a moment, then let himself go. Above him, his lightrope dissipated into the air.

Tal fell straight down into the strange fluid of the lake, only remembering to hold his arms out at the last moment, so his head didn't go under.

The mixture of ash and tiny crystals almost felt like water, but it was warm and dry, and it was much harder to move through. Luckily, it was easier to stay afloat.

Tal started swimming to the shore immediately. It would be daylight throughout the crater soon, and he had to find somewhere to hide.

He was halfway to the shore when he noticed that there was another noise beside the curious rustling sound of his own swimming. A sound that he could feel as a vibration through the ash, as well as hear. It was coming from behind him, so he rolled over to look, while continuing with a fairly clumsy back-stroke.

At first he couldn't see anything. Then a large and highly unwelcome shape briefly surfaced about a hundred stretches away, before disappearing again.

Tal saw a great long back of serrated blue and red scales, accompanied by the brief flash of a huge mouth surrounded by four long, questing tendrils.

Suddenly Tal's arms started thrashing through the ash with new strength and speed.

He knew what he'd seen. It was a Kerfer, one of the great carnivores of the lake. A creature played in Beastmaker for Strength or Special. Its Special ability lay in its six feathery tentacles. Four were several times longer than a man and sensed vibration and movement. Two were shorter, but oozed a paralyzing venom.

Tal looked again. The Kerfer briefly broached the surface, tentacles rising into the air before they splashed down ahead of its body. It had closed the distance between them by half in only a few seconds. He had no chance of outswimming it.

The Chosen boy stopped swimming, though his feet trod the ash to keep him afloat. He raised his Sunstone ring and concentrated on it. Red light grew in intensity there, until it was almost blinding.

A tentacle rose up out of the ash just a stretch away. One of the sensing tentacles — but the paralyzing tentacle would not be far behind.

Tal waited. The tentacle quested forward and touched his chest. He flinched, and it recoiled. Then came the target Tal had been waiting for. The Kerfer breached again, and he saw its cavernous mouth, a mouth lined with wriggling cilia instead of teeth.

Tal fired the Red Ray of Destruction at the highest intensity he could summon, straight between the monster's jaws.

Light exploded everywhere, the crystals in the ash picking up and multiplying the red flash. Tal was momentarily blinded. Something hit him, and he screamed, thinking it was the paralyzing tentacle. Ash filled his mouth. The Kerfer had reared up and splashed down, creating a huge wave.

Tal's vision cleared as he spat out ash. For a moment he couldn't orient himself, couldn't see the shore or the monster. Then he saw the Kerfer floating on the surface, its tentacles limp. It was either stunned or dead.

Tal didn't wait around to see which it was. He struck out for the shore as fast as he could.

He climbed up onto a beach of more solid ash. He didn't look behind until he was safely on rock and a good twenty stretches from the lake. Then he turned around, his Sunstone ready, in case the Kerfer was going to drag itself after him.

It wasn't. As Tal watched, the inert creature bobbed under once, then twice, as if something was nibbling on it.

Something was. Tal couldn't help retreating even farther from the lake as the whole Kerfer — a creature that would weigh ten times as much as Tal — disappeared with a sudden *pop*, leaving a deep whirlpool in the lake that was easily fifty stretches in diameter.

Tal shuddered. He was glad he hadn't encountered whatever *that* was instead of the Kerfer.

Now his priority was to find somewhere to hide, so he wasn't exposed out here in the sun. The crater wall had lots of caves. But was there one close by?

He ran toward the wall, jumping from one tumbled rock to another. There were a few promising patches of dark shadow ahead. One of them should be a cavemouth. And apart from the lake, the Chosen made sure that there were no creatures within the crater itself. So there should be no danger from a Cavernmouth, or any other of the horrendous inhabitants of the rest of Aenir.

At least, Tal thought, there shouldn't be any danger. But then he'd never gone into any caves that weren't on the path . . .

·CHAPTER· EIGHT

No Spiritshadows lay in wait for Milla, Odris, and Malen. As Milla cautiously crept out into the lowest of the Underfolk levels she wondered whether the three spiky-snouted Spiritshadows had perished from their wounds or lack of light. Or perhaps they had gotten lost, or had not reported their find.

Whatever had happened, she was grateful. Not that she was afraid of fighting shadows. She simply preferred the battle to be fought when she had a great host of specially armed and armored Icecarls behind her.

This trip was a raid, and airweed was the prize they sought. In fact, they could not return without it, for their own supply was now exhausted.

It took Milla a moment to reorient herself as

Malen climbed out behind her. She had taken extra care to memorize all the twists and turns of the heatways, but had not paid particular attention to the Underfolk levels. Even so, she had subconsciously mapped it all in her head, as any good Icecarl would do.

"This way," she said decisively, pointing down the plain, whitewashed corridor. Its ceiling held occasional, weak, undersized Sunstones, and consequently the hallway had many shadows. Natural shadows, Milla was pretty sure, though she was ready to strike with the Talon if necessary.

Odris noticed the tension in Milla's hand and stayed back with Malen. Not that the Crone liked this. She kept trying to move away, only to have Odris keep up with her.

"We have to go along here, and then down a stair, through a belish root forest, then down a steep tunnel into the lake where the airweed grows. From there it's fairly easy to get to the Freefolk Fortress," Milla explained quietly after she had checked the next intersection.

They turned the corner, but Milla didn't keep going. Instead she stopped and frowned in thought. "Though there's bound to be an easier way — if only we can find one of the Freefolk. Perhaps we should wait a little while here. They found us easily enough before."

"I would not be sorry to rest a little," said Malen. As before, she hadn't complained. But the heat, the bad air, and the pace Milla had set had clearly taken their toll. Her golden hair, normally perfectly straight, was bedraggled and her face was flushed. Only her strange Crone's eyes were unchanged, still that deep, luminous blue.

"Rest, then," Milla said. Malen gratefully sank down, putting her back against the wall. Odris sat next to her, ignoring the Crone's angry look.

Milla didn't rest. She paced quietly back and forth, keeping an eye down both corridors while she thought about how much airweed they would need. Assuming an average of two bulbous nodules were required per person to get through the patches of bad air, a force of two thousand Icecarls would need four thousand nodules.

That was a lot of airweed to get to the far reaches of the heatways, particularly since whoever carried it would also need to use four nodules, there and back. Yet one person could probably carry twenty or thirty strands, each with six nodules. That was 120 per trip, less the four they used themselves, was 116 . . .

Milla kept calculating. She wished she had a tally stick, a flat piece of bone with holes and pegs that shipmasters and clan chiefs used in their calculations.

Leading Icecarls into battle wasn't as easy as Milla had imagined. She had always assumed it was simply a matter of leading the battle from the front, that someone else would have to think about food and supplies and all such matters.

A distant noise interrupted her calculations. Instantly she was on the alert. Malen heard it, too, and leaped up. Only Odris stayed sitting. In fact, she yawned.

Though Milla hadn't recognized the initial sound, she knew those that followed it. Footsteps. Stealthy footsteps. She could only catch them every now and then, a slight scuff or a less-than-totally-careful footfall. Someone . . . or several someones . . . were creeping along the corridor from the heatways.

Milla knelt down and looked around the corner, keeping low.

She saw four shapes creeping down one side of the corridor, staying as much in the shadows as they could. Milla smiled as she saw them. The leader was a tall boy with sandy hair held back with a white bone comb. He was followed by a blond girl, then a little farther back by a small boy who walked with a hesitant step. Last came a stocky, solid girl who had an oversized apron over the grimy Underfolk robe that they all wore, along with a string of airweed over her left shoulder.

All of their robes had been painted with the letter *F*.

It was Clovil, Gill, Ferek, and Inkie.

Milla kept watching them, to see if they were followed by anyone else. There was a slim chance they had been taken by the enemy, or were being forced to do Sushin's bidding.

Milla couldn't see anything following them. When they came to the hole where Milla had climbed out, they spread out around it and drew their knives. Clovil peered down quickly, then stepped back.

"No one there," he said quietly. "Guess we'd better go down farther and take a look."

Milla stepped out into the corridor.

"What for?" she asked.

All four Freefolk jumped, and Ferek let out a nervous squeak.

"You!" Clovil exclaimed.

"Milla!" Gill cried. "You didn't die!"

Gill had been the one to show Milla the way to the heatways, and they had talked quite a bit. She now looked very pleased to see the Icecarl again.

Ferek shivered and stayed silent. Inkie scowled. As far as Milla knew, Inkie never spoke at all.

Milla clapped her fists together in greeting. The Freefolk nodded or waved or did nothing, according to their natures.

"Where's Odris?" asked Gill.

"I'm here," Odris replied, drifting out behind Milla, taking a wide berth around her left hand and the Talon.

"I have another Icecarl with me, too," said Milla. "The Crone Malen."

Malen stepped out and clapped her fists. The Freefolk hadn't flinched at Odris, but they were obviously cowed by Malen. Milla tried to remember what she had told them about the Crones.

"I greet you," said Malen. "As do all the Crones of the Clans."

The Freefolk approached warily, though they did put their knives away.

"What's with the crown?" asked Clovil, pointing at the bone circlet on Milla's head. "And I thought you were going to freeze yourself to death or something, weren't you?"

"I wasn't allowed to go to the Ice," Milla replied stiffly. "It's hard to explain . . . The circlet is because I have become . . . well, it's either because I'm the Living Sword of Asteyr or the War-Chief of the Icecarls . . . I'm not sure which."

Clovil and Gill were clearly impressed by this news. Ferek looked afraid. Inkie looked the same as she ever did. Imperturbable.

"Uh, what does that mean?" asked Gill. "And why did you come back?"

"I will explain," said Milla. "But we should go to your fortress. There were Spiritshadows in the heatway tunnels, and they may have alerted Sushin or others to our presence."

"Spiritshadows?" asked Clovil urgently. "Free ones, without Chosen? Were they with some of the Fatalists? Underfolk, I mean? We heard that two water-stirrers were forced to carry lanterns for them, and one of Ebbitt's alarms went off, so we thought they'd gone down here. In fact, when the alarm sounded again, we thought it was probably them coming back."

"They won't be coming back," said Milla. "The Spiritshadows killed them."

"Killed them!" exclaimed Gill and Clovil, as Ferek shivered even more. "But why?"

"I don't know," said Milla. "Come — we mustn't keep talking here. We must go to your fortress, and talk to Ebbitt and Crow."

The four Freefolk looked at one another.

"You haven't heard, then?" asked Gill hesitantly.

"Heard what? We've only just climbed out of the heatways!"

Gill was at a loss for words. She looked at Clovil. He opened his mouth, but didn't say anything.

Everyone got a surprise when Inkie spoke.

"Your friend Tal fought with Crow," she said in a deep and husky voice. "Crow threw his knife. Tal brought the ceiling down on him — and us — and cracked a steampipe. Ebbitt arrived just in time to make a shield of light around us all. But Crow had already been hit on the head, and the spell took a lot out of Ebbitt. They're both unconscious back at the fortress. Jarnil thinks they're going to die."

313

·CHAPTER·
ΠIΠE

The first cave Tal found was too small. The second was too wet, water dripping through it constantly. The third was just right. Long and narrow, it zigzagged into the crater wall for about fifty stretches. Tal went past the second zigzag and found a shelf of rock that would make an uncomfortable bed. But that was better than none at all, and it was far better than being discovered.

Tal sat on the shelf. The fight with the Kerfer had left him exhausted. With the weariness came a renewed sense of guilt. Sleep beckoned as a tempting refuge from remembering.

Only it wouldn't be very sensible, Tal concluded, as he fought to stay awake.

The cave kept on going, Light knew where. He didn't feel quite so confident about the crater wall being free of creatures. Not in this narrow cave, with his only avenue of escape out into the light, where he would be spotted by Sushin's minions.

He needed Adras to watch over him. But where was the Storm Shepherd? He'd been gone for quite a while. Nothing could have happened to him, or Tal would feel a lot worse than a slight ache in his stomach. Part of that ache was probably hunger, Tal suddenly thought. He hadn't eaten for ages. No wonder he was tired.

"Adras, come back," Tal whispered. He imagined himself sending out a thought to the Storm Shepherd. He pictured his thought like a small bird, flying out of the cavemouth, up into the sky, searching everywhere for a cloud that moved against the wind. "Come back, Adras, come back."

Tal concentrated on that thought for several minutes, but he had no idea if it had worked or not. He certainly didn't feel any of Adras's thoughts or feelings, as he sometimes did when the Storm Shepherd was close.

A moment later his head snapped up. He'd fallen asleep!

"I must stay awake," Tal whispered, pinching himself along his wrists. "Until Adras gets here."

Perhaps he could talk to Lokar, Tal thought. He

undid the knot in his sleeve and got out the Red Key-stone. But when he focused upon it, all he could hear was continuous mad laughter. He could see Lokar, but she did not look up from her constant pacing, and no matter what Tal said, she did not stop her crazy giggling, not even for a second. Tal put the Keystone away. He would keep himself awake.

But only a few minutes later, Tal caught himself nodding away again. Shaking his head, he slipped off the shelf and tried pacing up and down. It was even harder than swimming in the Lake of Ash. He was just so tired.

Before long he was simply staggering a few paces, turning around, and staggering back again. Each time he turned he nearly fell over.

"Come on, Adras, come on," Tal whispered again as he turned.

This time he did fall over, because as he turned, he ran straight into the cool, cloudy body of the Storm Shepherd. Judging from the fact he could hardly fit in the cave, and the healthy white puffiness of his body, Adras was clearly full of water and completely revitalized.

"I'm here!" Adras boomed. His voice was so loud that Tal felt sure that every Chosen on the lake would hear it. Hopefully they would think it was distant thunder.

"Good," said Tal sleepily. "Watch. Please. Too tired."

With that, he collapsed onto the shelf and fell straight into a sleep that was deeper than any light-dive.

Adras yawned and floated himself along next to the ledge.

"Why is it always me who has to stay awake?" he said, a little more softly than before. "When is it my turn?"

Tal woke in darkness, though sun had been leaking into the cave before he slept. For a moment he panicked, until he could raise his Sunstone and bring forth a soft, gentle light.

Adras was still floating by his side, his great cloudy chest rising and falling in a steady rhythm. Every now and again a crackle of thunder came from his nose. He was sound asleep.

Tal slipped down from the ledge and, shielding his Sunstone, crept to the cave entrance. It was night outside, but there was a crescent moon, its silver light cool and calm across the Lake of Ash.

Other lights sparkled among the houses of the Chosen Enclave and along the bridges and walkways. Like the Castle, there were many Sunstones set everywhere, stones constrained to shine only when darkness fell around them.

There was a light breeze, soft on Tal's face. He enjoyed the cool touch of it for a moment before he went back inside. He had to figure out how to get to the Empress's island, and for that, he needed to consult Lokar.

Tal felt a bit guilty as he undid the knot in his shirt and got out the Red Keystone again. He probably hadn't tried hard enough to interrupt her crazy laughing fit, which was unforgivable now that he knew how awful it was to be trapped.

"Lokar," he said, staring into the fiery depths of the Sunstone.

The Guardian of the Red Keystone still danced in a circle, her Spiritshadow eternally hopping around her. But she didn't answer Tal, at least at first. She was making a noise, though, and it wasn't the mad cackle of before. Tal focused even harder to try and hear what it was.

Singing, he realized. Lokar was singing the same song over and over again. It was a Chosen lullaby.

Sunbright stay and hold me tight
All the day's dawning, till I'm yawning
Starlight come at night, moonshine give me light
Till sun returns, till sun returns, till sun returns

Tal listened to the song twice. He'd never paid any attention to it before, but it was a pretty weird song for a Chosen of the Castle. While they enjoyed the sun in Aenir, it was a holiday place, not home. Home was covered by the Veil. Tal had never heard a Chosen say a word about missing sunshine, starshine, or moonshine. Yet there it was, in a nonsense song for children.

It had to be a very old song, predating the Veil. It was hard to remember that the Chosen of long ago had raised the Veil as a defense against Aeniran shadows. Back then, they had nowhere else to go, as travel to Aenir was forbidden. It was no wonder they sang about the sun. . . .

Lokar started singing again. Tal snapped back to the problem at hand.

"Lokar! Lokar!"

Finally the woman answered.

"What? Tal?"

"Of course it's Tal."

"How long has it been since you spoke to me?" asked Lokar. "A day, a week, a month?"

"Less than a day," replied Tal worriedly.

Lokar mumbled something to herself, then asked, "So where are we?"

Tal told her and asked her for any suggestions about how he could get to the Empress's island.

"Can't walk across the Big South Bridge," answered Lokar quickly. "No, no, no. Maybe sneak along one of the runner-ways? No. Nighttime. But where is it dark? Not on the bridges, not on the walkways, not near the houses. Where is it dark?"

"Where is it dark?" Tal repeated. "What do you mean?"

"To get across to the island unseen," Lokar explained, "you must go in darkness. All the bridges, the walkways are lit by Sunstones. How can you cross unseen?"

"Oh, no," said Tal. He could see where this was going.

"Yes," Lokar whispered. "You will have to walk across the lakebed. Under the ash."

·CHAPTER·
TEП

The Freefolk Fortress hadn't changed. Milla hadn't expected it to. Apart from the entry over the forbidding crevasse with its lava flows far below, it was a pathetic sight. Just a big cave with seven ramshackle cottages built around a central well. Even knowing that the cottages had larger, better-maintained rooms dug into the rock below them didn't impress Milla.

An old, short, and generally dried-up-looking man with razor-short gray hair was drawing water from the well, using only one hand. He looked up as Milla and the others approached, and dropped the bucket.

"That is the former Brilliance Jarnil Yannow-Kyr of the Indigo Order, once Chief Lector, is it not?"

whispered Malen to Milla. "Now self-appointed leader of the Freefolk?"

"Yes," Milla confirmed shortly. Like all the Crones, Malen had not only heard everything that had happened to Milla but had walked through her mind and seen a lot of her memories as well.

Jarnil didn't seem overly pleased to see Milla again, particularly in company with another Icecarl. But he did come to greet them. Milla noticed that he now wore a Sunstone openly, on a gold chain around his neck. She hadn't seen it before. It was a large stone, about as big as a baby's fist, and shone with an indigo light.

"Milla of the Far-Raiders," Jarnil said, formally bowing and giving the briefest flash of light from his Sunstone. "To what do we owe the honor of your return?"

"I have come for airweed," said Milla bluntly. "I want to enlist the Freefolk to help me deliver it through the heatways."

"What!" croaked Jarnil, his face losing all its color. His bad arm twitched and quivered. "Airweed? What for?"

It was Malen who answered him. She strode forward and gripped his shaking hand.

"Long ago, our peoples joined together to defeat

the creatures of Aenir. To prevent them coming as shadows here, we raised the Veil and cast the Forgetting in Aenir. But your Chosen did not keep the pact of long ago. You have been to Aenir and brought back shadows. Now the creatures of Aenir have broken the Forgetting and seek to break the Veil. They must be stopped. As the Chosen have fallen into error, it lies upon the Clans to do what must be done."

"Who are you?" whispered Jarnil. He couldn't stop himself from looking into the Crone's deep, luminous eyes. "What are you doing to my arm?"

"I am Malen, daughter of Arla, daughter of Halla, daughter of Luen, daughter of Rucia, daughter of Nuthe, in the line of Grettir since the Ruin of the Ship. Your arm has been twisted in your mind. I am untwisting it."

Milla suppressed a gasp as she heard Malen's full lineage. No wonder she had not been fully introduced to her before. It was a Crone's privilege to speak her full name or not, and Crone Mothers were simply known by their titles. Even so, Milla wished she had known before. Malen was the daughter of Arla, the Shield Mother who Milla had fought and killed in her desperate rush to the Ruin Ship to warn the Crones.

"Let me go!" Jarnil protested. He was almost weeping. Whatever Malen was doing, it obviously hurt a lot. The Freefolk by Milla's side shifted nervously, but didn't do anything.

Finally Malen let go. Jarnil slumped at her feet. But when he pressed his hands against the floor to get up, both arms moved normally. Jarnil stood and stared down at his open palms, flexing his fingers and rotating his wrists.

"I . . . I thank you," he mumbled. "Yet, I cannot . . . cannot condone what you intend. It is not right that the Castle . . . I will forbid the Freefolk to gather airweed. There, I have said it. You will get no airweed!"

Only Milla listened to him. The Freefolk were all staring at Malen.

"That was great!" said Clovil.

"Do you think you can make Crow better?" asked Gill. "And Ebbitt?"

"Bennem," said Inkie, surprising everyone again. "Make Bennem better."

Bennem was Crow's older brother. He had been twice in the Hall of Nightmares, and was now lost in dream.

"Let us see," replied Malen. "Take me to them."

"No airweed," Jarnil repeated. His usually smooth voice broke.

"The world is changing," said Milla. "You cannot hold a Selski. You can only kill it or get out of the way. Even if you kill it you must still get out of the way."

"I don't understand," muttered Jarnil.

"We will get airweed," said Milla. "Icecarls will come. I will make sure you are not harmed."

Jarnil sighed and, with an effort, drew himself up to his full height — a head short of Milla. He bowed again, this time both his arms moving gracefully into the perfect position. He did not give light from his Sunstone.

"Do what you must," he said and turned away.

"Do not leave this place," Milla instructed.

Jarnil didn't answer, but he left the bridge and went into his own cottage, gently shutting the door behind him.

Milla watched him go and wondered if she should have killed him. Somehow she didn't feel like it, even though he was undoubtedly planning something against her and the Icecarls.

Nothing was as easy as she had once imagined. She had always thought that when you saw an enemy, or thought someone might be one, you killed them.

But when it came down to it, Milla remembered very few actual killings of people among the Clans, because there were few real enemies. There were plenty of fights, and plenty of blood was shed, but it rarely ended in a death. The deaths that did occur were always in the heat of battle. There seemed something basically wrong about killing a little old man who was more like a Crone than any sort of fighting Icecarl.

Perhaps Jarnil would attack her, Milla thought, so she could kill him without having to think about it.

She shook her head at this notion and strode off to the cottage where the others had gone. If Malen — *Daughter of Arla* echoed in her head — could help Crow and Ebbitt, they might be able to tell her what had happened to Tal. She did not believe that he had been killed by Crow. Milla was bound to Tal, after a fashion, by Icecarl oaths as well as the magic they had experienced together. She thought she would know if he was dead.

Odris followed her at a safe distance, always keeping to the right, away from the Talon.

·CHAPTER· ELEVEN

"I can't walk across the lakebed!" exclaimed Tal. "I'll be eaten in a minute!"

"There is a way," replied Lokar. "It is fortunate you have a Storm Shepherd on hand. First, you will have to make a suit of Chromatic armor. Make it a hand-width too large in all ways, so the Storm Shepherd can cram in with you."

"Chromatic armor?" asked Tal. "What's that?"

"Don't the Lectors teach anything anymore?" grumbled Lokar. "It's armor made of light, of course. In this case you have to make sure it's air-tight."

"But how do I make it?" asked Tal. He couldn't help but be fascinated by the idea. "And how do I breathe?"

"The Storm Shepherd," said Lokar. She paused

then, as it was clear Tal didn't get the idea, she continued, "He's made mostly of concentrated air and water vapor."

Tal wrinkled his nose.

"So I'll be breathing Adras?" he asked. "That sounds disgusting."

"You won't even notice," said Lokar. "Nor will he, as long as you don't stay in the armor for more than a few hours."

Tal considered this. It was pretty revolting, but it did seem the only way he could cross the lakebed. Then another nasty thought struck him. He remembered the Kerfer being sucked straight under.

"So I'll be in armor," he said. "But what if something swallows me whole?"

"Chromatic armor can be fashioned to radiate intense heat. You'll be comfortable inside, but to anything outside you'll feel like a red-hot belish root. Nothing will want to eat you, I promise."

"I'd better ask Adras," Tal said. The Storm Shepherd was still snoring in midair. Tal prodded him in the arm. Nothing happened, so he punched him lightly, his fist sinking into the cloudy shoulder.

"What!" boomed Adras, sitting up with a start. "I'm awake! I didn't fall asleep."

"Yes you did. But that doesn't matter since we

seem to have survived. Now, how do you feel about crossing the bottom of the lake inside armor made of light while I use your air to breathe?"

"What?" asked Adras again. He shook his head and cleaned out one huge ear with a puffy finger. "What did you say?"

Tal explained. Three times. He explained they couldn't fly because they'd be seen. Adras's main problem with the plan was going under the ash. He didn't like the idea of that at all.

When Adras finally agreed to give it a try, Tal looked back into the Red Keystone.

Lokar was sighing again.

"How long have you been gone?" asked the Guardian.

"Only fifteen minutes, at the most."

"Fifteen minutes..." Lokar shook her head. "Gone with the hours, gone with the days. Listen, Tal. I will explain how to make a suit of Chromatic armor. Are you familiar with Indigo crafting and Blue welds?"

Tal had to admit that he was not.

"Violet bonds? Yellow crimping? Red shifts? Orange weaves?"

Only the last two were familiar to Tal. He said so, and Lokar sighed again.

"Then I will begin with the basics. Listen carefully. We will take it in stages. I will explain, then you will do what I have taught you, then we will go on to the next step."

For the next six hours, Tal labored under Lokar's directions. He made several false starts, and was continually having to begin again. But slowly the suit of Chromatic armor began to build in the cave. It looked like a man-shaped sarcophagus made of rainbows, all seven colors swirling through it. It was fashioned in two parts that hinged down one side, so Tal could get in and close it on himself.

Finally, the Chromatic armor was ready. It lay glowing on the floor, colors constantly chasing and mixing across its surface. It looked solid and heavy, but Tal had no trouble standing it up and opening it a bit more so it stood upright on its own.

"How do I see out of it?" he asked Lokar. As far as he could tell the suit was all rainbow light, with no transparent parts, even in the helmet.

"You will be able to see from inside when the suit is closed," replied Lokar. "Provided you've made it correctly. It is particularly important that the unraveling cord is in the right place on the outside."

Tal looked at the suit. Sure enough, there among the moving rainbows in the middle of the chest plate was a solid circle of violet light. When it was time to open the suit, he would grasp that and pull it, springing the suit open. The unraveling cord was essential. Tal remembered the near disaster he'd had creating the minor veil, trapping Adras in its making, and almost asphyxiating himself and Crow.

"I guess we'd better go, then," he said. "I'll talk to you as soon as I can, Lokar."

Lokar didn't answer. She was singing the song again. Tal looked away, breaking contact. He tied the Red Keystone into his shirt once more, for safe-keeping.

"Time for us to get in," Tal announced to Adras, who had been floating near the ceiling. The Storm Shepherd grumbled a low thunderous rumble, but lowered his legs to the floor.

Tal opened up the two halves of the suit a bit more, then stepped back into it, shuffling his feet into position and setting his shoulders in place. The suit, as instructed, was too large. When it was closed there would be a good handspan between Tal and the sides.

Adras drifted over and stared at him.

"Where am I supposed to go?"

Tal hadn't thought about how they would actually get in. After a moment's reflection, he stepped out.

"You get in first, and then I'll squeeze in against you," he said.

"It's pretty small," Adras objected.

He started to go in face first, until Tal stopped him and made him back in. Though Adras was much bigger to start with, he compressed well into the armor. His cloud body could shrink and expand enormously.

"Shrink a bit more," Tal instructed, as he backed in himself. "We have to both fit."

"I don't like this," said Adras. "It's a prison."

"No it isn't!" exclaimed Tal. "It's only for a few hours. There!"

He was in. It was weird being pressed up against the Storm Shepherd. He felt like a clammy sponge. Tal hoped Lokar was right about Tal being able to breathe some of the air that Adras was made out of.

He reached forward and grabbed a thin blue circle that had held constant among the rainbows of the other half of the armor. He pulled it and it came apart in his hand, breaking into a thousand tiny motes of blue light.

"Dark take it!" cursed Tal. He thought he'd broken it. Then the suit of armor started to close. Tal quickly pulled his arm back into position and kept absolutely still. Adras squirmed a bit around him.

"Stay still!"

Slowly the other half of the suit closed in on Tal. He watched it inexorably shutting and had a moment of panic. What if he'd made it wrong, and the suit crushed him? What if he couldn't breathe? What if Adras had too much water vapor in him and not enough air and they ran out halfway?

The suit closed. Rainbows danced across Tal's face. He took several deep breaths, and was relieved that there seemed to be something to breathe.

Slowly the rainbows in front of his face faded. He could see out into the cave, though flashes of red and blue did keep crossing his vision.

Experimentally, Tal raised one arm. It moved easily enough. Tal could see his armored limb rising, rainbows coruscating all over. But as he raised his arm higher, it got harder to move, until it was stuck and no matter how he strained it would not move at all.

He tried to move his other arm. It went a few inches and then froze, too.

Fear hit Tal again. He'd made the armor incorrectly and now he couldn't even reach the unraveling cord.

They were stuck in here forever!

·CHAPTER·
TWELVE

Ebbitt and Crow were in one of the cellar rooms, lying in beds arranged directly under the single weak Sunstone in the ceiling. Crow's head was heavily bandaged. Ebbitt looked uninjured, but he was unconscious, too. His great cat Spiritshadow lay across the end of the bed. It raised its head as Milla and Odris entered, but didn't get up.

Malen was already examining Bennem. The big man sat quietly on a stool at the end of Crow's bed. The Crone was staring him in the eye, with one hand on his forehead. Gill, Clovil, Ferek, and Inkie were all ranged alongside Crow's bed, watching the Crone intently.

Malen withdrew her hand. Bennem smiled and turned back to look at Crow.

"He is gone too deep," said Malen. "I think that

he might be brought back, but I do not have the skill for it. Perhaps when one of the Crone Mothers comes, or one of the others who knows more healing than I do."

"What about Crow?" asked Milla. She wanted to talk to him about Tal, and also to ask his advice about attacking the Castle. Crow had spent many years making plans to defeat the Chosen. He would have useful knowledge.

"I haven't looked at him yet," said Malen. She walked to the head of Crow's bed and bent down to listen to his chest. Then she took the pulse at his neck and lifted one eyelid. The other Freefolk continued to follow her every move, obviously fascinated.

"Who bandaged him?" she asked. "I need to remove it."

"Jarnil," said Gill. "He knows the most healing. He did light magic on the cuts on Crow's head, and that stopped the bleeding. But he hasn't woken up."

Malen nodded thoughtfully. She started to unwind the bandage, but stopped as Bennem got up from his stool, obviously distressed at what she was doing to his brother.

"I need to see," Malen said to him. She looked him in the eye and repeated her words. Whether he understood them or not, Bennem was calmed, and sat back down.

Malen undid the last of the bandages, revealing a nasty, puckered, and very new scar across the top of Crow's forehead. It was partially healed, but looked red and inflamed. Milla had seen wounds like that before. Usually people died of them, if the Crones didn't arrive in time.

Malen peered closely at the cut. Milla looked, too. She knew some healing light magic, but she didn't mention it. A head wound was a Crone's business, not for someone with only a basic understanding of Sunstone healing.

"I will need to clean and treat this," Malen said. "I have some of the medicines I need with me, but I will require boiled water and kriggi."

"Boiled water's easy," replied Clovil. "What are kriggi?"

"Ah, little white grubs that eat meat," replied Malen. "Do you know of them?"

"Maggots," said a voice from the next bed. "Twisty little beggars. Try the composting tunnels at the southern end of Underfolk Five."

Everyone looked across. It was Ebbitt who had spoken. Everyone but Malen knew his voice. But he still lay there, apparently asleep.

"Ebbitt," said Milla.

One of Ebbitt's eyes opened a fraction. The pupil moved until it was looking straight at Milla.

"Nice crown," said Ebbitt. "Interesting fingernail. Where did you get that?"

"The heatways," said Milla. "The same skeleton that had the Sunstone you split for Tal and me. Are you all right?"

"Weary," said Ebbitt. He shut his eye and opened the other one. "Stonkered. Worn out. Too old for emergency light magic."

"You saved us, though," said Clovil. "We are grateful."

Ebbitt gave a tiny shrug.

"Couldn't stand the thought of the mess," he said. "Besides, Tal didn't mean it. Accident."

"Inkie told me that Crow threw his knife at Tal," said Milla. "Do you know what happened to him?"

"Knife missed," said Ebbitt. "Should have had a fork as well. Maybe a spoon. Whole set."

Milla was used to Ebbitt and his *unique* way of talking. She continued her questions.

"Do you know where Tal is now? Odris says Adras has gone back to Aenir. Could Tal have gone, too?"

"Maybe," said Ebbitt. "He had the Red Keystone.

Should have brought it to me. Then again, he probably thinks I got squashed. Who knows where the caveroach goes? Ask Crow when your charming companion has opened his head. Should use healing magic but too tired. Get Lokar to do it properly this time. Anyone seen the Codex?"

Everyone shook their heads. Malen looked at Milla, obviously thinking that the old man was sick and raving. Milla whispered that Ebbitt was always like that.

"I have," added Ebbitt. Then he rolled over, closed both eyes firmly, and refused to answer anyone else's questions.

Gill went to get hot water while Malen removed a small case of Wreska hide from under her light furs. She unfolded it on the bed, revealing lots of tiny pockets filled with medicines made from seaweed and the many beasts of the Ice. Milla only recognized a few of them, like the powdered Merwin horn, still faintly glowing, and a vial of very rare Ursek tears.

While the healing preparations were under way, Milla explained to Clovil her plan to enlist the Freefolk to transport airweed to the halfway point in the heatway tunnels. Clovil listened intently, but wouldn't commit himself or any friendly Freefolk or Underfolk until they could talk to Crow about it. Milla wanted him to make a decision without Crow.

"We need to move quickly," Milla urged. "Right now all the Chosen are in Aenir, their bodies sleeping above us. If I can bring enough Icecarls equipped with shadowbags and other such weapons into the Castle, we can capture or destroy the Spiritshadows that guard them before the Chosen can come back from Aenir. A surprise attack will mean there is less damage to the Castle — and fewer people will die, including Underfolk. Just think what a full-scale battle will mean to your people, even if they're trying to stay out of the way."

"And when we have won," she added, "your help will ensure that all Underfolk are treated properly. Icecarls are always faithful to sworn allies."

"Crow is the leader," Clovil answered uncomfortably.

"I think . . . I think . . . we should help Milla," said Ferek. He glanced anxiously at Crow. "The Icecarls will come anyway. Best we be friends from the start."

"What's that?" Gill asked, as she staggered back in with a huge crystal tub of hot water, her face red from the steam rolling off it and the effort. She put the water down next to the bed.

"I found some old biscuits, too," she added, taking a handful out of her pocket to put on the bed. A whole lot of maggots fell out onto the blanket. "Are those kriggi?"

Malen nodded and herded the squirming maggots into a neat pile, ready for use. Then she dropped some medicines into the pot of steaming water and stirred it with her knife. When the blade came out it was bright purple.

Everyone except Milla looked the other way as the Crone began to cut.

After a few seconds of strained silence as everyone tried not to hear the Crone at work, Clovil explained to Gill what they were discussing.

"We might as well get started right away," said Gill. She didn't seem to think there was any difficulty in joining forces with the Icecarls. "There's no point in waiting for Crow, Clovil. He won't be better for ages. I'm sure we can get Korvim to come back for this, and he'll bring others!"

"It's a big decision," warned Clovil.

"Of course it is," said Gill. "But haven't we been waiting all this time to do something big? This is it! This is our chance! Everything is going to be different. No more Chosen lording it over us. No more Hall of Nightmares! Freedom for our people!"

"I hope so," said Clovil. He looked at Milla. "Perhaps we will just be exchanging one lot of rulers for another."

"You are free to choose now," said Milla. "I promise you we will help you decide your own fate in the future."

Clovil looked into her eyes. Whatever he saw there made up his mind.

"We'll get the airweed. Tell us where it has to be taken."

"Good," said Milla. "I will draw you a map. When Malen is finished with Crow, she will tell the Crones to expect you, and to prepare for the assault!"

341

·CHAPTER·
THIRTEEN

"Adras!" yelled Tal. "We're stuck!"

"Don't shout," grumbled Adras. His voice was incredibly loud, right at Tal's ear. "Do you mean I don't have to stay still?"

Tal's arms suddenly spread wide and his legs shuffled forward. The suit toppled. Reflexively, Tal tried to put his hands down to break the fall, but his arms were wrenched the other way.

They bounced once, got halfway up, then Tal found his knees bending and his arms windmilling. Finally he realized what was happening. Adras had stopped Tal moving before, and now the Storm Shepherd's movements were directing the armor. Tal was so much weaker that he was just a passenger inside the suit.

"Adras!" he ordered. "Stay still for a moment. We have to work together."

Adras obeyed and the suit slowly settled down.

"Right. Adras, please follow my motions, but don't use too much strength or overdo it. I'm going to raise my left arm now."

He started to raise his arm, felt Adras join in, and then the limb was jerking all over the place.

"Ow! Ow! Easy!" exclaimed Tal. "Now the right arm."

It took quite a lot of practice, but eventually they managed to work out how to move inside the suit. Tal moved first, then Adras would join in, using only a fraction of his strength.

Tal was glad no one could see them as they jerked about the cave, occasionally crashing into the walls and falling down. Even when they'd worked it out, their movements were still stiff and clumsy.

They headed out of the cave. Tal wanted to stop near the entrance and have a look around, but mistimed stopping, so they staggered out and tipped over. While they got up, Tal cursed and Adras complained, until the Chosen boy suddenly realized that he didn't know if sound traveled outside the armor or not.

That shut them both up. Fortunately, they didn't

seem to have attracted any attention. At least not with the noise. Tal was further alarmed to see just how bright the suit was out in the night. Not as bright as a Sunstone, but the rainbow surface did glow, even before he started the defensive spells that would make it burn red-hot.

They needed to get under the ash quickly. Tal started for the lake and quickly waded in. He had a moment's worry as the ash closed over his head, but the suit was airtight. Or at least ash-tight.

Even though the ash was mixed with clear crystal, it was still very hard to see more than a few stretches through it. Tal took a few steps down the steeply shelving lakebed before he thought about another problem.

Without knowing where he was going, he could easily get lost or turned around. How was he going to find the Empress's island?

He thought of Milla then, and her unerring sense of direction on the Ice. What would Milla do if she were here?

Follow a bridge, came the answer.

Tal smiled as he thought of Milla telling him what to do, but the smile faded as he recalled that she was probably dead, too, gone to the Ice. Someone else who was dead because of his actions.

He was alone.

"Stop it," mumbled Adras.

"What?"

"That feeling in your head, when it gets all heavy and your heart aches," replied Adras. "It makes me sick."

Tal didn't answer. Instead he started moving along the lakeshore, keeping his helmet just a fraction out of the ash. The Big South Bridge — one of the main bridges to the central cluster of Chosen houses — was about eight hundred stretches away. He would follow the shoreline to it, then follow the bridge's foundations out.

As he got closer to the bridge and its steady Sunstone light, Tal went deeper into the ash to avoid detection.

He was surprised to find as he went deeper that the lakebed was not smooth as he'd imagined. It was often broken up, and there were deep holes and crevasses. He had to pick his way carefully and several times he almost fell into what might be a very deep pit. The biggest problem was that he only ever saw them at the last second, because the visibility was so bad.

At least that was the biggest immediate problem. Tal couldn't help remembering the sudden disappearance of the stunned Kerfer. Something really big and really hungry was down here in the ash. He really, really hoped it wasn't looking for dessert after its Kerfer dinner.

It took what seemed like hours before he reached the Big South Bridge. In fact, he almost walked straight under it and continued on, but he ran into some cut squares of stone. That made him turn back to shallower waters, carefully poke his head out, and check his position.

He was under the bridge. Sunstone light shone down to either side. He could certainly hear through the suit, he discovered, because there were heavy footsteps above, and the sound of voices. Tal tried to hear what they were saying, but they were too far above. All the bridges and the houses stood at least forty stretches above the lake, probably to ensure the Chosen's safety from things with long tentacles.

Tal strode back down the sloping lakebed in what he hoped was the same direction as the bridge. It was, as discovered before long when he almost walked straight into a pylon, built of massive blocks of shaped stone. It was hard to tell in the constantly changing light from the suit, but to Tal it looked like the stone was a dark green — not volcanic gray or black — which meant it had been quarried somewhere else and brought to the crater.

Tal slowly worked his way around to the other side of the pylon. He was about to launch off deeper into the lake in the hope that the next pylon wouldn't be far away when he saw a faint glow off to his right. A soft violet light, diffused by the ash.

He hesitated for a moment, then decided to investigate. Just in case, he kept one finger on the red loop on his chest, the one that would make the suit super-hot on the outside — and only on the outside. He hoped.

When he got closer, Tal saw that the light came from a cluster of Sunstones. They were grouped at the top of a long pole that was thrust deep into the lakebed. Tal lumbered closer still, and saw that it wasn't a pole. It was actually a giant harpoon, made from Chosen crystal, one of the few materials that was identical in both the Dark World and Aenir. There were Sunstones all along the shaft, though most were long extinguished. Only the cluster at the end of the harpoon and some Sunstones on the part of the point that was exposed were still shining.

"Weird," said Tal. Why was a giant harpoon stuck in the lakebed?

"How long do we have to stay in here?" Adras

347

asked plaintively. "I want to fly. I need to see the sky."

"Soon," soothed Tal. The harpoon was an interesting mystery, but Adras was right. They shouldn't be wasting time. He turned away from it and started walking.

Fortunately the Chosen who had built the bridge had also smoothed the lakebed underneath it. Tal discovered that this helped his navigation a lot. Whenever he encountered tumbled stones or broken ground, he worked back to where the lakebed was undisturbed.

Even on the smoother ground it was hard going. Adras tried to cooperate, but they had both reached the limits of their dexterity in the suit, and still rolled, lumbered, and tripped up. Their Chromatic armor walking would make a great show for Chosen children, Tal thought as they got their legs unsynchronized and came to a sudden, swaying halt.

As they got going again, Tal saw another glow ahead. It looked the same as the one he'd seen a hundred stretches back. Had they gotten turned around somehow?

He headed up to it, and for a few seconds was convinced that they had ended up back where they'd been. There was another harpoon, glowing with Sunstones.

But, Tal noticed, this harpoon had different patterns. It was another one, so at least they hadn't turned around.

This time he went right up to the harpoon and gingerly touched the crystal. It didn't move at all, even when he pushed quite hard. He was about to withdraw his hand when Adras suddenly decided to help, shifting his cloud-flesh around to the front of Tal and exerting his full strength.

The harpoon shifted very slightly. Instantly the remaining Sunstones on it flashed brightly and Tal felt a vibration run through the lakebed and up through his boots.

"Stop!" he shouted. He pulled his hand back, but it just bounced on the inside of the glove. Adras did stop, but not for a second or two. In that short time, the harpoon shifted a finger-width, and the Sunstones flashed again.

This time the vibration through the lakebed was strong enough to shake Tal's teeth. He looked down and saw faint cracks running through the stone around the harpoon's point.

"We'd better leave this alone," Tal said. Whatever the harpoons were part of, it was serious magic and he had been stupid to interfere with it.

"You don't want me to pull it out?" asked Adras. Tal had the unpleasant sight of the Storm Shepherd's eyeball floating under his chin so Adras could take a look. "It could be useful. We could stick Sushin with it, like Milla did."

"No," replied Tal hastily. "Come on."

They backed away, almost falling over, then took a wide circle around the harpoon. As Tal had half expected, there was another pylon just beyond the harpoon. He went around it and when he saw a familiar glow on the other side, didn't go and investigate.

"Concentrate on the task," Tal whispered to himself as he successfully put one foot in front of another.

"What?" asked Adras. The Storm Shepherd apparently couldn't walk and talk at the same time, because the next step stalled as Tal moved his leg forward and Adras didn't. They only managed to recover by taking a series of tiny, hopping steps that Tal knew looked particularly stupid.

"What did you say?" Adras asked again.

Tal took a deep breath. Adras wasn't the only one who wanted out of the suit.

"I didn't say anything to you," Tal said, as calmly as he could. "I was talking to myself."

Adras snorted, nearly blowing Tal's eardrums in. "How much farther is it?"

"I don't know!"

Adras didn't talk after that for quite a long time, as they found and went around two more pylons. Unfortunately it wasn't a companionable silence. It was a sulky semi-silence punctuated by snorts and long-suffering sighs. Adras also kept his eyeballs floating around at the edge of Tal's vision, just in front of the boy's ears, though he could see perfectly well if he left them on Tal's shoulders.

Tal was thinking they should hit the sixth pylon soon when Adras spoke again.

"What's that?"

"I don't know!"

Tal answered automatically, before he even saw what Adras was referring to. When he did see it, his hand went instantly to the red loop and pulled it.

For once, Adras cooperated perfectly. Unfortunately they should have stopped first. Their last, fateful step had carried them straight into the thing Adras had spotted a second before.

A wall of white scales, higher than Tal, stretched as far as he could see to the left and right.

As they touched it, the scaly flesh rippled, but the thing didn't move. Tal looked up and along, his heart hammering in his chest. It was some sort of worm or snake-thing, but far larger than it had a right to be. As far as he could tell, it was actually wrapped around the next pylon.

The scales rippled again. The worm flexed a little and the section in front of Tal slid along a few stretches, sending waves through the ash.

"The head must be that way," Tal whispered. He didn't know why he was whispering.

He started moving the other way, but as he moved, the worm moved, too. It seemed to be irritated, the huge body rippling sideways as well as moving forward.

Tal looked down at the front of the suit. It was no longer rainbow-colored, but a deep red that was verging into black. Tal felt no difference, but the armor was clearly working as Lokar had promised. It was turning red-hot.

It was turning red-hot while they were right next to a gigantic worm, which at any moment could get annoyed and sweep its body across and turn Tal and Adras, armored or not, into pulp.

"Back up," Tal said urgently as the worm got more and more agitated. It was sliding back and forth and rolling its body, the scales lifting as if it sought to cool itself underneath.

The worm rolled again, its vast body crashing down right where Tal had been a moment before.

"Back, faster!" shrieked Tal. He was windmilling his arms to stay upright as they staggered back. If they fell now, it would be all over.

Then they hit something else. Tal tried to turn left and Adras tried to turn right. Adras won, but the suit spun out of control, pitching them to the lakebed.

They landed face-up. Tal stared as the worm rolled closer and closer. Then he looked to see what they'd run into.

He caught the briefest glimpse of a cavernous, bony mouth big enough to snap up a dozen suits of armor.

Then it closed over him.

·CHAPTER·
FOURTEEN

Whatever had swooped in and eaten them accelerated away so swiftly that Tal momentarily blacked out. Then he started to struggle, punching wildly and kicking, until Adras joined in to help and made it too difficult.

In his initial panic, Tal hadn't looked around. Now he saw that they were still in the creature's mouth. Whatever it was didn't seem bothered by the heat, possibly because the armor was totally surrounded by ash swallowed at the same time.

Tal tried to sit up, but fell over as their swallower suddenly tilted one way and then the other. It felt like it was still moving very quickly, though it was hard to tell from inside.

"At least it hasn't swallowed," Tal said after a while. It was still impossible to sit up. They'd twice flipped over completely and if he hadn't been cushioned by Adras, Tal would have been seriously bruised inside the armor.

"I want to get out," replied Adras. "Out of the monster, out of the armor, out!"

"So do I!" said Tal.

He thought furiously. What was the story Milla had told him? About Ulla Strong-Arm when she was swallowed by a broken-jawed Selski? She'd cut herself out of the Selski's stomach. But he didn't have a sword. Maybe he could burn his way out . . .

Tal started swimming through the ash to reach the side or the floor of the creature's mouth. But every time he got close there was nothing to hang on to and the next sudden swerve or turn threw him back where he started, suspended in the middle.

Then Tal saw two protruding bulbs of flesh at the rear of the mouth. They were about as big as he was. Though they were constantly quivering, he could at least try and hold on to them.

They weren't tonsils, but Tal thought they might be the monster's equivalent. If he could tickle them, or annoy them, or burn them, the monster might throw up.

"Let's grab whatever they are and see what happens!" he said, and pointed. A moment later he was hurled across the mouth by a sudden zigzag, but Adras got the message. Together they struggled to swim across to the fleshy appendages.

It was a case of two strokes forward and one fall back, but finally they were close enough. Tal hesitated. For a fleeting moment he wondered if it could get any worse. Then he embraced the closer appendage with his now black-hot arms.

It wriggled and shook as Tal held it, but the exposed gray-blue flesh didn't seem to burn. He gripped it tighter and tried to throw himself backward and forward. But it was like holding on to a tree trunk in a gale. It went wherever it wanted to and Tal only just managed to hang on.

Then the mouth opened a fraction and a fresh current of ash swept through the mouth. Tal shouted in triumph, and prepared to let go so they could get vomited out.

But the monster didn't vomit. The mouth snapped open wide and a huge wave of ash came crashing in. Tal was picked up and hurled past the tonsil-things and down a tunnel that was all too gulletlike. Halfway along, the suit was gripped by a tremendous suction and fired like a spitball down a tube. Tal and Adras were twisted and turned and spun about so Tal could hardly see where they were.

They exploded out into a large chamber that Tal guessed was the creature's stomach. It was only half full of ash and crystal, and besides Tal and Adras in the armor, there were several things floating on the surface. Things that had obviously once enjoyed some sort of life in the lake.

Two long gray tendrils came out of the stomach wall, reached down, and picked up a big chunk of what looked like a Kerfer. The tendrils held it above the ash while another thicker tendril moved across it, coating it with a sticky yellow substance. Then the first two tendrils shoved the Kerfer tidbit hard against the stomach wall. A tiny hole there expanded to admit the chunk. The tendrils pushed it in and the hole snapped shut.

"I feel sick," said Tal.

The tendrils swooped back down. They almost touched Tal, but recoiled at the last moment. The third tendril hovered close, but it didn't touch the suit, or spew forth any of the yellow mucus.

Then the suction started again. Ash rose up all around Tal and Adras, almost pure ash without the crystals that made it more see-through. The ash coated the suit's helmet so they couldn't see at all.

A second later Tal was slammed down one end of the suit as it was gripped in a mighty suction. The suction increased. The suit was being buffeted and Tal shook around like a pea in a pod as they accelerated. There was an explosion that deafened Tal and rattled his teeth and they spun end over end before coming to a crashing halt that would probably have killed Tal if Adras hadn't spread around him and cushioned the blow.

After a few seconds of wondering what in the name of Light had just happened, Tal wiped the front of the helmet, to clear the ash. After a few wipes, he had it clear enough to see that they had collided with a huge block of stone.

They were out of the monster, free and clear in the lake. Tal closed his eyes and breathed a sigh of relief. It wasn't how Ulla Strong-Arm would have done it, and it wasn't the stuff of legend. But he didn't care.

He looked up at the stone. It was smaller than the bridge pylons, but it was shaped stone and it went straight up. It was probably the foundation of a Chosen house.

"Let's climb up and see where we are," he said to Adras. "The sooner we get out of this lake, the better."

It was a long climb. Evidently the creature that had swallowed them was a denizen of the deepest part of the lake.

It was a nervous climb, too. Tal found that it took all his willpower to concentrate on the climb and not look over his shoulder every few minutes. He kept expecting to see the shadow of those giant jaws. What if the thing decided to keep them next time?

By the time they reached the top, Tal had almost decided not to go back under again. Whatever the risks of detection, they would leave the suit and sneak along a bridge. Then he would steal a boat to get to the Empress's island. He couldn't face being eaten and . . . *ejected* . . . by a monster again.

But when they got to the top of the stone, Tal discovered that it didn't join a bridge or a house. It just stopped, about half his height below the surface.

Tal crouched on top of the stone and looked around. It was still night, which was good. Without having his Sunstone accessible to check the time, he had feared it would be past dawn already. The moon had risen, though, and it was two-thirds full and far too bright for comfort.

It took him a while to get his bearings. They had been brought by the monster to the other side of the lake, the less inhabited side. There was the main cluster of Chosen homes off in the distance, and the Big South Bridge. There was the East Bridge, and the Orange Common House he knew well.

And there, no more than two hundred stretches away, was the dark shape of the Empress's island. He could only see the bright pools of light from a few Sunstones on it, most on the far side closer to the main part of the Enclave. There were no lights at all on the lakeshore facing Tal.

Tal looked at it carefully. There was a time when he would have just headed for it straight away. He was more thoughtful now. Why was the island and the closer shore the only place that wasn't lit up? How was it defended against all the creatures that could crawl up its shores out of the lake?

"Out," said Adras, cutting into Tal's thoughts.

"Soon, very soon," said Tal. He thought for a moment longer. There was no way he was going to climb back down and walk across the lakebed to the island. They would have to take a chance, even with the moon shining so brightly.

"Adras. Are you strong enough to fly us both to the island?"

"Yes," Adras confirmed instantly. Tal worried about that for a moment, since he knew Adras would say anything to get out.

"All right. I'm going to open the armor. As soon as I step out, I want you to pick me up and fly me just to the edge of the island. To the edge. Got that?"

Adras nodded, pushing Tal's head forward so sharply he nearly cricked his neck.

Tal grabbed the violet loop and pulled it, before Adras could nod again.

·CHAPTER· FIFTEEN

The suit of armor didn't open. It blew apart. Thousands of red-hot shards flew in all directions, falling into the lake like strange hail. One fell near Tal's foot. He could feel the heat from it, even through the ash and crystal.

Adras didn't spring up into the air as Tal had planned. He stayed where he was, until the last flaming fragment of the armor fell to earth.

"Lokar didn't tell me it would do that," croaked Tal. His mouth had gotten suddenly dry. "What if I'd been standing next to someone?"

"They'd be very cross," replied Adras. He was slowly billowing out to his full size.

"I hope no one . . . nothing noticed." Tal looked around. The surface of the lake was still and there was no sign of any activity off in the lit-up areas.

Adras launched out of the ash and floated above Tal's head. He didn't look any the worse for having supplied breathing air for several hours, or for being compressed in the suit of armor. But he was clearly much happier to be out.

Tal held up his arms and winced even before Adras grabbed him. For some reason the Storm Shepherd knew only one shoulder-dislocating technique for picking Tal up.

Cloudy hands met around Tal's wrists and the expected savage jerk came. For a few seconds Tal's legs trailed in the ash, bringing unpleasant images of fishing expeditions and brightly colored lures. Then Adras rose higher and Tal came free.

"Don't get too high," cautioned Tal as they rose up to forty or fifty stretches above the lake. The moon was bright, bright enough to cast a shadow from the flying Storm Shepherd and the Chosen boy dangling beneath him. Tal watched the shadow flicker across the lake. It was strange to think that here in Aenir, shadows were only ever dark reflections and nothing more.

The Empress's island looked peaceful enough by moonlight. Looking down at it, Tal could see that most of the place was taken up by carefully ordered gardens. There were statues spread among the gardens, and several pools of what must be real water, silver in the moonlight. Off on the southern side there was an L-shaped house, its windows mostly dark. It was roofed with crystal tiles that had to be sprinkled with Sunstones, for they twinkled in different colors rather than reflecting the moonlight. In front of the house there was a courtyard covered by a canopy of crystal leaves. There were Sunstones shining brightly under that canopy, but Tal couldn't see what they illuminated.

It all looked very pretty and comfortable. But there must also be guards of some sort, Tal thought. He would have to evade them, and somehow get enough time to tell the Empress of the danger Sushin presented, of the threat to the Veil and the whole Dark World.

Adras glided down as instructed and set Tal down on the very edge of the island. The landing was as gentle as could be expected, which meant that Tal fell over. He was surprised to find that he had landed on soft grass. As he got up he saw that it grew right up to the lakeshore and the ash. No normal grass would do that. It felt normal enough, though, just like the lawns in the garden caverns of the Castle.

There was a path not far away. Tal cautiously crossed the grass to it, and studied it before he stepped onto it. It was made of bricks, but not normal ones. These were violet crystal and had Sunstone fragments suspended in them. As his foot came down, the bricks under it sparkled, but nothing sinister happened.

Adras hovered in the air behind Tal.

"Something smells funny," whispered the Storm Shepherd. "Oily."

Tal sniffed the air, but he couldn't smell anything oily. All he could smell was the fresh scent of grass and the pleasant perfume of the flowers that grew on the tall bushes ahead.

Tal walked along the path for a while. It looked like it circumnavigated the island. Other paths ran off it, into the interior. One of them headed in the direction of the house.

Tal took it. He walked a little slower as the path headed between two overhanging flower bushes. Something about the whole place made him uneasy. Perhaps it was the moonlight, he thought. It made everything look creepy.

He took a few more steps before he realized what it was.

There was a light breeze blowing from behind his back.

But the bushes were leaning toward him.

Tal stopped and looked at them. They were taller than he was. Big bushes with broad clusters of green leaves. Both had two large red flowers about two-thirds of the way up.

"They're only plants," Tal said aloud. "Only plants."

But he didn't walk toward them. As he watched, first one flower then another slowly swiveled to face him. Then, with a horrible sucking sound, both bushes lifted their roots out of the ground and glided forward, rustling. The roots they moved on were sharp and pointed, more like multiple talons than anything else.

Tal backed away. But he had only gone a few paces when Adras said, "Uh-oh."

Tal looked behind. Two of the statues he'd seen from the air were coming down the path. They were humanoid, a little larger than an adult Chosen, and made of the same golden metal as the Ruin Ship. As they closed in, Tal noticed the oily smell Adras had mentioned before. They moved like Tal and Adras in the Chromatic armor. Slowly and clumsily.

"Time to fly," said Tal, reaching up his arms. Adras swooped down and grabbed him, and this time it really hurt — because Tal's feet wouldn't leave the path.

He looked down and saw strands of violet wrapping themselves around his ankles, forming shackles of light.

The flower creatures glided forward, piercing roots questing ahead of them. The statues shuddered up behind, their massive fists rising and falling.

"Let go, I'm stuck! Try to hold them off!"

Adras let go. Instantly Tal focused on his Sunstone. If he could make a Violet Key he could unlock the shackles on his ankles. Thanks to Lokar, he had some idea of what he had to do.

But could he do it before the statues clubbed him down or the flower creatures stabbed him?

·CHAPTER·
SIXTEEN

Malen kept working on Crow for several hours after the Freefolk left to gather airweed and take it to the Icecarl advance guard. Milla watched the Crone's quick and clever hands for a while, then decided to make sure Jarnil hadn't tried to sneak away.

She found him asleep in his bed. Milla looked down at him, wondering again whether she should do anything. She was about to leave when something triggered a memory. Jarnil was sleeping in an odd posture. He had his hands linked on his chest, under the blanket.

Milla pulled the blanket back. As she'd suspected, his hands were clasped around a Sunstone.

Jarnil wasn't asleep. He'd gone to Aenir. Without leaving a Spiritshadow to guard the body he left behind, because he didn't have one anymore. It had been taken from him in the Hall of Nightmares.

Yet even though he had been cast out and made an Underfolk, and eventually one of the Freefolk, in the end it hadn't been enough to break his life-long loyalty. There was only one reason Jarnil would have gone to Aenir.

He was going to warn the Chosen about the Ice-carl invasion.

Milla's knife came out of her sleeve and into her hand. She held it lightly, poised above Jarnil's throat. Then she sighed and put it away. Nothing would be gained by killing Jarnil's body. She didn't know if it would kill him in Aenir, and in any case, he was a brave man to do what he had done. Plus, he was asleep and defenseless. There would only be dishonor if she slew him now.

Milla climbed back up to the central courtyard and splashed some water from the well on her face. When Jarnil gave them a warning, the Chosen would swiftly return. They would also learn about this fortress. If Milla stayed here, she could be cut off from her forces, the Freefolk fortress being too easily besieged with its single bridge over the lava crevasse.

But her knowledge of the Castle and the Underfolk levels in particular was too limited. How could she be a War-Chief if she didn't know the territory where her people would fight?

"I need maps," she shouted angrily, releasing the tension she felt at her own mistake in leaving Jarnil unwatched. "Where can I find maps?"

A splash from the well answered her question. Instantly, Milla leaped back from the rim, her Merwin-horn sword and dagger in her hands.

A door-sized rectangle of crystal slowly floated up through the water. It was horizontal at first, but then it levitated upright, water splashing down on every side. Even after the water fell, its face was liquid and shining.

Icecarl runes formed upon its surface.

"Maps may be found in many places within the Castle. I have many maps within me."

For once Milla stared. This was the Codex of the Chosen, the magical artifact she and Tal had risked their lives to bring back from Aenir. They had left it hidden in the Mausoleum higher in the Castle, only to learn from Ebbitt that the Codex could wander of its own accord.

"You have come back," Milla said.

The Codex didn't answer. It was its nature to only answer questions.

"How do I get to the Underfolk levels from here?" Milla asked.

Silver lines appeared on the shining surface of the Codex. They drew a map. Milla studied it intently. There was another way out of the Fortress of the Freefolk, she saw, but it was narrow and difficult and led only to a distant part of the heatways.

"Where is the best place for a raiding party of five hundred Icecarls to gather in the Underfolk levels so they can quickly attack the higher Chosen levels?"

Another map formed, showing a huge chamber labeled as The Assembly of the Miners. Milla smiled as she studied the map. Even if the Chosen did come back, the Codex would help her defeat them. There were so many secret ways and passages that the Chosen wouldn't know. The Codex, on the other hand, knew everything.

If she could make sure it stayed around.

"Malen!" she called, half turning away. "Malen!"

As she turned back, the Codex sank into the well again. Milla snatched at it, and for a moment held a corner fast. But it shrank under her fingers and slipped away. In seconds the Codex was the size of a large fish and it zipped away like one, down into the deep waters of the well.

Malen came out as Milla scooped vainly at the well, spraying the Crone with water.

"War-Chief!" exclaimed Malen, affronted.

"The Codex! It was here!"

Malen rushed to the well, but there was nothing to be seen. She looked at Milla, her blue eyes already clouding over as she prepared to share whatever Milla said with the other Crones.

"The Codex of the Chosen," said Milla. "It was here. It came out of the well. I asked it to show me maps of the Castle. Tell the Crones with the advance guard to tell the Shield Maidens to ask the Freefolk to show them the way to the Assembly of the Miners on Underfolk Level Seven. We will meet there. Also . . . I have made a mistake. Jarnil has gone to Aenir to warn the Chosen."

Milla paused and waited for Malen to speak. But the young Crone was silent for some time. When she did talk, it was with the strange, gestalt voice of all the Crones, the voice that sent shivers down Milla's spine.

"You must keep the Codex if it comes again. It is of the highest importance."

Malen stopped talking and nearly fell into the well. Milla steadied her.

"Sorry," said Malen. She suddenly sounded like

her nose was blocked. "I'm not . . . not used to carrying the Voice. I've only had the basic lessons."

For once Malen didn't sound like a Crone. She sounded like a young Icecarl with a touch of the chill-fever, an Icecarl who wasn't too confident she could do what had to be done, but would try anyway.

Milla liked her the better for it.

"How is Crow?" she asked.

"I think he will recover," answered Malen. She coughed and stood straighter. The blue in her eyes grew brighter and she sounded more confident. "He will sleep normally now, and should be able to speak when he wakes."

"Can he be moved?" asked Milla. "If Bennem carries him?"

Malen frowned. "If he must."

"And Ebbitt, can he be moved?"

"Who knows? He is old and has overexerted himself. If he were an Icecarl, I think he would give himself to the Ice."

"But he is not," said Milla. "And the Castle is not so hard a place for the old as a ship. He is also very wise and powerful with the Chosen's light magic."

"It is different here," Malen acknowledged. She shivered and said, "I fear that it will change us, coming here."

Milla was silent. She had been changed beyond recognition already, so much she hardly knew who she was anymore. So few things were certain. One was her responsibility as War-Chief of the Icecarls.

"We will move," she ordered. "All of us, before the Chosen return. Bennem will carry Crow, Odris will carry Jarnil, and Ebbitt will ride on his Spirit-shadow's back. We will go to the Hall of Miners to meet the advance guard — and prepare for the attack."

·CHAPTER· SEVENTEEN

Adras swooped down and tried to topple the closest statue. It rocked back momentarily, but even the Storm Shepherd's strength could not prevent it from moving forward. Its mighty fists slammed into Adras's cloudy chest and sank in.

"Owwgh!" gasped Adras. He reeled back. "That hurt!"

The flower-creatures were advancing, too. Long, sharp roots slid ahead of them, as the trunks and branches crept inexorably forward.

Tal didn't look. He kept concentrating on his Sunstone and the shackles of light. They were violet, and all he had to do was find the right Violet Key to make them let him go. He had to bring the correct light forth from his Sunstone.

"I can't . . . can't stop them!" puffed Adras as he was flung aside by a huge golden arm.

Tal heard the Storm Shepherd's voice as if it were far away. All his concentration, every scrap of willpower was focused on his Sunstone. Light shone there, first red, then it flickered through orange, yellow, green, blue, indigo . . . and violet.

But it was a weak violet, lacking the fire and strength of the true color. Tal bent all his thought upon it, trying to intensify the light, to make it true. He had to have pure violet to make his key and escape.

The statues grew closer. A sharp root, ahead of the rest, sliced across Tal's shin, drawing blood. He ignored it. The light was intensifying. It was almost there. Another root slashed across his leg. A flower bent toward him and some part of Tal's mind noted that its petals were as sharp as steel as they came toward his face.

Then something clicked inside Tal's head. He felt totally attuned with his Sunstone, as if he and it were the only things that existed in the whole world.

Violet, thought Tal.

The Sunstone flared into bright, pure violet light.

It grew brighter and brighter — Tal had to close his eyes and shield his face with his arm. Violet light was everywhere, all around, and he couldn't see, couldn't make it undo his shackles. Any second the flower would cut his face and the statues would smash him to the ground . . .

The light faded. No flower cut came, no crushing blow. Tal opened his eyes and let his arm fall. The flower-creatures were retreating to their groves along the path. The statues had turned around and were lumbering back to resume their stolid poses. Adras was floating just off the path, rubbing his chest and groaning.

There was still a faint remnant of violet light. Tal looked down. His legs were only lightly scratched and the blood was already drying. The light shackles around his ankles were gone, and the path sparkled innocently. The violet light came from his Sunstone.

Tal held his hand close to his face. The Sunstone had changed. It had been generally yellow with flecks of red before, and occasional twinkles of all the other colors. Now it was a pure deep violet, all the way through, down into hidden depths it hadn't had before.

"Thanks," said Adras. "Those statues *hurt*."

"I . . . I don't know what I did," said Tal. He let his hand fall. The Sunstone dimmed a little, but his fingers were still washed in violet light. "Come on."

There were a lot more flower-creatures along the path, and several more statues. Tal felt a strong urge to run past them, but he didn't. He just kept walking. The flower-creatures rustled as he passed, but made no move to attack. The statues' heads swiveled to watch him, but didn't step off their plinths.

It made for a very creepy progress in the moonlight. Tal kept expecting a flower-creature to go from a rustle to a sudden stab, and the statues to suddenly move and bar his way.

Finally, they came to the house. As Tal had seen from the air, only the courtyard was lit up. The crystal leaves that were woven into the canopy above the courtyard shone green and silver in the moonlight, and tinkled in the light breeze.

There were several people in the courtyard, despite the fact that it was very late. Or very early, depending on how you thought about it.

Tal paused next to a flower-creature to get a proper look before he went into the open. It wasn't a very successful reconnaissance as he kept one eye on the closest branches and tried to do his spying with the other.

Because the crystal leaves hung over the sides as well as making up a canopy, it was hard to see what was going on. As far as Tal could tell, there were two people sitting down in the very center of the courtyard, and two others waiting on them, occasionally going back and forth to the house.

The two sitting down were probably Chosen, as Tal caught brief flashes of light from their Sunstones, brighter and differently colored than the ones that were set in the corner-posts. The two servants . . . he wasn't sure about. They didn't seem to be human-shaped.

One of the sitting Chosen had to be the Empress, Tal thought. With a courtier, and two servants of some kind. Who else could it be?

He looked nervously around for the guards. But there didn't seem to be anyone else nearby. The house was dark and quiet. Perhaps here the Empress relied totally on the flower-creatures, the statues, and the magic in the paths.

So there was no one to stop him from walking over, bowing before the Empress, and giving light. He could tell her about Sushin, the Veil, his father . . . everything.

"I need a drink," whispered Adras. Or in his idea of a whisper. It made Tal jump into the flower-creature. If it hadn't leaned away he would have been sliced to pieces.

"I don't understand this place," Tal whispered

back when he recovered his balance. In some ways it was worse than being out on the Ice. At least there he knew he didn't know anything. Here in the Chosen Enclave, he felt like he ought to be more knowledgeable. He should know why the Sunstone harpoons were in the lakebed, he should know why his Sunstone had gone Violet, he should know why the guards of the Empress's island had suffered a change of heart.

But he didn't. And at this very last minute, he was having doubts about the wisdom of going before the Empress. Yes, she did have the power to put everything right. But he hadn't followed the correct procedures to see her, even if it was impossible to do so with Sushin in control of the Guards and so much else. It wasn't the Chosen way to just saunter across in the middle of the night and address the very highest of the Chosen.

Yet there was no other way. This was the choice he had made. He had to be brave and take the opportunity.

He stood up and walked across the grass. Adras billowed along behind him. They went to an arched gateway and stepped under the canopy of crystal leaves.

Tal looked across the courtyard. Two slim, long-armed semi-human creatures with large green eyes and fuzzy black fur looked back at him. One carried a silver tray with a bottle on it, the other a golden tray with two crystal goblets. Neither creature seemed at all perturbed by Tal and Adras. After a moment's glance, they looked away again.

There were also two Chosen, seated in the middle of the canopy. They paid the new arrivals no attention at all. They were both engrossed in a game of Beastmaker. The game was in its final stages, all cards played and the beasts already created in the battlecircle. A star-shaped thing with many mouths was wrapped around a scaly, two-headed insectoid. The latter had a long tail-sting that it struck with every few seconds, hitting itself as often as its opponent.

Both the Chosen players wore flowing violet robes and many Sunstones. They were both indescribably ancient, extremely thin, and had very long white hair. It took Tal a moment to work out that the one with the violet cap trimmed with Sunstones was female, and thus almost certainly the Empress, and that her bareheaded counterpart was male. They were obviously closely related. Brother and sister, or perhaps mother and son. They were so old it was hard to pick any difference in their ages.

Tal approached, but they paid him no attention. When he was only a few stretches away, he sank to one knee, raised his Sunstone, and gave them respectful light.

At the same time, the insectoid beast expired. The star creature flexed up on one point and did a strange little dance. Then the game was over, and both creatures vanished in a stream of tiny sparks of light that circled round and round the polished gameboard and back into the deck of cards.

Only then did the two Chosen turn to face Tal. Each held out a hand, the Empress her right and her relative his left. The two semi-human servants placed a goblet in each hand and then poured out something frothy and black.

They drank and threw the goblets behind them, which were dexterously caught by the servants.

Tal waited, still on one knee. Eventually, he gave light again. He'd meant to give an orange glow appropriate to his station, but somehow it came out violet.

This got the Empress's attention.

"Oh! It's him!" she wailed. "It's him!"

·CHAPTER·
EIGHTEEN

"No it isn't, Ildi," said the other Chosen. "Don't be stupid. Who are you, boy? You look familiar. Gronnius's son?"

"I am Tal Graile-Rerem," announced Tal. "I bear important news for Her Imperial Highness."

"Never heard of you," said the man. "What are you doing here with important news? Tell it to Sushin. We're busy. Got a Beastmaker series to finish. Best of a hundred."

"Yes, go away," pronounced the Empress. At least Tal was pretty certain she was the Empress. He'd only ever seen her in the distance before, at important events, when she wore full robes of state. But he thought Ebbitt had said her name was Kathilde, and the man had just called her Ildi.

"Um, you *are* Her Imperial Highness?" he asked hesitantly.

"Of course I am . . . that is, we are," the old woman retorted. "Why does this doubt . . . this treachery . . . this carping disbelief continue?"

"I don't doubt, Highness," Tal assured her hastily. "It's only I've never been so close to you before, and your . . . um . . . radiance is blinding."

"Well, that is true," the Empress conceded. "You are a well-brought-up boy. But I cannot recall your parents' names among our Violet personages. Perhaps they are newly risen? We are so busy that we fear we get a trifle behind from time to time."

Tal glanced down at the Sunstone on his finger, and its glowing violet pulse. Obviously the Empress thought he was of the Violet order, the child of a Shadowlord and lady. Time to change the subject.

"Highness, I bring grave news," he said again. "There is a plot against the Chosen by the shadows of Aenir. Some of the Keystones have been unsealed, and the Veil is threatened. Our whole world is in danger."

The Empress smiled and shook her finger at Tal.

"Now, now, if you want to present a light-puppet drama to us, you must apply to our Light Vizier first."

"And I'll tell you straight off that your story sounds stupid, it's been done before, and anyway we'd rather play Beastmaker than watch some incompetent stripling fumbling about with light puppets," said the man.

"You're the Light Vizier?" asked Tal. He had a terrible sinking feeling in his chest. They were both so old, and they didn't appear to be listening to him at all!

"Uthern Lalis-Offin, Light Vizier to . . . to her," replied the man. He waved his hand vaguely and a faint violet glow came off his Sunstone.

He leaned forward and almost fell out of his chair, both furry servants arriving only just in time to catch him.

"Confidentially, my boy," he whispered, "I'm the elder brother. I should have been Emperor after we kicked Mercur out. But *she* was in more with the Violet and the Indigo."

Tal's nose wrinkled as Uthern leaned back. The Light Vizier wasn't just old. He was drunk, and so, by the look of her, was the Empress.

"I'm not pretending," he said urgently. "I'm telling the truth. Sushin is in league with the Aenirans and they are unsealing the Keystones!"

At Sushin's name, Empress and Light Vizier

looked at each other like children caught in a Lector's glare.

"Not our business," announced the Empress. "Ceremonial duties only. Made quite clear. Long ago. You may leave us."

"But you have to listen," urged Tal. He jumped to his feet and stood over the Empress. "You have to do something! My father is trapped inside the Orange Keystone! Lokar is trapped inside the Red. Look!"

He undid the knot in his shirt and pulled out the Red Keystone. It flared brightly as he raised it, and both the Empress and Uthern whimpered and tried to shield their eyes.

"We don't want it!" shrieked the Empress.

Tal stared down at the two of them, cowering in their chairs. He couldn't believe these were the highest and mightiest of the Chosen, the pinnacle of Castle society. What was wrong with them?

"Look into the stone," he pleaded. "Your Highness, you have to use the Violet Keystone to release Lokar! You have to."

"Haven't got it," whimpered the Empress. "Foundation of doubt."

Tal lowered the Red Keystone and stepped back.

"What do you mean you haven't got it?" he whispered. "I've come so far ... gone through so much ..."

"She never had it," said Uthern with a vindictive look at his sister. "Mercur had a back way out, all the way down to the Underfolk levels. He took it. The Violet Keystone, the Claw of Ramellan, the secret knowledge. But I struck him as he ran."

The old man raised a skinny arm and mimed throwing a bolt of light.

"I never had it," repeated the Empress. "No one could know. We agreed, Uthern. But you told the shadow."

"I didn't," hissed Uthern. "It was you, you."

"What shadow?" asked Tal slowly. "What did you tell the shadow?"

"Sharrakor, Sharrakor, Sharrakor," crooned the Empress. "How we wish he had never slithered across our path."

"Sharrakor?" asked Tal. "Your Spiritshadow?"

The Empress and Uthern laughed, a mad giggle that raised the hair on the back of Tal's head.

"Not mine, no, no," cackled the Empress. She gestured at the furred servants behind her. "There are our Spiritshadows. No one to guard us in the Castle. No loyal Spiritshadows to make sure we survive. Sharrakor is his own master."

Tal stared aghast at the little black humanoids. Apart from the fact that as bound servants they should be guarding the two Chosen's bodies back in the Castle, they were obviously completely harmless and were totally unsuitable to be Spiritshadows to any Violet Chosen, let alone the Empress and the Light Vizier.

Yet everyone thought Sharrakor was the bound and true servant of the Empress. Sharrakor, who was regarded as the most powerful Spiritshadow of them all.

"And Sushin?" he asked. "What is Sushin?"

"Shadow-pawn," said Uthern. He had stopped laughing and was weeping now, the tears sliding down his aged and wrinkled cheeks. "Shadow-pawn of Sharrakor."

"You have betrayed us," said Tal. He couldn't believe it. They'd undermined everything. It was their fault that his father was trapped in the Orange Keystone. They were ultimately responsible for the disappearances and the deaths. The Pit and the perversion of the Hall of Nightmares. "You have betrayed us all to the shadows."

"No," said Kathild. "I am the Empress of the Chosen. I am Most High!"

"No," said Uthern, but his voice quavered and

the tears still fell. "I am Light Vizier. Nothing will change. The Chosen will go on. The Castle will stand. The Veil will hold."

"No they won't!" screamed Tal. He was almost sobbing himself, but with rage, not sorrow. "I should kill you both! It's what the Icecarls would do to traitors!"

He stepped back still farther and raised his own Sunstone. It swirled with violet light. Tal fed his anger into it, and the violet light grew and strengthened. Tal didn't know what he was going to do, or what spell he could cast. He just let all his rage, frustration, and fear fly into the stone.

Violet lightning began to spit out of the Sunstone, crackling and flashing. It shot out and around Tal, spinning a barrier of violet streaks. Tal tried to make it stop circling and strike the two Chosen, but it wouldn't be directed. It rose higher and higher until there was a spinning storm of violet lightning bolts flashing over Tal's head.

The Empress and the Light Vizier stared up at it, white-faced. Then they fell out of their chairs and prostrated themselves at Tal's feet, sobbing and clutching at his ankles.

"Spare us! Spare us, Mercur, Ramellan, whoever you are!"

·CHAPTER·
ΠIΠETEEΠ

Tal stared down at the two Chosen, then up at the crackling violet light above his head. It had formed into the shape he knew well. The Jagged Lightning Crown, worn by the Empress on the Day of Ascension and Dark Return.

Why was this strange light replica of the crown hovering over *his* head?

"I'm so sorry, Highness," sobbed Uthern. "She made me do it!"

The Empress hissed and scratched at Uthern. In a second, they were rolling around on the ground, weakly kicking and hitting each other, more like children or baby animals than people.

Tal bent down and pulled them apart. They were so thin and light, he could have picked one up in each hand. He sat them back in their chairs and their servants hurried forward to straighten their clothes and hair.

"Why do you call me Highness?" he asked. The anger had all gone out of him now, though the crown of violet light remained. He felt cold and hard now, without anger.

Or mercy.

"You wield the Violet Keystone," whispered brother and sister together. "Are you Ramellan come again, to punish us?"

Tal looked at the stone on his finger, now revealed in all its Violet glory. He remembered the skeleton in the heatway tunnel. It must have been the late Emperor Mercur, who had not quite managed to escape the traitors who had supplanted him.

He also remembered Ebbitt splitting the Sunstone. What he wore on his finger now was only half the Violet Keystone. The other half was probably atop the mast of the Far-Raiders ship. Or lost with Milla upon the Ice, he thought with a pang.

But even half the Violet Keystone might be enough to release Lokar and his father. It might be enough to reseal the Keystones and save the Veil. It might be enough to rally the Chosen and turn them against Sushin and Sharrakor.

But only if Tal had the courage and the strength

to use the Keystone properly. Now there really was no one else he could go to. It was all up to him. He had to make the right decisions, starting right now.

Tal felt like he had before he decided to climb the Red Tower, in a life that seemed long ago. That simple decision had changed everything. Now he stood on the brink once more, in the frozen moment before he did something that could not be undone.

He felt every muscle in his body tense, as if he were a spring being compressed as far as it would go. What would happen when it was released?

Tal stared at the two cringing Chosen. What was he to do with them? What was his next step? He couldn't kill them, he realized. He might not really be a Chosen anymore, but he wasn't an Icecarl, either.

He was prevented from making a decision by a shout from Adras, who had drifted off to suck up water from an ornamental pool nearby.

Tal turned to see what was the matter. As he did so, Kathilde and Uthern both leaped forward, drawing crystal daggers from the arms of their chairs.

"Die!" they screamed.

Tal twisted back, but he was too slow to do anything else. The daggers flashed down — and were met by bolts of violet lightning from the crown above his head. Crystal exploded into powder, and then more lightning struck, straight at the hearts of the Empress and the Light Vizier!

Tal reeled back and was caught by Adras as the violet lightning jumped the gap between Kathilde and Uthern and struck their servants as well. There was a tremendous flash, a boom louder than any of Adras's thunder, and all the crystal leaves were blown off the canopy.

Tal and Adras were thrown to the ground. Through slitted eyes Tal saw Kathilde and Uthern struck again and again by bolts of violet lightning. It played over their bodies, striking every part of them, the flashes blinding and the thunderclaps deafening. Sunstones on the Chosen's clothing absorbed some of the lightning, and for a few seconds the two continued to struggle, to try to get away. But in the end the last Sunstone exploded into dust and the Empress Kathilde and her Light Vizier were still.

The violet crown that had been above Tal's head drifted across to them, and the bands of light rearranged themselves into a vaguely human shape. It hovered above the dead Chosen, raised its arms in triumph, and disappeared in a fall of violet sparks.

"Did you do that?" asked Adras. "I liked the lightning."

"No," said Tal wearily. "That, I think, was the death curse of the Emperor Mercur. I just delivered it."

He got up and dusted himself off. He didn't go and look at the bodies. There wasn't much left of them, and the ground around them was still smoking.

"What were you going on about just then?" asked Tal.

"Hmmm?" asked Adras. He was inspecting the burn marks on a nearby pole. "Oh, a ship."

He pointed. Tal looked. Sure enough, a large boat was approaching the island. It was brightly lit with Sunstones and crammed with the Empress's Guards and other Chosen. A familiar rotund figure was standing at the bow.

"Sushin," groaned Tal. Now was not the time to confront him, or to try to win the Chosen over. Not with the Empress and the Light Vizier dead at his feet.

"I hope you haven't had so much water you can't fly," Tal said.

"Why?"

"Because we have to fly, of course!" shouted Tal.

"There's no need to shout," sniffed Adras. "Where are we going?"

Tal shook his head. He felt incredibly tired again.

"I don't know. Away from here before that boat lands."

"Too late for that," said Adras. "It just did."

"It can't have," said Tal. He didn't bother to look. "It was hundreds of stretches away."

"No," explained Adras patiently. "The other ship. The one I didn't see before."

Tal looked. Another boat full of Guards had grounded on the western shore. The first Chosen were jumping off the bow. They saw him, and an angry shout went up.

Tal's tiredness disappeared. He turned to run, tugging at Adras's hand.

"Come on," he shouted, holding up both arms. "Running takeoff!"

"I feel sick," announced Adras. But he pushed off the ground and grabbed Tal's arms as he lifted him into the sky. The very low part of the sky. Tal was dragged along the ground, and only saved from being sliced apart because two flower-creatures leaned over backward to let him past.

"Higher!" Tal screamed. For a moment his feet rested on the shoulders of a golden statue. He jumped off and they gained a bit of height, only to lose it again as Adras groaned and dipped.

They were almost at the lake on the far side of the island when Adras finally managed to get properly airborne. He kept heading toward the crater rim, mindful of all the Chosen and their Sunstones that were behind him.

Tal breathed a sigh of relief, only to lose it in panic as he realized something truly horrible.

He'd dropped the Red Keystone when they were knocked over back in the courtyard.

·CHAPTER·
TWENTY

"Take us high," said Tal bitterly. "Then you can drop me."

"How high?" asked Adras.

"High enough," muttered Tal. How could he have been so stupid? He'd been so careful not to lose the Red Keystone. That Icecarl Crone had prophesied truly when she said, "Sunstones fall from you, yet into other's hands."

"Um, Tal, why am I going to drop you?" asked Adras.

"You're not," said Tal shortly. "I'm just angry at myself. I don't really mean for you to drop me. Is that cloud up there? Let's join that for a while."

"Sure," said Adras. There was a long strand of cloud drifting over the crater. "Why are you angry at yourself?"

Tal bit back an angry response. There was no point in yelling at Adras.

"I dropped the Red Keystone," he said dully. "I've practically killed Lokar, just like everyone else."

"The Red Keystone?" asked Adras. "Is that the red Sunstone?"

Tal took a deep, slow breath. "Yes, it is the red Sunstone."

"Oh, I picked that up," said Adras. "I thought you'd want it."

"You picked it up?" Tal repeated. He looked up at the Storm Shepherd, who was smiling down at him. "Where is it?"

"I put it in my pocket."

"Your pocket? You haven't got a pocket . . . um . . . have you?"

"When I want to have a pocket I have a pocket," replied Adras proudly. "Look!"

He let go of one of Tal's arms and the Chosen boy swung wildly underneath. But Tal didn't panic. He just gripped a little tighter himself.

Adras reached into his stomach area and two big puffy fingers pulled out a small red-glowing Sunstone. He started to hand it over to Tal.

"No, you keep it for now," said Tal urgently. "You've earned the right to look after it."

He didn't add that the last thing he wanted to do while hanging beneath a Storm Shepherd a thousand stretches up was take an irreplaceable Sunstone from two oversized cloud fingers and try to tie it in his shirt.

When they rendezvoused with the cloud, Tal had Adras stay a fraction beneath it, so he could watch what was going on down below. There was a lot of activity, not only on the Empress's island, but all over the Chosen Enclave. Sunstones were flaring brightly everywhere, in houses and on walkways and bridges. It was a colorful sight from a safe distance.

While the death of the Empress was bound to cause a stir, Tal couldn't figure out why absolutely everybody was dashing around. There were even Chosen running back from the tunnel that went through the crater wall.

Tal and Adras stayed with the cloud for some time. The sun had risen and the last of the night darkness was slipping from the crater below when Tal finally figured out what was going on.

"They're going back," he said, disbelief in his voice. "The Chosen are going back to the Castle. But it's months yet to Dark Return!"

Even the death of the Empress would not prompt a return to the Castle. It was unheard of. From the Day of Ascension to the Day of Dark Return, all

Chosen were in Aenir. It was as simple as that. But there was no mistaking what was going on below. The Orders were gathering in their respective areas. Tal could see the different colors in their Sunstones as they assembled along the major bridges. There was his Orange Order on the West Bridge, every single one of them.

Tal peered down. He wished he had a telescope. There were a number of litters with the Orange Order, for the sick and the infirm. His mother would be lying on one. She had to be. He refused to consider that she might now be dead.

A bunch of Chosen around the edge of the Orange ranks suddenly disappeared, leaving a prismatic afterimage. Tal blinked. That was even more unusual than the fact that the Chosen were returning. There was a set order to going back to the Castle. Red went first, from lowest to highest, and then it went in order of seniority through the other colors.

A group of Blue Chosen suddenly shone and then they were gone, too. Then a couple of Indigo, and a bunch of Yellows.

"Let's go lower," Tal instructed. "I need to see this."

They sank lower, but no one looked up. They were all too intent on getting back to the Castle.

Tal watched as the transfers became even more

confused. People seemed to be transferring back as soon as they were ready. A lot of children and sick Chosen were being sent back even when they weren't ready. Tal saw one little boy running away from his mother when he was struck by a kaleidoscopic whorl that signaled the transfer.

It took Tal a few minutes to realize that what he was seeing was a panic. The Chosen were desperate to return to the Castle and the Dark World. But why? Had the Spiritshadows already revolted? Surely that would be accompanied by an attack here in Aenir as well?

Whatever was going on, Tal knew it was an opportunity for him. He looked down at the steadily thinning ranks of the Chosen. If it was chaos here, with everyone translating back, it would be even worse in the Castle.

Now was the time to go back and give the water spider antidote to his mother . . . if he hadn't lost it. Tal felt the other knot in his shirt, the one he had never undone. Two vials of precious antidote were there. Provided they weren't harmed by the transfer to Aenir and then back, they should bring Graile out of her coma and make her well.

"Take us to the crater wall," said Tal. "We're going back home."

"This is home," said Adras.

"The Dark World," said Tal. "You'll be a Spirit-shadow again."

"Hhmmph," snorted Adras. But he headed for the crater wall.

Home, thought Tal. Where was home now? Almost everything he had thought was true about the Chosen and the Castle was a lie. The Empress had proved to be a usurper and a coward, her Light Vizier likewise. The Dark Vizier was the puppet of a shadow.

And back in the Castle, like a dark stain across his life, there was the memory of his failures, the accident he had caused, and the deaths for which he was responsible.

Atonement was the answer, Tal thought bleakly. He had to make up for what he had done. He must release Lokar and his father and the other Guardians trapped in the Keystones. He must defeat Sushin and Sharrakor and save the Veil. Not just for his people, but also for the Icecarls. He owed Milla that, and more.

It was all up to him.

"Fly to that ledge," he said, pointing. "We will transfer back from there."

·CHAPTER·
TWENTY-ONE

The Assembly of the Miners was a vast natural cave that had long ago been adapted into a splendid auditorium. Its sloping floor had been shaped into broad terraces and the protruding rock at its southern end sculpted into an imposing pulpit.

In its heyday, during the construction of the Castle, it had regularly held gatherings of twenty or thirty thousand people. That time was long gone, and much of the vast chamber was dim now, the Sunstones on the ceiling far above faded.

The Underfolk used a fraction of one of the terraces to store stone bottles of oil, but otherwise the hall was deserted.

The Assembly was an ideal gathering place for Milla and her Icecarls. It had many entrances and exits, most importantly a very broad corridor leading to the Clear Ascendor, one of the major stairways of the Castle, that led all the way from the lowest Underfolk levels to the beginning of the Violet.

Milla's strange cavalcade of Crone, Spiritshadows, damaged Bennem, spirit-departed Jarnil, dozing Ebbitt, and wounded Crow had arrived in the Assembly without difficulty. They had seen Underfolk on the way, but they had quickly scuttled away when they saw the Spiritshadows.

Apart from them, the lower levels of the Castle were quiet. They saw no other Spiritshadows, and there was no sign of any general alarm. There had not been any attempts to close the many doors and gates that had probably not moved for centuries, or decades at least.

Malen made her patients as comfortable as she could near the pulpit, while Milla and Adras traversed the terraces of the Assembly. Satisfied that there was no ambush there, and that it would be easy to both attack or retreat from, Milla returned to the others to wait for her first warriors to arrive, and to speak to the Crones through Malen.

It wasn't a really long wait — less than eight Chosen hours — but it felt like one. Milla was acutely aware that the Chosen, forewarned by Jarnil, could return at any time. Or the free Spiritshadows already in the Castle might decide to attack both the Chosen and her little band. Milla wondered what the bound Spiritshadows would do if they were confronted by their brethren. Would their bindings force them to fight? After all, the Chosen employed a variation of the Prayer of Asteyr, which, as far as Milla knew, could not be thwarted.

The free Spiritshadows probably wouldn't attack until the Veil was destroyed. They would have to bring a vast host from Aenir to overcome both the Chosen and their bound Spiritshadows. They couldn't do that until the Veil was destroyed and the light made them more powerful.

The question was, how damaged was the Veil already? Milla wished Crow was conscious, so she could ask him what he had learned in the Red Tower. She knew that he and Tal had gotten the Keystone, but not much else.

A slight sound alerted Milla to movement near one of the nearer entrances. She crouched, knife and Talon ready. Odris slid across the ground to her right side and reared up.

An Icecarl slipped around the corner. A Shield Maiden. She saw Milla and gave her the good-hunting sign, two fingers held straight down and whisked to the side. Milla returned the sign.

The Shield Maiden disappeared back beyond the doorway. A moment later, she returned. A Shield Mother came next, followed by a tide of Shield Maidens and hunters. The Shield Mother clapped her fists briefly at Milla, then turned to direct her followers to fan out as they entered the chamber, tapping each one as they passed and pointing them in different directions.

All the Icecarls carried airweed draped across their hunting packs, in case they had to fight their way back through the heatways. Milla was pleased to see that forethought.

More and more Icecarls poured in. Another four Shield Mothers arrived, each clapping their fists to Milla before joining the first Shield Mother to confer briefly, then direct their Maidens or Hunters to join different groups.

Milla waited patiently. This was always the way of the hunt. Only when everyone was in a proper position would the lesser leaders come to the Icecarl who led them all.

She was surprised by the next arrival. A gigantic Icecarl, his chest and arms bare, bent his head to fit through the door. His feet and all his skin save a small circle around his nose, mouth, and eyes were stained a deep, rich blue. He wore only trousers, his feet bare. The trousers were made of the shimmery, scaled skin of a rare and extremely dangerous Norr-worm. Around his waist was a heavy chain of golden metal, the links as thick as Milla's hands.

Only one Icecarl went barefoot on the Ice and lived to walk again. He had to be the famous Sword-Thane Jarek Bloodswimmer. Not only had he killed two Norrworms, he'd had to swim in their blood for three sleeps, until it seeped out of the ice cave where they died. The blood had permanently transformed his skin, making it very tough and resistant to cold and fire.

Jarek was a Wilder. The chain was his weapon.

At his side was a small woman, who at first glance looked like a regular Shield Maiden, until Milla noticed she wore her furs in a strange fashion, had six differently shaped knives at her belt, and her low boots were also made of Norrworm hide.

Milla knew her, too, for her legend was twined in Jarek's own. She was Kirr, a Shield Maiden who had been given leave to wander with the Sword-Thane. She was Jarek's companion, the only Icecarl who could control, at least a little, his Wilder rages. He never harmed her, and she could bring him out of the fury. The Crones considered this to be an important service, so she was not required to join a Hand.

Jarek and Kirr saw Milla, and clapped their fists to her before heading up to watch yet another entrance. Milla was surprised, caught staring at them. She was almost too slow to clap her fists in return. She had seen some other, less famous Sword-Thanes on the Mountain, but had no idea that Jarek and Kirr had joined them.

More Shield Maidens came in, then two Freefolk, Gill and Ferek. They started to head toward Milla, then hesitated, not sure they should approach, because the Shield Mothers hadn't done so.

Milla beckoned them over.

"Don't worry," she said. "The Shield Mothers are just getting everyone sorted out. Where are Clovil and Inkie?"

"They're showing some of your people the air-weed lake," Gill reported. She kept staring at all the arriving Icecarls, obviously excited by the activity. "Then they're going to try and convince some of the Fatalists that the time has finally come to break free!"

"Good," said Milla. "I'm glad you have come back, because I wanted to ask you if you will be guides. We will need you, and as many other Freefolk as you can gather, to show us the way to different parts of the Castle. Particularly the Chosen levels."

"Sure!" exclaimed Gill. "My parents were table-washers for the Red, Orange, and Yellow Commons. I know those levels really well."

Ferek was silent. Milla saw him swallow and twitch nervously.

"Though we will need someone here, too," she added quickly. "This will be our ship-home, for the Crones and the wounded. We will need a Freefolk here, one who knows these lower levels. It's an important job. Perhaps, Ferek, you will stay here and do that?"

Milla had once valued courage above all else. But since then she had been in the Hall of Nightmares, and she knew what that place could do to a child, one who did not know how to call the Crones to save them from bad dreams. Ferek was such a child.

"Yes, yes, I will," said Ferek, looking relieved.

"Good," Milla replied. She saw the Shield Mothers turn and approach. There were twenty of them now, which meant twenty Hands of Shield Maidens, two hundred and forty in all. Plus maybe another hundred hunters and Jarek and Kirr. "Perhaps you will see how Crow does?"

She moved away from them, toward the Shield Mothers. This would be the first real test of her command. They were in enemy territory now, and their full force still on its way. Would the Shield Mothers obey her?

Out of the corner of her eye, Milla saw Malen leave Crow's side and hurry over. The Crone was not going to let Milla talk to the Shield Mothers alone.

"I greet you, Shield Mothers," Milla announced, hurriedly closing the gap. At least she would get a few words in before Malen caught up.

"War-Chief," rumbled the reply. Some of the Shield Mothers said the title more easily than others, Milla saw.

"Come," she said. "We will take council. Ah, there is the Crone Malen. I will ask her to join us."

Since Malen was at that time only a few stretches away and obviously not to be left out, the Shield Mothers knew that this simply meant Milla was not going to wait for the Crones to tell her what to do. Some of them nodded slightly in approval, but at least as many had faint, barely impolite scowls.

They were not going to make this easy for Milla.

·CHAPTER· TWENTY-TWO ☉

The Shield Maidens gathered around Milla in a semicircle. Malen stood with them, rather than next to Milla. Even though she didn't want the Crone to join her, Milla felt keenly alone.

They all waited for her to speak.

She ran her gaze along the Shield Mothers. She had met most of them, and knew most of their names, but not much else. Little could be told from their faces or garb. All of them wore light, in-ship furs in the colors of the Hand they led, and Selski-hide armor. Some had polished shell armor plates over the top as well. Most carried swords and spears of Selski or Wreska bone treated with the glowing algae the Crones had given them, though there were two who had bright Merwin-horn swords.

Without their face masks, they were much easier

to tell apart. They ranged in age from five or six circlings older than Milla to the vastly experienced Shield Mothers who might have had thirty or forty circlings leading Shield Maidens upon the Ice. For the latter, this would probably be their last great expedition before they went out alone to wrestle with the wind and test the warmth of the Ice against bare skin.

Milla found her throat dry and didn't know what to say. They were all staring at her, waiting. She had never imagined that this would be worse than confronting a Merwin, or escaping a Hugthing in Aenir.

But she must not show her fear. Or do any Rovkir breathing, because they would notice it. She must simply speak.

"The Chosen have been warned of our attack," she said, talking too quickly. "I think that even now they scurry back from Aenir. It was my plan to attack before they knew we were here, but that chance is lost to us now. Now I think we must make these lower levels our own, and hold them until sufficient airweed is delivered for our full host to come through the heatways."

The Shield Mothers nodded. They would not speak until Milla invited them to.

"I will show you where we are. Who has a hide

and a drawing-stick?" Milla asked. Immediately several rolled-up Wreska hides were offered to her, and a variety of writing-sticks, from basic charcoal to a thin brush and bottle of Thrill-ink.

Milla spread the hide out and knelt down, sketching quickly with the charcoal. She drew a very basic plan of the area around the Assembly, then a rough cross section of the Castle, showing the Underfolk levels and the major stairs that she knew.

"We will hold the top Underfolk level at these stairs and this ramp, and at any others that we may find, " she said, pointing to several different points. "Then the Chosen will not be able to get food or have their servants attend to them. Most of the Chosen are soft, and will suffer greatly. That will help us when the time comes for the full attack. We must move quickly to have every possible stair and way between Red One and Underfolk Seven blocked."

A Shield Mother sliced the air with her palm.

"Speak," responded Milla.

"What of the Underfolk? Will they resist?"

"Perhaps," said Milla. "But it is my wish that they are not to be harmed unless there is no other way. Some may try to go to work in the Chosen levels, but they must be turned back. We will have some

Freefolk to help explain to them, and others who will guide us."

Another Shield Mother sliced the air, one of the older ones, with many scars upon her face and hands. Milla nodded.

"This is a straight plan, War-Chief, but to make sure I have it in my old head, may I repeat it? We hold all stairs and ramps and ways between us and the Chosen, kill or capture Chosen or Spiritshadows, be wary of Underfolk but treat them well, and die before retreating."

"Yes," said Milla. "We must hold these levels, until the arrival of the main host."

Another slice through the air.

"Yes?"

"Perhaps we should speak no more, War-Chief, but hurry to find all stairs and ramps, and be ready before the enemy strikes."

Milla nodded. "This place shall be our clan-ship. Send all messengers here. Beware the shadows, for they are more dangerous than the Chosen, even with their light magic. Now, who shall go where? Speak freely."

The Shield Mothers gathered even closer, and spoke quickly, sometimes over the top of one another. But it was soon decided which Hands would go where, and as each decision was made, the relevant Shield Mother would turn away and hurry to gather her Shield Maidens and hunters.

Finally only one Shield Mother remained. The older one, with many scars. Her name was Saylsen, Milla remembered.

"I will stay here, with my Hand, to guard the shipplace and the War-Chief," said Saylsen. She glanced at Malen, and Milla caught a slight nod from the Crone. Obviously this had been decided already.

"What do the Crones say of our plans?" asked Milla. She had seen Malen's eyes go cloudy through nearly the whole meeting of the Shield Mothers.

"You are War-Chief," replied Malen, neatly avoiding an answer. Then she added, "The Freefolk boy. Crow. He is conscious. You wished to speak with him?"

"Yes!" Milla looked across at the pulpit. Sure enough, Crow was sitting up. Ferek was giving him a drink. Gill had left a little earlier, proudly leading a Hand of Shield Maidens.

Milla also saw Jarek and Kirr. They were sitting on a ledge beyond the pulpit, playing the knife-hide-stone game.

Saylsen saw her look. "Jarek and Kirr are with my Hand. The Crones asked it of them."

Guards, Milla thought. She wondered if they were there to protect her, or to protect Malen from her. After all, if anything happened to Malen, then Milla would be free to do as she liked, until the Crones sent a replacement.

That prompted a thought.

"Are more Crones coming?" Milla asked.

"Not until the battle is won," replied Malen. "It is not the place of a Crone to be in battle."

"What about you?" asked Milla. Malen wet her lips and looked troubled.

"You know Crones must never join any fighting. There was a lot of talk about even sending me here, where battle may come anywhere. As for the wounded —"

"Wounded live if they are meant to," interrupted Saylsen with a shrug. "If there are no Crones, there are no Crones. Warriors fight and warriors die."

"I was speaking, Shield Mother," said Malen.

Saylsen did not seem repentant. She gave Milla a look that seemed to say, *This is our business, not the Crone's.*

"Come and talk to Crow with me," said Milla to Saylsen. "He knows the Castle well, and is a sworn enemy of the Chosen."

·CHAPTER·
TWENTY–THREE

The rainbow colors cleared away, leaving only a steady violet light. Tal blinked and felt the stone lid of the sarcophagus above him.

"Adras?" he whispered. He felt cool shadowflesh across his arm as Adras slid out and up the side of the sarcophagus.

"Yes?"

"Just checking," whispered Tal. "Are you all right?"

"Aenir is better than here," replied Adras. "I don't like being a shadow."

"You'll get back there," said Tal. He said it automatically, but it stuck in his head and he paused to think about what he was saying. What would he do with Adras? It was now certain that Milla was right when she said that the Chosen should not have Spiritshadows. In addition to saving the Veil, Tal would have to make sure all the Spiritshadows the Chosen now had were sent back to Aenir and made to stay there. This would include Adras.

And what would happen to the Chosen when all their Spiritshadows were gone, and — as Tal admitted had to happen — the Underfolk were freed?

Tal shook his head. Best he think like an Icecarl and worry about the Ice in front of him, not what lay behind or far ahead.

"There is something sharp . . . and hot . . . cutting into me," complained Adras. "Can we get out now?"

"Sorry," apologized Tal. It was time to act, not lie there thinking.

With Adras's help he raised the lid of the sarcophagus a fraction and looked through the gap. The Mausoleum was silent and there were no bright lights disturbing its perpetual twilight. Tal could hear a lot of shouting in the distance, but it was far off and didn't seem to be coming any closer.

He slid off the lid and climbed out. Adras flowed out after him.

The Red Keystone was lying in the sarcophagus. Tal reached in and picked it up.

"The pocket doesn't work when I'm a shadow," said Adras, rubbing his stomach.

Tal knew Spiritshadows had difficulty handling Sunstones, though they had no problem with normal items in the Dark World. He supposed it was another part of the mystery of their transformation between the worlds, the transformation that made them Spiritshadows.

Together they replaced the lid with its statue of the long-gone-to-dust occupant's Spiritshadow. Then Tal held up the Red Keystone, his forehead wrinkled in thought.

"I suppose I should release Lokar," he said, looking down at the half of the Violet Keystone on his finger. "If I can."

Adras nodded firmly. "Prison bad. Better to be free in the air."

"We'd better find somewhere to hide first," Tal said. He could still hear the shouting, and he wanted to know what was going on. But Adras was right. Now that he knew he might be able to release Lokar, he should do so as soon as possible.

The Antechamber where the Underfolk sculptors did the basic work on the statues that decorated the sarcophagi was deserted, as Tal had expected. He found a shielded spot between two columns of un-worked stone and crouched down to concentrate on the Red Keystone.

As before, he saw Lokar slowly swim into view. She was singing again, her Spiritshadow still hopping.

"Lokar!" Tal called out. "Lokar!"

She paid him no attention.

Tal called her name several times more before he realized that Lokar was particularly far gone this time. In desperation, he raised his own Sunstone until it was adjacent to the Red Keystone, so he could focus on both at once.

He didn't really know what he was doing, but he concentrated on the violet stone. Some instinct told him to try and build a wash of violet light that would flow over the Red Keystone and push its own light back.

Violet light built and started to bleed into the red of the other Keystone. As it spread, Lokar suddenly stopped singing. She looked up, stretched her hands toward Tal, and cried out.

"Highness! Release me! Release me!"

For the first time that Tal had seen, her Spirit-shadow stopped circling, too. It mirrored Lokar's actions, stretching its paws to the sky.

Violet light washed across them, a broad band against the red. Tal, still not knowing why he did it, directed it to loop behind and underneath Lokar. The light swept around her, and she threw herself into it.

The next thing Tal knew he was knocked to the ground and there was someone lying on his chest. He crawled out and gently helped Lokar up. She sobbed and clutched at him, then turned to run her hands along the stone before embracing her Spirit-shadow.

Out of the Keystone, she was older and smaller than Tal had imagined she'd be. Considerably older than his mother, and only two-thirds his height, she was a tiny, fine-boned woman with short silver hair and piercing brown eyes. She wore the robes of a Brightness of the Red, but had no Sunstone. That had been taken by Sushin when she was first trapped in the Keystone.

Her Spiritshadow was larger than she was. It was a Leaper-beast, in Aenir an inhabitant of swamp-land and marshes. Its bulky triangular body had massive hind legs, powering impressive leaps. Its forearms were smaller, and ended in sharp claws. It also had a long and highly flexible tongue. Leaper-beasts had learned to handle basic tools with their

421

tongues, as well as weapons. They could sling a large stone several hundred stretches, an ability the Spiritshadow form probably retained.

It took Lokar a minute to stop sobbing and regain control. She pressed her palms against her face for a moment, then straightened up and looked at Tal.

"Thank you," she said. She stared around her and added, "I saw the violet light. Where is the Empress?"

Tal bit his lip. Instead of answering, he held up his hand, with his piece of the Violet Keystone shining there.

Lokar looked puzzled, but slowly sank to one knee. She made an instinctive move to give him light, before remembering she had no Sunstone.

"I don't understand," she said. "You are Tal, aren't you? How do you come to wield the Violet Keystone?"

"You'd better stand up — or sit on that stone," Tal said. "It's kind of complicated."

As quickly as he could, he told Lokar everything that had happened since he first fell from the Red Tower. That seemed like a very long time ago.

When he had finished, Lokar looked up at the ceiling and released a long, troubled breath.

"So the Empress is dead," she said. "And Sharrakor effectively rules the Chosen through Sushin. But why has everyone come back before the Day of Dark Return?"

"I think," Tal said cautiously, "that the Icecarls might be doing something. Milla . . . Milla thought they would."

He found it hard to say the Icecarl's name. Upsetting.

"What are you going to do?" asked Lokar.

"Find my mother and give her the antidote," Tal said firmly. "Then I will climb the Orange Tower and release my father from the Keystone there. After that, I will do whatever I can to stop Sharrakor and Sushin, to save the Veil."

Lokar nodded. Then she held out her hand.

"Give me the Red Keystone. It is sealed again now. I will return it to its rightful place in the Red Tower, so it may power the Veil once more. Even if Sharrakor does manage to unseal the other Keystones, or tries to lower the Veil from the Seventh Tower, the Red Keystone will keep it going. A single Stone will keep the Veil up for seven days by itself. That may be enough, some time to buy a chance of reversal."

Tal handed her the Keystone.

"But you won't have a Sunstone once you put it back."

"I might be able to get one on the way," replied Lokar. "But even if I don't, returning the Keystone is the most important thing."

She knelt again before Tal, and gave him light from the Red Keystone, despite his attempts to raise her up.

"Don't kneel to me," he protested. "I should be kneeling to you. You're the Guardian of the Red Keystone."

"And as a Guardian I can see that you are not just the wielder, but the true Guardian of the Violet Keystone," replied Lokar. "Which means you are also Emperor of the Chosen, whether you want to be or not. Wish me light and fortune, Highness."

"Light and fortune," croaked Tal. He was Emperor of the Chosen? The boy who couldn't even get a Sunstone a few months ago?

"Light and fortune to you, Highness. And to us all."

Lokar rose and left, her Spiritshadow hopping after her as Tal stared and stared into space.

"Does that make me Emperor of all Spiritshadows?" asked Adras, who had been very interested in Lokar's obeisance.

"No," replied Tal in a faraway voice. "It doesn't make me Emperor, either, no matter what Lokar says."

He shook his head. Think like an Icecarl, he told himself. The immediate object was to get to his mother. She was probably in his family rooms, but even with all the confusion, Sushin would still make sure Graile was guarded, or there would be traps.

The first thing to do was find another disguise. A mid-ranking Chosen's robes, and he would have to work out how to stop his Sunstone being so obviously violet.

Then he would check to see exactly what was going on, and what all the panic in Aenir and the shouting here was about.

·CHAPTER·
TWENTY-FOUR

Crow was weak, but he had come back to his full senses. Ferek was helping him sip a cup of water, and telling him what had been going on. As Milla approached, Crow gently pushed the water back into Ferek's hands.

"Greetings, Crow," said Milla. She indicated the Icecarl at her right. "This is Shield Mother Saylsen, and I believe you have spoken already to the Crone Malen."

"Greetings, Milla . . . uh, that is War-Chief, and er . . . Shield Mother, and greetings again, Malen," replied Crow. His voice was scratchy, but Milla noticed another change. Crow had always almost snarled at her before, his voice permanently angry. That anger was gone. He simply sounded tired and weak.

"Has Ferek told you that I have come back with my people to put an end to the Chosen's use of Spiritshadows and save the Veil?" asked Milla. "We will help your people, too, if you let us."

"Yes," said Crow. He gave a wry smile. "I will do everything I can to help you, if you help us in return to be truly free. That is, if you don't kill me first."

"Why would we kill you?" asked Milla, puzzled.

"I mean you personally, not the Icecarls," said Crow. He stopped, took the cup from Ferek, and wet his throat before he continued. "I tried to kill your friend Tal and steal the Red Keystone."

Milla shrugged. "I've tried to kill him myself, but he survived."

"I'm serious," Crow protested. He shook his head as if he couldn't believe what he had done. "I just went crazy. I thought we had to have the Red Keystone for ourselves. Tal was a Chosen and he would always side with the Chosen. I hit him on the head, and then I threw my knife at him."

"Did you hit him?" said Milla.

"No," said Crow. "I only got his coat."

"You should practice harder."

"Is that all you have to say? I *really* tried to kill him. For no good reason. I would have gotten Ferek, Inkie, Gill . . . all of us killed if Ebbitt hadn't been there."

"It is for Tal to forgive or punish you," said Milla. She couldn't understand why Crow was so concerned. "And for you to forgive or punish him. It has nothing to do with me."

"I . . . I was rude about you," said Crow. "I insulted you, to Tal."

He looked down, unable to meet her eyes.

"Do you want to fight me?" asked Milla. She was genuinely unable to understand this Freefolk. He had fought Tal and lost, and had nearly been killed. That was all. "Speak your insults again and I will kill you. But if I have not heard them, then it is as if they have never been. They are lost on the wind."

"I don't know," whispered Crow. "I just feel . . . I feel bad."

Now Milla understood. It was the head-wound talking. When it was better, Crow would return to his usual angry self.

"We need you to look at this map," Milla said. She quickly explained what the Icecarls were trying to do, and asked Crow to point out any stairs or entrances from the Chosen levels that they might have missed.

There were quite a few. Milla marked them on her map, and wished for the perfect drawings the Codex could do. If only she'd managed to grab it before.

As each new stair, ramp, or entryway was marked, Milla and Saylsen briefly discussed how to defend or block it. Then Saylsen would send one of her Shield Maidens or hunters off to tell one of the other Shield Mothers to include the new place in her area.

Crow was still going over the map when an Icecarl hunter burst in and came at a run toward Milla, Saylsen, and Malen. When he was a few stretches away, he clapped his fists.

"War-Chief, Shield Mother, I bring word from Shield Mother Kyal," he panted. "The Chosen have attacked. Two tens of them, with shadows, have tried to force the . . . the Red-West Roundway Down."

He stumbled on the strange place-names, but Milla had already found it on her map, her finger stabbing the hide.

"And?" she asked sharply as the hunter took a deep breath.

"We hold it," the Icecarl said proudly. "We have taken four shadows and killed three Chosen. Two of our own are wounded and one slain. Shield Mother Kyal asks for more shadow-bottles and that is all."

Milla looked at Saylsen. She did not know whether there were any such things to spare.

"Go to Anrik, there," snapped out Saylsen,

pointing. "He has four shadow-sacks. Take three. Go!"

The hunter clapped his fists and ran off.

Before anyone had a chance to say anything, another panting runner burst in from one of the closer gateways. Also a hunter, he jumped the last terrace and landed with a clatter of polished shell armor. His breastplate bore the scorch-marks of a Red Ray of Destruction. If he hadn't been wearing it, he would have been cut in half.

"War-Chief! Shield Mother Verik says more than four Hands of Chosen and shadows contest the Underfolk Watercart Ramp. They have broken through the middle gate, but we hold the lower. We need mirror-shields and shadow-sacks!"

Milla shrugged the polished shell shield off her back and gave it to him. He seemed surprised, but took it. Saylsen handed him a shadow-bottle from her own belt.

"That's it! Take them and run!"

Saylsen turned to Milla and Crow. "There were few shadow-sacks and suchlike ready for us to bring through, and I know we will need many, many more. Do you know of any other weapons here we may use against the shadows, Crow?"

Crow shook his head. "Jarnil had some shadow-sacks, like yours," he said. "But I don't know where he got them. I do have a Sunstone I can use, a little."

"As can I," said Milla. "And there is the Talon."

"The War-Chief must not fight, not unless all will be lost," said Saylsen. "The War-Chief must stand apart, for clear thought and direction."

Milla frowned and made a fist.

"That is the Crone's will, too," said Malen. As she spoke, Milla felt the words like an undigested meal in her stomach, heavy and constricting.

"But the battle has only just started, hasn't it?" asked Ferek anxiously. "And we're winning. Aren't we?"

"Yes," said Milla confidently. "We only look to what might need to be done."

Another Icecarl burst in through a different entrance. A Shield Maiden this time. She ran down the terraces and slid to a stop, speaking even as she clapped her fists together.

"War-Chief! Shield Mother Granlee reports many Chosen gathering above the Old Grand Stair. A hundred or more. Some have armor that shines in different colors, and there are many shadows. The Shield Mother says we will die bravely, but that will not be enough. She asks for another Hand or two."

"The Chosen have been much faster than I

thought," said Milla, speaking too quickly, a sure sign of her agitation. She looked at Saylsen and Malen. "A hundred Chosen, and some of them Guards. We can't risk moving any of the other Hands, in case it is just a trick. I must go!"

"No!" said Malen. The single word gripped Milla in the stomach like a vicious cramp. "It is not safe for you! Send the others, but you must stay!"

"War is not safe," snarled Saylsen angrily. "You must let the War-Chief decide for herself, Crone."

Malen looked worried. She held a hand to her temples.

"I will ask the Crone Mother. Can everyone just be quiet!"

"There is no time to ask the Crone Mother," Milla said quietly. "I *am* War-Chief of the Icecarls, Malen. I wear the Talon of Danir. Our people will not die needlessly because I would not stand with them. I *will* go."

Malen kept her hand to her temple. Her eyes began to cloud.

Milla ignored the pain in her middle and started to walk away. Saylsen walked with her, summoning her Hand with a wave. Jarek and Kirr were the first to join them, falling in behind with a passing clap of their fists.

Milla kept walking, though the pain was a fire inside her. She heard the mighty Crone voice, too, echoing inside her head. Next to her, but far enough to be out of reach of the Talon, Odris staggered through the air, clutching her stomach and her head.

Every step was agony. But Milla was too proud to give in. The Crones had decided her fate. They had laid a great task upon her. It was not a task she could complete if they tried to control everything she did from far away.

She took another step, and another. Sweat poured from her face and her skin went whiter than the purest snow. But she was almost at her limit of pain and strength. Another few steps and she would fall.

She lifted her foot and slid it forward. As the pain increased, and the great Crone voice inside her head crescendoed, she heard Malen's soft voice cut through pain and noise.

"Go, War-Chief. The Crones say you are free. Free to fight as you think best."

·CHAPTER·
TWENTY–FIVE

In the same laundry holding area he'd used before, Tal found the robes of a Brightstar of the Yellow Order. After he changed into them, he added a bandage around his head. That would not be seen as too unusual right at the moment, Tal thought, as he listened to the continued shouting and the distant sound of what had to be fighting echoing up the laundry chute.

Adras was disguised, too. Tal helped him take on the appearance of a slightly malnourished Borzog, pulling at the Spiritshadow's shoulders and arms. Eventually Adras had the shape almost right.

The Violet Keystone took a little more work to camouflage. It simply didn't want to change color, and Tal had to use all his willpower to get it to revert to its former colors. Eventually he managed it, and it stayed yellow with flecks of red.

He was also pleased to find a packet of dried shrimps in another set of robes. While there was no real need to eat in Aenir, he couldn't remember when he'd last eaten in his normal body. The shrimps went down in a few quick gulps, accompanied by a long drink of water from the prewashing sink used by the Underfolk laundry people.

Disguised, and fortified with food, Tal ventured out into the main Yellow levels. Chosen were hurrying everywhere, yelling and carrying on, and there were a few Underfolk trying to go about their business. Tal kept his head down and walked slowly, as if he were injured.

It took Tal a while to realize that he was going against the tide of traffic. He was headed down to the Orange levels. Most of the Chosen were heading up, many of them with their Spiritshadows carrying their valuables, children behind them with their shadowguards carrying their toys and keepsakes.

But not all Chosen were fleeing what Tal guessed was a battle with the Icecarls. He had to press himself against the wall of a colorless through-corridor as a disciplined troop of Guards jogged past, side by side with their thin-waisted Spiritshadows. Behind them hurried twenty or thirty determined-looking Chosen of all Orders, Red to Violet, carrying improvised weapons and many Sunstones. Their Spiritshadows danced around them, up and down the walls and across the ceiling. Tal checked them out from the corner of his eye, but couldn't see any extras. So far the free Spiritshadows in the Castle seemed to be biding their time.

As the Guards went past, Tal took the opportunity to slide along to another Chosen, a Brightblinder of the Blue, who had also moved out of the way.

"What is the news?" asked Tal. He didn't bother to give light in respect. Nobody else was, either. Proper courtesy seemed to be the first thing to go.

"The same as before," remarked the Chosen. "Vicious monsters in the lower levels, with white faces. The Guards will sort them out."

He said the last without absolute confidence.

"What of the Empress?" asked Tal.

The Brightblinder stared at him without comprehension.

"She has announced that the weapons of the Seventh Tower will be used against the invaders," he said. "Is that what you mean?"

"No," said Tal. What were the weapons of the Seventh Tower? "No. I heard she was . . . I heard she was sick."

The Brightblinder shook his head. "I've heard all sorts of things today, but nothing as stupid as that. Hold! Where are you going?"

Tal had started to edge away, to follow the Guards.

"That's not the way, Brightstar! Hasn't your Lumenor told you where to report? We're clearing out everything from Indigo down!"

Tal didn't answer. He tried to look vacant and staggered across the traffic, which had resumed going the other way. He earned some angry cries, but by the time he'd threaded his way through, the Brightblinder was lost in the sea of fleeing Chosen.

After that, Tal took lesser-known ways down to the Orange levels. The Brightblinder had obviously known what he was talking about, as the lower Tal went, the more deserted it was. There were still Guards and irregular groups of Chosen with them heading down, but Tal stayed out of their way or pretended to be resting before continuing on up. In any case they were always in too much of a hurry to pay any attention to him.

Finally, he came to the familiar Orange levels that had been home for most of his life. They did not feel like home now. Tal realized he didn't really feel like a Chosen anymore, either. Certainly he had no desire either to join those fleeing upward, or the fighters heading down.

At the corner of the corridor that led to his family's rooms, Tal paused. He looked down it and saw the familiar door with his family's sigil. The orange Sthil-beast leaping over a seven-pointed star.

His eyes misted as he remembered rushing home when he first got the news of his father's disappearance. He had tried not to cry then, not wanting anyone to see his sorrow and fear. Sushin had been waiting inside.

It was unlikely Sushin was waiting inside now, not with the Icecarls attacking. But Tal was sure he would have left traps, and perhaps free shadows, to guard Graile. He had almost caught Tal before in a similar way, by using his brother, Gref, as bait.

"You see the door with the Sthil-beast?" Tal whispered to Adras. "Can you slide under and have a look around? Be careful. There might be traps, or enemies."

"Adras will break traps and tear enemies into three," declared the Spiritshadow.

"In half, I think you mean," corrected Tal.

"No, three. One piece left, one piece right, one

piece to trample on," said Adras. "It is the Storm Shepherd way. That's what Odris is doing now."

"Odris?" asked Tal. His voice sort of squeaked, in either nervousness or excitement. "She's in the Castle?"

Adras nodded and pointed one massive thumb at the floor.

"Down below. Fighting. I hear the wind tell me."

"And Milla?" Tal asked eagerly. "Is she still alive?"

"Don't know," said Adras. "Wind speaks only of Odris. But wind would not know Milla anyway."

"Maybe Milla's showing the Icecarls the way in," Tal said quietly. "They would need a guide, and she's the obvious choice. Maybe they wouldn't let her go to the Ice because she was needed."

Adras shrugged. He didn't know. He was happy to know Odris was close. He would see her soon.

Tal felt happier, too. He'd never really believed that Milla was dead, but he'd feared that she was. But if Odris was here, and fighting with the Icecarls . . .

"Do I go now?" interrupted Adras.

"Yes, yes!" said Tal. "But be careful. Unlock the door if it's locked, and don't touch anything suspicious."

Adras drifted down the corridor. Tal watched

anxiously as he slid under the door, every sense alert. But he didn't hear anything, and there was no sign of any alarm or trap.

Minutes passed. Adras did not return. Tal stayed crouched at the corner, tension mounting inside him. What had happened to the Spiritshadow?

Another minute passed. Tal stood up, crouched down, stood up again.

Another minute passed. Tal pushed his Sunstone ring up and down his finger nervously. Surely Adras would have opened the door by now? Something must have gone wrong.

Tal started to sneak along the corridor, his Sunstone hand held ready. Red light started to billow to the surface of the stone, as Tal prepared a Red Ray of Destruction.

He was almost at the door when it suddenly swung open. For a split second, Tal was about to fire the Red Ray at whatever came out. But he didn't, because it was Adras.

"What are you waiting for?" asked the Spiritshadow. "I unlocked the door ages ago. There's no one here anyway. Just one of your lot, sound asleep in a funny hot room at the back."

"That's not 'one of my lot,'" Tal said angrily. "That's my mother!"

·CHAPTER·
TWENTY-SIX

Milla danced a dance of death, the Talon's whip of light weaving around her like a razor-sharp ribbon. She mowed through the ranks of attacking Spiritshadows like a Merwin through a half-asleep herd of Wreska.

As the Talon cut, sliced, and choked through the Spiritshadows, it also deflected the rays of light and other magics that were sent against the War-Chief of the Icecarls. But quick as it was, faster than a Fleamite, the Talon could not fully deflect every Red Ray or Blue Burst the Chosen was firing from their makeshift barricade higher up the wide reaches of the Old Grand Stair.

Red light struck and Milla was lightly burned across both arms. But she did not fall back until the Spiritshadows were in full retreat. Even then, the

Talon tried to lash out behind Milla, and she only just managed to turn it aside as Odris grabbed her and dragged her back behind the Icecarls' own wall of partially reflective crystal panels, stacked against a breastwork of barrels, boxes, and anything else they could drag up from the Underfolk level at the end of the stair.

As Odris dragged Milla away, several Shield Maidens paused in their own retreat to raise their mirror-shields to guard the War-Chief. They did it not a moment too soon, as more Red Rays and an Indigo Cutter zapped down, blowing chips of stone out of the steps as they were deflected by the shields.

Momentarily safe behind the barricade, Milla and Odris hunkered down as about a dozen hunters stood up and hurled their glowing spears at the last few Spiritshadows.

Saylsen crept up to them, her head just below the level of the barricade. More Red Rays crisscrossed overhead as she approached.

"Well done, War-Chief!" exclaimed the old Shield Mother. "If only the cowards themselves would attack, instead of sending their shadows! Then we would show them!"

Milla set her teeth for a moment, as she began to feel the pain from her burns.

"They show good sense," she said grimly. "The Spiritshadows do not die easily, and their Chosen masters will survive their pain. I wish that we had Spiritshadows to die for us."

She looked around. They had been fighting on the stair for almost a Chosen hour by her Sunstone, and there had been many deaths and many wounded among the Icecarls.

"There is no honor here," Milla added. It was not like the old stories and legends. "There is only foul and unpleasant work that must be done."

She saw Malen tending to a dying Shield Maiden, and crawled down to her.

"What news of the main host?" asked Milla.

Malen shook her head. Her hands were shaking, Milla saw.

"I . . . I don't know," Malen whispered. "I can't hear them in the middle of this. I can't hear them!"

"It doesn't matter," Milla calmed her. "Just do what you can for the wounded. I've sent runners back. They will bring up the others when they come."

When they come, Milla thought. She hoped it would be soon enough. Even with the Talon, there was a limit to how many Spiritshadows they could stop. There had been six assaults so far down the stairs. Each time there had been more Spiritshadows, and each time they had been barely thrown back.

Milla looked across at the end of the barricade, where there was a considerable space after the main body of defenders. Everywhere else the line was packed tight with Shield Maidens and hunters, staying low until they had to confront the next attack.

The reason for the space was immediately clear. Jarek was there, staring through a slight gap between two panes of crystal. His vast blue-stained chest was rising and falling like a bellows, and he held his great chain of gold metal taut between two huge fists. Kirr was stroking the back of his neck and whispering in his ear. She had managed to get him to come back after each attack, a feat Milla would have believed impossible after seeing his intense rage and the carnage he wreaked among the Spiritshadows with his chain. The golden metal, like certain types of light, was all too solid to Spiritshadows.

As Milla watched, a Red Ray drilled through the gap and struck Jarek on the chest. Anyone else would have been killed instantly, but his skin, soaked in Norrworm blood, reflected the ray. It hit a barrel and sliced away a long wooden splinter.

The splinter flew through the air with an awful whir, and went straight into Kirr.

The Shield Maiden fell without a sound, crumpled over the next lower step. Milla ran to her, as fast as she could without exposing herself. Malen followed, her slim medicine pack in hand.

Even before they got there, they knew nothing could be done. The splinter was as long as an arrow, and by terrible mischance it had struck Kirr under the arm, where she had no armor.

Jarek looked down at his partner and touched her gently on the back. When she did not move, he rolled her over. Milla and Malen froze, seeing the madness in his eyes.

Jarek put Kirr down again. His head went back, and he gave the most terrible howl anyone had ever heard, Icecarl or Chosen. It was louder and fiercer than a Merwin's screech, deeper than the distant rumble of the Selski.

Time stood still. Even the Chosen stopped firing Red Rays over the barricade.

Jarek rose up and smashed his way through the barricade, whirling the great chain above his head. The awful howl continued, far longer than anyone's lungs could have sustained it.

Red Rays flashed and played across his body, but

he did not fall back. A Blue Burst broke over him, but he did not falter.

Milla didn't need to think twice.

"Attack!" she yelled. "For Kirr! Attack!"

In an instant, every Icecarl was up, including many wounded. The barricade was pushed aside or jumped or bulled through, as every Shield Maiden and hunter stormed up the stairs in the wake of the Wilder Jarek's chain and War-Chief Milla's terrible Talon.

·CHAPTER·
TWENTY-SEVEN

Tal advanced into the antechamber cautiously. Despite Adras's complacency, he was sure there was a trap. There was no way Sushin would have left Graile unguarded.

But he couldn't see anything. There were no strange Sunstones in the walls or ceiling. No shadows moving where they shouldn't be, no odd patches of darkness.

He checked the door to the sunroom. Adras had opened it, and it, too, seemed innocuous.

Tal edged through the doorway, ready for anything. As always, the heat hit him, and the humidity. The sunroom's walls and ceiling were covered in tiny Sunstones that constantly emitted light and heat. The humidity was explained by an onion-shaped dome in the corner, pricked with thousands of tiny holes that had steam wafting out of them. It was directly connected to one of the lesser steam pipes of the Castle.

Graile was lying on the bed, not moving. Tal felt a sharp pain in his chest as he saw her. She looked so gray and wasted. For a panicked second he couldn't see her Spiritshadow, then he spotted it under the bed. It, too, had faded, and was now only a sad remnant of the great shadow owl it had once been.

Tal stood absolutely still, looking at his sick mother. Was it water-spider venom that had made her like this? Water-spider venom given to her by Sushin? Or was it something else, something that the antidote he now clutched in his hand would be useless against?

Tal took a deep breath and knelt down by the bed. He opened the vial of antidote, then gently lifted Graile's head, supporting her neck. She was breathing very, very slowly and infrequently, and she did not respond to his touch. Her skin was also very, very cold.

Tal poured the antidote into her mouth, closed it, pinched her nose, and shook her a little.

For a few seconds nothing happened. Then she suddenly coughed, an explosive cough that almost made Tal let go of her. He did release his pinch on her nose.

She coughed again, a racking cough that shook her whole body. Then her eyes opened. She couldn't focus at first.

Tal eased her head back onto the pillows. Her eyes grew sharp, and she smiled at him as he plumped up her pillows.

"Tal," she whispered. "You've grown."

Tal smiled back, and a single tear slid down his cheek. He wiped it away as Graile saw the ring upon his hand.

"You've got a Sunstone," she added, her voice so faint Tal could hardly hear. "A Primary Sunstone. We will be able to go to Aenir."

Her own Sunstone lay on her chest, suspended on a silver chain. It barely sparked. Tal wondered what Sushin had done to it.

"It's a bit more complicated than that, Mother," Tal said hastily. He looked around. He knew Sushin must have trapped the room somehow. "A lot has happened. A real lot. We have to get away from here, for a start."

Graile nodded, but when she tried to get up it was obviously beyond her. Her Spiritshadow, which was also looking a little better, tried to help her, but it still had no strength.

"Adras will carry you," said Tal. "My Spiritshadow. Adras!"

"Your Spiritshadow!" echoed Graile. She smiled again. "A lot has happened."

"Adras!"

Adras came back into the room. He was holding a tiny, squirming fleck of shadow in two fingers.

"Look what I found. There were lots of them, but the others got away."

Tal stared at the tiny wriggling thing. It was the smallest Spiritshadow he had ever seen. He couldn't even clearly see what it was.

"It's the Spiritshadow of a Frox," explained Adras kindly. "This is what a swarm's made out of."

"It's speaking aloud," said Graile faintly. Tal thought she meant the Frox, until he realized she meant Adras. Chosen Spiritshadows never spoke in public. Only to their masters, in private.

"Adras is different," said Tal quickly. The Frox that got away were probably reporting to someone right now. They had to move quickly.

"Adras, please pick up my mother carefully," he said. "Her name is Graile. You must protect her as if she were me."

"Sure," boomed Adras. He bent over the bed and easily picked up both Graile and her Spiritshadow, which jumped onto her stomach at the last moment. In full health, the great owl was normally the same size as Tal. But it had withered to less than a third of his height.

"Where are we going?" whispered Graile. "How did you wake me?"

"You've been poisoned with water-spider venom," explained Tal quickly as he led the way out. "I got an antidote from . . . from Ebbitt . . . um . . . I'll explain . . . that is . . ."

A sound from beyond the outer door saved him. Footsteps.

Tal raised his Sunstone. All his anxiety and fear for his mother flowed into it. The stone took it in as raw power, and instantly shed its disguise.

Violet light filled the room. Graile let out a shocked cry.

"Violet!"

Tal cursed.

Someone tried the door.

"Back!" Tal whispered. They retreated swiftly back. Tal paused at the sunroom door, keeping it open a fraction. His Sunstone, now a vivid violet, shone ready. Once again, Tal didn't have a particular Light spell ready. Just a violent anger that he let build in the Sunstone.

The outer door opened. Two Guards crept in. They had their swords and Sunstones ready.

Sushin was behind them, his great bulk filling the door. He was wearing the robes of a Violet Shadowlord openly, and had even more Sunstones on his hands and body than ever before.

Tal didn't wait. He directed all his hatred through the Sunstone and out toward the three Chosen.

A terrible blast of raw violet light flew across the room. It blew furniture to pieces, picked up the Guards, and hurled them out into the corridor.

The blast sent Sushin reeling back, his Sunstones flashing as they absorbed the shock. Before Tal could loose another blast, Sushin threw something at him. A ball, about the size of a juice-fruit.

It hit Tal on the chest, and exploded everywhere exactly like a juice-fruit. Water flew up in Tal's face and dripped down his chin. But water tainted with something, something that smelled horrible and familiar. Tal couldn't place it for a moment. Then he knew.

It was spider venom!

A second later, Tal felt it flow through his veins. It might be slower than when it was injected by a spider, but he probably had less than a minute before he would be unconscious.

He slammed the door and staggered back. Adras was putting Graile down on the bed, the big Spirit-shadow already yawning.

"Mother!" Tal said, forcing the words out against the darkness that was descending inside his head. "Pretend to be sick still. When you can, go down to the Underfolk levels. Tell the Icecarls you're Tal's mother. Tell them to take you to Milla, if she lives. Tell her Lokar is released. Take the violet half . . ."

He tried to slip the Sunstone from his finger, but it was already too late. It was on too tight, and there was no strength in his hands. Then he remembered the last vial of antidote, still tied into his shirt.

Weakening fingers fumbled at the knot.

He almost had it undone when darkness claimed him.

THE VIOLET
KEYSTONE

·CHAPTER·
☉ΠE

Tal returned to consciousness in slow stages. The first stage only lasted a few seconds. He felt himself being carried upside down, his face almost scraping the floor. Then he blacked out again. The next time he came to, he tried to move his hands and couldn't, because they were tied behind his back. He was sick and threw up. Someone cried out in disgust and hit him, bringing the darkness back.

The third time he regained consciousness, it took Tal quite a while to work out where he was. It was still dark, but not the total darkness of the Ice outside the Castle. There was light not too far away, the constant light of a Sunstone. His arms were no longer tied, but when Tal reached out, he hit something. He tried to stand up and smacked his head. He tried to stretch his legs and couldn't.

Hunched over, Tal felt above his head. His hands slid across smooth crystal, a downward arc.

He was inside a globe. A crystal globe.

There was only one such globe that Tal knew of. He felt fear grab at his stomach and send a shiver down his back.

He was trapped in the punishment globe in the Hall of Nightmares.

Slowly Tal's eyes adapted to the dim light. He could see the outline of the globe around him. Beyond were the silver stands that held the Sunstones that powered the nightmare machine. Those Sunstones were dark now, the machine silent.

Tal heard a door scrape open. A single light flowered in the distance and grew bright. It came from a Sunstone — a Sunstone held in the hand of a man who was feared by all the Chosen, a man whose name was used by parents to threaten rebellious children.

Fashnek.

Half-man, half-shadow. Master of the Hall of Nightmares. A tall, almost skeletally thin man, his long black hair hung in unkempt tendrils on either side of his face. From his left shoulder down to his left hip, Fashnek was made of shadow. Long ago something had bitten away his arm and a good portion of his chest and stomach. He had been kept alive by his Spiritshadow, which had melded itself to his living flesh. Perhaps the result would have been bearable if the Spiritshadow had been vaguely humanoid. But it was not. It was a giant Aeniran insect, with six multijointed legs and a repulsive, elongated head that ended in a ring-shaped mouth, unpleasantly like a leech's.

Fashnek's walk was half a limp and half a slither. Two other Spiritshadows accompanied him, a few paces behind. They had to be free Spiritshadows — supposedly forbidden in the Castle — for there was no sign of their Chosen masters.

One was an Urglegurgle, a creature that resembled a giant upside-down mushroom. It bounced from side to side, occasionally tumbling completely over and snapping its disklike body together. In Aenir, Urglegurgles dug themselves into soft ground and bounced out upon their prey, completely closing over it, the central "stalk" spraying intensely concentrated acids upon its food. As a Spiritshadow, that stalk might spray a corrosive shadow.

The other Spiritshadow was one of the narrow-waisted, broad-shouldered humanoid creatures favored by the Empress's Guards. Tal didn't know what they were called.

Fashnek stumbled as he approached the globe that held Tal. Both his human hand and his insectoid shadow pincer grabbed at one of the dream machines, only just arresting his fall. Angrily, Fashnek hauled himself upright and flailed at the Spiritshadows.

"Be careful!" he shouted. "Keep your distance!"

The Spiritshadows retreated a little, even though it had clearly not been their fault.

Tal lay still. The Sunstones around the globe slowly sparked into life, triggered by Fashnek's arrival. The Chosen boy felt sick and disoriented. How had he ended up here?

Slowly he remembered. It was like putting the last few pieces of a light-puzzle together, to trigger the moving image. He had come back from Aenir. The Violet Keystone . . . Tal surreptitiously looked at his hand. His half of the Violet Keystone was gone. But had Sushin taken it, or had Graile — Tal's mother — somehow managed to get it? He remembered the ball of water-spider poison Sushin had thrown at him. Tal had said something to Graile then. But what? Had she managed to pretend she was still in a coma?

Someone must have given him the antidote to the

water-spider poison, though, or he would still be unconscious. Or perhaps the poison was weaker when it wasn't injected by a spider's hollow fangs.

Fashnek stopped, clattering into one of the Sunstone stands. He was either drunk or very nervous, Tal realized. This gave him some heart. Surely if his jailer was nervous that was good news for him.

Fashnek kept looking over his right shoulder, the human one. His nervousness was contagious, too. The Spiritshadows kept looking back toward the door.

Tal kept his eyes narrowed to slits so he looked like he was still unconscious. He desperately wanted to look around, because he could feel his own Spiritshadow — Adras — somewhere nearby. But that would not be wise. Better to lie still and hope for the chance to surprise Fashnek.

There was a knock at the door. Fashnek jumped, and the two Spiritshadows rushed back toward the sound. The door opened before they could get there, and a Chosen guard stepped in, his Spiritshadow close behind him.

"What news?" shouted Fashnek, almost toppling over as he swung around.

"The enemy is in the Red levels, but we are holding them there," said the guard confidently. "Sushin wants to know what you have learned from the boy about these . . . Icecarls. We need to know their weaknesses and how to recognize their leaders."

"I . . . I have not yet begun," answered Fashnek. "It is not easy. . . ."

"Hurry, then," said the guard. "The Most Violet Sushin desires a report from you within the hour."

With that, the guard turned and left the Hall, slamming the door behind him.

"Most Violet? Most Violet?" muttered Fashnek. "Now is not the time to take on such titles."

Tal watched as Fashnek hobbled closer to the globe, his human hand fumbling to draw a Sunstone out of the pouch he wore at his waist. So Sushin had declared himself *Most Violet*. That had to be a step toward letting the Chosen know the Empress was dead and declaring himself Emperor. Perhaps Sushin needed to do that in order to wield the Violet Keystone, the Keystone he would use to deactivate the Veil that protected the whole world from the Sun — and from the Aeniran shadows who Sushin ultimately served.

Tal had to stop Sushin. He almost laughed at himself as that thought struck home. Here he was trapped inside a crystal globe in the Hall of Nightmares and his overriding emotion was not fear but cold rage, a desire to escape and take on Sushin; his master, the Spiritshadow Sharrakor; and all the shadows of Aenir.

Fashnek moved one of the Sunstone stands. The stands ran on rails set into the floor, so they could be slid into different positions. Tal stared at the stones as Fashnek moved the stands closer. He could feel the power of the Sunstones deep inside himself, in a way he had never felt before. Tal recognized the unusual nature of these Sunstones, which had been so ill-used for so long. They were tainted with nightmares, fear, and pain. But he could use them for a while.

It was like a sixth sense. He knew he could reach out to them mentally and try to take control of their power.

Controlling distant Sunstones was the highest feat of Chosen Light Magic. Controlling someone else's stones was unheard of. But Tal knew he could do it. After all, even though the Violet Keystone had been taken from him, wasn't he the newly anointed Emperor of the Chosen, even if it was only in name?

Tal focused on the nearest stone. He would make it pulse, just to know he had control. He felt its steady blue light, reached out to it with his mind, and . . .

It pulsed. Once . . . twice . . . three times.

Now he knew he could wrest control of the stones and release himself. He remembered the light sequence Ebbitt had used to release Milla. All he had to do was reach out now to the other stones. Adras was somewhere close. With his help, and the element of surprise, Tal could take on Fashnek and the Spiritshadows.

Tal sighed in relief.

That was a mistake. Fashnek looked quickly over, and his human hand shot to a small bronze wheel set in the side of one of the dream machines. The wheel spun easily.

There was a hissing noise at Tal's feet and he smelled something sweet and sickly. He remembered what Milla had told him of her experience in the crystal globe.

Knockout gas!

Sure enough, a thick green gas had begun to waft about his feet. Tal held his breath and concentrated fiercely on the Sunstones. First one, then another came under his control. Sweat broke out on his face as he held them, changed their color, and moved on. Three Sunstones . . . four Sunstones . . . there were seven needed to release him.

Tal's lungs hurt. He desperately needed to

breathe. Five Sunstones, their colors winking. Fashnek was turning the wheel madly, and more gas was
flooding in. The Spiritshadows were closing, circling the globe.

Six Sunstones. Tal reached for the seventh. There
was a terrible, stabbing pain in his head. He gasped
with the pain and took in a breath.

For a fraction of a second, all seven Sunstones
were under Tal's control. But the colors were
wrong, and in that single second, the gas did its
work.

Tal slumped to the bottom of the crystal globe.
The seven Sunstones changed back to their normal
colors.

Fashnek wiped a sheen of sweat from his forehead with his good hand and looked in every direction, as if seeking some escape. But there was no
escape. Sushin demanded answers, and there was
only one way Fashnek could get them.

Slowly he approached the crystal globe, a Sunstone held high in his right hand while the shadow
pincer that took the place of his left arm slid
through the crystal. Fashnek hesitated for another
few moments, the Spiritshadows beside him moving
restlessly. Then his shadow pincer moved again and
cupped Tal's head.

·CHAPTER·
TWO ☉

Milla Talon-Hand, War-Chief of the Ice-carls, let her hand fall wearily to her side. The Talon of Danir she wore on one finger, which had only moments ago lopped the head off a Spiritshadow, shrank back to the size of a long nail. Only the glitter of light in its crystal shape hinted at its temporarily dormant powers.

"They have fallen back, at least for a time," reported Saylsen, the senior Shield Mother. She lifted her face mask to speak, revealing a scarred and battered face and eyes that had seen thirty or forty circlings of battle out upon the Ice. But nothing she had seen before had equipped her for fighting in the Castle of the Chosen, where their enemies wielded Light Magic and Spiritshadows stalked through floors and walls and doors. "What is the War-Chief's will?"

Milla looked around at her exhausted and diminished band. It included her own Spiritshadow, Odris, a unique companion for an Icecarl. As usual, Odris was keeping her distance from the shadow-slaying Talon on Milla's hand. Then there were Shield Maidens and Icecarl hunters, and the seemingly unkillable Sword Thane Jarek the Wilder, a berserk warrior whose skin was bright blue. The color came from soaking in Norrworm blood, which had transformed his skin into something tougher than Selski armor, save for an irregular patch around his eyes, nose, and mouth. Jarek was shirtless, his trousers another sign of his victory over Norrworms, since they were made of the creatures' scaly skin. His chosen weapon was a chain of golden metal that he wore twined around his waist when it was not in his hand.

He was sitting cross-legged and blank-eyed now, in the aftermath of his battle fury. It had left as rapidly as it had come, or he would still be chasing Chosen. Jarek was scratched and burned in a dozen places, particularly around his face. The Chosen had eventually realized they would have to put a

469

Red Ray of Destruction through an eye or his open mouth to kill him.

It was Jarek who had gotten them into their current predicament, though Milla had seen it as an opportunity at the time. After his companion, Kirr, had been slain, Jarek had led them all in a mad charge up the Grand Stair, his swinging golden chain smashing anyone who resisted into pulp, whether they be flesh or shadow. Chosen and Spiritshadows alike had fled before him, and from Milla and all the Icecarls who came charging up behind her.

They had cleared the stairway in one frenzied charge and kept on going out into a large chamber. But there the charge had faltered. Chosen reinforcements poured in from the higher levels, including many Spiritshadows and guards who were accomplished at the more destructive light spells.

Attacked on three sides by a fusillade of Red Rays and other light magic, Milla had ordered a retreat, only to find her small force cut off from the Grand Stair by a large group of Chosen, who had used their superior knowledge of the Castle's many hidden ways to get behind the intruders. Unable to go down, Milla had led the way into the Underfolk corridors, a maze of smaller passages that allowed

470

the Chosen's servants to move through the Castle without disturbing their masters.

But the Chosen had followed, and every turn Milla took it seemed they were there ahead of her. More and more Chosen and more Spiritshadows, steadily boxing them in. Milla had tried to break out through the weakest-looking bunch, but there were too many of them and they were too quickly reinforced. Milla alone, with the Talon, might have been able to fight her way through, but only at the cost of all her people.

"We'll stand here," answered Milla to Saylsen. *Here* was a large Underfolk storage chamber, a rough-hewn cavern easily two hundred stretches in diameter, with a very high ceiling. It had five doors of varying sizes, all of them now spiked shut by the Icecarls. Milla knew there were Chosen behind each exit. The doors wouldn't stop Spiritshadows, or hold the Chosen if they blasted through.

There was no choice but to make a stand.

"We will build a ship-fort here," Milla continued, indicating the barrels and full sacks that lined the walls. "We will hold it until the main host relieves us."

Saylsen nodded and immediately started to shout orders to the Icecarls. Milla counted them quickly as they ran to roll barrels together and build walls with the sacks. One sack spilled open, showering an Icecarl with an avalanche of shiny black seed-pods. It distracted Milla from her count for a second, but there were too few survivors for her to need to recount. Fourteen in total. Herself, Odris, Saylsen, Jarek, the Crone Malen, five Shield Maidens, and four Icecarl hunters.

Malen was standing alone, completely still, her hands cupped to her temples. Milla knew she was trying to make contact with the other Crones. Young and relatively inexperienced, Malen had found she could not reach the strange group mind of the Crones unless she was calm and silent, the absolute opposite of being in a battle.

Being unable to communicate with the Crones via Malen meant that Milla had no idea where the main host was. They might still be on the Mountain of Light, or even now they could be advancing up through the Underfolk levels. Similarly, Milla didn't know how the rest of her advance guard was faring, spread out as it was through the Underfolk levels. In retrospect, it had been a big mistake to go charging up the Grand Stair. Or at least to keep on charging after they had initially beaten the enemy away.

It was a mistake that Milla would probably pay for with her life, and the lives of everyone she led.

Malen dropped her hands, but even before she asked, Milla knew that the Crone had not been successful. It was evident in her face and defeated posture.

"News?"

Malen shook her head. There were tears in the corners of her eyes, not of sorrow, but of fierce concentration.

"I cannot still my thoughts," Malen said. "It is the first lesson of the Crones, but I have lost it. . . . I had not thought I could."

She drew herself up and clapped her fists together before continuing.

"I have failed you, War-Chief," she said. "If we should survive this battle, I will ask leave to go to the Ice."

Milla frowned. Was this how she had seemed to the Crones herself? A proud young Icecarl demanding death upon the Ice rather than facing up to the problems that confronted her?

"That will not be necessary," Milla said sharply. "You have not failed me or any of us. Crones do not go to battle, and I expect this is why. I am sure you will hear the Crones again. For now, I think we should both start shifting barrels. The Chosen will attack soon enough."

Malen clapped her fists together again, but Milla was not fooled. She knew that look. Malen *would* ask to go to the Ice. Well, that was a problem for later, Milla thought. There was only a small chance they would get out of here alive anyway. She turned her back on the Crone and went to help a pair of Shield Maidens wrestle a particularly large and sloshing barrel over to join their rapidly rising fort in the center of the cavern.

·CHAPTER·
THREE

Tal opened his eyes. The crystal globe was gone. He was lying on the floor somewhere, and there was a voice droning on in the distance. Tal sat up and saw that he was in the Senior Lectorium, up on the last tier of the auditorium, between two desks. The Lectorium was empty, save for himself and the Lector, who was speaking from the central pulpit.

It was Lector Roum, Tal's chief teacher. A tall and solidly built Chosen, a Brightstar of the Blue, and so proud of it he dyed his beard blue and wore tiny Sunstones woven into it.

"Your father is missing, believed to be dead," Lector Roum suddenly roared, pointing his finger at Tal.

As the Lector's shout echoed through the Lectorium, his skin split apart like a fresh fruit, revealing a Spiritshadow within — a huge Spiritshadow, a formless mass of darkness that kept spilling out of the Lector's body. It was a black tide, unstoppable, implacable, flowing up the tiers, reaching hungrily for Tal.

He turned to flee, took one step, and was suddenly stepping off one of the golden rods that suspended the Sunstone nets high above in the Red Tower. Stepping off into thin air.

Tal screamed and tried to grab something, his arms and legs flailing as he fell.

It was only then that he realized he was awake inside a dream. No, not a dream.

A nightmare.

Tal closed his eyes and the scream faded away. He still felt as if he were falling, and it was as cold as it had been when he really fell from the Red Tower. His shadowguard had saved him then. Perhaps that was what would happen in this nightmare.

Then he hit something. Tal opened his eyes to find that he was not falling anymore. He was floating in the reservoir beneath the Castle. The reservoir that was home to the water-spiders.

Desperately, Tal started swimming. But he didn't know what he was swimming toward. Unlike the real reservoir, this one was well lit, with an even white light that extended as far as he could see.

He couldn't see any water-spiders at first, but then in between two blinks of an eye, they were all around him. Huge, bulbous-bodied spiders, scurrying across the surface of the water. Their multifaceted eyes were glowing like Sunstones. Venom dripped from their fangs.

If they killed him in a dream, would he die for real?

"It's only a dream!" Tal shouted in panic. "It's only a dream!"

The water-spiders scurried closer. They were bigger than the real ones. They grew as they approached, getting larger and larger, their fangs sharper and longer, dripping with more poison.

Desperately Tal tried to remember what Milla had done to survive the nightmare machine. She had practiced her Rovkir breathing, he knew, a form of deep meditation. But he didn't know how to do that.

What he did know, he realized, was the deep concentration of Light Magic. Perhaps if he lost himself in that, it would have the same effect.

Tal shut his eyes and concentrated. He felt inside

himself for the deep, pure Violet of the Seventh and most important Keystone. He willed the light to fill his mind, to infuse his entire body. He used the Violet to force back all thoughts of water-spiders, one-eyed Merwin, Sushin, Sharrakor, and other horrors that might be summoned into his dreams. Worst of all was that awful moment when he'd brought the ceiling down, killing Crow, Ebbitt, and the others. He had to stop that nightmare somehow.

There was Violet. Only Violet. Nothing else existed.

Yet there was still one tiny part of his mind that kept screaming, one small remnant that screamed on and on, flinching with every second as it expected the stab of a spider's fangs, the pain of flowing poison. . . .

But no stabbing pain came. Violet light filled Tal's body. He felt calm and secure. Soon even the slightest remaining fear was banished. He was Emperor, wielder of the Violet Keystone. He was in command.

Tal opened his eyes. There was a violet glow all around him, but beyond that, there was nothing. He was floating in nothingness, in darkness. He could feel no breath of wind, no ground beneath him. He was somewhere beyond the reach of the nightmares, but beyond everything else as well.

For a moment, Tal almost panicked. But the violet glow fought against that. It lent him confidence, bathed him in self-assurance. He would find the way out. He must.

The Crones, thought Tal. The Crones had come to Milla and helped her out of the nightmare. Tal would have to call them.

But how? Unlike Milla, he had not been trained to call the Crones into his nightmares. It was a skill all Icecarl children were taught, but Tal was a Chosen.

Tal did have one link with the Icecarls. He bared his wrist, looking at the triangular scar there, the mark of his oath. The cuts had healed well but were still very obvious, thin lines of raised scar tissue. Tal had thought the Crone crazy at the time, to cut him so dangerously. But he had grown used to the scars in time, and even to the idea that they linked him to Milla and the Clan of the Far-Raiders.

Tal rested two fingers across the scar. He tried to remember the feel of the bone ship's deck, the freezing wind, the humming of the rigging of the iceship, the clap of the sails. He cast his mind back to that time, to the Crone of the Far-Raiders who had made the cuts, to the Crone Mother who had spoken in prophecy. He tried to call them with a silent, mental shout.

Nothing happened. Still Tal persevered. He kept up his call and tried to remember all the small details from his time on the Ice with the Far-Raiders. The smell of the Selski soup. The exact color of the Sunstone that was bound to the mast. The snort of the Wreska. The distant crash of Selski in their eternal pursuit of the Slepenish.

Slowly, he felt the void around him change. Wind came, a freezing wind. Then light, the particular color of the Far-Raider's Sunstone. He felt bone planks beneath him, shuddering and shifting as the ship rode the Ice.

The darkness retreated. Tal stood next to the main mast of an Icecarl ship, in the pool of light from the Sunstone high above. The ship was under full sail, streaking across the Ice, a star shooting through the darkness.

There was someone else on the deck. Not a Crone, as Tal first thought. A Chosen. Fashnek. A whole Fashnek, his body repaired in this dream, without his Spiritshadow half.

He looked scared, raising his arms in horror as

Tal stalked toward him, his violet glow forming a blinding nimbus around his head.

"Fashnek!" shouted Tal above the wind. "I am the Heir of Ramellan, Emperor of the Chosen, and you will be —"

Before he could say any more, Fashnek disappeared.

"Dark take it," swore Tal. He had hoped he could force Fashnek to release him, since there was no sign of the Crones. It did seem as if he had defeated the nightmare machine, but that was not enough. Even if he could choose his own dreams, he was still a prisoner. And who knew what was going on back in the Castle? Even now, Sushin might be using Tal's half of the Violet Keystone to destroy the Veil.

·CHAPTER·
FOUR

The Icecarls had barely finished rolling the last of the barrels into their makeshift fort when the Sunstones in the ceiling high above flickered and then grew much brighter.

Milla was the first to realize that the stones were being manipulated from a distance. The only possible reason to brighten them would be to make Spiritshadows stronger. Obviously the Chosen were about to attack!

"Into the fort!" Milla shouted, waving in the few Icecarls who were still carrying sacks over from the walls.

Within a minute, Milla's small force was at the ready, crammed into their tight circle of barrels and sacks. Milla looked at them, so out of place in this great stone room in their furs and bone face masks, made for a life out upon the Ice. She had led them badly, and not just them, but all Icecarls. The fate of their world had been put into her hands, and she had failed.

"They come," hissed Saylsen.

Milla looked over the barrier. Spiritshadows were slithering in through every still-closed door, sliding along the floor before standing up along the walls. Spiritshadows of all kinds, from the thin-waisted humanoids of the guards to strange, insectlike things with multiple body parts and too many legs.

More and more Spiritshadows kept pouring in and lining up along the walls. At least a hundred Spiritshadows, and more flowing through every second, to join the massed ranks on all four sides of the Icecarls' fort. There was no sign of any Chosen trying to open the doors and follow them. Milla wondered if they were free shadows, the forerunners of an invasion force from Aenir.

"They are bound shadows, not free ones," said Odris. The Spiritshadow could often tell what Milla was thinking. "I expect some of them won't make it far from the doors, unless their masters follow. They'll snap back."

"I don't think it will make that much difference," muttered Milla.

"The Chosen mean to overwhelm us with shadows," Saylsen observed. "Cowards!"

No, not cowards, thought Milla. It was only common sense for the Chosen to save themselves as much as possible from injury and death. Besides, they had to know that apart from Milla's Talon and Jarek's golden chain, the Icecarls had few weapons to use against the Spiritshadows. Just one Merwin-horn sword and some glowing algae-coated spears. They had long since used all their shadowsacks and shadowbottles.

As the Spiritshadows flickered and moved into position, Milla ran through everything she could do, all the weapons or tactics they could employ.

"A Shield Maiden thinks of all things possible and expected, then does the impossible and unexpected."

She didn't realize she'd spoken aloud until Saylsen looked at her approvingly. At the same time, Milla realized there was one weapon she hadn't thought of using, one that was particularly effective against Spiritshadows when used properly.

Her Sunstone. The only problem was that she didn't really know how to use it. Tal had given her a few lessons, and she'd practiced a little in the heatways on the way out, but that was all.

Milla stared down at the stone, watching the sparks of light inside it. What should she try and do? A Red Ray of Destruction? She'd seen enough of them. But hadn't Tal told her that Violet was the most powerful light of the spectrum? At this point, with the Spiritshadows outnumbering them twenty to one, surely it would be better to try a Violet Ray of Destruction.

Or better still, a Violet *Wave* of Destruction.

"Milla? What are you doing?" asked Odris nervously as Milla raised her hand and bent her head to focus on the Sunstone.

Milla ignored her. The flow of Spiritshadows through the doors was lessening, and their ranks were almost complete. They would attack very soon, unless she did something.

Focus, concentration, and visualization — that was what Tal had said. Milla bent her mind upon the Sunstone, shutting out everything else. It was rather like the second stage of Rovkir breathing, Milla thought, and was surprised to find that she'd actually started the breathing pattern.

Violet. Violet. Milla willed the Sunstone to produce Violet. She needed to make a great pool of Violet inside the stone, and then unleash it like an avalanche upon the Spiritshadows. Even if it only took out the ranks in front of her, that would give them a chance.

Milla remembered a real avalanche she had seen once. It was at a gathering between the Far-Raiders and their sister clan, the Frostfighters. Both clans had left their ships under skeleton crews to celebrate and feast upon the lesser peak of Twoknuckle Mountain. It had been a great but risky celebration, as the mountain was known to be dangerous. It was sheer bravado that had led the clans to choose it. Even so, the Crones had insisted on some precaution being taken, and hundreds of moth lanterns were laid in expanding rings around the central fires.

Halfway through the feast, the higher peak of Twoknuckle shrugged, sending down a vast wave of snow and ice. They had heard it first, a deep roar in the darkness, louder than any beast. The outer ring of lanterns was snuffed out in an instant, and for a few blinks the inner ring lit up the avalanche as it fell upon the camp. Milla remembered it well, a wall of icy death that swept away everyone who wasn't quick enough to find shelter behind the clusters of rock.

It was an avalanche she imagined now, one of solid Violet. She called it up out of the stone, using all the powers of concentration and all the discipline that made her such a dangerous fighter.

Violet flared. Icecarls gasped. Odris stepped even farther away and said something that Milla was too focused to hear. She could feel the avalanche coming, could feel the Violet power rising in the stone. Her hand was shaking, her whole body trembling, as if a real avalanche was roaring down upon her.

Instinct told her when to thrust her hand forward and let the power go — at exactly the same moment the Spiritshadows charged.

Milla shouted a war cry as Violet light leaped from her Sunstone and spread into a wave. It was as wide as the fort and tall as an Icecarl, rushing forward with a deafening crash and rumble. The wave swept every Spiritshadow before it, sending them crashing and tumbling back through the walls and doors.

The Icecarls cheered, but only briefly. One attack had been forestalled. There were still three forces coming from the remaining sides.

"Sell your lives dearly!" Milla shouted as she dashed toward the side the Spiritshadows would reach first. She was surprised to find Odris speeding ahead of her, and on the side she wore the Talon.

Nothing had ever made Odris come that close before.

"It's coming back!" Odris warned. "Look out!"

Milla looked behind her. The Violet wave had rebounded from the wall and was ricocheting toward them. It looked stronger and more menacing from this side, and showed no signs of weakening. It had veered a little to one side in the rebound. Only half of it would strike the Icecarls' fort.

"To this side!" Saylsen cried, her voice at full roar in an effort to be heard above the rumble of the wave. "To this side!"

Everyone was running to the safer side when the Violet wave hit. Milla watched aghast as it picked up huge barrels and hurled them toward the ceiling. Sacks were blown apart. One of the Shield Maidens, already wounded and slow, was lifted up, thrown down onto the floor, and then rocketed out the back of the wave. If two of her companions hadn't caught her, she would have broken her neck.

Still the wave of light kept going. Spiritshadows, attacking only a moment before, fled in all directions as the Icecarls hunkered down as best they could, shielding themselves from the spray of debris.

"Well done!" shouted Saylsen to Milla. "The enemy flees! Let it run one more time through, then stop it!"

"Stop it?" Milla yelled back. "I don't even know how I started it!"

·CHAPTER·
FIVE

Tal had just about given up on the Crones and any hope of escaping from his dream when he spotted a black-clad figure approaching across the Ice. A Crone, skating without skates, moving as fast as the ice-ship, though it was under full sail. Tal had tried to slow the ship down, but had only succeeded in changing the color of the Sunstone on the mast. Apparently he had to know how something worked in order to dream it properly. Or else thinking he had to know something stopped him from dreaming it. He could go mad thinking in circles like that.

Tal glanced away for a moment. When he looked back, the Crone was suddenly there, standing next to him. He jumped, then he realized it was the Crone of the Far-Raiders, the first Crone he had ever met.

She smiled at him, her silver eyes twinkling, but she didn't speak.

"Please feel free to talk," said Tal. "It's my dream, after all."

The Crone smiled again, but remained silent. She seemed to be waiting.

"Am I supposed to do something?" asked Tal politely. He couldn't quite remember what Milla said happened when the Crones showed up. Except maybe this wasn't truly a Crone. Maybe he'd just dreamed up a Crone, instead of having a real Crone entering his dreams, so she couldn't actually help. . . .

"Stop it!" muttered Tal to himself.

"Stop what?" asked a familiar voice.

Tal whirled around. Adras was floating behind him, but in his Aeniran Storm Shepherd form, not as a Spiritshadow. Which was impossible. All Aenirans turned into Spiritshadows in the Dark World.

"Where are we?" asked Adras, scratching his cloudy head with one puffy finger.

"In my dream," said Tal. "Are you you, or are you me dreaming you?"

"What?" asked Adras. "The last thing I remember is falling asleep."

"Yes, but I could easily dream you saying that,"

said Tal. "Oh, who cares! Hopefully we'll wake up soon."

He turned back to the Crone and jumped again. The deck was crowded with Crones now. Lots of Crones, and a Crone Mother sitting there in a high-backed chair of bone.

"Who are they?" Adras asked as he puffed himself up to full size. Lightning crackled in his fists. "Are they enemies?"

"No!" said Tal hastily. "They're Icecarls. Like Milla."

"They're a lot uglier than Milla," remarked Adras, but he let the lightning crackle away into the air.

The Crones slid forward. Tal watched them nervously, but didn't move as they clustered all around him. He had to shut his eyes, unable to meet their stares.

He felt the Crones pick him up and opened his eyes again. He saw the mast and its Sunstone high above, and the darkness beyond.

The Crones threw him up in the air. It was exhilarating to be thrown and caught again. The first time he went up half as high as the mast. The second time he was level with the Sunstone at the very top.

The third time, he didn't come back down. He

just kept going up and up and up into the dark sky. Then there was a tremendous flash of light and all of a sudden Tal was wide awake, crouched inside the crystal globe. Fashnek was only a few stretches away, frantically turning the wheel that controlled the green gas. Vapors were beginning to swirl around Tal's feet again, but he ignored them.

Without hesitation, he reached out to the seven Sunstones around him and took control. Each one flashed, then steadied into the appropriate color — the code to unlock the crystal globe.

There was a faint click and the globe split at its equator. Tal threw it fully open and jumped out. Fashnek shrieked, a strangely high-pitched shriek for a Chosen. He dropped the Sunstone he held in his right hand and scuttled back, both of his halves in total panic.

Tal snatched up the Sunstone as it skittered across the floor.

"No, no, it wasn't me," moaned Fashnek in one breath, and then in the other, "Get him! Kill him!"

His two Spiritshadow companions obeyed. The Urglegurgle bounced twice and launched itself at Tal's head, while the wasp-waisted shadow lunged forward to grab his legs.

Once again Tal acted instinctively, almost without thought. He stepped back against the globe. Still in tune with the seven Sunstones, he summoned a thin line of Violet from each of them, to form a fence of light around himself.

The Urglegurgle hit the fence as it came down and was split in two as cleanly as a cut apple. Each half landed badly and bounced away. They came together for a moment, failed to join, and then there was a *pop* as the Urglegurgle disappeared, either back to Aenir or destroyed for good.

The thin-waisted Spiritshadow was quicker. It twisted away, losing only a hand to the Violet wire.

Tal raised the Sunstone he had picked up off the floor. The Spiritshadow raised its remaining hand in a gesture of defeat and vanished. Its rapid disappearance troubled Tal. It showed that free Spiritshadows could retreat to Aenir whenever they wanted to. He hoped it was much harder for them to come back, though with the Veil weakened and possibly already failing, it might not be.

"Spare me, noble master," whined Fashnek, prostrating himself on the floor. "I am but a humble servant of the Empress."

"The Empress is dead," Tal said harshly. "Besides, I know your true master is Sushin. Where is my Spiritshadow?"

"A deal, an agreement, your Spiritshadow for my miserable life," Fashnek whimpered. "Oh, your generosity —"

Tal held his Sunstone high. Red light flared, bathing Fashnek in its glow, making the sweat on his face look like beads of blood.

"In the shadowbottle over there!"

Tal looked where Fashnek pointed. There was a bottle of golden metal on one of the worktables. But there were other bottles and containers strewn around the room.

"You open it," Tal instructed. "And I might let you live."

"Yes, of course, great lord," Fashnek replied. He slowly levered himself up and hobbled toward the table. Tal kept his distance, the Sunstone ready.

"You will be Emperor, I am sure," mumbled Fashnek as he struggled with the stopper on the bottle. "I saw the Violet in you. I know these things. And an Emperor always needs a Master of Nightmares, no? I will serve you as I served Her Majesty. Sushin, why, he is nothing, a nobody —"

"Shut up!" ordered Tal. "If I am ever Emperor, there will be no Hall of Nightmares at all!"

"So you say now, Master, so you say . . . ah!"

With a last heave from his good hand, the stopper

came free. A shadow erupted forth, a great stream of roaring darkness that rapidly assumed the familiar shape of Adras. A very angry Adras, shadow-lightning flickering not just from his hands but also from his eyes.

"Jailer, die!"

With that, Adras grabbed the shadow-half of Fashnek around its insectoid head and began to twist, shadow-lightning flickering all around and thunder rumbling.

Fashnek screamed. Tal started forward, shouting, "No!"

But it was too late. Adras bellowed in triumph as the Spiritshadow's head came off. He threw it on the ground and trampled on it, letting Fashnek's body fall to the floor.

"No one will lock Adras in a tiny bottle ever again!"

Tal knelt down next to Fashnek. The Master of Nightmares stared up at him, his eyes glassy with shock. The shadow-half that had sustained him was already fading into nothingness. Where it had been, there was no skin and Tal could see bone and internal organs, even though he tried not to look.

"It was a mistake," whispered Fashnek. "A terrible mistake. I was afraid of dying . . . yet there are things worse than death. . . . It was Sharrakor who wounded me, in dragon-shape, and Sharrakor who gave me life. I should not have taken it from his hands. But perhaps it has all been only a nightmare, all in my dream machines . . ."

"No," said Tal, thinking of Bennem and Crow's parents and Jarnil and all the people who had been tormented by Fashnek and his machines, many of them to their deaths. "*You* were the nightmare."

But Fashnek didn't hear him. He was already dead.

·CHAPTER·
SIX

There were no Spiritshadows left in the cavern, which was good, thought Milla. But there was nothing left of the makeshift fort, either, and her little band of Icecarls was tiring rapidly as they dashed from side to side in their efforts to avoid the Violet wave. It hadn't lessened in size or power at all, though it was becoming more erratic in direction and harder to predict every time it rebounded from a wall.

"Left!" shouted Saylsen, and they all ran left, until the Shield Mother shouted "Stop!" and then, "Dark take it! Right a bit!"

The Violet wave missed them by a few stretches, hurtling past toward the far wall. It would be a few minutes before it came sweeping back in at a new angle.

"Have you tried reversing whatever it was you did?" asked Malen. She didn't look at Milla. Like everyone else she kept her eyes on the wave.

"No," snapped Milla. Every time she started to focus on the Sunstone the Violet wave would come back. Someone would grab her and drag her out of the way, and her concentration would be gone. Besides, all she could think of was the avalanche. Trying *not* to think of an avalanche only made the image even stronger in her head. So even if she could concentrate on her Sunstone, it was likely she would just create another Violet wave. Two would kill everyone for certain.

"We'll have to try one of the doors again," Saylsen said grimly. "We can't run away from this thing forever."

"Odris! Have a look and see what's behind that one," ordered Milla, pointing to one of the doors. There were only two exits left to try, out of the five. One stone door and part of the corridor behind it had been totally smashed by the wave and was now impassable. Two others were so heavily barricaded and defended that there was no chance of getting through.

"I'll get my head pulled off if I poke it through," Odris protested. "*You* have a look if you want!"

"*I* can't stick my head through a closed door," said Milla. "You can. Would you prefer to get swept up by the wave?"

"*I'm* not tired," said Odris mulishly. "I can keep away from —"

"Left!" shouted Saylsen. "Left!"

Odris was the only one who hadn't been watching the wave. As Saylsen shouted, she moved right instead of left.

"This way!" yelled Milla. "*This* way!"

The wave rushed on. Odris, caught in front of it, didn't follow Milla. Instead she ran in front of the wave, before launching herself into the air and hurling herself at the door Milla had indicated. A second after she went through it, the wave hit with a deafening crash. Once again, it rebounded to groans from all the Icecarls.

"Surely it has to stop soon," puffed Malen. "I did not think Sunstones were so strong."

"Neither did I," muttered Milla. All the Light Magic she had seen before had only lasted as long as the caster concentrated on it. This thing she had created seemed to have a life of its own.

Milla anxiously looked at the door Odris had gone through. She could feel the Spiritshadow's absence — a sort of dull ache that was hard to pin down, rather like a toothache. But at least there was no worse feeling. If Odris was being hurt by other Spiritshadows, Milla would feel some of her pain.

"Head for the door," Milla ordered after a quick look to make sure they would still be able to avoid the wave's return passage. "Odris isn't fighting, so maybe we can get through."

They were halfway over to it when the door opened. But instead of Odris, there was a Chosen woman, a Sunstone in her hand and an unfamiliar Spiritshadow at her back, a huge bird-thing with eyebrows like horns.

Milla opened her mouth to order a sudden charge, but snapped it shut as another Chosen emerged behind the woman. This time it was someone she knew. Tal's eccentric great-uncle Ebbitt, now clad in a weird assortment of crystal armor plates in many different, shining colors. To top it all off, he was wearing a golden metal saucepan on his head, cushioned by a scarf of bright indigo.

Milla couldn't help smiling. From their very first meeting when Tal had taken her to his great-uncle's lair, she had liked Ebbitt. That meeting seemed very long ago. Now Tal was who knew where, she was surrounded . . . but just the sight of Ebbitt brought sudden hope.

"Quick! Quick!" Ebbitt called out. "This is an escape in progress!"

The Icecarls needed no urging. The wave was already rushing down upon them. Despite their weariness, they started to run for the door, which was wide enough for three people to pass through at one time.

"What is that?!" exclaimed Ebbitt as he saw the wave. The woman with him exclaimed something, too, then both of them raised their Sunstones as one, and twin beams of intense white light shot out to meet the wave.

As the White Rays hit, the wave faltered and slowed. But it did not stop fully, nor disappear, as the two Chosen seemed to expect.

"Too strong!" gasped the woman. "I cannot hold it!"

Her light snapped off, and she fell back to be caught in the gentle claws of her Spiritshadow.

Ebbitt kept up his White Ray, but the wave began to speed up again. Ebbitt started to back up, passing through the doorway with the last of the Icecarls, the Wilder Jarek, who was still in his post-fury state. He could move and fight quickly enough, but would not speak and his eyes remained strange and distant.

"Get . . . ready to . . . slam door," instructed Ebbitt. Sweat was pouring off his face as if he were physically holding back a great weight. His Sunstone was so bright that Milla could not look at it, and the White Ray was equally blinding.

"Now!" shouted Ebbitt, and the White Ray disappeared.

Milla and Saylsen hurled the door shut and stepped back, just as the wave hit the other side.

503
•

·CHAPTER·
SEVEN

Stone screeched and the door shuddered. For a terrible moment Milla thought it was going to explode inward, but then it stilled. The wave had rebounded again.

"Quick, quicker, quickest!" said Ebbitt as he dashed down the line of Icecarls. "We must away!"

He led them down a corridor, past four dead or unconscious Chosen, to a T-junction where Odris was busy prying loose stones out of the end of the corridor and piling them against a door.

Ebbitt went to the seemingly solid wall opposite the door and pressed carefully in several places. Nothing happened. He looked puzzled for a moment, then pressed in entirely different places. He was answered by a deep rumble under the floor. The wall pivoted in place to reveal a narrow entry and a flight of steps leading down.

"The out-way. Go help Odris!" cried Ebbitt, going over to pry out a stone himself from where Odris had begun to demolish the wall. The stone was bigger than he expected, came out suddenly, and fell on the floor, narrowly missing his feet.

As the stone rolled to a stop, a spot of blue light suddenly appeared on the door, smoke curling up from it. The light began to fizz and spit wood chips, steadily cutting through and down the door. Someone was breaking in from the other side.

"More stones!" boomed Odris. The Icecarls rushed to help her, forming a chain to pass on the stones that the stronger Spiritshadow pulled out of the wall.

In a few minutes, the door was buried beneath a cairn of stones. Blue light still flashed up through the gaps, but even after the Chosen cut through the door, the piled-up stones would delay them for a little while.

"Down with the established order," said Ebbitt. "Hurry! I shall shut the gate."

Though Saylsen tried to get in front of her, Milla led the way down the steps. Not because she didn't trust Ebbitt, but if it was some sort of trap, she at least had the Talon to deal with it.

The stair led down to a very damp, wet room with walls that wept beads of water. Algae was slowly dying all around, making it clear that the whole place had been submerged until very recently.

Milla heard the wall grind shut above them as the last of her Icecarls entered the room. Shortly after, Ebbitt appeared. He pressed several stones on the floor in a particular combination, which made a section of the wall slide across to block the stairway behind them.

"There's another way out, isn't there?" asked Milla as Ebbitt took off his saucepan helmet and wiped his brow with a patchwork handkerchief that he pulled out from under his shoulder plate.

"Out? Out? We've only just got here," replied Ebbitt. "*Of course* there is another way out. We'll have to hope that no one else knows how to control the surge system, though."

Milla looked around at the algae and the dripping water and sighed. It was good to have gotten away from the Violet wave and the Chosen, but she was still cut off from the rest of her forces. She felt the frustration of it deep inside every muscle. She wanted to run and shout and attack the enemy, but that was not wise.

"Malen, see if you can reach the Crones," she ordered. "We will rest here for a little while."

"We thank you for your rescue," Milla said formally to Ebbitt and the Chosen woman.

"I haven't seen anything like that wave since Mercur's day," said Ebbitt thoughtfully.

"Then you've never seen anything like it, because you aren't that old, Uncle," said the woman. With the help of her Spiritshadow, she stood up and looked at the assembled Icecarls. Her eyes fell on Saylsen. "Are you Milla?"

Milla looked back and drew herself up on her toes a bit. The Chosen woman was quite a bit taller. She looked much more shaken by her efforts to control the Violet wave than Ebbitt. Her skin was very pale and her Spiritshadow was surreptitiously helping her stand up.

"I am Saylsen, Shield Mother. That is Milla Talon-Hand, War-Chief of the Icecarls," pronounced Saylsen as she pointed at Milla. "Who are you?"

"I am Graile Parel-Kessil," answered the Chosen. She seemed a bit surprised by Milla's age and Saylsen's announcement. "Tal's mother."

"Tal's mother!" exclaimed Milla. "But he said you were sick, likely to die."

"I was poisoned," said Graile. "Tal brought me the antidote."

"Tal is here?" asked Milla. "That is good. Why is he not with you?"

"He was captured when he came to me," Graile explained. "Ebbitt says he has been taken to the Hall of Nightmares. The Codex told him."

Milla frowned. Her first priority was to rejoin her forces and find out where the main host was. But Tal in the Hall of Nightmares? For all his failings, she did not want him to be killed, or end up like Bennem, wandering inside his own head forever.

"Tal must be rescued, though I cannot see yet how it can be done," pronounced Milla.

"Ebbitt told me that —" Graile said.

"When did you speak to the Codex?" interrupted Malen.

"Er, quite recently. The Codex also told me that Sushin has Tal's Sunstone," said Ebbitt. For once his voice didn't quaver and he didn't sound half-crazy, though his fingers were beating on his crystal breastplate in a nervous way. "Half of the Violet Keystone, the Codex said. I didn't believe the thing, for I had split that stone myself. But then I saw the Violet wave, and I am guessing that was your work, Milla Thingummy-Hand. So maybe it is true."

"I did make the wave," said Milla.

"May I see your Sunstone?" asked Ebbitt.

Silently, Milla raised her hand to show her ring. Her Sunstone shone there as usual, a deep yellow shot through with red sparks. Ebbitt raised his own Sunstone, and shone a thin ray of Violet at Milla's stone. The ray hit, and Milla's Sunstone exploded into vibrant Violet light, flooding the whole room with its brilliance.

"It *is* the Violet Keystone!" exclaimed Graile. "Or part of it."

"Hmmpff," said Ebbitt. He seemed annoyed that he hadn't realized it before. Then he slowly and creakily sank down on to one knee, his crystal armor clanking. "I suppose this makes you Empress or something."

"No, it is Tal who should be Emperor when the time comes," said Graile swiftly. "The candidate must be ratified by the Assembly, and Tal is a Chosen and also bears a Violet Keystone."

"Not if Sushin's stolen it," Ebbitt grumbled. "I rather like the idea of an Icecarl Empress. Of course, we'll have to get rid of the old one."

Graile flinched as Ebbitt spoke this treason and looked away.

Milla stared down at the old man. She was tired and, though she would not admit it, slightly in shock from the fighting they had been through. What were they going on about?

"Because I have the Violet Keystone I am the Chosen Empress?" she asked. "But doesn't that mean that if Sushin has the other half now the Chosen will say he is the Emperor? And Tal must be rescued whether he's Emperor or not."

"Oh, Crow's gone off to rescue Tal," said Ebbitt airily, waving his hand around as if it suddenly had

a life of its own. "And since Sushin is going off to destroy the Veil with his half of the Violet Keystone, it is hardly likely anyone will want to call him Emperor."

Milla shook her head. She felt like she wasn't hearing properly. Crow and Tal were practically sworn enemies.

"You've sent *Crow* to rescue Tal? And who is going to stop Sushin from destroying the Veil?"

Ebbitt stopped waving. He pulled his arm back and bent his hand as if he were imitating a bird for children, moving his thumb and fingers like a beak. Then his hand-puppet spoke, with Ebbitt throwing and changing his voice so realistically that the Ice-carls jumped.

"Crow feels bad about Tal, so he will do his best to save him. I think he will succeed. Who will stop Sushin? Why, Milla, of course! And Ebbitt and all the little Icecarls will help."

"Should we kill him?" asked Saylsen, frowning. This sort of madness could be contagious.

"No," sighed Milla. "I fear that he is speaking the truth. We will have to stop Sushin. Only I don't know how, or even where we should go to find him."

"The Seventh Tower," said Ebbitt, dropping his hand and speaking in his normal voice. "The Violet Tower. Everything will come together there, for better . . . or worse."

·CHAPTER·
EIGHT

Tal looked down at the pathetic remnant that had been Fashnek. Adras stood next to him, still rumbling with distant thunder.

"'It was Sharrakor who wounded me, in dragon-shape, and Sharrakor who gave me life. I should not have taken it from his hands,'" Tal said quietly, repeating Fashnek's last words. "What in Light's name does that mean? How can a dragon have hands?"

"Jailer die," said Adras, which wasn't much help. "Where do we go now?"

Tal considered for a moment, biting his lip in anxiety. There was no point in looking for the Underfolk, not since he'd accidentally killed Crow, Ebbitt, and the others. But perhaps he could join the Icecarls who were attacking the Castle. Adras had sensed that Odris was with them, so Milla must be there, too. At least Tal fervently hoped so. Otherwise she would have gone to the Ice, and that would be another death on his conscience.

But Tal knew he couldn't just go and join the Icecarls. There was Sushin, always the enemy. Tal had to admit there was very little chance his mother had taken the stone before he passed out. Sushin almost certainly had Tal's half of the Violet Keystone, so he finally had the ability to destroy the Veil.

"I guess we have to go up," Tal said slowly. "Up to the Violet Tower. The Icecarls won't know what Sushin can do, at least not until it's too late. Even if Milla suspects Sushin, she won't know how to stop him."

"Sushin is the one who throws poison?" asked Adras. He puffed himself into a ball that was a reasonable imitation of Shadowmaster Sushin.

"Yes."

"I don't want to go there," said Adras. " I want to go to Odris."

"We have to go to the Violet Tower," repeated Tal. The more he thought about it, the more the urgency grew inside him. Sushin could be using the

Violet Keystone right now, as they wasted time talking. They had to get to the Violet Tower and stop him from destroying the Veil.

"I'm not going," announced Adras, folding his arms. "You can't make me."

Tal was about to let his anger burst out into words when they both heard someone open the door. Instantly Tal ducked behind one of the workbenches, and Adras shot up to the ceiling and spread himself out among the shadows there.

The unknown intruder was trying to be very quiet. The door only opened a little way, and Tal saw someone slide in. In the dim light he couldn't even tell whether it was a Spiritshadow or someone wearing black.

Adras drifted over, ready to drop on the intruder. Tal lifted his Sunstone, and it began to swirl with red light in preparation for a Ray of Destruction.

It was a person, Tal saw, not a Spiritshadow. All dressed in black, with a black hood drawn tightly around his face. Tal saw a dagger in the hand held close by the intruder's side. He moved from shadow to shadow, until he could see the open globe and the body of Fashnek. He stopped suddenly then and looked around.

"Tal?"

It was a voice from the past, a voice from the dead.

Crow's voice.

But that was impossible. For a moment, Tal thought he might still be under the control of the nightmare machine. But the Sunstones on their silver stands were dark, the globe still open.

"Tal?"

Tal stood up slowly. Crow faced him and slowly undid his hood. He was very pale, and there was a partly healed scar across his forehead.

"I thought I killed you," whispered Tal.

"Ebbitt saved us," said Crow.

"Ebbitt's alive, too?" exclaimed Tal. He felt relief flood his entire body, making him feel weak. He needed to sit down.

"We all survived," said Crow. "I thought I'd killed *you*. And I did hit you on the head. I . . . I'm sorry. I guess I went crazy. . . . There is so much the Chosen have done to my family. . . . "

"I've been in the nightmare machine," said Tal. He didn't need to say anything else.

Crow nodded and went over to look down on Fashnek's body.

"It took too long to come to this," he said.

"I'm sorry, too," said Tal after a moment. "For

bringing down the roof. For everything my people have done to yours."

"It's all changing now," said Crow. "The Icecarls will win. They have agreed that we will be free."

"I hope that happens," replied Tal. He was surprised to find that he meant it. He had come to learn that there was no such thing as the natural superiority of the Chosen over everyone else. In fact, Tal realized with surprise that there were more Underfolk and Icecarls who he admired and looked up to.

"I came to rescue you," said Crow. "The Codex told Ebbitt where you were. Or so he said. Only you seem to have rescued yourself."

Silence fell awkwardly between them then. Tal still wasn't absolutely sure Crow could be trusted. Too much had happened between them in the past. Could the Freefolk boy have changed so much?

"Um, I have to go," Tal said after a few more seconds of uncomfortable silence.

"Where?" asked Crow.

"The Violet Tower," Tal answered slowly. "Sushin has part of the Violet Keystone. It's probably enough for him to destroy the Veil. The Sun will come again and melt the Ice. There will be an invasion of shadows. Thousands and thousands of shadows. I have to . . . I *have* to stop him."

"You will need help," said Crow.

"Like you helped me in the Red Tower?" asked Tal.

Crow shook his head.

"No. I swear it in my parents' names. We fight together now."

He clapped his fists, Icecarl-style, then drew out a Sunstone. For a moment Tal almost shot a Red Ray at him, but he forced himself to wait. Crow simply gave light in respect, and Tal let out the breath he didn't know he'd held.

"All right," Tal agreed. He clapped his fists, too, and let the red light fade from his Sunstone in order to give light in return. It was Violet that shone forth, though he had not tried to make it so. Perhaps even without the Violet Keystone something of the imperial majesty clung to him.

"We'll fight together."

"Adras fight, too," boomed the Spiritshadow from the ceiling. "Only can we fight someone easier, not Sushin?"

Tal ignored him.

"You said Ebbitt told you where I was? He didn't get hurt too much?"

"No. He was hurt, but he's all right now."

"And Milla is with the Icecarls?"

Crow laughed for a moment, then grew suddenly serious again.

"Milla is the *leader* of the Icecarls! She has a magical fingernail of crystal and Sunstone chips they call the Talon of Danir, and she is called Milla Talon-Hand, War-Chief of the Icecarls and Living Sword of Asteyr. She has grown, I think — if not in size, in something . . . something you can't see. You have grown, too, Tal."

"What do you mean?" asked Tal. He looked down at himself. He didn't seem any taller or stronger or anything.

"You seem . . . more important," Crow said hesitantly, as if he wasn't sure himself. "Less a boy, and less a Chosen. You have become something else, something more."

"You have changed, too, at least in your choice of color," Tal said, with a slight laugh. He wasn't sure he liked Crow being strange and mystical any more than he had liked him being aggressive and antagonistic.

Crow looked down at his black robes, so different from the white normally worn by Freefolk, or the white with black lettering of the Underfolk.

"It's true I've changed," he said. "Deeper than my clothes. I know what's really important now."

Tal tried to smile again, but found he couldn't.

"I'm glad Milla leads the Icecarls," he said. "She knows about the danger from Sushin. How far have the Icecarls penetrated into the Castle? And where is the current fighting? I know a few ways to get to the Violet levels, but they may be blocked off or defended."

Crow nodded. "Come, let's talk as we go. There is no fighting close by, at least not yet. There are also Underfolk ways to the Violet levels. I will show you. Follow me."

·CHAPTER·
ПIПE

"I have to find out what is happening with the main force before we can go anywhere," Milla said sternly. She looked across at Malen, who was once more standing still in absolute concentration.

Ebbitt looked at the Crone and wiggled his eyebrows, trying to distract her. But Malen did not see him, though her pure blue eyes were open.

"There are many of your people in the lower Red levels," said Graile. She was lying down, exhausted, supported by both her own and Ebbitt's Spiritshadows. "At least, that is what I overheard a Chosen saying. Thousands of them, he said. I am still not entirely sure why you are invading our Castle. But Uncle Ebbitt says we need you to stop Sushin from destroying the Veil, and I find myself believing him, which is not always the case. And my son sent me to you, not to any Chosen."

"Thousands?" asked Milla. "The main host must have arrived!"

Saylsen shook her head. "The Chosen may simply be afraid. Remember, 'In fear, nothing is certain. A single sharik becomes a swarm. Only the calm Shield Maiden can count.'"

Malen's eyes clouded. There was an instant hush. All the Icecarls leaned forward, as if they, too, might hear what Malen heard.

"There is a Crone at the exit from the heatways below. She will come no farther. She says that she has counted two thousand of our folk through and still they pass. Some wounded have come back, they say. . . . They say we are victorious in the Red levels, and the Chosen retreat upward into Orange!"

"Ask her to tell a Shield Mother that Milla Talon-Hand lives," instructed Milla. "That I must now fight my way to the Violet Tower. Tell her that the most senior Shield Mother should assume command, and that they must keep attacking up through the levels, and try to join us in the Violet Tower as soon as they can."

"Feyle One-Ear will command if she still lives,"

said Saylsen. "We should send her a messenger as well, to be sure."

Milla looked around the green and dripping walls of the room.

"How do we get out of here?" she asked Ebbitt. "And how do we get to the Violet Tower?"

"It is a secret, but some can go by steam to the topmost Violet level," whispered Ebbitt, holding his finger upright next to his nose. "But first we must all jump in the bucket."

He pointed at the wall opposite the stairway they'd come down. There was no sign of any bucket, or a hidden door or stairway, but the Icecarls moved apart so Ebbitt could press his palms against various stones in a complicated sequence.

Nothing happened. Ebbitt scratched his head. Then he pressed his ear against the wall. Whatever he heard satisfied him, and he stepped back.

Everyone waited for another minute, watching the wall, before Odris spoke to Milla in her Storm Shepherd whisper, which could probably be heard through the wall as well as by all the Icecarls and Graile.

"Is something supposed to happen?"

"Yes," said Milla.

As she spoke, she felt a rumbling underfoot. All

the Icecarls shifted nervously. It felt like breaking ice, and their instinctive reaction was to run away from it as fast as possible.

"Um," said Ebbitt. "Perhaps it was the floor —"

He jumped back as the floor suddenly slid away under his feet, revealing a deep hole. Two Shield Maidens caught him and rushed him back still farther, joining the general dash to the other wall.

When the rumbling stopped, almost a third of the floor had slid away, revealing a ramp that led down into a dark and stagnant pool of water.

"Damp," said Ebbitt. He started down the ramp, his Spiritshadow easing out from behind Graile to glide along at his heels. The old man paused at the edge of the water, pulled his breastplate away, and spoke down, apparently to his own chest. "I advise you to hold your breath through here."

Before anyone could ask him what he was doing, his Sunstone shone brightly and a globe of green light formed around his head. His Spiritshadow went first, then the old man followed it confidently farther down the ramp. Both of them disappeared underwater.

"Oh, Ebbitt," sighed Graile. "There's probably a perfectly easy and dry way out of here, but he has to choose the dirtiest and most difficult."

She started to get up, but even with her Spirit-shadow's help she would have fallen if Milla had not caught her elbow.

"Thank you," gasped Graile. "I am still . . . very weak. Perhaps you could help me with a globe of air?"

"That is what Ebbitt made just then?" asked Milla. "To breathe under the water?"

"Yes. It is Green magic, not difficult. Air is compressed into the light. I don't think I could hold my breath at all, so I will need it."

"How do I begin?" asked Milla tentatively. She remembered the Violet wave all too well. What if she made a mistake and formed a globe around Graile's head that had no air in it?

"I will show you with my Sunstone," whispered Graile. "You need only follow what I do, but with more power. You regulate power with will — it is a matter of how fiercely you think it. I am sure you can do that."

Milla nodded. But before Graile could begin, Saylsen interrupted. All the Icecarls had been suspicious of Sunstone magic in the first place. Milla had only made it worse with the Violet wave. It made her feel strange deep inside to know that not only did she have the ability to use Sunstone magic, but that the Icecarls feared her for it.

"We should send someone through the water to take a look," the Shield Mother said. "To see that there is air on the other side, and that the way is clear."

"Odris can go," said Milla.

"The shadow does not breathe," said Saylsen. "We need to know that we can make it through without magic."

"Milla could make you each a globe of air," said Graile weakly. "It would not take long."

Milla saw the resistance on every Icecarl face, but no one spoke. If she ordered it, they would accept. But she would not order them, and once again she felt a pang in her heart, as she was reminded how distant she now was from the Shield Maidens and hunters who stood before her.

"Send who you will," Milla said. "But tie a cord to them first, in case of trouble."

She turned back to Graile.

"Show me," said Milla. "I will make a globe of air for you, but we will cross the water without magic. That is the Icecarl way."

·CHAPTER·
TEN

After three attempts to cross one of the major colorless corridors to get to an essential stairway, Tal was forced to accept that he would have to ask Crow to show him an Underfolk way to the Violet levels. Every time they were about to run across, large groups of armed Chosen, usually led by a guard, would appear at one end of the corridor, hurrying along. It was clear that the entire adult population of Chosen, including some older children, was being mobilized against the Icecarl invasion.

Many of them would be killed or injured, Tal thought sadly, all of them fighting for a lie. They were not defending themselves, but were simply dupes of Sushin and Sharrakor. The Aeniran plan to destroy the Veil and take over the Dark World had long been in action. Even the Empress had been controlled by Sharrakor.

"Go, don't go, back, stop," grumbled Adras. "This is a silly game."

"It's not a game, Adras," said Tal. "Crow, do you know a way we can get up through Orange and Yellow?"

"I know a way to get right up to Violet One," said Crow with a slight smile. "But it's not pleasant or easy."

Tal didn't like the look of that smile. It reminded him of the old Crow, the one who had hit him on the head and stolen his Sunstone.

"What is it, then?"

The smile disappeared and Crow grew more serious. "You know the laundry chute?"

Tal nodded. Everyone knew the laundry chute. But you couldn't climb it — it was made to slide down. Besides, he'd used it to escape from Sushin before. It was sure to be guarded.

"There is another, similar chute," said Crow. "Except that it's a vertical shaft, without any turns. It runs from the Underfolk serving kitchen on Violet One all the way down — down to the heatways or even lower. It's called the slopdown."

"The slopdown?" asked Tal. That didn't sound too good.

Crow saw the look on Tal's face and nodded.

"It's for the kitchen garbage from each level. So it smells bad, and it's pretty slimy. But there is a metal ladder that goes all the way. I think."

"You've climbed it?" asked Tal.

"Only as far as Indigo Seven," said Crow. "That's why I don't know whether the ladder goes the whole way. But you can get out at any kitchen on any level. The main danger is the slipperiness, or hot slops."

"Slipperiness? Hot slops?"

"A lot of cooking oil and grease goes down, so the ladder is very slippery," explained Crow. "We'll have to climb with a grit bag and grit up every now and then. And sometimes the assistant cooks pour out things like hot soup."

"They might not be cooking with the Icecarl invasion going on," said Tal hopefully.

Crow shook his head at Tal. "They'll be cooking more than ever. Fighters need feeding. But the ladder is on the far side of the shaft from the kitchen hatches, so only a long throw or a lot of stuff coming down could get to us."

Tal thought about it for a moment. There didn't seem to be any alternative. He had to get to the Violet levels as quickly as possible, and from there into the Violet Tower. This *slopdown* seemed the best and most secret way.

"All right. But you go first."

Crow nodded. "This way," he said. "There's an old kitchen back here somewhere."

Of course, Crow knew exactly where the old kitchen was. Like most places around the Hall of Nightmares, it had not been used in many, many years. The rows of ovens were cold, their Sunstones dead. The cupboards were empty, doors hanging open at odd angles, old hinges giving way.

Crow went to a gray iron hatch in one wall. It was hinged at the bottom, designed to be pulled open and down. Crow tugged at the handle, but it was stuck fast.

Tal and Adras came to help, and they pulled together. There was a grinding noise, then a sudden snap. All three fell over backward, still holding the handle.

But the hatch was open a fraction. An awful smell came wafting out from behind it. The smell of years-old cooking oil, the odor of ancient, putrefied meat, and the newer but no less disgusting reek of rotten vegetables.

Tal gagged and held his nose. Crow shook his

head as if he could shake the smell off. But Adras was affected even worse. He twisted up into a frenzied whirlwind, spinning round and round and roaring incoherently. Whatever he was saying wasn't clear, but his feelings were obvious. Adras was totally repulsed by the slopdown.

"Stop that!" shouted Tal as he ripped one of his sleeves to make a face mask, while Crow did the same with his new black robe. "It's . . . it's not that bad."

Adras stopped spinning.

"Yes it is," complained the Spiritshadow. "The air is dead and poisoned!"

"It's only food scraps and . . . and stuff," said Tal bravely. "And it's the quickest way to get to the Violet levels. We have to climb it."

"No," said Adras firmly. "I will go and find Odris."

"You'll get used to the smell," said Crow. "And there will be a bit of fresh air around each kitchen hatch. If they're open."

"Come on, let's get going," said Tal. He knew Adras would follow, no matter what he said. They were bound together. Adras could not go far from him, or vice versa. Tal thought his own willpower was stronger. Adras would give in and follow. "You go first, Crow."

Crow nodded. He tied his face mask on and climbed through the hatch. Then he climbed back in.

"Forgot the grit," he said, showing blackened, greasy palms to Tal. "The first few rungs of the ladder are really slippery just here. They usually keep some next to the hatch. . . . "

He rummaged about in the cupboards near the hatch, and eventually found two moldy bags of chalklike powder. After testing that the bag was not too rotten, he plunged his hands into it and wrung them, so that he got a good coating of the gritty substance.

"You tie the bag to your belt like this, so that it can still be opened with one hand," he said, showing Tal. "We'll probably have to grit up every level or so."

Tal took the bag, checked it was sound, and copied Crow. In the back of his mind he couldn't help thinking that climbing a greasy ladder was the perfect opportunity for Crow to take his revenge. All he had to do was tread on Tal's hands and he'd fall for sure.

"Right, I'll go again," said Crow. "Don't follow too close, in case I slip." He climbed through the hatch, and his feet disappeared as he pulled himself up the ladder inside the shaft. His voice came echo-

531

ing back down, along with another disgusting waft of awful smells.

Tal hesitated. Crow was warning him, and he appeared to be more honest and open than he had in the past. But was this all just an act to lull Tal into thinking he was safe?

"I'm not going," said Adras.

"Yes you are," said Tal, his voice very stern. "We don't have a choice. Stop your nonsense and follow me."

He climbed through the hatch. Adras *did* follow him, though the Spiritshadow made a small continuous noise that was very like a small child whining.

The smell was even worse inside, so strong that even with his mask Tal could only take shallow breaths. He knew if he really breathed in hard he would instantly vomit. The shaft was smaller than Tal had expected, and darker. He increased the light from his Sunstone, which was tied into the point of his collar, making it bright enough to shine through the cloth as if it wasn't there.

Crow was already a good twenty stretches higher up and making good progress. Tal watched him climb for a while, noting that the Freefolk boy always made sure he had one really solid hand- and foothold before he took another step.

The rungs were really greasy. If it wasn't for the grit on his hands, Tal wasn't sure he'd be able to hang on.

He looked down for a moment, but quickly looked back up. There was nothing below but darkness, the ladder disappearing out of sight. The smell already made him feel nauseous and looking down didn't help. Besides, with the danger of slops being thrown down from above, he would be much better off looking up.

He looked up and started to climb. It was a long way up to the Violet levels. Even if he didn't fall off on the way, once they got there he'd still have to find a way into the Violet Tower.

Then he would have to confront Sushin and the great shadow dragon who was Sushin's ultimate master.

Sharrakor.

·CHAPTER·
ELEVEN

The water was freezing cold. But the Shield Maiden who'd been through once already said that the flooded tunnel was only twelve stretches long before it sloped up into air again.

Twelve stretches wasn't very far, Milla thought. She suppressed a shiver as she took another step and the water rose above her waist. Something rippled in the water next to her and she almost struck at it with the Talon before she realized it was Odris swimming. Even as a Spiritshadow, Odris liked water. It was the stuff of life for a Storm Shepherd in Aenir. Or part of it, anyway. Air and water, that's what they were made of. Air, water, and magic.

Two Shield Maidens were close behind Milla, helping Graile's Spiritshadow with its mistress, who was still very weak. Milla was pleased with the shimmering globe of green light that surrounded Graile's head. It seemed to be working properly.

She took another step, and the water gripped at her neck. It was so cold it constricted her lungs. Still, she told herself, it was not as cold as a windstorm out on the Ice.

Milla breathed in and out slowly, several times. Then she took the breath that would have to last her through the flooded tunnel. As the last of it filled her lungs, she pushed forward, keeping one hand against the wall so she would keep going in the right direction. The water was too dirty and dark to see in, even with a Sunstone.

One step, two steps, three steps . . . it was hard going, walking underwater. The floor beneath her was slippery, too, so she had to be careful. If she slid over, she might get turned around, or smack her head and lose her precious breath.

Four steps . . . five steps . . . six steps . . . that had to be two stretches, surely? But she'd been taking smaller steps than usual, so maybe it wasn't. Already she felt short of air, the cold pressing on her lungs and throat.

Maybe she'd become weaker since she'd been to Aenir and lost her natural shadow. Maybe wielding the Talon and using Light Magic had weakened her, too. She was used to having magical or Spirit-shadow help, and some of her toughness had leaked away. Surely such a small crossing underwater wouldn't have worried her before?

Ten steps. Or was it eleven? Milla tried to move faster through the water. Her breath was almost gone and she couldn't bear the shame of drowning — or almost drowning and having to be rescued. That Shield Maiden Jorle had been through twice already and hadn't been bothered at all.

She had to keep going. It could only be a few more steps.

Unless she'd somehow found another branch of the tunnel. What if Jorle had been lucky and gone straight through, but Milla had somehow ended up taking a side passage? Maybe she was walking even deeper underwater, into blacker depths from which there would be no return.

A second later, she burst out into air and light, gasping a heartfelt breath. Ebbitt was standing farther up a ramp ahead, the green globe still around his head, not as bright as it had been.

"What took you so long?" he asked. "We have a locomotor to catch."

Milla climbed out of the water and up the ramp to Ebbitt. Then she shook herself, sending a spray across the old man. He flinched and grimaced and muttered about something called *towels*, but didn't retreat.

There was a loud splash below. Graile and the two Shield Maidens emerged — Graile completely calm but shivering, the two Icecarls spluttering and gasping for breath.

As soon as they looked up, Milla slowed her own breathing. She knew that a leader must try to appear calm and capable at all times. But she wasn't sure whether the Shield Maidens were fooled, particularly when they immediately tried to disguise their own panting for more air.

The next Icecarl to arrive was the Wilder, Jarek. He was still emerging from the strange condition that came when the berserk fury left. He seemed unaffected by the crossing, but did not speak or even look at anyone else. He trudged up the ramp and stood cradling his chain, his eyes blank.

Perhaps it was actually grief from the loss of his companion, Milla thought as she cast a cautious glance at him, and not the aftereffects of the fury. She did not know much about Wilders.

"Hurry up, hurry up," chanted Ebbitt. "I told you we have a locomotor to catch."

"This is not a time for hunting. We must get to

the Violet levels as quickly as we can," Milla said impatiently. "What is a locomotor anyway? Some sort of beast?"

"You'll see, you'll see," explained Ebbitt. "But it is not for hunting. Oh, no. We will catch it to ride it, and it will take us the first part of the way we have to go to get to where we're going."

"The Violet levels," reiterated Milla. She wanted to be absolutely sure Ebbitt knew where they wanted to go. Though even with constant repetition there was no guarantee.

"We are all here, War-Chief," called Saylsen from the bottom of the ramp. As Milla half expected, the Shield Mother was hardly out of breath and didn't even look as wet, bedraggled, and cold as everybody else.

"Come," said Ebbitt. He led the way to the top of the ramp and then along a sandy tunnel that cut straight through the rock, without smooth walls or stonework. There were no Sunstones set in the ceiling here, and the only light came from the stones of Milla and Ebbitt, aided by a dim glow from Graile's.

The tunnel went on for a long way. After a while, Milla heard a strange noise coming from up ahead. It sounded a little like the metalworkers of the Fire-keeper Clan, the Icecarls who held the secret of turning rocks into metal. They were the only ones who could use the special rock that was sometimes found around the hot pools of ghalt, or which fell from the sky like Sunstones. The metal they made wasn't as good as the golden metal of the ancients, but it was prized just the same.

The ring of metal and the dull thud of stone grew louder as they kept on. Ebbitt obviously heard it but was not concerned. Milla decided that if he wasn't, she wouldn't be, either. The Icecarls took their lead from her.

"Careful now," warned Ebbitt. He slowed down and held his Sunstone higher. Milla tensed, her Talon-hand ready. Odris, seeing that, slipped back.

"The tunnel ends above the locomotor road, up ahead," said Ebbitt. "We have to drop into one of the locomotor buckets, which will carry us along to a point where we can go by steam. Some of us, anyway."

"What is a locomotor and what is one of their buckets?" asked Milla.

Ebbitt didn't reply, but he gestured Milla to come forward and join him. Together, they walked slowly forward. The light from their Sunstones lit the way ahead, the tunnel walls giving way to a much larger open space where their light could only partly banish the darkness.

The tunnel ended at a cliff partway up the side of a large cavern. Below them, on the floor of the cavern, was a strange path that led into the darkness, a path that was marked by three metal lines, each about a stretch apart.

Something moved out of the darkness, something about the size of a juvenile Selski. It took Milla only a moment to recognize that it was not a living thing, but the source of the hammering sound. It was just a box of metal, open at the top, balanced on a platform that had two big wheels running on the outside metal lines. There were also little toothed wheels at each end, clacking along on the metal line in the middle.

"A locomotor bucket," explained Ebbitt. "The locomotor is at the back. It pushes the buckets around on those metal lines, which are called rails. There are many locomotors, each one pushing ten buckets. They come out of the darkness below, rise to where we want to go, and then disappear down into the darkness again."

Milla kept staring as more and more of the wheeled boxes Ebbitt called buckets came into view.

As he'd said, there were ten, all of them pushed along by the strange locomotor. Unlike the buckets, the locomotor appeared to be at least partially alive, a thing of strangely pulsing gray flesh that sat on the same kind of wheeled platform. The blob of flesh had powerful arms, each as long as a grown Icecarl, that turned the wheels. But there was no skin covering these limbs. Milla could see the muscles tensing and relaxing, and the sheen of bone.

"Line up along here," Ebbitt instructed. "When an empty bucket is beneath us, we just jump down."

"Where do we get out?" asked Milla. She had a vision of the strange locomotor pushing them somewhere they didn't want to go, deep beneath the Castle.

"There is a place ahead where the line steepens and the locomotors stop to gather their strength," explained Ebbitt. "We jump out there, right next to an Underfolk passage that goes to a steam riser and also out to Red Five."

"Where does the locomotor go after that?"

Ebbitt shrugged. "Down again," he said. "I don't know where. One day I'll find out."

The first bucket drew level with them as Ebbitt finished speaking. It was traveling not much faster than a walk, and was only four or five stretches below. An easy jump for an Icecarl. Even Graile, aided by her Spiritshadow, could do it, Milla thought.

"Everyone line up along the edge here," ordered Milla. "We'll jump in the last two buckets."

"No, not the last two," interrupted Ebbitt. "Stay at least one bucket away from the locomotor."

Milla looked at him.

"It has extra arms as well as the ones that turn the wheels," said Ebbitt. "And somewhere under all that flesh, I believe there is a mouth."

Milla wasn't sure whether to believe him, but it was better to err on the side of safety.

"You have done this before, haven't you?" she asked.

Ebbitt smiled.

"Get ready to jump," said Saylsen, who had kept her eye on the buckets and was timing their passage. "Avoid the last bucket, as instructed."

"You have, haven't you?" Milla asked again.

Ebbitt kept smiling, but made no move to answer.

"Jump!" Saylsen shouted.

·CHAPTER·
TWELVE

Tal climbed wearily out of the hatch and fell onto the kitchen floor. It had been a longer climb than he could have imagined, much farther than when he had climbed the Red Tower. His hands were raw, blood mixing with the grit, and one shoulder was caked in the foul-smelling residue that had come flying down the shaft when they were about halfway up. Fortunately it had been cold.

Crow was sitting close by, his face pale, obviously even more worn out than Tal. Adras was sliding across the ceiling, trying to get as far away from the odorous slopdown as he could.

Unlike the kitchen they'd left so far below, this one was still in use. Fires burned under many pots, and there were even some old Sunstone-powered hot plates that glowed yellow and red with permanent heat. A breeze constantly blew through the kitchen, taking smoke and cooking smells up into holes in the ceiling. There were benches laden with fresh ingredients being prepared by Underfolk cooks. Tal saw belish root, cave fish, shrimps, orange and red yaribles, blue mushrooms, and more — enough to make him remember he was hungry.

All the Underfolk were gathered at the far end of the kitchen, clearly scared by these garbage-encrusted intruders who had emerged from the slop-down hatch. Tal raised his Sunstone and it flashed Violet. Instantly, they all turned back to their allotted tasks, ignoring the unexpected arrivals.

"A flash of light and they know who's master," whispered Crow. But he said it without the anger that would have been there before. He just sounded sad.

Tal looked at the stacked crockery on one of the nearer benches. It was all of violet-colored crystal, confirming that this was indeed a kitchen on one of the Violet levels.

"Where do we go from here?" asked Crow. "How do we get into the Violet Tower? I hope we don't have to climb the outside of it."

"I'm not sure," Tal admitted. He knew very little about the Violet Tower. He remembered being taught that it was much larger and higher than the other six. But he didn't remember much else. He had seen the topmost part of it briefly from the Red Tower, but it had been the farthest away, and he hadn't been able to make out any details.

"You must have some idea," continued Crow.

"I have one idea," said Tal. "I'm just not sure it's a good one."

Crow looked at him expectantly.

"Well," Tal began, "the Empress must be . . . must have been able to get into the Violet Tower. And there's a children's puzzle song that might have something to do with it, only I can't remember it properly. It has a line that goes 'The first sat here, the second spied here, the third flew here, the fourth ate here, the fifth was born here, the sixth sang here, and the seventh grew here.' All I can remember of the answering part is that the first was an Emperor, the third a bird — probably a crow, I guess — and then it ends with 'the seventh was a tower.' And 'here' was the Audience Chamber, which has the Imperial Throne in it. Only I don't know where the Audience Chamber is."

"I know who we can ask," said Crow. He slowly got to his feet and looked at the Underfolk, who were keeping their distance. "If the Empress ever ordered a drink or food, someone from here would have taken it to her."

"I guess so," said Tal. He got up, too, ignoring the stabbing pains in the muscles of his arms and legs.

Crow singled out the most senior Underfolk, an old cook, and started to talk to him. Tal tried to stretch a bit, to ease the stiffness that he knew would come along sooner or later. He was tired, his weariness made worse by the aftereffects of the waterspider poison. He didn't really listen to Crow and the Underfolk cook until Crow called out to him.

"Tal! Come and hear this."

Tal pushed himself off the bench he was leaning against and walked over. Above his head, Adras glided across the ceiling.

"Tell him what you told me," instructed Crow.

The Underfolk man bowed nervously. He obviously didn't know what to make of Crow and he wasn't absolutely sure about Tal, even with his Sunstone and Spiritshadow.

"As it please you, Masters —"

"Don't call us Masters!" Crow interrupted.

The cook bobbed his head several times and cleared his throat.

"Yes, Ma — as it pleases you. The Audience

Chamber and the Imperial Throne are not used, haven't been used by Her Highness, not these many years. Well, never, I think, as my parents told me."

"But it must be cleaned from time to time," said Crow. "Everywhere is cleaned."

The cook shook his head.

"No, no. The doors cannot be opened, save by the Empress. In my father's time, under the old Emperor, the doors were always open, and I am sure we cleaned it most thoroughly. It is not neglect, Masters, not at all. I am sure the Cleaners would be very happy, most ecstatic to clean the Audience Chamber again. . . ."

"Can you show us where the doors to the Audience Chamber are?" asked Tal. "Can we get to them through Underfolk ways?"

"I am assigned here," said the cook nervously, casting an eye back over all the other Underfolk working over the fires and at the benches. "I cannot leave. But I could send one of our waiters, if it please you, Masters."

"Stop this 'Master' and 'if it pleases you' stuff," said Crow, some of his old anger returning. "You'll be free soon. The Icecarls have invaded the Castle and will win. The Chosen are losing."

The cook trembled at Crow's words and didn't

547
•

answer. The confusion in his eyes was clear enough. He had only ever known one world and could not imagine it changing.

"A waiter will be fine," said Tal gently. "As long as he knows the way."

The cook bobbed and nodded and hurried off, calling out a name.

"I hope the doors are still closed," said Tal.

"Why?" asked Crow. "How will we get in?"

"I'd forgotten that the Empress never had the Violet Keystone," explained Tal. "Mercur — the old Emperor she deposed — managed to escape with it. He died in the heatways, and that's how we got the stone that Ebbitt split in two for Milla and me."

"So?"

"I bet you need the Violet Keystone to open the doors to the Audience Chamber and to get into the Violet Tower. That's why the doors have been shut since Mercur's time. If they're open now, it means Sushin has already used the half he stole from me to get in."

Crow nodded thoughtfully.

"What do we do if we run into Sushin?" he asked. "I mean, if he's still there?"

"Hit him with everything we can," said Tal. "You can do a Red Ray of Destruction, can't you?"

"Yes," admitted Crow. Even though he was an Underfolk, he had stolen a Sunstone and had been secretly trained by Ebbitt and Lector Jarnil.

"Then do that," said Tal. "There's a spell I've been meaning to try on him, too, if I can do it. The Violet Unraveling."

"What does that do?" asked Crow.

"It dissolves anything it touches," Tal answered grimly. "I only wish I'd been confident enough to try it on him before."

The cook came hurrying back through the kitchen, dodging the workers as they moved between stove and bench and swung open ovens or sharpened knives. A young Underfolk boy, no more than six or seven years old, trailed after him, surreptitiously picking his nose. He stopped when he saw Tal looking at him and whipped his hands behind his back into the approved posture of a servant.

"This is Edol," said the cook. "He will show you through the serving ways to the Audience Chamber."

·CHAPTER·
THIRTEEN

"I can't truly say I have experienced this delightful ride before," replied Ebbitt, a moment after he landed with Milla in the metal bucket. "But I have read about it."

"I hope what you read is true," said Milla. "I do not like traveling this way, stuck to these metal rails. Even a Selski may be steered."

The other Icecarls in the bucket murmured their agreement.

The sloping sides of the bucket were too high to see over easily, so Milla ordered a Shield Maiden to climb up on the broad shoulders of Jarek to look ahead. Odris slid up and poked her head out so she could see, too.

"How will we know when to get out?" asked Milla. "Is there some sign or mark?"

"When the locomotor slows then we will know," said Ebbitt. "If the locomotor speeds, then we have gone past our needs."

Milla scowled and turned away. She had to think. If the main host had indeed arrived below and was attacking, then the rest of her advance guard would be relieved in time. Tal would probably be all right, since Ebbitt was sure Crow would rescue him, and she had a low opinion of Fashnek. But Sushin had half the Violet Keystone and with it he could finally destroy the Veil. He might already have done it, for all they knew down here. Down here in this metal box, trapped traveling in a straight line to who knew where . . .

"What's ahead?" she suddenly asked.

"It is very dark," answered the Shield Maiden. "I think . . . I think the rails ahead go down."

"Down?" asked Ebbitt and Milla at the same time.

"Yes," answered the Shield Maiden. "Definitely. I can see a locomotor ahead, but not the buckets it pushes — now it has disappeared, too. It must be a steep slope."

"Perhaps I misremembered," mused Ebbitt, ducking his head and scratching under his breast-plate. "Was it *ascends* or *descends* for the Underfolk corridor I mentioned before? Ascends, descends, upends, depends . . . oops —"

He turned to Milla and bowed deeply.

"I fear, my dear, that I have been unclear. We need to disembark from this equipage before it *descends*."

"Our first bucket is already over the edge," reported the Shield Maiden.

"Everybody out!" Milla shouted. "Jump!"

She jumped up and got astride the rim of the bucket, swinging her legs over to jump clear. Ice-carls jumped around her, but at the last instant Milla hesitated. Someone was missing. She looked back down and saw Graile still lying there, asleep, with her Spiritshadow sprawled next to her.

Milla looked ahead. The next bucket had started down the slope. It had to be an almost vertical drop, she realized, as the buckets disappeared immediately from sight.

"Graile!"

The Chosen did not stir.

Milla jumped back inside, shouting for Odris.

"What?" came a plaintive cry from the Spiritshadow, calling from some distance back along the path. She had obeyed Milla's order to jump.

"Come here!" screamed Milla. "Now!"

She bent down and shook Graile hard, but still

the Chosen didn't stir. She was breathing, but deeply unconscious.

Milla heard another bucket go over the edge, the regular clacking of the third wheel replaced by a much higher pitched and more frequent screeching.

She slapped Graile then, but the Chosen woman would not wake. Her Spiritshadow did not move.

"Odris!"

"I'm here," grumbled Odris, who was hovering overhead. "No need to shout."

Milla dragged Graile onto her shoulder. She was surprisingly light for her size, but even so, she was too heavy to boost up over the rim of the bucket.

"Take her," ordered Milla.

Odris dropped down and grabbed Graile with her two puffy arms. As she started to rise again, she gave out a surprised yelp.

"She's stuck," announced Odris. At the same time, Milla heard another bucket go over the edge. That was the third, and they were in the sixth. There were only five or six breaths before they would go over, too.

"What do you mean?" Milla asked frantically. Then she saw what Odris meant. Graile's Spirit-shadow was holding on to her with one claw, some-how weighing them both down. "Try harder!"

"I can't move!" wailed Odris. "The Spiritshadow has done something weird — it's too heavy!"

"Leave her!" shouted another voice. Saylsen. The Shield Mother had jumped back onto the side of the bucket and was looking down. "Leave her, War-Chief!"

Another bucket went over. Number four. Milla stood motionless, her mind traveling as fast as it had ever done.

"Light, Odris! What light is best for Spiritshadows? To make you strong?"

"I don't know!" shrieked Odris. "Can I let go?"

"Think! What color light?"

"White!"

"Look away, Saylsen!"

Milla pointed her Sunstone at Graile's great bird Spiritshadow and thought of pure, white light, the brightest she could imagine. At the same time she turned her head away and lidded her eyes.

Light burst out of the Sunstone. Pure bright light that lit up the bucket and the cavern beyond and made the two Spiritshadows stand out as if they were cut from black cloth and stuck on a white-washed wall.

Graile's Spiritshadow stirred and flexed its wings. One eye opened and it moved its beak.

"Jump, War-Chief!" pleaded Saylsen. Her cry was immediately followed by the sound of the fifth bucket going over the edge.

They were next.

Still Milla kept the light pouring into Graile's Spiritshadow. She raised her other arm and called to Odris.

"Odris! Lift me out!"

Odris swooped, Saylsen jumped, and the bucket started to tip. Graile slid down to the end, as Milla leaped into the air and Odris lifted her up. The white light snapped off, and the topmost rim of the bucket clipped Milla's boots as Odris groaned and carried her free.

555

They landed in a heap only a few stretches from the edge of the cliff, as the seventh bucket went over.

Saylsen was there, already back on her feet. But there was no sign of Graile or her Spiritshadow.

Milla hobbled to the edge of the cliff and looked down. It was a vertical drop, and it went down as far as she could see in the light from her Sunstone. Somehow the locomotor and its buckets stuck to the metal rails. But whatever was in the buckets would almost certainly fall out, down to a distant death.

Milla was suddenly furious with Ebbitt. She had

put up with his meandering, crazy ways, but now his absentmindedness had got his own brother's daughter killed. She turned back from the cliff edge to find him . . . just in time to see an extra arm come out from the locomotor that was approaching. A pink and grisly arm fifteen stretches long that ended in a three-fingered hand the size of a human torso, a hand that was about to grab Saylsen as the locomotor trundled past.

"Ware foe!" shouted Milla and she ran forward, the Talon extending from her outstretched hand.

Saylsen whirled, knives ready, even as the hand closed around her. She stabbed at it over and over again, sending out spouts of gray, watery blood. But the locomotor did not let go and the last bucket went over the cliff and the locomotor began to tip up as Milla reached it and struck.

A brilliant line of light shot out of the Talon and whipped across the creature's wrist. Sparks shot out everywhere, momentarily blinding Milla. She threw herself to the ground in case another arm attacked her while she couldn't see, and rolled farther away from the cliff edge.

When her vision cleared, she saw Saylsen struggling on the ground, the severed locomotor hand still gripping her tight. Milla got up and rushed toward her, in case the hand was somehow strangling the Shield Mother even after it was cut off.

Then she heard movement behind her, the sudden rush of displaced air. Thinking the locomotor had somehow reversed, Milla flung herself aside and spun around, the Talon ready.

But it was not the locomotor.

It was Graile's Spiritshadow, its huge wings fully extended for the first time Milla had seen. It rose above the metal lines, wings beating furiously, then glided in to hover well clear of Milla and her Talon. The Spiritshadow held Graile tenderly in its claws. It hovered in place for a few seconds, then gently deposited the Chosen on the ground and slid down next to her.

Only then did Graile wake up. She stretched and yawned, then looked around with puzzled eyes. She saw Milla, and Saylsen clambering out of the locomotor's severed hand, and Ebbitt and the rest of the Icecarls hurrying up from where they'd jumped.

"I'm sorry," she said. "I fell asleep. Did I miss something?"

·CHAPTER·
FOURTEEN

Edol led Tal and Crow through a series of ever-narrowing corridors used by the Underfolk waiters. It became clear why the waiters were mainly young children, as there were several places where Tal and Crow had to crawl or squeeze through gaps as the serving way ran under floors or inside a wall. Sometimes there were peepholes to look through, or hatches where food could be left, but Edol led them at a cracking pace and there was no time to steal a glance.

Finally they came to an intersection of four equally narrow corridors. Edol pointed along the left-hand one, which ended in a small door, and said, "Through there's the Grand Parade. Doors to the Audience Chamber across the Grand Parade."

Then he scampered away along the opposite corridor, his forefinger already jammed in his nose again.

Crow squeezed along the corridor, Tal following a little way behind, with Adras at his shoulder. Tal still wanted to keep Crow in front, where he could see him, though the Freefolk leader had behaved perfectly so far.

"Dark take that boy!" swore Crow softly as he examined the door.

"What is it?"

"This isn't really a door," said Crow. "It's a hole in the wall, with a painting or something hung over it. I'm going to have to push the painting off the wall and it's bound to make a noise. If there's anyone on the Grand Parade they'll know about it."

"You can't lift it off quietly?" asked Tal.

"No. It's too heavy."

"Can you cut through it?" asked Tal, thinking of the portraits of former Lectors that were hung in the Lectorium. They were painted on cloth stretched on metal frames.

Crow tapped the obstruction again and shook his head.

"It's made of something solid. I think . . . I think it's a thin sheet of metal. It might even be a mirror."

"I guess we'll just have to risk it," Tal said finally. "And hope that everyone is down fighting Icecarls."

Crow nodded and began to push at the top of the sheet. It slowly shifted, with a screeching sound that set Tal's hair on edge.

"Hurry up!" he said. The continuous screech of metal on stone was bad enough, let alone any other noise. "Adras, help him!"

Adras flowed around Tal and pushed with his huge puffy arms. Almost immediately the screeching stopped, and the whole sheet of metal fell forward, letting in bright Violet-tinged Sunstone light from the broad corridor beyond.

Crow, Tal, and Adras watched the rectangle of metal fall, all of them tensed for the sound it would make. But none of them was prepared for the tremendous crash that did eventuate, nor the ringing sound that continued afterward, a ringing that echoed everywhere.

Light flashed everywhere, too, for the sheet *was* a mirror of highly polished silver. It quivered on the floor, sending wild flashes in all directions.

"Quick!" said Tal, and the three of them squeezed out into the Grand Parade. With the ringing still in their ears, they looked every which way for possible enemies and somewhere to run to.

Then they all stopped and stared.

Diagonally opposite them were two enormous arched doors. They were made of the ancients' golden metal, but studded with tiny Sunstones so that they shone in all colors, ripples of rainbow light constantly shimmering across their surface.

Both doors were partly open. But neither the Sunstone-laden doors nor the fact that they were open had stopped Tal and Crow in their tracks.

It was the piled-up bodies of dead Chosen sprawled in front of the doors. More than a dozen of them, including Chosen in Violet robes and guards. There was no sign of any Spiritshadows.

The last echo faded away, and the silver mirror lay still.

"Sushin did get here first," said Crow.

Tal nodded and tore his gaze away, to check along the Grand Parade. He'd never been here before, though he had come to the Violet levels once. The Grand Parade lived up to its name, as a sweeping, broad corridor that went for stretches and stretches in either direction, before it curved away.

There was no one in sight, at least no one alive. Tal went forward to examine the dead Chosen. They all looked surprised, rather than afraid. None of them had Sunstones in their hands, or anywhere visible, and the guards' swords were still sheathed. There was also no obvious cause of death. No wounds, no burn marks, no other signs of fatal light magic.

"I wonder why he killed them," muttered Tal as he moved between the bodies, Crow close by his side, both of them with their Sunstones held ready. "And how."

A slight movement near one of the doors made them spin nervously, red light flashing in their Sunstones. One of the guards, propped up against the wall, was not dead after all and she had moved her hand.

Tal recognized her. It was Ethar, a Shadowlord of the Violet and a senior officer of the guard. Her hand twitched again, and Tal realized she was trying to get him to approach.

"Who walks there?" whispered the woman, raising her head a little. Her eyes did not focus on anything. With a start of horror, Tal knew she was blind.

"Tal Graile-Rerem," he said, stepping over a body to get closer. He was still ready for a sudden attack, but he did not think one would come. At least not from Ethar. Her face was as pallid as the dead Chosen, and he knew she would not live long.

A momentary smile crossed Ethar's lips.

"The Beastmaker boy," she said, and coughed. With the cough came a froth of bright red blood that bubbled out of the corner of her mouth. "You played well."

"Did Sushin do this?" asked Tal. "Has he gone into the Audience Chamber?"

Ethar did not answer immediately. Her chest heaved, and more blood stained her lips. Then she said, "Yes and yes. We protested, for all that he was the Dark Vizier and could command us, he had no right to try the doors. . . . He showed us the Violet Keystone and told us to be silent, that he would be Emperor and do as he willed. But even with the Keystone, the Assembly must decide, and we told him . . . we told him he could not pass."

Tal waited as she stopped and drew in a racking breath.

"He blinded us then, with the Keystone, and in the darkness spoke words, words that felled our Spiritshadows in an instant. I felt my Kerukar go, torn away from me, and I almost went with him. But I did not. Duty . . . it is my duty. . . . You must stop him, Tal, for he should not be Emperor. . . . He must not be. . . . "

"I will stop him, if I can," said Tal.

"I ask one small boon before you go," whispered Ethar. "From one player to another. End this game."

"What . . . what do you mean?" asked Tal, but he knew what she meant.

"A Red Ray," whispered Ethar, her hand crawling across to tap weakly against her heart. "Here. Do not let me linger."

Tal raised his Sunstone. Red light swirled inside it, building in intensity. Then a single thin ray snapped out, striking Ethar exactly where she'd indicated. Her body jerked, then slowly subsided down the wall.

Tal wiped his eyes and turned away.

"I never did . . . I never did kill anyone, you know," said Crow quietly. "Not a single Chosen, for all my talk. I couldn't do what you . . . I couldn't . . . "

"I couldn't, either," croaked Tal. "Before I met the Icecarls, before . . . before everything."

Crow was about to say something else, when Adras suddenly reared up and looked down the Grand Parade.

"What is it?" asked Tal. "Is someone coming?"

"Yes," said Adras. "A monster."

·CHAPTER·
FIFTEEN

Milla looked at the steps going down, the steps going up, and the narrow passageway that led farther on, while Ebbitt hesitated at the intersection, scratching his head.

"Where do we go from here?" asked Milla. "Think carefully, Ebbitt. I don't want down when it should be up, or left when it should be right. You almost got Graile killed!"

"A failing of mine," sighed Ebbitt. "Perhaps if I tied ribbons of different colors to my wrists, I might know left from right. But I am *absolutely* sure of our whereabouts now and about where we shall go. Though I'm afraid only four of us can travel by steam to the Violet levels. Everyone else will have to take those stairs back down to Red Five. I am sure it will be in Icecarl hands by now."

"Why only four?" asked Milla. "And what do you mean to 'travel by steam'?"

"Only four will fit in the envelope," said Ebbitt. "Which is propelled upward by steam rising in the aptly named risers. Though the return pipes for the condensed water are not called fallers, which is strange —"

"Fit in the envelope? What is an envelope? Something like those metal buckets?"

"Not at all," replied Ebbitt. "An envelope is what you put a letter in. An appropriate envelope, depending on the letter. A formal response to an invitation, for example, should be placed inside a square envelope that is either the color of your order, or white, if seeking to depress pretension —"

"Ebbitt!" snapped Milla. "What is this envelope we can travel in?"

"Oh, that is an envelope of Light Magic. Otherwise we would get scalded by the steam. It is an invention of my own. I suppose it could be called a caul, or a second skin, or a container, or a shroud, though that is rather morbid. . . . "

Ebbitt's voice trailed off into a mutter and he started counting on his fingers, enumerating all the things you could call this envelope of magic he used to travel by steam.

"Perhaps we should try to find some other way," said Milla to Saylsen and Malen. "Graile? Do you know what Ebbitt means? And if we can get out to Red Five we could get to the Violet levels from there, surely?"

Graile was half asleep again, but she opened her eyes as Milla spoke and answered softly, "I don't know exactly what Ebbitt means, but I presume he has found some way to travel through the heating system of the Castle. There are steam pipes that carry steam from the depths throughout the Castle. But yes, if you can get out to the Red levels, there are many ways from there to the Violet levels."

"But not as quickly as by steam," interrupted Ebbitt. "You would have to fight every stretch of the way through Orange, Yellow, Green, Blue, Indigo. By steam, we would be in Violet in a matter of minutes. Oh, dark take it, I've lost my count. Where was I? Yes, forty-three, a sac, forty-four, a paldroon . . . "

"I suppose we will have to chance this steam passage," sighed Milla. "I will go, of course, and Malen, you had best come with me. That leaves one to choose. Perhaps Graile . . . "

But Graile was asleep again, slumped against her Spiritshadow, which had folded one dark wing over her as if she were a chick to be sheltered.

"No. She is still too weak," Milla answered herself.

"I will come, War-Chief," said Saylsen. Milla shook her head. Even though Saylsen had said nothing, Milla was sure from her slightly odd posture that the locomotor hand had broken some of the Shield Mother's ribs, if not inflicted more serious injuries.

"No. I need you to lead the others back to the main host and assume command. I think . . . Jarek."

"War-Chief —" Saylsen began, but Milla cut her off with a sign.

"We will face the strongest Light Magic," she said. "Jarek can survive it, as we have seen."

"He is a Wilder, War-Chief," warned Saylsen, ignoring Milla's attempt to cut her off. "If the fury takes him, you might not be able to steer him straight. It were best I come with you instead."

Milla met the Shield Mother's fierce gaze and tried to look commanding. But was Saylsen right? Someone had to lead the others back, and Milla was sure Saylsen needed to have her ribs bandaged, or perhaps even to be taken back out to the Crones waiting in the heatways.

"I have spoken," she said finally. "You will lead the others back. I will take Malen and Jarek with me."

For a moment, Milla thought Saylsen would refuse, and she wondered what she could do about it. Then the Shield Mother dropped her gaze and clapped her fists.

"As the War-Chief wills," she said. "We will hurry, and I will join the host. We will meet again in the Violet levels, as soon as may be."

"Malen?" asked Milla, to be sure the Crone — and all the other Crones — would not object to this plan.

Malen's eyes clouded for a moment, making contact. Then she shook her head, rather dispiritedly. She had not been the same since she had been cut off from the group consciousness of the Crones earlier. Some vital spark of life appeared to have gone out of her.

"You are War-Chief," Malen said shortly and clapped her fists. "You will be unfettered by my counsel."

"Jarek?" asked Milla, raising her voice. "I want you to come with me."

Jarek strode through the Shield Maidens, standing out head and shoulders above them all, his strange blue skin glistening in the light from Milla's Sunstone.

The Wilder had finally come out of his post-fury

state. He stopped in front of Milla, towering above her, and clapped his fists together. He did not speak, but simply nodded very slowly to indicate that he had heard and would obey.

"Good hunting," said Saylsen and she clapped her fists again, before leading the remaining Shield Maidens and hunters down the steps. Each of them clapped his or her fists as they passed Milla, and she answered in kind. The last two helped Graile up, her Spiritshadow flitting backward and forward behind her.

Graile weakly gave light from her Sunstone to Milla.

"May the Light protect you," she said. "If . . . if you should meet up with Tal, tell him that he has my love, trust, and hope. May we all meet again, under the Veil."

"That is also my wish," said Milla. "We will do everything we can to secure the Veil."

"Farewell, Uncle," Graile added as she started down the stairs. But Ebbitt didn't hear her. He was in a world of his own, mumbling and counting, until Milla tapped him on the shoulder.

"We are ready," she said. "Take us to the steam and the Violet levels."

·CHAPTER· SIXTEEN

For once Ebbitt was right about where they were. He led Milla and the others farther along the passage that ended in a small room totally dominated by a large metal door, with a wheel set in the middle of it.

"Here we are, here we are," declared Ebbitt. "Gather close, everyone, gather close. No, closer still, please, Master Blue. Odris, you do not need to join us. Steam does not hurt shadows."

Jarek did not seem displeased by being called Master Blue, Milla was relieved to see. They all clustered close around Ebbitt. When they'd finished shuffling and were all practically shoulder to shoulder, the old Chosen raised his hand, and the Sunstone ring on his finger suddenly shone with a pure indigo light.

"One, two, around Master Blue," chanted Ebbitt, moving his hand in a complex gesture, a trail of light following the motion. "Three, four, can't take any more."

Milla watched with interest as Ebbitt used the light like a weaver would a shuttle, building up threads of light into a solid cloth that wrapped all around the four of them. It extended under their feet, too, and finished with Ebbitt bringing it in over the top as well.

"Walk with me, stay near," ordered Ebbitt. He shuffled toward the metal door. Then he pushed his hands against the indigo light that surrounded them, and it stretched out without breaking, giving Ebbitt indigo mittens. He turned the wheel, but did not open the door, looking to his Spiritshadow.

It looked back, then slowly slipped under the door. This was not made of the golden metal, Milla observed, for that was impervious to shadows, and there was no crack between floor and door. It was merely iron or something similar.

The feline Spiritshadow did not return for a minute or two. Ebbitt tapped his foot impatiently and whistled through his teeth. Finally the Spiritshadow slipped back out and nodded its great maned head.

Ebbitt opened the door, and steam poured out all

over them. The three Icecarls started, but the steam was repelled by the indigo light, splashing harmlessly around them.

Beyond the door, Milla could just see a deep shaft, filled with steam. Obviously this was one of the risers Ebbitt had mentioned.

"In step now," said Ebbitt. "Don't think we'll fall, because we have a very pretty floor."

He stepped off with the others shuffling behind. For an instant, he looked like he would fall, despite his words, with the indigo light giving way under his feet. But it simply bounced a little and supported both him and the others as they followed him into the shaft. The two Spiritshadows slid along the wall and then slowly slipped through the envelope of light that surrounded Ebbitt and the Icecarls.

"It tickles," giggled Odris as she rose up next to Milla. "Tickly light."

"Great gouts of steam," muttered Ebbitt as he shuffled around and closed the door behind them, the indigo light still wrapping his hands when he pushed against it. "Huge great gusts of great steam. That's what we want."

Nothing happened for another minute.

"Gigantic gusts," said Ebbitt hopefully. "Super surges. Gales. Hurricanoes."

Still nothing happened.

"What is wrong with the stupid steam system!" Ebbitt shouted. He knelt down and put his ear to the glowing floor of light. "Come, steam! Come!"

Milla opened her mouth to ask Ebbitt what he was doing, but before she could speak, a titanic force hit the envelope and threw them all against the walls and floor as they accelerated at a speed none of the Icecarls could have imagined. Desperately, they clung to one another and tried to get upright again, as the envelope rocketed up.

"Steam, glorious steam, there's nothing quite white as it," sang Ebbitt. Then he started counting very loudly.

It was hard to hear him, with the roar of the steam and the whoosh the envelope made as they went faster and faster and faster. Milla began to worry that they would collide with something at the very top of the shaft and be splintered into pieces, like an iceship running into a rock under full sail.

As Ebbitt counted, "Sixty!" he grabbed the indigo wall in front of him and pulled it in as hard as he could, to let the steam that had propelled them rush past the envelope. At the same time, his Spirit-shadow sunk its rear claws into the floor and reached out through the light to sink its front claws into the stone wall of the shaft. With a terrible bone-tingling screech the envelope skidded to a halt, with everyone ending up tumbled together on the floor.

"Perfect!" declared Ebbitt proudly as he crawled out from under Milla and Malen. He reached across, the light stretching around his hands, and grasped the locking wheel of another door. "Violet One, as promised."

"Stand ready!" ordered Milla sharply as Ebbitt spun the wheel. She raised her hand and the Talon started to glow with its harsh red-gold light. Jarek unwound his chain. Malen stepped behind them.

Steam spiraled out as they left the riser and stepped out into an antechamber with a corridor beyond. Ebbitt slammed the door behind them, spun the wheel, then waited a few seconds for the steam to dissipate before dismissing the protective envelope with a pulse of multicolored light from his Sunstone.

There was no sign of any Chosen or Underfolk. Jarek went to the corner and looked out cautiously, then signed that there were no enemies in sight.

"Right here," said Ebbitt. He pointed left with his right hand, then he used his left hand to pick up his right hand and point it right. "That way."

"Lead on, Jarek," ordered Milla.

"This will take us to the Grand Parade," said Ebbitt. "From there we can get to the Audience Chamber and Milla can open the doors for us."

Milla nodded. She didn't ask Ebbitt why she would have to open the doors. It was better not to ask. He would probably want her to sweep the floor next.

·CHAPTER·
SEVEПTEEП

"A *blue* monster," added Adras.

Tal and Crow huddled down behind the bodies and Adras slid to the wall, as they watched a huge, manlike creature come cautiously around the bend in the Grand Parade. He was bright blue and had shimmering, metallic legs. He carried what looked like a chain in his hand.

"What is it?" asked Tal.

Crow stood up. He seemed nervous, but in a strange way.

"Jarek!" he called. "We're friends."

"What are you doing?" hissed Tal. He felt a momentary panic. This was where Crow betrayed him. He had to do something before —

Someone else came around the bend, following the blue man. Tal started in recognition, forgetting all thoughts of Crow and his possible treachery. He'd know that white-blond hair anywhere, even if it was topped by something that looked like a crown. That was part of being War-Chief of the Icecarls, he supposed.

He was about to stand up and shout "Milla!" when a shadow flashed past him, bellowing like thunder, his arms spread wide.

"Odris!"

This shout was met with the cry of "Adras!" and an answering shadow leaped into the air from behind Milla. The two of them met halfway, with a clap of thunder that shook the mirror on the floor again and made both Tal and Milla wince as they shared the shock of the Storm Shepherds' meeting.

Shouting "Milla!" after that seemed a bit pointless. Instead Tal got up slowly and walked forward. He felt strangely nervous. He hadn't seen Milla since they'd parted company down in the Underfolk levels, he to climb the Red Tower again and she to go to the Ice. An awful lot had happened since then. To both of them, it seemed.

To make matters worse, Tal realized he had never really been sure whether they were friends or not. They had been comrades in adversity, but had also fought and troubled each other a lot. What was going to happen now? Maybe Milla still wanted to kill him, as she had when they'd first met. . . .

Milla was thinking similar thoughts as she watched Tal approach. She wasn't certain of her own feelings. There was a familiar irritation at the sight of him, but that was coupled with a relief that he was still alive and looked unscathed from the Hall of Nightmares.

They met in the middle of the corridor, ignoring their two Spiritshadows, who were still spinning around and chasing each other up and down the corridor in sheer joy.

"Milla," said Tal, and stopped.

"Tal," replied Milla.

A heavy silence fell between them, then both spoke at once.

"I'm glad you're alive," said Tal.

"I met your mother," said Milla.

"My mother! Is she all right? I wasn't sure if the antidote —"

"She is weak, but well, and under our protection down in the conquered levels. She sends you her love and knows you will do what must be done."

"Sushin has the Violet Keystone — my half, I

579

mean," said Tal hurriedly. It seemed easier to talk about that than anything personal. "He will use it to destroy the Veil. We have to stop him."

"We know," said Milla, with that calm, confident tone that always annoyed him. "That's why we're here. Where is Sushin?"

"Um, I don't know," replied Tal awkwardly. "We only just got here. But he's opened up the Audience Chamber and probably got into the Violet Tower already, so we have to hurry."

"Then why are we standing and talking?" snapped Milla. She turned back and shouted, "Hurry up!"

She pushed past Tal and strode down toward the open doors.

The enormous blue man who had stood behind her looked at Tal, a look that scared and shook him. There was madness deep in his eyes, and Tal knew it could erupt into full force at any time.

"You must be Jarek," he said weakly and clapped his fists together. "I'm Tal. I'm a . . . sort of honorary Far-Raider. . . ."

Jarek did not return the greeting, but continued after Milla.

Tal was just about to follow him in turn when he saw Ebbitt and another Icecarl, a young woman who must have been some sort of apprentice Crone or something. She had Crone robes on, anyway, though her eyes were a remarkably bright blue.

"Great-uncle Ebbitt!" Tal called and ran over to him, embracing the old man with sudden fervor. "I am so glad I didn't kill you!"

"Then let go," replied Ebbitt. "Before you strangle me to make sure of your botched job."

Tal laughed and let go. He suddenly felt so much better. Having Milla and Ebbitt with him made the odds so much better for facing Sushin.

"This is the Crone Malen," said Ebbitt. "Very interesting person. Could teach you a thing or two."

"Uh, I'm s-sure," stammered Tal. He clapped his fists to her, too, and unlike Jarek, she answered, though it was more automatic than heartfelt.

"I know much about you," said Malen coolly.

"From Milla?" asked Tal.

"No," said Malen. "The War-Chief has not the time for speaking tales. I have walked through her mind, with the other Crones. I have seen her memories, seen Aenir through her eyes, and you."

"Oh, good," said Tal weakly as he tried to remember how he would have showed up in Milla's memories. Not too well, he suspected.

"Ebbitt, Sushin has the Violet Sunstone," he said

as they hurried after Milla. "And the Empress and the Light Vizier are dead, and they told me that Sushin is the shadow-pawn of Sharrakor —"

"Shadow-pawn? Shadow-pawn?" exploded Ebbitt. "They said that?"

"Yes," replied Tal, surprised by the violence of the old man's reaction. "What does it mean?"

"No idea," said Ebbitt. "But it sounds bad."

"Hello, Tal."

"Oh, hello, Odris," replied Tal, waving at the Spiritshadow above him.

"Adras says you went back to Aenir and you stuck him in a funny suit and he got eaten by a thing and then when you returned here he got put in a box and after that he had to climb up a really smelly pipe," said Odris sternly. "You should be more careful with him. He has a weak constitution."

"I will be more careful," said Tal mechanically. Somehow this reunion wasn't going as well as might be expected. "Ebbitt, do you know how to get into the Violet Tower?"

"I have an inkling or two," said Ebbitt. He looked down and tugged his crystal breastplate away from his chest, a strange gesture that Tal supposed was meant to be an indication of modesty — or maybe was just a new kind of twitch.

"Lokar is free, by the way," continued Tal earnestly. "She's going to try and replace the Red Keystone. She said that it might be able to keep the Veil going for a little while even if the Violet Keystone is unsealed."

"Lokar is the Guardian of the Red Keystone?" asked Ebbitt, raising one frosty eyebrow. "Lokar! Whoever will they think of next?"

"But you knew that," said Tal. "She's Lector Jarnil's cousin. . . ."

His voice trailed off as they reached the doors and he stepped inside for the first time.

Into the Audience Chamber. Into a vast hall, as large or larger than the Assembly of the Chosen he knew down in the colorless midsection of the Castle between Yellow and Green.

The Audience Chamber had a domed ceiling that was bright with thousands of Sunstones around the rim but stretched into darkness at its apex. The floor was tiled in all seven colors of the spectrum, but every eighth tile was a mirror, reflecting the light from the Sunstones that rimmed the dome, so that light flowed and shimmered everywhere, making it very difficult to see anything in the huge room.

Tal shielded his eyes with his arm. He could make out Milla, Jarek, and Crow ahead of him, and there was some sort of construction right in the middle of the chamber, but that was all. He could not see Sushin, or any other doors, stairs, or other exits or entrances. There was no clear way from here to the Seventh Tower.

"Come," said Ebbitt, seeing the question on his face. "The answer lies in the throne."

·CHAPTER·
EIGHTEEN

The lonely structure in the center of the Audience Chamber was the Imperial Throne of the Chosen. Carved from a single rainbow crystal, it was an ornate and enormous chair wide enough to seat three people. The back of it rose ten stretches from the seat, and was finger-thin. Light shone through it as if it were a thick pane of beautiful, multicolored glass.

A ring of Sunstones was set in the floor around the throne — large, violet Sunstones soldered in place with gold.

"So what is the answer?" asked Tal as they all stood looking at the throne. He also cast a suspicious eye at the ring of Sunstones. They were too big and too purposefully placed to be decorative. They had some function, probably defensive. They might project heat or flame, or something equally dangerous.

"The way to the Violet Tower," said Ebbitt, "lies on the throne. Though only the bearer of the Violet Keystone may use it."

Tal looked at Milla. He felt ashamed — Milla would never have lost her half of the Keystone to Sushin, and she probably despised him for letting their enemy get such a vital thing.

Milla met his gaze. Then she twisted the Sunstone ring off her finger and threw it to him.

He caught it reflexively, more surprised than he ever had been in his life.

"Milla!" exclaimed Malen. "What are you doing?"

"Returning the Emperor of the Chosen's Keystone," said Milla calmly. "Though I would like your other Sunstone in return, Tal."

Wordlessly, Tal threw her the Sunstone he had taken from Fashnek. Then he slipped on the half Keystone. It pulsed with sudden Violet, a light that was answered by the ring of stones in the floor.

"Take it back," said Malen, her voice cool. Her eyes were cloudy, Tal saw. She was communing with the other Crones. "The stone is the Icecarls' now. Take it back, War-Chief."

Jarek grunted and started toward Tal, but stopped as Milla raised her hand.

"I do not know how to use it to its fullest strength," she said, speaking not to the Crone in front of her, but all the other Crones beyond. "Tal has the power, and the right. What is more important? Squabbles between Icecarls and Chosen, or saving the Veil?"

Malen was silent. Tal could not know what was happening, but Milla did. The Crones were arguing among themselves and needed to vote.

"How exactly does the throne tie in with the way to the Seventh Tower?" whispered Tal to Ebbitt as the silence dragged on.

Ebbitt shrugged. Tal noticed the old man was keeping a wary eye on Jarek.

"Sit on it and we'll both find out," whispered Ebbitt.

Malen coughed. Everybody stood absolutely still. Jarek's chain slowly unfolded from his hand, link by clanking link.

"Very well, War-Chief," Malen said in the strange combination voice of the massed Crones, her words echoing through the chamber. "Once more we follow your lead. We have chosen well."

Trust the Crones to congratulate themselves for giving in, thought Milla.

"Thank you," Tal said to Milla. "Ebbitt thinks I should sit on the throne."

"We should all sit on it," said Ebbitt, who was peering down at the Sunstones in the floor, then back up at the dome high above them. "Tal, you go first."

Tal looked at the Sunstones in the floor, too, and remembered his earlier thoughts. To be on the safe side, he summoned Violet from the Keystone once more, letting it wash all over him. Then he stepped across the ring.

The stones in the floor glowed, but did nothing else, not even when Ebbitt and the others followed Tal.

The throne was cold and hard. There was a dusty cushion on the seat, but it had long lost any comfort it once offered and was so dusty that Tal sneezed every time he moved even slightly.

Ebbitt came and sat on his left, and Milla on his right. Crow crouched next to Ebbitt, and Malen squeezed in beside Milla. Jarek knelt down in front of Milla and Malen, watching Tal balefully. Ebbitt's maned cat flung itself down in front of the throne, under all their feet. Adras and Odris drifted up to hang on either side of the throne's back, like strange heraldic retainers.

"Bit crowded," remarked Tal. "What do I do now?"

No one answered.

"Great-uncle Ebbitt? What do I do now?"

"You're the Emperor," snapped Ebbitt. "How would I know? Do something imperial, you idiot."

Tal bit back a hasty reply. If he was the Emperor, surely he deserved to be addressed as something more respectful than "you idiot." Not that there was much hope of that from Ebbitt.

Still, perhaps the advice was good, however it was offered. Tal raised his hand and summoned forth more Violet, sending a beam of it straight at the circle of Sunstones on the floor.

The stones answered immediately, flaring so brightly that everyone had to shield their eyes. At the same time, the Sunstones in the rim of the dome shone brighter, and rays of Violet struck down. Hundreds of distinct rays, from every part of the rim, connected with the circle around the throne.

"Well done," said Ebbitt.

"It looks pretty," said Tal dubiously, watching the dust rise through the Violet streams. "But it doesn't seem to be doing anything."

"Apart from lifting us up, you mean?" asked Milla.

Tal looked at her, then back down at the floor. As usual, she was right. The throne and the circle of floor around it were slowly rising toward the dome, suspended on the hundreds of beams of Violet from the rim. They were already a good twenty stretches up.

"Yes," he said weakly. "Apart from that."

"Well, the dome is opening at the top," added Crow. "I suppose that could be counted as something else. I guess that's how we get to the bottom of the Violet Tower."

"Sure to be," said Tal, trying to sound confident. "But Sushin may have set some sort of trap there, or he might be there himself still. We'll have to be careful."

Silently and steadily, the throne continued to rise. Tal tried not to think of what might happen if the magic failed part of the way up. Odris and Adras might be fast enough to save him and Milla, but the others would fall to their deaths. They were already a hundred . . . no, a hundred and fifty stretches up . . . with a hundred to go, and a very hard floor below.

The magic did not fail. The throne passed through the circular gap in the dome and came to rest in another, much smaller room. It was also completely bare, and there were far fewer Sun-stones set in the ceiling. A broad staircase made from a pale green, highly polished stone wound up in one corner.

"Welcome to the Seventh Tower," said Tal as they stepped off the throne and walked toward the stairs.

His voice sounded strange and doom-laden, even to him, and he wished he hadn't spoken.

591

·CHAPTER·
NINETEEN

As soon as Tal left the circle of Sunstones, the throne began to sink again, back down to the Audience Chamber. Ebbitt, who had been lingering, had to jump out, assisted by his Spiritshadow, who lifted him by his collar much as it would carry a kitten.

There was no sign of Sushin, or any visible trap. Even so, Milla gestured to Jarek to go ahead of them, up the green stone stairs. He was not only tough enough to withstand a light trap, but was also a very experienced hunter, likely to detect any ambush.

The stair led up to another level, and another chamber that was empty and bare. But the stair did not continue farther, and there were four large doors to choose for further exploration. All the doors were made of the golden metal, Tal noticed, and the walls were also lined with a close mesh of golden metal against the stone. No Spiritshadows could pass through doors or walls here.

"Dark take it!" swore Tal. They couldn't afford any delay by going the wrong way. "That's all we need. Which one do we take?"

"Just follow Sushin," said Ebbitt. "Elementary tracking, my boy."

Tal looked at the stone beneath his feet and stamped in exasperation. As he'd expected, even stamping left no mark on this floor. There wouldn't be any tracks to follow.

Or so he thought, until he saw Jarek at one of the doors. The Wilder licked his finger and ran it along the joint between door and wall, before examining the result. Then he sniffed around the door handle, which was made of Violet crystal and golden metal. He did this at all four doors, running between them, before pointing at the door on the eastern side.

"What?" asked Tal. "How can he tell?"

"Dust," replied Milla. "Or the lack of it. And a hand leaves oil or sweat on metal. Come on!"

"But he couldn't smell that," said Tal. "Could he?"

Milla didn't answer. She ran toward the door and

stood off to one side, the Talon ready. Odris glided over to the other side, Adras next to her.

Jarek tried the door handle. It didn't turn, even when the huge Icecarl began to exert his full strength.

"The Keystone!" snapped Ebbitt. "Use your head, Tal. We can't wait around for you to get on with it!"

Tal flushed and raised the Keystone, directing a beam of Violet at the door handle. It was reflected back, and suddenly the handle turned under Jarek's hand, and he thrust it open.

The Wilder sprang through, drawing his chain as he ran. Milla followed him, the Talon extending, followed by the Spiritshadows and Tal and Crow, with Ebbitt and Malen behind.

All of them expected some sort of trap, or enemy left behind by Sushin. But they didn't expect to see a gigantic insect, an awful thin-bodied creature at least fifty stretches long, with hundreds of segmented legs, serrated mandibles longer than Jarek, and two huge multifaceted eyes.

Light flared in Sunstones, the Talon extended into a whip of light, and Jarek whirled his chain above his head.

594
•

Then everyone stopped. The light faded. Milla let her hand drop to her side and Jarek's chain slowed its terrifying whirl and came to what would be a bruising stop on anyone's side but his own.

The giant insect was dead. Or had never been alive. As they moved forward, Tal saw that it was actually a machine of some kind. It was made of something like the golden metal, though this material had a greenish sheen on the gold. And the great multifaceted eyes were actually made up of hundreds of Sunstones. Dead Sunstones.

It had a sort of saddle high on its back, behind the head with its terrifying mandibles, and the two closest legs had blunt bristles that could be used like rungs on a ladder, where all the other legs had razorlike protrusions.

"A war beast," said Milla in awe. This would be a terrible foe. It was thin enough to slip through anywhere a human could stand upright, but those mandibles could cut a warrior in two, and the legs slice a hundred foes into pieces.

"A Wormwalker," said Ebbitt. "Fascinating. I always thought they were made up."

"They?" asked Crow. "There are more of them?"

"According to the stories, at least a score," said

595

Ebbitt happily. He produced a measuring tape from one of his ample pockets and stretched it between the Wormwalker's mandibles.

"Not now, Great-uncle," said Tal firmly, taking the old man by the elbow. "We're in a hurry, remember?"

They walked quickly past the Wormwalker, careful to keep away from its sharp legs. The insect machine was actually positioned along a curving corridor, and as they rounded the bend, they saw another war machine. Only this Wormwalker was posed differently, its head and part of the body behind reared up, as if it were about to strike down an enemy.

It appeared as dead and frozen as the first one, but everyone slowed down again except Jarek, and even he circled the head warily and kept his chain at the ready.

"I wonder how many Sunstones you'd need for each one of these," Tal wondered as they passed. There was a third Wormwalker ahead, like the last reared up in an aggressive attitude.

Ebbitt looked at something under his breastplate and answered absently.

"Seven hundred of at least strength-eighty stones in each eye for full operation. They have not been used since the time of Ramellan and the Shadow Wars."

His Spiritshadow had to nudge him aside from the Wormwalker's legs as he spoke. It was finally clear that he was reading something, something he had stuffed down the front of his robe, against his chest. It wasn't just a weird new habit he'd chosen to annoy Tal.

Tal had a good idea what Ebbitt had concealed there, though he couldn't work out how the old man was carrying it, when it weighed as much as he did.

Ebbitt caught Tal's frown, looked down inside his robe again, and coughed.

"I was going to tell you," he said. "But it slipped my mind."

"I thought it couldn't change its weight," complained Tal. "It nearly dislocated my arm before!"

"It can't do some alterations itself; you have to ask it the right way," said Ebbitt. "Fortunately I have researched some of the phrases for commanding its obedience. Though not all, by any means, and it is a tricky bit of . . . of whatever it is. . . . "

"Milla!" Tal called out, for he and Ebbitt had slipped a little way behind. "Ebbitt has the Codex!"

Milla turned back to look but Jarek continued on past her. As the Wilder walked on toward the third Wormwalker, Tal saw a sudden glint appear in its eye — and multiply like fire across a pool of oil.

·CHAPTER·
TWENTY

"Look out!" screamed Tal, but even as the words left his mouth the Wormwalker struck. Its mandibles snapped down at Jarek, gripping the Wilder around the waist. He dropped his chain, and his mighty arms pushed against the creature's jaws, trying to keep them apart. Anyone else's hands would have been sliced through, but Jarek's strange skin resisted the mechanical insect's serrated mandibles. Even so, strong as he was, it was clear the Icecarl would soon be crushed.

Tal immediately raised his Sunstone and fired off a Red Ray of Destruction, only to see it absorbed by the Sunstones in the Wormwalker's eye. Adras and Odris flew forward, but as they tried to grip the creature's mandibles to help Jarek, they found themselves repelled by the green sheen on its surface, which was now sparking — another Sunstone-powered effect.

Milla attacked, too, whipping a light rope around the Wormwalker's head. But just as the Spiritshadows could not touch the metal, the rope of light was repelled.

Crow threw a knife at one eye, and was gratified and surprised to see a few Sunstones fall out, but not enough to make a difference.

Jarek roared, the Spiritshadows boomed and shouted, Milla cried a war cry, and Ebbitt said something to Tal as he fired another Red Ray, this time aiming at the thing's front set of legs.

"What?" shouted Tal. Ebbitt was bobbing around at his side and muttering while trying to read something from the Codex he had under his breastplate.

"The top of its head!" shouted Ebbitt. "In front of . . . in front of the saddle. You have to pull its . . . er . . . brain out."

Tal looked at the Wormwalker, which was shaking Jarek back and forth, its long body undulating wildly behind it all along the corridor. Milla was dancing about in front of it, whipping the light rope from her Talon across its eyes. With every third or fourth stroke, a Sunstone would fail to resist and explode, but there were too many for that tactic to work.

"In front of the saddle?" asked Tal quickly.

"Yes!"

Tal sized up the Wormwalker's motion and started to run. As he ran, he shouted to Adras. "Adras! Adras! Throw me onto the thing's head!"

Adras turned at his voice, but didn't seem to understand. Tal had a momentary vision of the Spiritshadow simply stepping aside to let him slide under the Wormwalker and into the forest of its razorsharp legs.

"Throw me!" he screamed. "Onto its head!"

The Spiritshadow finally got it. He cupped his hands a second before Tal reached him. The Chosen boy leaped, had his feet caught for an instant, and was thrown through the air, over the mandibles and the still-struggling Jarek.

He came down hard on the Wormwalker's head and started to slide off, the wrong side, down to the sharp legs. But the saddle was only a handsbreadth away, and he managed to stretch himself to what he was sure was much more than his usual height and grip on to it.

A moment later he had spun around and was in the saddle, holding on desperately as the Wormwalker arched, undulated, and shook in an effort to dislodge him.

Tal held on to a ring just in front of the saddle with one hand and clawed at a round panel set in the thing's head, which was the only possible clue to where its brain might be. All his nails broke, but he managed to flip it open. Underneath there was a single Sunstone set in the top of what looked like a crystal cylinder or tube full of a pulsing green fluid.

Tal forced his fingers into the receptacle and tried to pull the cylinder out. But he couldn't get a grip, and he was nearly thrown out of the saddle as the Wormwalker redoubled its efforts to shake him off. It was gyrating up and down from the floor and smacking itself against the ceiling, so that Tal had to fling himself right down on the saddle to avoid being crushed.

"Do . . . thing imp . . . !" shouted Ebbitt, his voice only just audible above the din. Tal took a second to translate this in his head as "Do something imperial!"

Tal grimaced, concentrated, and fired a pulse of pure Violet at the Sunstone atop the cylinder. It answered with a flash, and the cylinder popped half out of the receptacle. Tal grabbed it, pulled it the rest of the way out, and flung it over the side.

He almost went over himself, as the Wormwalker froze in midundulation. His hand, already sore from the climb up the slopdown, was burning and bleeding again and he had the familiar feeling of a nearly dislocated shoulder.

Climbing down, he found Ebbitt examining the long crystal tube. It was full of green lumps of something disgusting-looking, floating in what could be cooking oil but almost certainly wasn't.

"Well done," said Ebbitt, sliding the tube through his belt. "Very considerate of you to get one of these for me."

Tal shook his head. "I hope there aren't any more Wormwalkers ahead of us," he said. "Ebbitt, can you ask the Codex where Sushin is? It must have taken him quite a while to get this thing going again, so maybe he isn't too far ahead."

Ebbitt nodded, which to Tal meant yes, as he ducked under the Wormwalker's head to where Milla, Crow, and Malen were standing solemnly looking up at the body of Jarek.

One look told Tal that somewhere in those last few seconds of struggle, Jarek's strength had failed him, and the mandibles had closed.

"The fury did not come to him," said Milla.

"He did not want to live after Kirr was slain," said

Malen. "So it is with all Wilders. The fury only fails them when they do not need it anymore."

"I was too slow," said Tal. He looked away. "Too slow again . . ."

"You fought well," said Milla to Tal. "Almost like a Far-Raider. But we have all been too slow. We must not let Sushin have any more time to bring foes like this to life again."

"The Codex can't tell where Sushin is," said Ebbitt, appearing from under the Wormwalker, his breastplate pushed well away from his chest, a strange light now clearly visible shining through his rather grimy undershirt. "A power opposes it."

"What about the Veil?" asked Tal urgently. "Is the Veil still working?"

Ebbitt looked down and muttered a question.

"It's hard to read upside down," he complained. "But the Codex is not to be trusted if I keep it anywhere else, so —"

"The Veil, Ebbitt!"

"It's still up," replied Ebbitt with a smile. Then the smile disappeared, instantly wiped away. "But not for long. The Codex reports the Chamber of the Veil is in use. The Veil is being 'shut down,' whatever that is. Three of the Towers are already out, from Violet to Blue. Oh, no! Green is going!"

"Where is the Chamber of the Veil?" snapped Tal. "How do we get there?"

Ebbitt looked down, growled in exasperation, and ripped off his crystal breastplate, sending it clattering to the floor. There, tucked into his shirt, was the Codex of the Chosen, or a miniature version of it. A rectangle of pure crystal, its surface shimmered like the reflection of the moon on water.

Ebbitt pulled the Codex out, tearing his shirt, and set it against the wall. Its edges shimmered and then it slowly spread both sideways and up. In a few seconds it was the size Tal remembered, about as tall as Ebbitt and three times as wide.

"How do we get to the Chamber of the Veil from here?" asked Tal. He knew the Codex only answered direct questions.

Dark lines appeared on its surface. A map, with far too much detail for Tal to quickly take in. But there was also a line of text beneath the map, written in Chosen script and Icecarl runes.

Only one way, follow this spiral corridor to the top of the Seventh Tower.

·CHAPTER·
TWENTY-ONE

"How long will it be until the Veil is completely . . . ah . . . shut down?" asked Tal almost before he absorbed the answer to his previous question.

Twenty-nine minutes at current speed of procedure, answered the Codex, again in Chosen script and Icecarl runes, presumably so Milla and Malen could read the answer as well.

"Come on!" shouted Tal. He spun around and started running. From the map, there were at least three thousand stretches of spiraling corridor to run up. It should be possible to make it in under twenty minutes. Provided they didn't run into more Wormwalkers or other obstacles . . .

Milla, Crow, Malen, Adras, and Odris followed Tal without question. Ebbitt coughed and leaned against the wall.

"I'll catch you up," he shouted after them.

When he looked back, the Codex was shrinking and losing its form, becoming a stream of jellylike fluid that was climbing up the wall. Ebbitt pounced upon it and wrestled it back against his chest before starting off after the others at a quick walk.

The corridor wound past several more Wormwalkers, fortunately none of them operational. Tal tried not to slow as he approached each one, though it was hard not to. Instead he called Adras to come close to him, ready to throw him up onto its head if it proved necessary. Milla came close to him, too, with Odris at her side, obviously to mimic his tactic if required.

Crow and Malen ran together a little way behind. Tal had stopped worrying about the Freefolk boy. Either he had reformed completely, or he was not prepared to jeopardize his relationship — and his people's — with the Icecarls by doing anything to Tal.

The corridor narrowed a bit after the next turn, and there were many doors coming off it, one every twenty stretches or so on both sides. The doors were transparent, and as they got close enough, Tal looked left and Milla looked right, in unspoken agreement.

They saw strange things through the doors, but could not stop to look at them. There were many odd-looking machines, of metal and crystal and Sunstones, some of the latter still twinkling and glowing. There was room after room full of animals suspended in clear containers of fluid, animals that Milla recognized as being denizens of the Ice, or distant ancestors of them. There were things like newborn Selski, but not quite the same; and Merwins with no horns; and Wreska only a tenth of the size she knew; and Wrack hounds with strange skin instead of fur; and even shiny Norrworms, no larger than her finger and bundled up in balls of many worms, unlike the huge ones of the distant Ice that denned in pairs.

Onward and upward they ran, the spiraling corridor narrowing with every turn, and the doors showing glimpses of stranger and stranger secrets.

"Ebbitt," panted Tal, "will never get past all this. He'll open a door and forget what he was doing."

"We should have brought the Codex," said Milla. She was not really panting, but it took an effort to speak normally.

"No time to make it shrink," gasped Tal. "Besides, we know where Sushin must be."

Around another turn, Crow suddenly cried out

behind them, and half fell, half stumbled against the wall and immediately threw up. Malen stopped, too.

"Too much exertion, too soon," she said, feeling his forehead with her palm. "You must rest for a little while."

"Follow when you can!" shouted Milla, without stopping.

"So, it's just you and me again," said Tal as Milla increased the pace.

"And us!" interrupted Odris. "Why do you always forget us, Tal?"

"He's the Emperor now," said Adras gloomily. "Treats me like a servant."

"I do not!" protested Tal.

"Do too!"

"Save your breath," warned Milla. "It's getting steeper."

The spiral corridor was also winding itself tighter, and there were no more doors. It was like running up a very steep hill.

Tal started finding it harder to breathe, and a stitch began to grow in his side. He pushed his fist into it and ignored the pain. What was a stitch when the Veil was disappearing with every —

Then he saw it up ahead. The Veil. The corridor ended in absolute, clearly defined darkness.

"Is that . . . ?" asked Milla as they slowed down.

"Yes, the Veil," said Tal. "Adras and Odris, hold on to each other and on to us. Milla, take my hand. We should go through at a walk, and I'll keep my hand on the inside wall."

All four of them joined hands and Tal reached out to touch the inner wall.

"What if there is a trap inside?" asked Milla suspiciously.

Tal shook his head.

"I don't think you can do anything inside the Veil. It not only takes the light away, but breath as well. It's strange. It is not somewhere you could stay in long enough to set a trap."

Tal took a deep breath, Milla following suit. Then the two of them, and their Spiritshadows, plunged into total darkness.

All sound disappeared with the light. Even the touch of Milla's hand seemed distant and far away to Tal. He could feel the rasp of the stone under his other hand, but it was lessened, too. It would be easy to lose one's way in the Veil, to get turned around and blunder about until breath and senses failed.

It was even worse for Milla. She had expected the darkness of the Ice, but this was different. It was not cold, but somehow it leeched both energy and heat out of her, and made her shiver, something she rarely did from a simple chill. It also stretched on and on for much longer than Tal had said it would. She could feel his hand, but not the Spiritshadows', and even his hand felt strange and inhuman. The Veil was robbing her of breath and she was sure she would never see the light again —

When they burst out of the Veil, out into the Sunstone-lit corridor winding its way up and around ahead of them, Milla gasped in relief and swiftly looked at Tal to hide the small sign of her weakness. But Tal was gasping, too, and did not notice.

"That was bad," said Odris. "I do not think I would go through alone."

"I've been through three times," said Adras proudly.

"Let's hope it's still there when we come back," said Tal grimly. He broke into a run again, the stitch coming back straightaway.

"Will Crow and Malen make it through?" asked Milla.

"Crow's done it before," said Tal, though it took him a few seconds to get breath enough to answer. "He can help Malen. Or they could wait for Ebbitt, I guess."

Tal looked at his Sunstone, to check the time.

"Fourteen minutes gone," he said. "But we must be more than halfway."

They started to run again. Above the Veil, there were no more transparent doors, though there were side entrances every now and then, blocked by solid portals of metal or some material that might be wood.

Tal's stitch got worse, twisting deeper into his side. Finally he had to stop and bend over, almost retching from the exertion.

"I will go on," called Milla, but Tal reached out and grabbed her sleeve.

"No," he gasped. "Sushin is too powerful . . . and if Sharrakor is there . . . Adras, please, can you carry me?"

"See, he thinks I'm a servant," grumbled Adras.

"I said please," Tal coughed out.

"He did say please," confirmed Odris. "Shall I carry you as well, Milla?"

Milla frowned for a moment, then nodded.

"Yes," she said. "We should have thought of it before. The corridor is high enough, and it will be faster."

"I can't go too fast," said Odris. From the tone of

her voice she already regretted her offer. "I get tired as well, you know."

Milla and Tal held up their arms and felt the cool shadowflesh ripple across their wrists as the Spiritshadows gripped them. Adras and Odris were strong in the full, clear light of the corridor, and they lifted the Chosen and Icecarl with ease, and quickly accelerated up and around the bend.

It was much faster than the two humans could have run, though Adras had a tendency to cut corners and smack Tal into the side of the corridor, and Odris dipped every ten stretches or so and dragged Milla's feet along the ground.

After at least twenty more turns around the steadily steepening spiral corridor, Tal was dizzy. His stitch had gone, but he felt just as bad from the dizziness. If they kept going he would be in no state to face Sushin. He wouldn't even be able to see straight, let alone do any Light Magic.

"Stop!" he called. "We must be close!"

The Spiritshadows slowed to a halt and let go of their passengers. Tal staggered around for a few seconds, shaking his head until the dizziness passed.

"It can't be much farther," Tal said again. He

consulted his Sunstone. "Nineteen minutes. We have ten minutes until the Veil is gone."

"We should make a plan," said Milla. "What if Sushin has free Spiritshadows with him?"

Tal nodded. He had seen many free shadows in the Red Tower, above the Veil, brought across from Aenir to be the vanguard of an even larger force that would follow when the Veil fell.

"I think we have to concentrate on Sushin," he said. "Strike at him, as he's the one who can use the Violet Keystone. Adras and Odris can try to keep the free shadows off our backs."

"I cannot offer any better plan," said Milla. "We must hope fate favors us, and be bold and brave."

She held out her hand and turned her wrist up, showing the scars of her oaths.

"We have many vows between us, Tal," she said. "Let us add one more, without blood, for there is no time. Let us go together to save our world."

Tal held out his wrist, similarly scarred, and held it against Milla's.

"Together, to save the world. We will defeat Sushin and Sharrakor!"

Tal met Milla's eyes for a full second, and both of them saw something of themselves in the other's eyes. Somehow the Chosen had become almost an Icecarl, and the Icecarl was almost a Chosen. Emperor and War-Chief, both of them blending the best of their two peoples.

Then they broke apart and started off up the corridor, with their Spiritshadows behind. Two people of the Dark World, striding out together to face their enemy, the enemy of all life under the Veil.

·CHAPTER·
TWENTY-TWO ☉

The Chamber of the Veil was similar to the room at the top of the Red Tower, only larger and more impressive. It had four wide, arched windows that looked out to blue sky and sunshine. The floor was not checkered, but set with tiny Sunstones that shone with soft violet light that mixed with the golden sunshine.

Tal and Milla came to it sooner than they expected, the corridor simply turning steeply and merging into the floor of the chamber. They ducked down as they saw the edge, then peered up over the lip of the ramp.

There was no tree of bells as in the Red Tower, Tal saw, but there was a somewhat similar pyramid-shaped plinth in the center of the chamber. Parts of it shone like a Sunstone, in distinct colors. With a shock, Tal realized that the entire plinth was actually carved out of an enormous Sunstone, one that must have had a diameter of three stretches or more. He didn't know you could carve a Sunstone into any shape — let alone a pyramid.

As Tal watched, the horizontal band of yellow light in the pyramid went dark, and he saw with a feeling of terror that this was a progressive darkness, and that more than half of this enormous Sunstone had ceased to shine. Five distinct bands were dark, from the base of the pyramid up, and only two still shone. Orange and Red.

Then Tal saw Sushin. The bloated Chosen was on the far side of the pyramid, holding the Violet Keystone in his hand. He was sending pulses of Violet into the pyramid, pulses that Tal instinctively knew were closing — no, what was the term the Codex had used? *Shutting down the Veil.*

Sushin's Spiritshadow, a monster of spikes, with four hooked claws and two massive horns sprouting from its head, loomed up behind its master. But there were no other Spiritshadows in the Chamber, at least that Tal could see. He felt a rising hope build inside him. Sushin was a dangerous enemy, but he was alone.

"Attack on three?" he whispered to Milla, and she

nodded. Tal saw that the Talon on her hand was already glowing as she held it out from her body.

Tal held up three fingers. Closed one, his heart pounding. Closed two, his heart going faster than it ever had before, red light pulsing in his Sunstone. Closed three —

"Go!"

Everything happened too quickly then. There was no time for thought, only instinct.

Tal jumped forward and fired a Red Ray at the Spiritshadow, because Sushin was protected by too many Sunstones. It hit the thing between the eyes, and it reeled back, clasping its head with two hooked hands.

Milla charged straight at Sushin, the Talon fully extended, a long lash of light twisting and curling from it as if it had a life of its own.

Sushin didn't move. He stood there like a statue, the Violet Keystone on his finger continuing to pulse at the pyramid stone.

The Orange band of light went out. Sushin's Spiritshadow dashed forward, only to be met by another Red Ray from Tal as he advanced. Adras and Odris zoomed ahead, to grab the enemy Spiritshadow.

Milla struck at Sushin with the Talon, and Sunstones flared on every hem of his violet-colored robe. The lash of light from the Talon was deflected, whipping back over Milla's head. Without a second thought, the Icecarl flipped a bone knife out of her sleeve and tried to stab Sushin with a more physical weapon. But the Sunstones flared red, and the knife was burned away in an incandescent flash.

Milla howled in fury and tried to punch the Talon into Sushin's face. More Sunstones flared, this time blue and green, and she found herself picked up by some unseen force and thrown over the Chosen's head. Somersaulting in the air, she landed on her toes and rushed back, as Tal ran forward to join her, half his mind focused on forming the beginnings of the Violet Unraveling in his Sunstone.

Milla struck again first, and was once more thrown aside by Sushin's defensive spells, sliding across the floor with an angry scream. On the other side of the chamber, Adras and Odris were twisting the Spiritshadow's claws behind its back and holding it so it couldn't use its horns or teeth. Then they proceeded to tear it apart, bellowing and thundering with every wrench.

"Stay clear!" shouted Tal. A Violet cloud was spewing out of his half of the Violet Keystone. With a flick of his wrist, he sent it spinning into Sushin.

Every Sunstone on Sushin burst into brilliance as

the Violet Unraveling hit. For a moment, it looked like they might resist it, or even turn it back. Then they started to explode, one by one, as the Unraveling bit into them.

Yet Sushin still didn't move, keeping his half of the Violet Keystone on the pyramid. Even as his last Sunstone vaporized and the Unraveling started to eat away at his clothes and exposed flesh, he did not look away or lower his hand.

Then the last band of color in the pyramid went out. All seven bands were dark.

Sushin moved swift as a cavernmouth, turning his part of the Keystone back to bathe himself in Violet light of a different shade from the Unraveling. They canceled each other out, in the very second that Tal and Milla attacked again.

Tal's Red Ray was the strongest he'd ever dared, a finger-thin beam of vicious light aimed directly at Sushin's head. But Sushin caught it on his Keystone, deflecting most of it to the ceiling, though his hand was burned.

Milla came in low, sweeping the lash of light from the Talon across Sushin's legs. With inhuman speed, Sushin countered with a shield of Violet, but he was not quite fast enough and the lash cut deeply into his legs, just above his ankles.

As before, when Milla had thrown her Merwin-horn sword at him, no blood came out of these wounds. But Sushin did fall to the ground, his hamstrings cut. He wriggled like a Wormwalker around the pyramid, shrieking as he scuttled. "No, it's not me! It's not me! Don't kill Sushin!"

Then another voice came from somewhere inside him, a deeper, stranger voice, louder and more horrible than anything that came from any human mouth.

"You have lost! The Veil is destroyed! The time of Sharrakor has come!"

Then it spoke a quick series of words, words that neither Tal nor Milla knew, but somehow still recognized.

"Nvarth! Ghesh gheshthil lurese!"

Then it spoke words they did know, words that hit them like physical blows.

"Adras eris Aenir! Odris eris Aenir!"

With those words, Adras and Odris disappeared. To Tal and Milla it was like having something torn out of their bodies, a pain so terrible that both of them were instantly felled, toppling to the floor like chopped trees.

Through a haze of crippling pain, Tal saw Sushin crawling back around the pyramid, crawling toward him. He tried to focus on his Sunstone, but everything was blurry and he could not make his hand do what he wanted.

Milla tried, too, and actually managed to drag herself closer to Tal and raise her hand with the Talon. But no light whip came, and she could not keep going. All her strength was gone.

They were dying, Tal realized, though he could not think clearly for the pain. This was what had happened to Ethar and the other Chosen outside the Audience Chamber. Sushin — or whatever was *in* Sushin — had sent their Spiritshadows back to Aenir and the sudden shock had killed them.

"I shall take that," said Sushin in his normal voice, as he crawled up next to Tal. One blubbery hand reached across and slid the Violet Keystone from Tal's finger. The Chosen boy tried to resist, but it was no good. His arm just flopped and the pain stabbed through his eyes into his brain. "I think this is best put back together."

Sushin sat up and inspected the half Keystone he had taken. But before he could slip it on his own finger next to the half he already had, a beam of intense red light shot out and struck him full on the hand. The Keystone ring fell to the floor and bounced away.

The voice inside Sushin growled then, a sound that drove fear even through the pain in Tal.

Another Red Ray struck Sushin in the chest, smoke curling up as it drilled a hole right through him. He growled again and struggled to get to his feet, forgetting his hamstrings and bulk. He fell over again and started to slither along the ground like a snake or worm, toward the pyramid.

Through the deep cuts and rents in the Chosen's robe, Tal saw not flesh and blood, but shadow.

Tal rolled over, crying with the pain, and saw Crow standing near the entrance. The Freefolk boy was holding out his Sunstone in the approved manner taught in the Lectorium, his face wrinkled in concentration. Red light bathed his hand, growing in intensity as he prepared another Red Ray. A second later, it shot out, striking sparks as it cut through some metal on Sushin's robes.

But it still did not slow whatever Sushin was. He reached the pyramid and dragged himself up, using it as a prop so he could aim his Sunstone at Crow.

"Not! Not a man!" screamed Tal, the words interspersed with sobs. "A shadow! Malen . . ."

He could say no more, his strength exhausted.

·CHAPTER·
TWENTY–THREE

As Tal's words echoed in the chamber, Sushin fired a globe of shimmering Violet back at Crow and Malen's voice filled the air. A quavering, uncertain voice, speaking the words of the Prayer to Asteyr.

Crow dived aside and the Violet globe sailed past him, struck the wall between two windows, and exploded straight through, out into the air beyond, followed by a great plume of stone chips and dust.

The effect of Malen's voice was equally spectacular. Sushin froze, his mouth open, his hand extended. Then his whole body blurred. There was his human form, and then there was a dark double that was separating out of him, stepping back from the human version.

It was a shadow leaving the flesh it had hidden in. As it came out, it changed and grew, growing larger and more menacing. Slowly it assumed the shape that only Tal had seen before.

A monster. A dragon. Sharrakor himself.

Fully out of his fleshly host, his reptilean body stretched from floor to ceiling. His head was long and spiked, his many-toothed mouth big enough to snap up Tal in a single bite. His wings were furled, as they would not fit in the chamber. His tail was long and ended in a bone shaped like a butcher's cleaver.

"Asteyr herself could not bind me alone," roared Sharrakor. "How could you succeed where she failed and died for her failure? I do not see Danir, Susir, and Grettir come to do her work!"

The shadowdragon's voice momentarily drowned out Malen's, and for a moment Tal thought she had stopped. But then her voice came back again. Quiet, slow, but unafraid. Whether her prayer could bind Sharrakor or not, he clearly didn't like it.

"Speak your spell!" he roared again. "I shall not stay to hear it. But you I shall seek out, witch of the Ice, if you still live when I return. Go now and tell your peoples that the Veil is destroyed! That Sharrakor will soon finish the war your ancestors so foolishly began!"

With that, the shadowdragon's head flashed down

and bit off Sushin's hand. It held it in its mighty jaws for an instant, then the Spiritshadow disappeared, and the hand fell to the floor — minus the Sunstone ring that had been there a moment before.

Malen kept reciting the Prayer to Asteyr, even though the object of it was no longer visible. Crow rushed over to where Tal and Milla were writhing on the ground.

"What happened?" he asked. "Where are you hurt?"

"Spiritshadows," said Tal. He could barely speak between sobs of pain. "Sent back. Aenir. We . . . must . . . follow. Get Ebbitt. Get ring. Please . . . please . . ."

Tal watched Crow turn and pick up the ring. This is where it happens, his shocked brain thought. This is the betrayal. This is where Crow takes the ring and walks away. There, he is turning now. This is the end —

He was still thinking that when Crow slipped the half Keystone back on his finger.

"I know the Way to Aenir," said Crow. "Ebbitt showed me once. But I never went. Now seems the time."

"Get Milla," whispered Tal. He couldn't concentrate. "You . . . reflect the light into our stones. . . ."

Milla had already crawled a little closer. She did not speak or make any sound of pain when Crow grabbed her and dragged her next to Tal, rolling them both onto their backs and resting their Sunstones on their chests, their heads on his lap.

"Milla," muttered Tal. "Watch . . . Sunstone . . . follow . . . repeat . . ."

Crow began to visualize the colors and speak the Way to Aenir. His Sunstone flashed and he directed beams from it to the Sunstones clasped in Milla's and Tal's hands.

Through the pain, Tal tried to repeat the words Crow was speaking. He knew that they must get to Aenir. They had to find Adras and Odris, who must be dying there. They had to get back and repair or raise the Veil again, and prepare for Sharrakor's invasion. . . .

Milla followed the words without thinking of anything else. The words and colors were all that mattered. She had to survive. Her people were depending upon her. She had failed them already and had not defended the Veil. She must live to reverse her defeat. . . .

Malen finished the Prayer to Asteyr. But she did not feel its success. Sharrakor must have returned to

Aenir to avoid the spell. He was not lurking, somehow invisible.

Malen saw Crow sitting with Tal and Milla cradled against him, with waves of many-colored light washing across all three of them. She saw Sushin dead or dying next to the pyramid, blood flowing freely now that the shadow in him was gone.

Then she saw a flash of light at the very apex of the pyramid. It had been completely dark, but now the top began to shine with a weak red light. Malen watched it, thinking the light might spread, but it didn't. Only the top glowed.

She heard a noise behind her and whirled around, suddenly afraid. She was effectively alone, a Crone disconnected from her mothers and sisters, without Shield Maidens or hunters to protect her.

It was Ebbitt, puffing and straining as he climbed the ramp. He saw Malen staring at him, wild-eyed, and Sushin behind, the almost totally dark pyramid, and the rainbow-cocooned trio of Crow, Tal, and Milla.

"What happened?"

Malen shivered and found herself unable to speak, the words caught in her throat. Ebbitt rushed past her, and after a further glance at the three who had clearly gone to Aenir, he knelt beside Sushin, his Sunstone glowing as he called up healing magic. Ebbitt's Spiritshadow sniffed at Sushin, then wandered over to sniff at the point where Adras and Odris had pulled apart Sushin's spiky Spiritshadow.

"He . . . he had a shadow in him," blurted out Malen. "Sharrakor. A dragon. He made Adras and Odris disappear and Tal and Milla fell down. We were watching and Crow used Light Magic and I tried the Prayer of Asteyr but Sharrakor said the Veil was destroyed and he'd come back. . . ."

"The Veil isn't destroyed, it's just fraying at the edges," said Ebbitt sharply. There was no indication of his usual dodderiness. "The Red Keystone is keeping it going, at least for a while. Though not as strongly as it should, perhaps. What did Sharrakor say about coming back?"

"He said he'd come back and finish the war," said Malen. "Oh, I'd better . . . I'd better report . . ."

She stood up straighter and put her hands to her head. But the more she tried to reach the other Crones, the more she heard Sharrakor's awful voice, and his threat, that he would find her. . . .

"That'll hold you," said Ebbitt.

Sushin opened his eyes. "Thank you but that will be quite . . ." His voice trailed off and an expression of total bewilderment spread across his face. "Where am I? Who are you?"

"Rest now," soothed Ebbitt. "You've had an accident."

"I was in Aenir," said Sushin. "Having breakfast with Julper Yen-Baren. He was going to help me climb to Yellow. . . ."

He paused for a moment.

"I dreamed," he said after the pause. "A terrible dream. My head was opened and a stranger poured himself inside —"

His voice was getting more and more shrill as he spoke, building toward hysteria. Ebbitt hastily raised his Sunstone and a green light fell down on Sushin's face. The Chosen's eyes closed and he slumped back against the pyramid.

"I'm not sure whether it will be more merciful to help him live or die," remarked Ebbitt. "I suppose as in so many things, fate will decide. Imagine his last memory being breakfast with Julper Yen-Baren! More than thirty years ago. I bet it was a rotten breakfast, too. Julper was a mean fellow. Come on, then."

"Come on?" asked Malen. "Where?"

"Aenir," said Ebbitt impatiently. "You'll have to share my Sunstone for the transition. Just stare at it and repeat what I say."

"Aenir!" exclaimed Malen. "I can't go there!"

"You'll be needed," said Ebbitt. "From what I read in the Codex."

"What do you mean?"

"Ah, that would be telling," replied Ebbitt.

"Yes it would!" said Malen, stamping her foot. "So tell me, you . . . you old hoarder!"

Being called a hoarder was a serious insult among Icecarls, for sharing food and essentials was a central part of any clan's survival. Ebbitt, however, was not offended.

"Oh, put like that, I suppose," he said, rubbing his nose. "Having got rid of the Veil, or close enough, Sharrakor's next step must be to undo the Forgetting. Since it was your Crones — or the historical equivalent — that did the Forgetting in the first place, it seems to me that you'll be required."

"But I'm only a young Crone," protested Malen.

"You're the *only* Crone who's right here right now," answered Ebbitt, taking her arm. "Just stare into this Sunstone."

"But I should inform —"

"No time for that!" cried Ebbitt. His Spirit-shadow had sidled up to his side, and his Sunstone was already changing color, beginning the sequence that was part of the Way to Aenir. "They'll figure it out. Remember, say the words after me!"

He started reciting, and Malen, despite herself, stared into the Sunstone and repeated the words. Aenir! She was going to Aenir, where no Icecarl save Milla had been for a thousand circlings or more!

Neither of them noticed a trickle of silver slide out the back of Ebbitt's shirt and roll across the floor. The Codex of the Chosen had spent too long in Aenir, and it had no plans to return.

·CHAPTER·
TWENTY–FOUR

Tal, Milla, and Crow fell onto a stone platform that wriggled under them and tried to crawl away. The weaker sunshine of Aenir fell upon their changed bodies, the Aeniran versions of themselves. They were a little shorter, and slimmer, and their skin glowed with a slight luster.

The pain was still with Tal and Milla, but to a much lesser extent. Tal could feel Adras some-where. Too far away, but not totally absent. So the Storm Shepherd was still alive, thank the Light.

Tal sat up and looked around. They didn't seem to be in immediate danger, though the stone slab moving under him was a bit creepy. It was not the only apparently solid object that was moving. The remains of a nearby wall were also slowly shifting away, trailing old mortar.

"Ruins," said Crow. He was standing up, shaking his head a little as he looked around him and down at his changed self. "So this is Aenir. I always wanted to see this."

"Can you see any enemies?" asked Milla. She stood up, too, then sat down again rather too quickly and began massaging her legs and doing exercises with her arms.

"No," replied Crow. "At least I don't think so. There are a lot of stones moving around. Very slowly. Where are we, anyway?"

"A ruined city," said Tal, which was pretty obvious to everyone. At least that was what it looked like. You never could be too sure in Aenir what anything really was, as opposed to what it seemed to be. Certainly they were surrounded by many ruined buildings, and there were plenty more as far as he could see, rising up into the hills around.

"What happened?" asked Milla. "I felt Odris . . . wrenched . . . away. It was worse than when the Merwin gored me."

Tal shook his head.

"I'm not sure. Somehow Sharrakor sent them back here. But they're coming. I think."

"Yes," confirmed Milla. "I can feel Odris getting closer. But they are far away."

"We failed," said Tal, after they were both silent for a moment. "The Veil is gone."

"The Ice will melt," said Milla quietly. "The Slepenish and the Selski will die, and my people with them."

"And any who do survive will be slain by the shadows Sharrakor will lead back there."

"Not if we stop him," said Milla. "Perhaps we can do this one small thing, when we have failed in so many others."

"We must try," said Tal. He was thinking of his family, back in the Castle. He had saved Graile, there was a good chance his father, Rerem, could be rescued from the Orange Keystone, and Gref and Kusi reunited with them. But for what? So they could all die together when Sharrakor invaded?

"No," Milla contradicted him. "We must *succeed.*"

Tal and Crow nodded grimly in agreement. Tal forced himself to his feet. He tottered a little and had to put his hand on Milla's shoulder to balance. Crow offered a steadying hand, but Tal refused it. He managed to stand unassisted and look out in the direction he felt the Storm Shepherds were coming from. Seeing nothing, he slowly turned around in a circle.

There was a speck on the horizon, and for a moment Tal thought it was Adras. But it didn't look right, and after a second he realized it was flying away. He pointed it out to Milla and Crow.

"What's that?"

Crow looked but couldn't see it. Milla shaded her eyes with her hand.

"A dragon. Sharrakor," she said, the name sending a thrill of fear through each of them. "He is not dark like a shadow here, but bright as a mirror shining in the sun."

"Watch him as far as you are able," said Tal. "We'll have to follow when we can."

A movement attracted his attention and he whirled unsteadily. But it was only a boulder crossing between two walls, in a slow and stately progress.

Tal sighed and sat back down. There was nothing they could do for a little while. They had to regain their strength and wait for Adras and Odris to arrive.

But it was not Adras and Odris who arrived. There was a shimmer in the air next to them, and a sudden rainbow. Tal and Milla scurried back, readying Sunstone and Talon. Crow took cover behind the wall and picked up what he hoped was an inanimate rock. His knife had not come across with the transfer, but some of his other odds and ends had, though perhaps not without some transformation.

"Chosen!" snapped Tal. "Coming through from the Castle!"

The rainbow grew brighter, there was a flash, then Ebbitt and Malen were standing in front of them, accompanied by a dark green cat with a light green mane. Ebbitt was clutching his chest, and for a moment Tal thought he was having a heart attack, until the old man stamped his feet and launched into a tirade.

"Dark throttle the thing! Just when we needed it the most!"

"Hello, Great-uncle," said Tal. "What was it you needed?"

"The cursed Codex," shouted Ebbitt, flinging himself facedown on the stone to beat at it with his fists. His maned cat sat next to him and started licking its paws. "It got away from me."

"Welcome, Malen," said Milla, clapping her fists. "I am glad you are with us."

Malen was looking around, watching the creeping rocks and shivering walls. She stared back at Milla and belatedly clapped her fists in return.

"Greetings, War-Chief. I wasn't sure, but Ebbitt

insisted . . . I have to help stop Sharrakor from undoing the Forgetting, before the Veil fails."

"What?" snapped Tal. "What do you mean *before the Veil fails?*"

Ebbitt stopped beating at the stone with his fists and rolled on his side. His cat moved aside a little crossly to give him room, then resumed its toilet. Tal noticed that while its short hair was green, its eyes were yellow and its claws remarkably white.

"Lokar replaced and resealed the Red Keystone," he said. "Or the other way around. Anyway, it will keep the Veil going — at less than full strength — for about seven days, by my calculations."

"Your calculations!" exclaimed Tal.

637

"The Codex helped me with the hard bit, carrying the decimal point all over the place," admitted Ebbitt. "We talked about it as I was coming up after you hotheads. Always best to plan for the worst, I say."

"Seven days!" exclaimed Tal, and Milla echoed him, as Ebbitt frowned.

"It's not long, but I could be out an hour or two —" Ebbitt started to say. He stopped as Tal and Milla laughed and cheered. Crow smiled briefly, but kept watching the surrounding ruins and the sky.

"Seven days!" Tal exclaimed again. "We thought

the Veil was already gone! This gives us . . . this gives everyone . . . a chance."

"Yes, it's all quite simple," growled Ebbitt. "Find Sharrakor, stop him from undoing the Forgetting and raising an army of tens of thousands of Aenirans, get the other half of the Violet Keystone back, return to the Castle, restore the Veil, settle the war with the Icecarls, free the Underfolk —"

"Yes!" interrupted Crow.

"As I was saying, free the Underfolk, and . . . I've lost my locomotor of thought."

"The Storm Shepherds!" interrupted Crow again, pointing at the sky. "At least, I hope that's what they are."

Tal and Milla turned together and held out their arms. Two huge figures of cloud swooped down and embraced them so vigorously they would have fallen over again if they hadn't been almost crushed in puffy arms. Odris cried as well, rain pouring out in streams from the side of her head, making Ebbitt's cat give a strange yipping cry and jump aside.

"We almost died!" sobbed Odris. "And we ended up back at Hrigga Hill and it tried to eat us!"

"I want to give your shadow back," said Adras. "It hurt too much."

"Yes," said Tal, pushing Adras's arms aside and stepping back. "I think it is time we undid the binding between us. We should go into the next fight as we mean to go on. Without Spiritshadows or bound companions."

·CHAPTER·
TWENTY-FIVE

"I will be sorry to see the old cat go." Ebbitt sighed. "But I see your point."

"Oh, I didn't mean your —" Tal started to say.

"We've had one rule for some and a different rule for others for too long," said Ebbitt. He leaned over and rubbed his green cat under the chin. It purred and shifted its head so he would scratch the best spots. "Got to set an example for you young folk, don't I? Now, how do we go about it?"

"Um, I don't know," said Tal. "I thought you might."

"Not on the curriculum." Ebbitt sighed again. "Finding and binding, that was it."

"I know," said Malen quietly. "You use a variation of the Prayer to Asteyr to bind them in the first place. I can see it in the Aenirans. I can undo the binding between Tal, Milla, and the Storm Shepherds. I don't know about yours, Ebbitt. The . . . cat . . . was unwilling originally and the binding is very old and strong."

"Do it, then," said Milla. She would get her own shadow back! It was a step toward being a normal Icecarl again, a step she never thought she would be able to take. Yet at the same time, she had become used to Odris, and the Storm Shepherd had been a good and helpful companion. If a trifle annoying at times.

"Stand in a line," ordered Malen tentatively. "Next to one another."

They all shuffled into a line, Ebbitt still scratching the neck of his cat. Tal noticed that there were the beginnings of tears in the old man's eyes, but he didn't say anything. He was sad himself. All his life he had wanted a powerful Spiritshadow, to help him gain a high place in the Castle. But all that was gone. If they survived, they would live in new times, and there was no place for Aeniran — or human — slaves.

Malen began to chant as they stood silently in front of her. The words were familiar, many of them from what Tal now knew was the Prayer to Asteyr, but with a different cadence and rhythm. He felt the words resonate deep inside his bones, sending a shivery, feverish feeling through every part of his body.

The chant grew faster and stronger, and Malen began to stamp around in a circle, punctuating every ten words or so with a heavier stomp, sending dust flying.

Slowly, in answer to the words, shadows began to creep out of the three Aeniran creatures. Human shadows, which flowed slowly across the stones toward the feet of their original casters.

Malen shouted the last word and came to a sudden stop. Tal felt his shadow reconnect, and the connection he had with Adras was totally severed. For a moment, he felt thick in the head, as if he had a cold. Then he realized that the sense of the wind and the weather that came from Adras was gone.

Tal turned to Adras, and Milla to Odris.

"Well, that's that," said Tal in a small voice. "Thank you for everything you've done for me, Adras."

"I thank you, too, Odris," said Milla. "I hope you bear no ill will for the times I have been hard with you. Farewell."

"Farewell?" asked Odris. "We aren't going anywhere without you. Certainly not back to our old life at Hrigga Hill. Far too boring."

"We're going to come and watch you fight Shar-rakor," said Adras. "We'll even help if we can, though he is the Overlord and all that."

"The Overlord?" asked Tal. His mind was only half on the conversation, as he was watching Ebbitt kneel down by his cat and bare his neck, as if inviting it to bite him or something. Milla had seen it, too, and was already moving across, ready to intervene.

"Sure," said Adras. "The King or whatever. Odris said."

"What?" asked Tal, tensing as the green cat leaned forward and opened its mouth, revealing teeth as white as its claws, but much larger. Would it kill Ebbitt for enslaving it for so long? Milla took another step closer, the Talon extending.

"That's why we had to obey back in the Dark World," said Odris. "Sharrakor holds the oaths of most Aenirans from the old times, including our parents. But we don't have to obey him in everything. At least, I don't think so."

The cat licked Ebbitt's face, making him splutter and almost fall over, and jumped away, a green flash speeding through the ruins.

"That's what my shadowguard did," said Tal.

"He was with me for sixty years," said Ebbitt. He

sighed and accepted Milla's help to get up. "Well, we had best be getting on, children."

"Where?" asked Tal. "Where will Sharrakor be? And how does he undo the Forgetting?"

No one answered him. It was clear from the looks on the faces of humans and Storm Shepherds alike that no one knew the answer to his questions.

"I don't know," said Milla. "But I do know someone we can ask."

"Who?"

"Zicka the Kurshken," said Milla. "At Kurshken Corner. Wherever that is."

"Kurshken Corner?" said Odris. "I know how to get there, provided it hasn't moved lately. Assuming this is Rorn, which I guess it must be."

"Rorn?" asked Tal.

"Rorn?" echoed Ebbitt.

Milla and Crow looked at their shocked expressions.

"Rorn is forbidden to the Chosen," explained Tal. "Though I don't know why. We were taught never to go there . . . come here."

"The penalty is death," said Ebbitt. "I always wanted to take a look myself. This must be it. I know Rorn was a ruined city, heavily staked."

"Staked?" asked Crow.

"Staked through with Sunstone stakes," said Ebbitt. "Like the Chosen Enclave. To stop it from moving around. If we see some of those, then it must be Rorn. I wonder whose city it was and who lived here."

"Sharrakor, of course," said Odris. "Even *I* know that. It was the capital, before the Forgetting. All Sharrakor's people lived here before they got killed in the war. He's the only one left."

"This was a city of dragons?" asked Milla.

"No, silly," said Odris. "Sharrakor isn't a dragon all the time. He's a doubleganger, or maybe a triple-ganger. A shaper. He can turn into two or three different things, big like the dragon, or small like a mind-drill. The really bad ones that climb into your brain. That's what the shapers used to do a lot. That's one of the ways they ruled everyone else in the old times."

"Why didn't you tell us this before?" exclaimed Tal. "It would have been useful to know that Sharrakor could become a . . . a shadow mind-drill . . . back in the Castle."

"You never asked," said Odris primly. "And I never heard you mention Sharrakor at all, so it's *your* fault, not mine. And Adras didn't know because he never paid any attention to my lessons."

"Never!" announced Adras proudly. "Too boring."

Tal sighed. If only he had taken Odris with him instead of Adras when they met the Empress and the Light Vizier. If only he had taken Odris with him full stop. But that was an old and familiar feeling by now. Adras was Adras, as Ebbitt was Ebbitt. They both had their advantages, he supposed.

"Let's assume this is Rorn," said Milla, bringing them all back on track. "How far is Kurshken Corner, Odris?"

"Half a day's flight, maybe less," Odris replied with a shrug. "If it hasn't moved."

"Three or four days' walk," mused Milla. "Too long. Is there some way we can all fly?"

"I could carry Tal and someone else," declared Adras. He flexed the muscle in his puffy arms. "I am the strongest!"

"I can only carry Milla," said Odris. "We could leave Ebbitt or Crow behind. Or Malen."

"No," said Crow. "It is my fight, too. The Freefolk should be represented."

"We can't leave anyone behind," said Tal. He was thinking as he spoke. Perhaps there was a way to use the Storm Shepherds more effectively. "Ebbitt, what if we made a boat of light and sort of . . .

crossed it with a Hand of Light. If we could keep it going, it could lift us up and Adras and Odris could push or pull it."

A little of Ebbitt's usual spark returned to his eyes. This was the sort of thing he liked. A crazy idea that most Chosen would refuse to even think about.

"You have half of the Violet Keystone, which is very powerful," he mused. "If we bond the mesh with Violet, and weave it Green . . . Blue traces . . . yes, yes . . . What are you waiting for? There's not time to stand around! You start on a backbone of Violet and I'll do the planking in Green with Yellow perhaps. . . ."

Tal smiled. It was a little forced, but still a smile. Then he began to focus on his Sunstone. He and Ebbitt would build a flying boat of light, propelled by Storm Shepherds, to take them to Kurshken Corner and beyond.

·CHAPTER·
TWENTY–SIX

Kurshken Corner looked very odd from the air. It was a huge flooded field filled with giant leafy balls of yellow vegetation, a lot like vastly over-grown sprouts, outsized versions of the ones the Underfolk grew in their subterranean greenhouses. Most of the sprouts were the size of a Chosen family's greeting room, but some were much larger. They were clearly inhabited, as Kurshken could be seen coming and going between the different plants, skipping through the shallow water or racing along the many raised levees that crisscrossed the field.

Not that Tal had much time to look. Their flying boat, modeled on Asteyr's Orskir, required constant attention to stay both airborne and together. It was drawn by the two Storm Shepherds pulling on blue traces, but the actual lifting came from a variation of the Hand of Light spell, and Tal or Ebbitt had to keep it going with constant infusions of power from their Sunstones. Crow and Milla had each helped them from time to time, but were not practiced enough to take over completely.

With varying levels of power, the boat flew along at an erratic speed, depending on the Storm Shepherds' way with the winds and their own endurance. There were sometimes quite alarming variations in altitude as the various Sunstone-wielders changed shifts and combinations. The only person who wasn't worried was Malen, who had fallen asleep. The unbinding of the Aenirans had taken its toll and she had not been able to stay awake, much as she wanted to see the strange territory they flew over and the Aeniran denizens they encountered in the air or spotted on the ground.

The arrival of the flying boat at Kurshken Corner was greeted by the Kurshken with some alarm. There was some alarm on board as well, as the boat lurched and bobbed down to a heavy, skidding landing in a vacant area next to one of the levees. As soon as they were safely down, Tal and Ebbitt made sure Malen was awake and everyone was standing up, then they let the boat of light fade away. The Storm Shepherds, relieved of the blue traces, flitted back to float above the rest of their party.

Before everyone could climb out of the ankle-deep water to the levee, they were surrounded by scores of knee-high green lizards, each of them bearing a bow with a nocked arrow. The arrows had bright blue heads and looked highly poisonous.

"Peace!" called out Milla. "We are friends of Quorr Quorr Quorr Quorr Ahhtorn Sezicka!"

Tal shut his mouth. He'd been about to blurt out the short form "Zicka," which was all he could remember of their friend's name.

The name relieved the tension somewhat. The Kurshken lowered their bows but did not, Tal noticed, return their arrows to the quivers on their scaly backs. In the rear ranks, he saw several lizards turn and dash away, skipping across the water without actually going through it.

One lizard, who had two huge ivory teeth bound into the shoulders of his woven-grass harness, approached and bowed.

"I am Quorr Quorr Quorr Quorr Quorr Jak-Quorr Jareskk Yazeqicka," the lizard announced, his voice deeper than anyone who had not met a Kurshken before would suspect. "You may call me

Yazeq. Four of you I suspect I know from my triple-sister's second-clutch fifth-birthing's report — you know him as Zicka. You I think are Milla, and Tal, and the Storm Shepherds Odris and Adras."

Everyone bowed in return, Adras nearly colliding with Tal's head. Milla confirmed their names, and introduced Ebbitt, Malen, and Crow.

"Come," said Yazeq, with a particular glance at Ebbitt. "You must be tired. You may rest in our guest roro, or as you may wish to call it, roroqqolleckechahen."

"I'll say roro," Ebbitt replied weakly. Tal took his arm and looked down at his great-uncle with concern. Since his Spiritshadow had left, Ebbitt seemed older and more tired. The — admittedly rather lunatic — spark in his eyes had dimmed, and he looked pale, the Aeniran glow absent from his face. Maintaining the flying boat had also taken far more out of him, Tal saw, than Ebbitt would admit. Tal felt bad about it, for he had taken his great-uncle's power, skill, and endurance for granted.

"Are you all right, Ebbitt?" asked Milla.

"I am weary," said Ebbitt. "Very weary indeed. It comes from having to do more than my share of the work, but perhaps Tal will be less lazy in the future."

Tal scowled, but only because it was clear Ebbitt's heart wasn't in the insult. His great-uncle really was tired.

The roro turned out to be one of the huge sprout vegetables. The outer, living leaves concealed a solid husk, which was hollow and had been outfitted most comfortably with rugs and carpets woven from various natural fibers. As it was a guest roro, there were also a number of wooden chairs of different sizes, and drinking horns that varied in length from finger-sized to one as long as Tal's arm.

As they settled down on chairs, on rugs, or in the air and accepted suitably sized drinking horns filled with a sweet juice or sap, the leaves parted to admit another Kurshken. Though all Kurshken looked remarkably similar, something about this one made him instantly known to Tal and Milla.

"Zicka!"

"Indeed," said the lizard. "Welcome to Kurshken Corner, that in our tongue we call —"

Ebbitt interrupted with a fit of sudden coughing. Tal would have been concerned if he hadn't seen the faint glint in his great-uncle's eyes.

"I had not looked to see you so soon," continued Zicka as he sat down and accepted a drink. "But I am glad to see you escaped the Waspwyrm. Did you manage to return the Codex to its rightful place?"

"Sort of," replied Tal, sharing a glance with Milla. "But we have a bigger problem now, one that we hope you can help us with."

Speaking quickly, taking it in turns with Milla and ignoring the occasional interjections from Adras, Odris, and Ebbitt, Tal told Zicka and Yazeq about the situation in the Castle and how they had followed Sharrakor back to Aenir to stop him from undoing the Forgetting.

"So you see we must kill Sharrakor soon," finished Milla as Tal paused. "We cannot allow him to free every Aeniran and lead them back to our world. We hope you can tell us where he is, or will be."

Zicka and Yazeq looked at each other and spoke in a rapid tumble of words that all seemed to run together.

"This is disturbing news," said Zicka. "We had thought Sharrakor — or Skerrako as he was sometimes called by your ancestors — was still imprisoned beneath the ruins of Rorn."

"Imprisoned?" asked Tal. "How?"

"He was bound into a single shape by Asteyr, who died in the doing of it, then was overcome by

Danir, Susir, and Grettir," said Kurshken. "They did not wish to slay him, for he was an honorable enemy in their thinking. They bound him in chains of ethren, the golden metal, far beneath the ruins of his city. Someone must have released him, though I am surprised that even a shaper could live so long."

"The Empress and her brother, I guess," said Tal, shaking his head. "Looking for some power to help them overcome the Emperor Mercur."

"He will not be as strong as he was so long ago," continued Zicka. "Which is as well for all of us who would remain free. Sharrakor will not forget that we aided Asteyr and her daughters, and Ramellan, too, for that matter. And he will have many to help him, if he undoes the Forgetting and frees them from their bounds."

"So where *will* he undo the Forgetting?" asked Milla.

"There is only one place," replied Zicka. "The Old Khamsoul. It usually inhabits the deserts a day or so south of here, but I will find out where it was last seen."

He called out in the complex language, and a slightly smaller lizard popped its head in. There was a quick exchange, then the other lizard withdrew.

"The Old Khamsoul is possibly the most ancient

entity on Aenir," said Zicka. "It knows all secrets, all names. Sharrakor will need the names of all those bound by the Forgetting in order to release them. The names, and a source of power."

"What power?" asked Milla.

"The Violet Keystone will do," replied Yazeq. "Or the half of it."

"So we have to find out where the Old Khamsoul is," said Tal. "Then go there and stop Sharrakor."

"Go there and *kill* him," said Milla. "Danir should have killed him long ago."

"There is a difficulty you should know," said Zicka. "A most grievous difficulty, I fear."

Everyone looked at the little lizard.

"Sharrakor will be actually *inside* the Old Khamsoul."

"Inside?" asked Crow. "What do you mean *inside?*"

"The Old Khamsoul," explained Zicka, "is a whirlwind. A whirlwind of dust and spinning stones."

·CHAPTER·
TWENTY-SEVEN

"A whirlwind?" Tal shook his head. "Great."

"The whirlwind may not be part of the Old Khamsoul, but merely some form of protective layer," said Yazeq. "There is a pillar of stone at the center of the whirlwind, and some argue that this is in fact the Old Khamsoul. But no one knows for sure."

"If Sharrakor can get into the whirlwind, so can we," said Milla.

Zicka's tongue flickered in and out in agitation.

"No," he said. "The flesh would be stripped from your bones. It is not possible to enter unless the Old Khamsoul allows you. It would not grant that permission if Sharrakor is already there. It never allows more than one being to consult with it at any time."

"There must be *some* way," Tal protested.

"A Shield Maiden thinks of all things possible and expected, then does the impossible and unexpected," said Odris unexpectedly from above their heads. "I know a way into the heart of the Old Khamsoul."

"Odris knows a way," repeated Adras smugly.

"How?" asked Tal and Milla at the same time.

"It's a whirlwind," said Odris. "You don't fly *into* a whirlwind. You get above it and fly down through the eye."

"But the Old Khamsoul is no ordinary whirlwind," cautioned Zicka. "It reaches up to the very margin of the world, high above the clouds. How could you fly above the whirlwind?"

Odris sniffed.

"We can fly higher than anything, if we feel like it," she said. "Up and up and up, and then . . . a dive straight down through the eye."

"I have climbed high mountains," said Yazeq. "With height comes cold, and there is little air to breathe. You Storm Shepherds may fly high, but your companions would die."

"No we wouldn't," said Milla. "We could make globes of air with green light and warm ourselves with our Sunstones."

"I do not have a Sunstone," said Malen quietly.

"You may use mine," said Ebbitt. He slipped off the Sunstone he wore in a silver ring and held it out to Malen. "I am afraid that I cannot come with you any farther, children."

Malen protested, and Tal started to say something, but Ebbitt dropped the ring in Malen's lap and held up his hand to Tal.

"I am very old and very tired," he said firmly. "And I would undoubtedly lose my false teeth if I went diving into whirlwinds, and with them any dignity I have left. I have almost every confidence in your ability to deal with Sharrakor without my help."

"You don't have false teeth," said Tal.

"That is totally irrelevant," answered Ebbitt. "Now I am going to go to sleep. Good luck."

With that, the old Chosen curled up on one of the thicker rugs and closed his eyes. Tal half expected to see his maned cat slink in and curl up next to him.

Milla and Malen both slowly clapped their fists and then made a sign the others didn't know, crossing their palms one above the other and then gesturing out toward Ebbitt.

"What was that for?" asked Tal.

"He prepares to go to the Ice, in his own way," said Milla. "We honor him."

"He's just tired, that's all," insisted Tal. "Just tired. He's not going to die. Crow, you know him. He's just tired."

"Yes," agreed Crow, but Tal did not know who he was agreeing with. The Freefolk boy did not meet his eyes.

Tal looked back out at the entrance to the roro. He could remember so many times he had gone to Ebbitt, seeking help and advice, or simply to hide away from trouble. It was Ebbitt he had gone to when his father had disappeared, when he had to find a Sunstone. . . .

But he could not let himself grieve now. Ebbitt might have decided to die, but that didn't mean he would.

"Look after my great-uncle, please, Zicka," he said, looking back at Milla, Malen, and Crow. "Perhaps . . . perhaps he will be better in the morning. When we return."

He tried to say the last three words with the confidence of an Emperor, but it did not come out as well as he would have liked. There was an unspoken *if* hanging in the air instead of that *when*.

If we return . . .

"We'd better plan how we are actually going to do this," said Tal. "Adras, Odris, are you prepared to risk yourselves flying into the eye of the whirl-wind?"

"Yes," said Odris. She nudged Adras and he repeated her answer.

"Will we be able to take a boat of light through?"

"No," said Odris. "But we could take it above the eye, then I can carry two if we're just dropping straight down."

The Storm Shepherd's answer chilled the air for a moment as they all visualized dropping straight down the eye of a whirlwind, a whirlwind that rose higher than any mountain.

"We will have the added advantage of surprise," said Milla. "We will be able to strike at Sharrakor before he even suspects we are there. If we manage to actually drop *on* him —"

A lizard poked its head in and babbled something before she could continue.

"The Old Khamsoul is indeed in the Hrykan Desert," said Zicka. "Two days' march away for one of us."

"A few hours' flying," said Milla. "We could be there by the time the sun falls. What is that time called?"

"Dusk," replied Tal.

"A good time to attack," replied Milla with satisfaction. "We will surprise Sharrakor and I will cut his throat with the Talon."

Zicka and Yazeq exchanged a look. Yazeq's tongue flickered sideways.

"Please excuse me," said the older lizard. "There is something I must attend to."

"If we're going to get there by nightfall I'd better give Malen some lessons on how to use Ebbitt's . . . *her* Sunstone," said Tal. "Then I guess we'd better make some globes of air. Though . . . I don't suppose there's any point in waiting until early in the morning, and attacking at dawn?"

"Waiting feeds fear," said Milla. "Courage comes with deeds."

"Let's get it over and done with," added Crow.

"Yes," agreed Malen. "The longer we wait, the more the Veil weakens."

Adras and Odris nodded their agreement, huge heads of cloud bobbing up and down.

"The Kurshken wish you good fortune," said Zicka. "And success."

·CHAPTER·
TWENTY–EIGHT

They came out of the roro an hour later, blinking in the sunshine. All had globes of green light around their heads, and Malen kept flinching slightly as warmth flowed in waves out of the Sunstone on her finger and onto her skin.

Tal was surprised to see hundreds of Kurshken massed in the field in front of them. As they emerged, the lizards gave a deep-throated cry and waved their bows in the air.

"What is this?" asked Milla as four Kurshken advanced bearing an ornately carved stone box between them. They knelt before her and offered her the box.

"We are returning something," said Zicka. "Please open the box, Milla."

Milla lifted off the lid and handed it to some more Kurshken who rushed forward. Her hand hovered above the box, an expression of surprise and wonder fleeting across her face before it was suppressed, as she tried to suppress all signs of emotion.

"What is it?" asked Tal, craning his neck.

Milla didn't answer, but she reached in and pulled out a small, shining nail of Violet crystal, the twin to the one she already wore. Milla slipped it on to the forefinger of her right hand and felt the band constrict and become secure.

"The other Talon of Danir," whispered Malen in awe.

"One Danir gave to Ramellan," said Yazeq. "The other she gave into our care. Now we give it back to her daughter's-daughter's-daughter, unto the fortieth generation."

"It is a good omen," declared Milla, holding her hands up in the air so that both Talons caught the sun, glittering violet and gold. "Now we go to slay Sharrakor!"

The Kurshken shouted and drummed their paws, sending water splashing up around them in bold fountains. Milla and Tal led the way down an avenue between splashing and shouting Kurshken, out to the field where they had landed, and where a space was being kept for the re-creation of the flying boat of light.

"Are you sure you can make it by yourself?" whispered Milla as Tal raised his hand and focused on his Sunstone.

Tal nodded and began to work. Soon the keel of the boat began to shimmer on the water, and ribs curved up and out. Planks of yellow started to weave between the ribs and blue traces arched up into the sky, where they were grabbed by the waiting Storm Shepherds.

"Let's go," said Tal, without looking around. He had to keep most of his attention on the boat and his Sunstone.

When everyone was in, Tal changed the focus of the Keystone's power to lift the entire boat up as well as keep it together. With a lurch, the boat rose straight up into the sky, before the Storm Shepherds were able to drag the traces taut and apply some horizontal force.

Down below, the Kurshken kept splashing and drumming long after the four heroes, the flying boat, and the Storm Shepherds had disappeared from sight. Then they began the process of evacuating Kurshken Corner, to various boltholes and refuges, for they were rational creatures and believed in hedging their bets. They were also lizards of their word, and they carried Ebbitt with them.

It was a long climb to the highest reaches of the atmosphere, to get above the whirlwind that either was or cloaked the Old Khamsoul. It grew colder quickly, but their Sunstones warmed them, and though the air grew thin, they were sustained by their green globes. Tal did worry that they would not last, but he forgot about it as they continued to climb higher and higher and they saw new and strange sights.

First they saw the world curve away beneath them, truly round. Then they broke through cloud, and entered another world again, one where the ground beneath them was white and puffy and constantly changing. They rose above great bluffs of sculptured cloud, and then through long wisps of white that could hardly be called clouds at all.

Wind buffeted them mercilessly at some altitudes, only to die away completely as they continued to rise. In any case, the Storm Shepherds could work the wind to some degree, and change both its direction and force. Any wind they could not master they rose above, or passed aside.

Milla saw the Old Khamsoul first and pointed. From far away it looked like a solid spire of stone, reaching up to the heavens through a permanent and very wide hole in the cloud layer, a great circle that declared a no-man's-land around the whirlwind. *Pass here at your peril*, the space seemed to say. *Cross the line and be eaten by the spinning wind.*

"We are so high, and yet it stretches higher still," said Milla. "And down in its heart lies Sharrakor and our destiny."

Her eyes were shining. Tal watched her, catching glimpses in between focusing on his Sunstone. Truly she was the War-Chief going into battle. He knew there was no such light in his eyes. He just felt scared. Scared that he would die and scared that they would fail. That Sharrakor would kill them and go on to raise his army, return to the Dark World, and finish what he had started.

"Soon!" shouted Odris. "Higher, Tal! Higher!"

"Milla, Crow," said Tal, trying to keep his voice as matter-of-fact as he could. "Blue light into the keel, please. Malen, you just keep yourself warm."

Milla and Crow turned back from the bow where they had both been looking at the Old Khamsoul. They summoned blue light from their Sunstones, sending it pouring into the keel. Tal reinforced it with Violet, and the flying boat shot up sharply, easily keeping pace with the Storm Shepherds' own climb.

"Is it getting warmer?" Malen asked suddenly. "Or am I getting better with my Sunstone?"

Keeping warm with his Sunstone was now so automatic for Tal that he had to concentrate to see how much warmth he was drawing from the stone. He was surprised to find that he wasn't using it at all, though he certainly had been lower down.

"It gets warmer for a while up this high," shouted Odris. "But it will get colder again. We still have a long way to go."

They climbed in silence for an hour or more then, and once again Tal began to be concerned about the green globes. Theoretically the green glow could contain days' worth of air, but they were rarely used for more than an hour or two. If one of them failed now, it would be impossible to do anything. There had to be air around to compress it into the globe in the first place.

They were close to the Old Khamsoul now, the bare patch in the clouds far below them. They were near enough to see that the whirlwind was not made of dark cloud, but solid particles so that it appeared not gray, but black as night upon the Ice. The whirlwind was made visible by dust and rocks and whatever else it had snatched up, all spinning furiously, far faster than the flying boat or even the Storm Shepherds at their swiftest. Anything that it sucked in would be instantly destroyed. Flesh would be torn from bone, all moisture sucked from a magical cloud. Death would be instantaneous, for human or Storm Shepherd.

The whirlwind was broad at the top, Tal was relieved to see. But then it drew in closer and closer, funneling air down to what looked like a very narrow tube near the ground. Tal could only trust that the eye would be wide enough down there for them to get through without being ripped apart.

"Higher!" shouted Odris and once again the Sunstones shone brighter and the flying boat lurched up.

"We're higher than the whirlwind!" announced Malen, who was looking over the side.

"We need to get quite a lot higher," said Tal, who had only just realized what they would have to do. "Because when we dissolve the boat, the Storm Shepherds will have to swoop down and catch us before we get blown off track and sucked into . . . into that."

He pointed over the side, and everyone snatched a brief look at the churning vortex of darkness.

"Ready!" shouted Odris as the boat passed the very center of the whirlwind, the top of the vortex about five hundred stretches below. She and Adras kept the tension on the traces so that the wind could not blow the boat off station.

"This is it, then," said Tal. His throat was so dry the words came out in a deep Kurshkenlike croak. His heart was hammering so fast it felt like it was shifting position inside his chest.

"Tal, Milla," said Crow suddenly as they all took deep breaths, "if anything . . . if I don't survive . . . remember the Underfolk. Remember our freedom."

"I swear it," said Milla. Even her voice sounded strained and strange.

"I will remember," Tal whispered. "Everyone ready? Odris? Adras?"

"Yes!" came the answer, from Freefolk, Icecarls, and Storm Shepherds.

"Go!" shouted Tal.

He fired a burst of Violet that dissolved the boat of light around them, and suddenly they were falling, falling much too quickly toward the vortex, as the Storm Shepherds spun around and hurled themselves down as fast as they had ever flown.

·CHAPTER·
TWENTY-NINE

As Tal fell he grew strangely calm. He had fallen before, in darkness and cold, on another world. That had been the beginning of everything, in a way, and now maybe this was the end. Whichever way it went, it was the end. Maybe Adras wouldn't catch him and he would plummet to his death, or the wind would take him out of the eye, into the reach of the whirling destruction of the Old Khamsoul, or Sharrakor would laugh and slay him in an instant. But he would have done his best. His father would be proud, he knew, and his mother. And not just his parents. He had done many good and great things, just like the Sword Thanes of Icecarl legend, in the songs that always ended with them being brought home dead. After they had defeated the enemy, of course. So he had to defeat Sharrakor. . . .

Milla fell with thoughts of what was going to happen next. She had no doubt Odris would catch her, Odris being able to fly faster than anything could fall. Sharrakor was Milla's concern. He had surprised her in the Chamber of the Veil, with an attack she could not counter. What if he had more tricks, more secret weapons? What tactics could she employ, other than the surprise of falling from the sky?

Crow fell silently, his thoughts, as always, of the long struggle to free his people. Fashnek was no more, but the Hall of Nightmares still stood. The Chosen would be defeated by the Icecarls, and he trusted the Icecarls to stand by their word. But the greater danger to the Underfolk was themselves. They had been held in servitude so long that it would be hard for them to come out of it. But there were Freefolk to help them, provided that Sharrakor did not win and kill everyone. Perhaps, he thought, what the Underfolk needed most of all was something — or someone — to believe in. So they knew that an Underfolk could be the equal of any Chosen. . . .

Malen fell with the mental discipline of a Crone. She emptied her mind of all thoughts, and simply acted as a recorder. This was an experience all the Crones would wish to share, and she only regretted that she could not reach the others to share it immediately. But if she survived, many would want to walk in her memories, to see Aenir, and to fall forty thousand stretches down the eye of a whirlwind. . . .

The next thought all four of them had was overwhelming relief as strong cloud arms closed around their waists. They were still falling, but under control, Adras holding Tal under one arm and Crow under the other, Odris with Milla and Malen clutched close to her chest.

The roar of the air rushing past and the constant din of the whirlwind made it impossible to talk as they fell, even if they had wanted to. Every now and then someone would gasp as they looked below and it seemed as if the eye had narrowed too much for them to get through, but a few seconds later they would find that it was all an illusion. The eye did narrow, but it was always at least a hundred stretches wide, which looked like nothing from very high above.

They were falling for so long that it was a surprise when they suddenly saw the rocky spire that was the heart of the Old Khamsoul, and the desert ground below it. Tal's calm disappeared in an instant, to be replaced by panic. The top of the spire was flat, but it was no larger than the deck of an ice-ship, and they had to land on it.

That landing space grew closer with awful rapidity. Tal saw a bright shape upon it, a shining blot impossible to make out, but he knew it was Sharrakor. The blot grew larger and sharper, and became a dragon, a dragon that shone like a mirror in what little sunlight came down the vortex from above.

All four of them screamed in the last second, joining with the booming shouts of the Storm Shepherds. Tal screamed in a mixture of fear and anger, Milla screamed a war cry, Crow screamed for his people, and Malen didn't even know she was screaming.

They hit the rocky surface of the spire harder than expected. Tal fell over, rolled once, thought of the edge, and stopped. Milla landed on her feet, both Talons already extended, whips of light dancing from her hands. Crow landed well, too, and had his Sunstone in his hand. Malen smacked her knee and doubled into a ball to clutch at it, but it did not stop her from beginning the Prayer to Asteyr, her voice and gaze directed straight at the dragon who reared up at the other end of the spire.

For a second, Sharrakor kept speaking names out

into the vortex, his half of the Violet Keystone pulsing where he held it dwarfed and tiny in one enormous claw.

Milla dashed forward as Sharrakor turned. She struck with the Talons, light streaking out to lash at the dragon's forelimbs. But Sharrakor flapped his wings and rose above her, and the Violet Keystone flashed red.

Tal sat up and interposed a Violet Shield of Discontinuity between Sharrakor and Milla. A moment later a Red Ray flashed out, hit the shield, and disappeared.

Sharrakor flew higher, as Milla leaped and lashed out again, her twin lassos of light barely missing his tail. Crow shot a Red Ray up at the dragon, and Tal fired, too, but both were met by a blue defensive shimmer that Tal didn't know. He changed to a blast of pure Indigo, but that, too, was countered, and still Sharrakor flew up, until he was beyond the reach of Crow's Sunstone. Tal knew his own spells would be too weak.

The Storm Shepherds rose up after the dragon, roaring a challenge. Tal couldn't hear what they said, but Sharrakor's voice was clear, penetrating even the constant drone of the whirlwind that surrounded them all.

"Emechis! Gheshthil arrok Adras! Gheshthil arrok Odris!"

The Storm Shepherds screamed. Both stalled, hanging in the air for an instant. Then they dropped as if they were suddenly made of stone rather than cloud. As they fell, they were sucked sideways toward the whirlwind — and certain destruction.

"No!" screamed Tal. He raised his Sunstone and, without thinking, sent out two shimmering clouds of pure Violet. They enveloped Adras and Odris a second before the two Storm Shepherds were ruthlessly sucked into the spinning wall of debris. The Violet cocoons were visible for a moment, then they were gone.

Tal had no idea what he had done, whether it had worked, or if Adras and Odris had survived. He had no time to think about it, either, as Sharrakor sent a beam of Indigo into the whirlwind, plucked out a giant, jagged stone, and sent it hurtling down toward them.

Once again Tal acted instinctively. He made an instant Hand of Light from pure Violet and tried to slap the missile away, at the same time that Crow hit it with a Red Ray of Destruction. But the Hand was too weak, merely deflecting the rock, and the Red Ray only scored its surface.

The rock hit the edge of the spire and splintered into thousands of pieces of deadly shrapnel. Everyone threw themselves to the ground, and Tal just managed to raise a shield of discontinuity in time. Even though they weren't hit, the missile had served as a distraction.

Sharrakor followed the missile down, swooping with his wings folded, only spreading them to brake at the last second. He struck Tal in the back with a foreclaw as the Chosen boy sprang back up, and knocked Milla over with a sweep of his mighty tail. Crow managed to roll aside from the dragon's other claw, and Malen was ignored as she lay on the edge of the Spire, still bravely chanting the Prayer to Asteyr.

Tal felt blood running down his back as he struggled to turn over. But Sharrakor was too quick, and even as Tal got free and raised his hand, the claw came smashing down, pinning him to the rock. Milla was pinned, too, caught in the rapidly tightening coils of the dragon's tail, the Talons of Danir held too close to her own body to be used.

Crow ducked under the dragon's body and fired a Red Ray at point-blank range. But the beam splashed across the dragon's mirrorlike scales, and Sharrakor laughed. His mighty jaws snapped down as Crow stood fearlessly firing Ray after Ray into the creature's open mouth.

Crow ducked as the dragon struck. The terrible jaws closed, but not entirely on air. The hood of Crow's robe was caught. Sharrakor lifted him up and twitched his head, and the Freefolk boy was sent flying into oblivion.

Tal closed his eyes, only to open them again a moment later as Malen's voice rose to a shout on the last word of the Prayer to Asteyr, and the weight on his chest disappeared.

The dragon had vanished. In its place was a man. Or a manlike creature, for his skin was still mirror-scaled, and his eyes were the deep black eyes of Sharrakor. He held the half of the Violet Keystone, which he used casually to fire a Red Ray at Malen. The Ray hit her as she rushed to attack, a lump of rock in her hand. The Ray seared across her legs and she tumbled over, almost to the edge of the spire.

"Inconvenient," said Sharrakor as he walked over to the Crone and raised the Keystone again. "Release me, Crone, so that I may take my grander shape, and I will let you live."

"No," said Malen. She started to speak again, but Sharrakor set his foot upon her throat.

Tal tried to raise his hand, to point his Sunstone

at Sharrakor, but a familiar pain intervened. His arm was dislocated again, and useless.

"Milla!" shrieked Tal. "Kill him!"

But Milla was lying unconscious — or dead — twenty stretches away, the breath squeezed out of her by Sharrakor's tail.

Tal reached across with his good arm, dragged his right hand across his chest, and started to pull off the Sunstone ring. The movement attracted Sharrakor's attention. He raised his foot from Malen's throat and turned, his own Sunstone flashing red.

Tal screamed with pain as he jerked his useless right hand up so he could see into his Sunstone. He summoned Violet and raised a shield as Sharrakor's Red Ray struck.

The Red Ray snapped off. Through the Violet glow of his shield, Tal saw Sharrakor stalk off to one side. Ignoring the pain in his shoulder, Tal rolled around as well, and moved the shield just as another Red Ray snapped out.

Sharrakor laughed and began to walk back in the other direction. Tal groaned in pain and misery. Sharrakor was playing with him, moving too quickly for Tal to be able to do anything but defend. But he had to do something. He was the only one left.

Then Tal saw a slight movement from Milla. She

was moving her head very slowly so she could see what Sharrakor was doing. And she was looking at something behind him. . . .

For a second Tal lost concentration and his shield wavered. Sharrakor immediately fired a Red Ray, and laughed again as Tal only just managed to get the shield back up.

In that moment of lost concentration Tal had seen something that gave him hope. Crow had climbed back up over the edge of the spire, and was right behind Sharrakor. The Freefolk boy had something clutched in his hand, but it was too small to be a knife and Tal could not see his Sunstone.

Crow crept closer to Sharrakor. Tal groaned again, louder, to distract Sharrakor. If the Aeniran turned now, he would blast Crow before he could do anything.

Crow was three steps away . . . two . . . Tal saw Milla tense . . . one step . . . Tal let his shield down and screamed, and Milla jumped up shouting. Crow leaped upon the enemy, wrapping his legs around Sharrakor's waist and his left arm around his neck while with his right hand he smashed a small bottle into Sharrakor's face and a dark fluid splattered everywhere.

Tal stared as a clear fluid dripped down Sharrakor's face, and for that instant, he wondered what Crow had done. Then he recognized the sickly scent of caveroach poison, poison that was death to touch. But was it still poisonous in Aenir?

Tal was answered by a scream from Sharrakor, a scream that cut through all other sound, that intensified and grew louder and louder until Tal had to push his finger in one ear and grind the other against the stone to keep out the sound. Milla clapped her hands to her ears, the Talons sending crazy lines of light around her head like a halo.

The scream stopped as suddenly as it had begun, Sharrakor scraping at his own face as he and Crow teetered on the very edge of the spire. But while Sharrakor fought to wipe the poison away, the Freefolk boy did not. He fought only to take the Sunstone from Sharrakor's hands, and when he had it, he threw it toward Tal.

As the Sunstone flew through the air, Crow threw his arms back. Locked together with Sharrakor, the two teetered on the brink, an image caught forever in Tal's mind.

Then they fell, Crow's final cry cut off as the poison did its fatal work.

"Freeeeedom! Free —"

·CHAPTER·
THIRTY

Tal crawled to the edge of the spire and looked down. Far below, on the red desert sands, he could see a speck of black still wrapped around something that glittered and glowed.

Milla bent over him and gripped his wrist and elbow. Tal gritted his teeth, but could not help crying out as she put his arm back into the shoulder socket.

"He was brave," said Milla quietly. "Brave as any Icecarl, as any Sword Thane of legend."

"First of the Freefolk," whispered Tal. "He saved us all, in the end. With caveroach poison . . ."

He started to laugh, but it turned into a sob, a sob that racked his whole body until he managed to get himself under control. Then he felt tired, more tired than he had ever been. He just wanted to lie down and sleep for years. They had defeated Sharrakor. Let someone else take over now. . . .

But he was not left to lie there. Milla helped him up and practically dragged him across to where Malen lay. She was so still that fear struck Tal again.

"Is she . . ."

"She lives," replied Milla. "Her throat is bruised and she is burned, but I have put a healing light upon that. She will wake soon."

Tal looked at her. "An Underfolk defeats a monster, an Icecarl wields Light Magic," he said. "And a Chosen doesn't know what to do — except look for Adras and Odris. But how do we get out of this old whirlwind?"

"We all have to return to the Castle," said Milla. "The Veil must be restored, and peace made between all our peoples. That is what we must do."

"Yes," replied Tal. "And we must free the Underfolk."

He looked down at the half Keystone Crow had thrown to him, and slid it upon the finger where he wore the half Keystone Milla had given him. As the two Sunstones met, there was an intense flash of Violet, a stinging pain in Tal's finger. The ring was whole once more, the Sunstones become one.

"You can help us all get back to the Castle from here, can't you?" asked Milla.

Tal did not hear her. He was staring down at the Violet Keystone, lost in its depths.

Milla smacked him on the back and repeated her question.

"What? No. That is, I don't know. . . ." began Tal. Then he stopped to think about it and was surprised to find inside himself an absolute confidence that he *could* lead them back from anywhere in Aenir. "Yes. I suppose we can go from here. You'd better wake up Malen. I'm just going . . . for a walk."

Milla frowned. There was nowhere to walk to, atop the spire. But she bent down and propped Malen up against herself, wincing as her bruised ribs and back complained.

Tal walked to where Sharrakor had stood, right on the edge of the spire. The rock was worn glassy smooth there, as if by many feet. It would be treacherous if it was wet, but Tal guessed it never rained here, in the heart of the whirlwind.

"Khamsoul!" he shouted. "I have a question."

The sound of the whirlwind did not change, but somehow Tal heard a quiet voice above it, a voice

683

that was old and slow and mellow, gentle and vaguely amused at the same time.

"Of course you do, Tal Graile-Rerem, Emperor of the Chosen of the Castle. I will grant you one question, and one answer."

"Did you kill Adras and Odris?"

"I do not kill my children," breathed the Old Khamsoul. "Even my children's-children's-children, beyond the count of years. They live, and now know their ancestry. You may ask another question."

"Could . . . could I have done anything differently?" asked Tal. "Was there some way to do everything better? To defeat Sharrakor, without Crow . . . without Crow dying, or Jarek . . . or all the other people, all the Aenirans?"

"I cannot answer that," whispered the whirlwind. "I can only say what is, and what has been, not what might have been or what might come to pass. You may ask another question."

Tal stared out at the whirlwind.

"Who started the war between our worlds?" he asked.

"Which one?" The Old Khamsoul sighed. "Which one? There have been so many wars. And even I cannot always say how they began."

Tal was silent.

"I have not answered. Do you have another question?"

"No," said Tal slowly. "I do not know what to ask. I will come back someday, if you let me."

"You may come," said the Old Khamsoul. "I shall be here."

Tal turned and walked back to Milla and Malen. A minute later, three Sunstones flashed, and three voices spoke the Way to the Dark World. A rainbow shone, and the spire of the Old Khamsoul was empty.

·EPILOGUE·

The Great Gate of the Castle had been shut for more than a thousand years. Now the vast gate of golden metal stood open to the Dark World beyond. But it was not dark, for in the Hall of Welcome a thousand Sunstones shone, and out on the road beyond there were scores more Sunstones, hundreds of moth lanterns, and many oil-soaked torches burning with blue flames.

Tal stood in front of a crowd of Chosen and Freefolk. He was clad in simple white robes rather than violet, though the Violet Keystone shining on his hand splashed him with color. His natural shadow fell on the floor behind him. Only natural shadows flickered among this gathering, though there were still renegade Chosen, their Spiritshadows, and free shadows elsewhere in the Castle.

Opposite Tal, in front of a throng of Icecarls, stood Milla. The Talons of Danir glowed violet on her fingers, and the crown on her head was newly polished. Her Selski hide armor had been repaired and cleaned, and once more she wore her Merwin-horn sword at her side. She also wore a Sunstone ring, which shone indigo and was larger than the half Keystone she had given up.

"Farewell, at least for a circling," said Milla, clapping her fists together in a gesture to Tal. "Or more, perhaps. We will be busy."

Tal nodded in understanding. Though they had saved the Veil, it had been temporarily weakened, causing a shift in temperature and changing both the weather and the Ice. The pattern of Selski migration had altered, and with that alteration had come many conflicts among the Icecarl clans who had to depart from their traditional routes and hunting grounds. As always, the Crones would decide these disputes, but they had asked Milla to assist in their decisions. She would lead a special force of Shield Maidens and Crones who were to circumnavigate the world, ruling on the new boundaries and prerogatives.

"I'll be busy too," he sighed. Despite the collapse of the old regime, the vast majority of Chosen had still acclaimed him as Emperor. The Freefolk, led by Crow's brother Bennem — who had been cured by the Crones — had agreed to that acclamation, provided he was called Emperor of the Castle, not just the Chosen.

Tal, mindful of his promise to Crow, had accepted for the time being. Now he had the task of trying to make the new society work. It was a tall order when within the Castle there were rebel Chosen, recalcitrant Chosen who didn't want to do anything useful, former Underfolk who couldn't imagine change, and Freefolk who were bitter and wanted the Chosen to serve them or to be punished for their past.

"I wish Ebbitt —" Tal began to say, when he was interrupted by a scrawny, rather stooped Icecarl who seemed to be having difficulty with his facemask.

"Wish what?" said the Icecarl, lifting the mask to reveal a familiar long nose. "Wish I'd been bored to death by those Kurshkens?"

"No," Tal said, embracing his great-uncle. "You know what I wish."

"Hmmph," snorted Ebbitt. "I'll be back. Couldn't miss this opportunity, you know. There I was, on my last breath . . . or perhaps the second-last breath,

I can't be sure . . . and I thought if I die now I'll never see the Ice. Beside, there's those Crones. I like the sound of them."

Tal let Ebbitt go, but pressed two fingers against his great-uncle's chest. Something moved under the curs, something other than skin and bone.

"Ebbitt!"

"What can I say?" exclaimed Ebbitt. "It wants to come with me. We've been playing Beastmaker and I'm winning a hundred and six games to one hundred and eight."

The Codex beat against Ebbitt's chest and the old man hastily added, "The count is a little in dispute. It could be one hundred and six even."

Tal frowned. The Codex was too valuable to lose. But there was no guarantee he'd be able to consult it even if it did stay in the Castle. At least if it was with Ebbitt he'd be able to find it when he had to. Besides, Malen was going to stay in the Castle and several other Crones were gong to join her, as part of a permanent embassy. Tal would be able to communicate with Ebbitt and the Codex via the Crones.

And with Milla, too. There would be much to talk about.

"Farewell, Milla," said Tal. He held out his wrist,

showing the scars of the oaths they had made together. Milla bared her wrist, and they touched scars, cool skin against cool skin.

Milla smiled, a smile that Tal had not seen before. He smiled back and looked into her eyes. In their joined gaze, they both saw everything they had been through together, from their meeting on the Ice to the fall of Sharrakor.

Everyone was silent as they stood together. Time ticked over in Icecarl breaths and Chosen seconds, counted in sparks within their Sunstones. Finally, Milla raised her hand, and Tal's fell away.

Milla held her hand high above her head. A Talon flared and a violet whip spun overhead, before falling into motes of light as Milla closed her fist and lowered her arm.

Icecarls shouted, their calls reverberating through the great hall. Then they shouldered their burdens and set out on the long road down the Mountain of Light. Down toward the Ice and the Living Sea of Selski, down to their windborne homes, the clan ships of the Icecarls.

Milla did not look back.

Tal watched for a moment, then turned toward the shining Sunstones, to the thousands of halls and rooms and corridors of the Chosen and the Freefolk, the people of the Castle.

But even as friends and strangers alike came to his side to ask questions or beg favors or tell him things, his thoughts were only on one small part of the Castle. A suite of rooms with the front door marked by an Orange Sthil-beast leaping over a seven-pointed star.

Beyond that door his family was together again. His father, Rerem, who had been rescued from the Orange Keystone, was regaining both his sanity and his strength. His mother, Graile, had almost totally recovered from the water-spider poison. His brother, Gref, had been cured so rapidly by the Crones that he had already gotten into several sorts of minor trouble. And Tal's little sister, Kusi, seemed to have forgotten that anything had happened at all.

Tal smiled again, a smile tinged with the weight of memory and responsibility. So much *had* happened, and so much lay ahead.

But everything could wait, thought Tal, as he made his way through the crowd.

For Tal Graile-Rerem was finally going home, and he had a Sunstone.